HARROWED HEARTS

BERONIKA KERES

IMMORTAL
WOODS BOOKS

Cover design by www.trifbookdesign.com

ISBN 978-1-7390443-0-5 (paperback)
ISBN 978-1-7771514-8-5 (hardcover)
ISBN 978-1-7771514-9-2 (ebook)

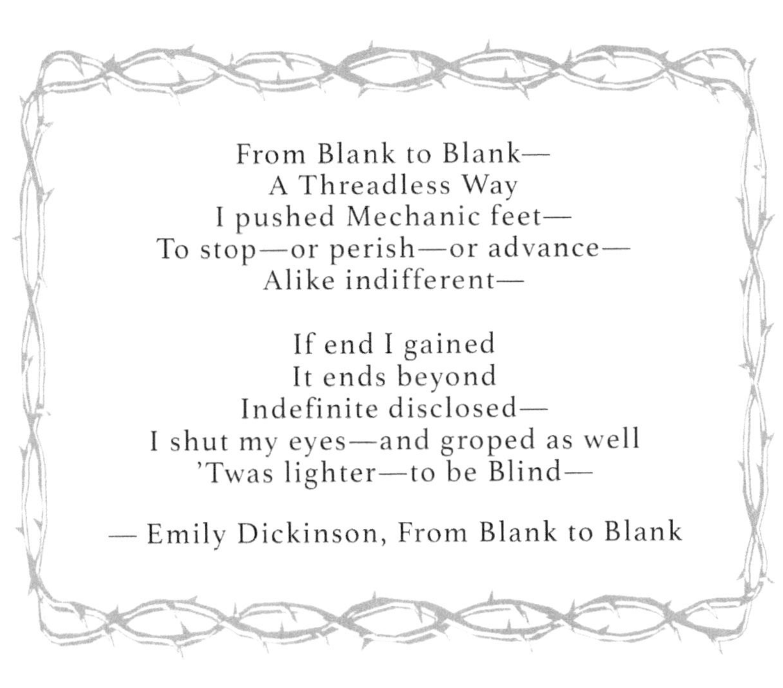

From Blank to Blank—
A Threadless Way
I pushed Mechanic feet—
To stop—or perish—or advance—
Alike indifferent—

If end I gained
It ends beyond
Indefinite disclosed—
I shut my eyes—and groped as well
'Twas lighter—to be Blind—

— Emily Dickinson, From Blank to Blank

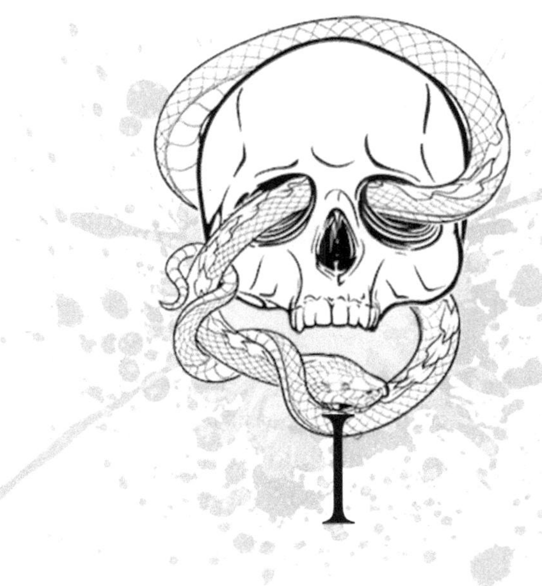

Terror binds me as vampires transport me to Hell through a never-ending stretch of trees blanketing the vast hills and mountains of Romania. The light of the moon intermittently cuts through the heavy night weighing on the forest, and I catch glimpses of branches and valleys beyond the truck window. It's likely the last time I'll ever see beyond cold stone walls.

It feels like hours have passed since disembarking the plane. I didn't glimpse buildings or roads since Mateo moved me so swiftly through the dark to this truck. I wouldn't have been able to escape anyway.

My face is swollen from crying, my eyes sore and dry from a long and sleepless flight from Washington state. With the blue lights from the truck's dashboard, my faint reflection stares back at me in the window past Mateo, who's on guard beside me on the cramped backseat.

One of Viorel's men—Asil, a suspiciously friendly man with a thick brown beard and muscles—drives without headlights as we crawl through the forest on a sparse, nine-hundred-year-old path kept alive over the years by castle guards. The passenger, a Darkling man with a warrior's scowl and a long, vertical scar across the left side of his dark cheek, hasn't said a single word since he met us with the truck.

I can feel Denendrius nearby, though I can't pinpoint the unlit truck he's in behind us. He must be in helpless agony with each second he spends locked in the steel coffin they loaded onto the covered flatbed.

Is he hoping for Sergei to swoop in and help us? Or do they both know such an attempt would be futile?

Carol, Derek, and Rayonne follow behind them in a third truck. It's terrifying to be alone with three Darkling men, but the excitement emanating from them has me glad for the separation.

Maybe they'll be lucky in the castle. At least they won't be locked in a room with a ten-thousand-year-old vampire who has been stewing in anger and plotting revenge for over fifteen-hundred years.

The random steep inclines, declines, and bumps are disorienting. My heart thumps along, my limbs sore from shaking sobs and flooding adrenaline. My chest aches, and I wish I could fall asleep and wake up in our house in Bellevue with human Denendrius sleeping beside me.

Everything would be so different if he never changed back. Maybe he would've snapped and stabbed me to death like in Ziggy's friend's vision, but at least I would have had three more years. It would have been a quick death too, unlike whatever Viorel has planned for me.

Mateo's ringed hand appears on my back, his Spanish-accented words low. "It's okay, we're almost there."

The realization everyone in the truck can hear my heart only makes it beat faster. Can they smell the layer of sweat fear cakes on me too?

What will Viorel do to me first? Is he going to start slow with the torment, or go straight for blood and pain?

I'm rigid with panic, wide eyes darting from window to window to locate the castle. There's nothing but darkness.

Mateo speaks from beside me. "We're here. Let him know."

I'm breathless as my balance tilts, vision blotting as my blood pressure drops.

Oh god.

The unnamed vampire in the passenger seat pulls out a large phone. He angles the green-lit keypad away from me while dialing, then has a quick conversation in a language I've never heard before.

When Asil turns on the headlights, yellow-tinted trees and worn tire tracks appear through dead grass.

I fight for breath to say, "Where—"

In a blink the trees vanish, a fortress appearing in front of me as we pass through a stone archway and over a matching road, the masking ability Rayonne told me Viorel has at play. I must have wandered into a dream. The gray, stone castle looms over us from atop a steep hill with dozens of yellow-lit windows. It's something from a Gothic film, its turrets and tall walls nearly convincing me I've been drug into the Middle Ages. It's so massive I can't see the highest points of it through the windshield.

The headlights bounce over manicured grass and the outlines of shrubs and flowers lining the winding road we race up.

It may be Hell, but it's undeniably beautiful.

The truck hauling Denendrius passes us and disappears into the dark on another stone road.

"Where are they taking him?" I demand as if I don't already know he's going to be tossed in the dungeon.

Nobody answers me, and I know in my aching heart I'll never see him again. It makes me want to scream and try kicking through the truck window for freedom since Mateo flipped the child lock on earlier.

The road turns into a wide, circular stone path in front of an arched passageway opening into the darkness leading inside. My mind spins images of what could be inside as the third truck pulls up beside us. We stop in near unison.

My hands shake, teeth chattering as my stare locks on it. Is Viorel there waiting for me?

Mateo touches my shoulder. "Let's go inside before you decide."

A tear drips from my bottom lashes, and I quickly wipe it. I shrink away from him and press myself into the seat. "Please, no," I cry. "I don't want to."

"You have to." He shoves his door open and climbs down, extending his hand to me.

I hunker down and shake my head as Asil and the passenger climb out, boots crunching against the dirt on the old stone.

"Come on . . ." Asil coaxes, his thick accent encouraging and bright. "Don't embarrass yourself. You'll be fine, we promise."

Mateo sighs, tucks his shoulder-length, wavy brown hair behind his ears, and reaches in to wrap his ringed fingers around my bare biceps. I'm stiff as he pulls me across the seat and sets me on my bare feet—my shoes in my luggage since I kicked at everyone who brought them to me, like I thought refusing them would make it harder for them to make me travel.

I pull the chilly, pure air into my lungs and shudder as I look up. Bright stars freckle the sky, and I must crane my head back to see the castle's tall turrets and the winged gargoyles.

I take in my surroundings—since this is probably the only time I'll ever see the outside of the castle—as the other truck empties.

Solar lights stick out of the grass and flower beds, illuminating the array of well-tended flowers and shrubs surrounding the massive yard. Does it circle the entire castle?

From where we stand at the top of a hill, I stare down across an endless sheet of forest, so far it's like there's no world but blackness beyond it. There are no city lights twinkling in the distance. No highways or roads. No sign of life beyond the castle.

Is it another trick, like how the castle doesn't exist for those excluded from finding it? Am I not allowed to see the world beyond, or is the forest simply vast?

The chilly wind spins my hair around me, and I hold it out of my face to watch Rayonne, Carol, and Derek approach. Rayonne's eyes glitter, mouth open in a wide grin as she takes in the castle. Carol sucks in a loud breath, only releasing it when Derek gives her a small smile and laces his fingers between hers.

Rayonne gives me a gentle, red-lipped smile—she spent the plane ride primping—when her eyes land on me. "We're here with you, Marianna."

I ignore her, my barefooted steps hesitant over the chilled stone, with Mateo's hand on my arm as he gently pulls me along into the mouth of the castle. The blackness tightens and chokes me as heavy doors slam behind us.

My pulse pounds in my temples, my eyes probing for something in my blindness. My ears ring, and the panic is building so high inside me it's only a matter of time before I crash down onto the hard stone under my soles.

"It's okay," Mateo says. "We'll be inside momentarily."

Metal grinds and groans behind me, and my breath turns rapid.

"It's the gate," Mateo whispers.

The racket cuts out with a slight shake of the ground, and one of Viorel's men moves through the shadows in front of us.

Metal squeals with the ghostly creaking of hinges. A vertical line of light grows in front of me as two doors part.

A long and empty hall cast in thick shadow from the overhead candlelit chandeliers awaits us, where I see the stone walls lined with iron-barred and moonlit windows.

Squinting, I spot another set of doors behind a metal gate at the end and notice how beyond the barred windows to my right is a glass room full of flowers and benches.

"What's the point of this hall?" I mutter as we trudge on, eyes grazing over arched ceilings and ample iron making me feel like I'm in a hall waiting for the right foe to turn it into a cell.

Steps echo around me, the cold space amplifying the sound of Mateo's flat explanation. "Safety."

Asil chuckles, adding, "Sunlight fills this hall most hours of the day."

My eyes narrow, and by the time we reach the gated doors, the hair is standing up on my arms.

I swallow and hold my breath as the gate groans and lifts, Asil reaching out before it's fully lifted to push the wooden doors apart.

A tall gymnasium-sized room lays before me. The amount of red and gold, lace and velvet, is astounding. Patterns clash, but the gray stone walls and candlelight hold everything together. I'm a statue as I take it in. There are at least a hundred vampires taking turns looking in our direction from the antique couches and tables scattered between us and the massive fireplace burning with hungry flames directly across the room. When a handful of vampires stand and leave down one of the wide hallways leading away from either side of the wall the fireplace is on, I can't help but think it's because of my arrival.

The faces—the black, red, and colorful eyes—blur together, though I don't miss the plain curiosity, the sneers, the eye rolls, and the fanged mouths shaping Denendrius's name.

It might embarrass me to stand before so many people shoe-less, sweaty, and disheveled if I weren't so terrified.

I drop my eyes to the floor, feeling as pathetic as I must look.

"Welcome home," Mateo murmurs, his thumb rubbing against my sore arm.

The welcome is nearly as cold as I expected.

Rayonne chirps gleefully beside me. Carol looks woozy with her mouth parted and her green eyes wide. I can't read Derek's composed expression. I wish I could put on as brave of a face as him, but tears prick my eyes and I don't have the strength to brush them away, not that I want to draw attention to the fact I'm about to cry.

A flurry of playing children pulls my attention from the crowd, and I glance to my right in time to see a blur of short figures disappear up a grand stone staircase, a woman scolding them from behind.

Vampire children are here.

Asil turns to Carol and Derek, jerking his head toward the grand staircase. "I'll show you two to your room."

Derek follows without hesitation, Carol taking a single step with them—her gaze locked on me—before halting. She shifts her weight between her white sneakers as she looks back at Derek and Asil. Derek gives her hand a little tug, but she resists.

Carol sets her eyes on Mateo. "Where—" She clears her throat. "Where's Marianna going?"

Mateo's expression pinches with impatience. "We've discussed this."

Her grip tightens on Derek's hand. "I was hoping to see where she's staying—"

Mateo's hand tightens slightly on my arm. "No. Viorel doesn't like many eyes around his chambers. I promise she'll be safe."

Carol presses her teeth into her bottom lip as her eyes

flicker to me and back to Mateo. "Will the two of them be alone?"

My heart aches for Carol. She must be understanding the dangerous truth Denendrius, and I already know.

He pushes out an annoyed breath. "Yes—"

"Her own bed, at least?" she half-squeaks.

Mateo's hand relaxes on my arm, the next flow of words kinder. "Carol, she's down there for her own safety. It's unsafe for her to stay in general population, and for you to be near her while she's marked. I promise she has her own bed, in her own little room."

Carol's swallow is visible, her emerald eyes watery and locked on mine.

Rayonne adds, "Trust them, Carol. She'll be fine."

I break her gaze by staring down at my dirt-stained feet.

"Love you, Marianna," Carol says carefully, unable to fully hide the worry in her voice. "Okay?"

"Love you too," I whisper.

I watch her shoes as she plods away.

"All right," Mateo starts as I lift my head, the encouraging tone of his voice only making my stomach twist tighter. "We'll get you downstairs to settle in bed. It's nearly sunrise."

From the other side of Mateo, an unnamed, salt and pepper haired vampire approaches. "Viorel wants to speak with Rayonne before she's taken to the ward."

Rayonne beams. "He does?"

I submit to Mateo's pull and force movement into my aching, weak legs. Rayonne basks in the room's glow as she waits to follow behind us, her twinkling eyes making me nauseous.

Is she happy now? She should be. She got exactly what she wanted.

Will she believe Denendrius once I'm harmed, if they ever

hear about me again, or will she come up with a way to keep Viorel the hero in her mind?

Back in Lorimer, while Rayonne and I were waiting for Denendrius to wake up after Agatha gave him the cure for vampirism, she started to convince me Viorel might be the good guy too. That it didn't matter if she couldn't get in touch with her contacts, because once we found a way to contact Viorel's men on our own, we'd reap the rewards of turning Denendrius in. She sold me on a shiny new life in Romania and told me Viorel would be so elated to have Denendrius under lock and key that he'd probably give me my own room in the castle and a happier existence to go with it.

But once Denendrius woke up like he stepped straight out of ancient Rome and unlike the immortal man I knew, the fog slowly cleared. After spending time with him—forced to pretend to be his wife to keep him under control—I realized she was only looking out for her own well-being. Once Denendrius could speak English properly again and recall the centuries he had forgotten, he validated all of my worries and more.

Viorel is the devil, and Denendrius knew the horrors awaiting me now. Out of Carol, Derek, Rayonne, and me, I was the only one willing to listen. I just wish I'd listened sooner and hadn't been so hasty in my decision to get Denendrius out of my life. Even Ziggy alluded to the castle not being the best place for me when we met him at his blood club to put the word out about how we had Denendrius. I should have taken him seriously, considered he might have meant more in the words he chose than he felt safe to say.

But it's too late now. No amount of regret is going to unseal my fate.

I stare at the stone underfoot, my hair blocking the peering eyes around us as we move toward the far-left hall. My breath is untamed, my empty stomach ready to flip inside out with each step. The air is warmer the closer we move to the fire. When we pass the crackle of flames, my feet hit the worn red carpet, and I stare straight ahead down a hall. It seems to go on forever. It's painted dark red, a dozen wooden doors along both sides of the hall with massive, framed paintings hung between them.

Fat tears dash down my sweaty cheeks as we inch closer to Viorel. I wish I could drop dead right here from a fear-fueled heart attack.

After passing half a dozen rooms, I spot a young man standing in his open doorway wearing a loose white T-shirt and black leather pants, his scarlet eyes darting between Mateo and me. His lips twitch with inaudible words, a ruby-beaded rosary clutched in his hand. When his eyes connect with mine, he swallows hard while kissing the rosary's silver cross. He runs a shaky hand through his short, dark brown hair while stepping a few feet back from my sight as we come within a few yards of him.

Mateo barks "kitchen" at him while taking hold of the room's glass doorknob, slamming it closed between us and the vampire as we walk by. He's so swift I can't catch a glimpse of the vampire's room. Mateo grumbles to himself in indistinguishable Spanish as he adjusts his grip on my arm to pull me along.

"Was—was he *praying for me?*" I squeak. My legs burn, begging me to twist out of Mateo's grip and run . . . *anywhere.*

Do the vampires here know what awaits me too?

Mateo huffs. "Don't mind him, he's cuckoo."

"Maybe he's praying for you to feel better," Rayonne suggests from behind me. "You look like you've been through the ringer."

I furiously wipe my eyes before curling my hands into fists. "Shut up," I snarl through gritted teeth. "I was fine until you all showed up to Bellevue and kidnapped me."

Rayonne says nothing.

Despite my anger, I grab her hand with both of mine and cling desperately as we approach a silver steel door a handful of minutes later, an ocean-eyed girl with a fanged and friendly smile leaning against it. Rayonne gives me a shaky smile, the pity in her eyes almost breaking my grip. But I don't have the emotional energy left to care about my dignity.

"How was the flight?" she asks Mateo, a single blond eyebrow quirking up below her pale pixie cut.

He sighs. "Please, I'm exhausted, Sascha."

She chuckles and rights herself while pushing the door open. "Down we go?"

Mateo forces out a tired grunt and asks the man with salt and pepper hair—who he calls Seth—to collect my luggage.

The door hinges groan as Sascha pulls it open. With a soft smile, she says, "You and Rayonne won't be able to see anything for a bit. I promise it's me and you haven't gone spontaneously blind. Once we reach Viorel, I'll let you see again."

Rayonne nods—like this is mundane—and gives my hands a squeeze.

Blackness falls over my sight, and as Mateo guides us forward, my feet stumble over the inability to ground myself.

My panicked breath fills my ears, cold air rushing in and out of my lungs as I feel my way down the frigid steps. I try to count them, but I'm too dizzy—my thoughts in too much of a flurry—to keep track.

Another door creaks open, and I hear hollers and chatter to my left. An echoing pained shriek forces my eyes wide as a surge of adrenaline rips through me.

My voice comes out high. "What the fuck—"

"The ward," Mateo explains. "It's where all the newborns and vampires go who need extra care. Rayonne, you'll return here for your transformation once Viorel finishes speaking with you."

"Not too bad. Cozy," Rayonne says confidently like she can see what he's talking about. "Oh—okay, blinders again."

Stairs continue underfoot, then stop for a long stretch before continuing a few times for small landings on the long and silent descent. My breaths are fleeting, the damp, chilly air heavy in my lungs. A shiver rips through me and I grip Rayonne's hand so tightly she cringes and mutters curses.

I feel like a scared child trapped in a dream of monsters.

"We're almost to Viorel," Mateo says, carefully adding, "Marianna, I suggest you don't give him a lick of the attitude you gave us on the trip here. You're safe, but he'll have little patience left after this entire ordeal."

My knees wobble, and I choke on a sob.

Rayonne gives my hand another squeeze. "You'll be okay, Marianna."

I hiccup, only able to shake my head in response. My vision trickles back in as Sascha turns to face us in the claustrophobic landing. There's an iron door between two flickering candles behind her. The longer I stare with my heartbeat smashing itself against my ribs, the taller the flames seem to stretch.

Sascha presses her palm against the door and pushes out her bottom lip. "It's all right, Marianna."

Does the sound of my heart echo against the surrounding stone?

My legs fail me as the door opens with a groan, and Mateo scoops me tighter against his side and drags me into Viorel's chambers.

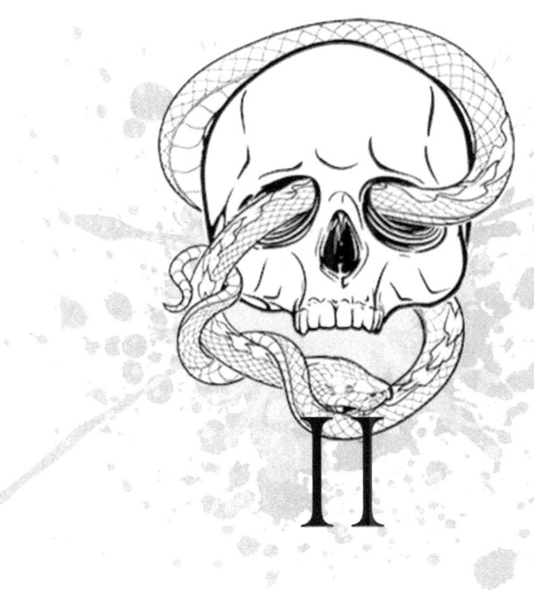

Through my flood of tears, Viorel appears as a black shadow in the flickering candlelight.

I wipe my eyes with my limp hand while trying to plant my feet against the floor in protest, my right still latched between Rayonne's fingers as her hushed voice tries to convince me I don't need to be scared.

Viorel pins his scarlet gaze on Rayonne, a fanged grin shaping his pale face as she walks into the sitting room.

He's inhumanly pale, blue veins below the crimson hue of his lower lids. He looks as cruel as when I met him in my dream-state. He even wears a similar floor-length black silk gown.

I almost expect Mateo to drop me in front of Viorel like an offering, but he pulls me past him to rest me on an antique, green velvet sofa on the right wall.

I can't bear to look at him, so I focus on the painted, faded flowers covering the wall across from the doorway. The gray stone dulls what might have once been vibrant hues of pinks, purples, reds, and greens. The gold accents on the occasional petal look real. Centered on the wall, there's a large, ornately carved wooden throne with a high back and gold-dipped feet. It must be from the Middle Ages.

There's a long, heavy-looking wooden coffee table in front of me that my knees knock against. Left of an antique teal chaise and dusty cabinet is a dark doorway cut from the stone. The ring of candles hanging from the low, curved vault of the ceiling isn't enough to light more than the vague curve of something slim and wooden in the shadows.

I clutch the stiff sleeve of Mateo's canvas coat as Viorel cheerily greets Rayonne and tells her how grateful he is of her, how she managed what his men couldn't in so many years.

"Marianna helped too," Rayonne imparts with rosy cheeks and starry eyes.

My heart beats at the base of my throat and I fight to get breaths past it as the room spins around me. I want to appreciate the pleasant light she attempts to shine on me, but I wish she'd avoid drawing extra attention to me. We both know it won't make a difference.

He's going to hurt me *horribly,* and I doubt he'll care about the ways I helped when I then aided Denendrius to evade captivity.

"Everything's okay now." Mateo gives my knuckles a comforting kiss after breaking my grip.

I scrutinize Viorel, studying his straight, chestnut hair falling halfway down his back, while wondering how he feels so much larger than Denendrius when he's likely only five-foot-eleven and slim.

"Please don't leave me alone with him," I beg Mateo, my voice squeaky.

He brushes his fingers over my wet cheek and holds my hands tight on my lap. "Shh. *Don't.*"

Viorel has Rayonne recount her perspective of events, and I

listen intently to keep myself from running away with my thoughts.

She explains how she met Agatha and the two men she was in cahoots with at a bar, introducing herself after hearing them talking about Denendrius, and how they gave Agatha and her the cure to use on him. How after they looked for five years, Agatha forcibly used the spare vial of cure blood on her, knowing Rayonne had knowledge of his face and wanting to extend her search to daytime. She tells him how horrible the last year being human has been with crippling blood cravings, before trying to shine a good light on me again. Rayonne insists I helped her steal Denendrius from Agatha, how it was a team effort until my mark became too strong and allowed Denendrius to manipulate me and the situation.

"I'm sorry we couldn't stop Marianna and Denendrius from running off." Rayonne cringes.

Viorel's friendly chuckle only sends another stroke of terror through me. "It's all right. None of you bear the blame. The most important thing is how you guarded him from others so my men could bring him here to fulfill his punishment."

She dons a proud smile though it plummets before she says, "Thank you. I'm sorry for trusting Agatha and her leaders. I really believed they belonged to you but shouldn't have trusted them so blindly."

"How would you have verified their identities?" Viorel counters. "Most are not foolish enough to attempt such impersonations. They will be dealt with accordingly."

"Thank you. " Rayonne says, allowing her smile to return.

He scoops her hands up in his, his slim fingers wrapping around hers and making them appear dainty.

"Thank *you*, Rayonne," he says warmly. "I truly hope you enjoy your time here."

"I know I will." The apples of her cheeks only burn redder, and she bows her head.

"Seth will retrieve more information about the ordeal from you before your transformation."

Mateo drops my hands, wishing me well as he walks away. I clamber off the couch in protest. My legs crumple under me as Mateo reaches the door and stands beside Rayonne. Seth returns with my bag, disappearing into the dark doorway before returning with a smile for Rayonne as he stands next to Mateo.

Viorel dismisses them, telling Rayonne he hopes her transformation is successful.

"Rayonne—" I start, tears streaking my cheeks as her gaze flickers to mine. I want to beg her to stay, try convincing her Viorel is going to make me pay as soon as she goes. Yet with how nice he was to her, combined with my mark, she'll have no reason to hear me out.

"Everything is okay now, Marianna. You'll see once Viorel marks you." She nods optimistically, adding, "If I don't survive the transformation, now I'm glad we had one another's backs while we did. But I hope I do, so I'll see you soon, and we can have a grand time without having to worry about anything anymore. Okay?"

I shake my head, strands of my sandy hair sticking in the tears soaking my cheeks. "Rayonne—" My gasps stop the rest of my pleas.

She gives me an apologetic smile as Mateo and Seth guide her up the stairs into the darkness.

With them out of sight, Viorel presses the palm of his hand against the iron door and pushes it closed before he pulls a long and flat metal latch down into position.

Nausea rolls through me as he slowly turns to face me. What is my sweet Denendrius going through right now? Have they started torturing him already?

Viorel must have used up all his friendliness on Rayonne, as he glowers at me with nothing but disdain.

I'm like a whimpering, kicked puppy before him. I don't have a morsel of the valor—of audacity—I once met Denendrius with.

"*Please,*" I cry, nausea wringing my gut. "Please don't hurt me."

I once told Denendrius I wouldn't die begging him not to kill me when he took me into the woods. If only I had that dignity now.

He stares at me with a curled lip for what feels like minutes, turning his head toward the door a bit like he's waiting until everyone's out of earshot.

What does he not want them hearing? Was he honest with his own men about his plans for me?

"Stand." The depth of his command makes the hair rise on my arms.

I can't get my weak legs to move out from under me. "*Please,*" I beg. "What are you going to do to me?"

"Stand!" he roars as he rounds the antique coffee table to get to me. "Or I'll make you."

Not even the threat of pain is enough to unlock my joints. I stare at him with tear-flooded eyes, and a trembling lip.

He locks his cold hand around my biceps, the sharp ache of his harsh grip and the pinch of his long nails forcing a yelp from me as he pulls me up. When I can't get my legs to hold my weight, he shoves me backward onto the couch. I curl up against the velvet back, covering my face as I sob.

"As far as you're concerned, I am your god now," he proclaims. "You are to do exactly as I command, when I command it, and without question or there will be consequences."

Tongue limp, I manage a brief nod as I peek at him through my untamed hair.

After a debilitating bout of silence, he says, "I was told you gave my men quite a difficult time on the journey here."

I look to the stone floor to escape his ruthless stare.

Tone flat, he says, "You've refused to sleep and eat. You threw a full dish at one of my men and repeatedly tried to kick Mateo. You spat at him too. Is this true?"

I clench my teeth.

"Look up and answer me!" His voice reverberates off the walls.

"I did," I cry as I wipe the hair from my cheeks and take in his furious face. "I'm sorry."

"I recognize where your behavior is stemming from, but understand something, Marianna, I will not tolerate such treatment. You and that leech have drained the last of my patience. You will regret testing me." His crimson stare tightens on me. "This is your only warning."

"I'm sorry," I squeak, not sure how else to help myself.

He stares down his nose at me. "Follow me."

I want to beg him to tell me where we're going. Instead, I clamp my teeth together as I force my legs to work, stumbling into the dark doorway after him while hugging myself. Part of me suspects he's taking me to the room I saw in my dream-state with the bedposts made of human bones. I don't rule out a dark hole with shackles.

I identify the curved, wooden object as a long church pew against the wall on my left and glimpse another dark doorway to my right as we walk.

Twenty stumbling steps later and I make out the shadows of furniture and see the opening to another room glowing yellow ahead of him. The flames flicker brighter as he stops in the middle of a mostly empty stone room, the only items are the backside of a massive wardrobe and bookshelf facing another dim area with a row of furniture on its left wall.

In the far wall to my right, there's a cell with iron hinge pins protruding from the stone where a door must have once been attached. It's so small there's only two feet between the end of the twin bed shoved in the left corner and the doorway. There's maybe three feet between the bed and an antique, wood-paneled dresser. My bag waits on the green blanket.

"It's a jail cell," I whisper. "Mateo told Carol I had my own room."

Viorel scoffs at me. "Be grateful I allowed Mateo to remove the bars and add a dresser and bed. I could always have him undo it."

I desperately shake my head. *"No."*

He holds his hand out toward it. "Unpack now," he demands, a ring of authority in his voice. "In the dresser."

I waver to my duffel bag. My hand shakes violently as I try to grasp the zipper, holding my breath until I pinch it between my fingers. He's grumbling as I unzip it and stare into the bag at my dramatic mountain of underwear and half-assed chosen garments. When he takes a swift step toward me, I shrink away.

"You're dim," he decides. When he jerks his hand, I think it's in frustration until my bag tumbles on the floor and my clothes spill out.

I gape at the mess on the floor in defeat, wondering how dirty my clothes are now while trying to fight off the embarrassed heat creeping into my face.

"Open the dresser drawer by the handles, pick up your clothes, and place them inside," he explains, like it's a new task to me.

"I'm not fucking stupid," I whisper while peeking at him.

"I'm unsure," he says flatly. "You're dedicating too much time to contemplation."

I don't risk another word and use a terrified burst of adrenaline to scoop my clothes off the floor and back onto the bed. Holding my breath, I pull open an old wooden drawer and move clothes over the three-foot space between the dresser and bed as his piercing gaze follows my hands.

"Where's your nightgown?" he asks as I near the end of the pile.

I assess the remaining garments, knowing I didn't shove any in the drawer. "I didn't bring pajamas," I realize, and fight the urge to explain how I didn't exactly have time—or care—to think about what I was packing.

"Yet you stand here and try to convince me you possess some sort of intelligence? You can't even pack a bag." His head tilts to the side. *"Stay."*

As he drifts away, I listen intently after him while stuffing the last few items—some jeans and my favorite baby blue velour tracksuit—into a second drawer. The only sounds I make out are the iron door opening and low whispers.

"Open the drawers," he instructs as he returns.

My heart drops, and I already know the issue he's about to take with me as I slide the first messy drawer open, followed by the second.

Slowly, he shakes his head. "That's the disorder I expected from a girl dim enough to add another month onto my waiting time for Denendrius."

"I'm sorry," I mumble, staring down at the tangle of fabric. "I'll fold them."

"Fold *and* sort." He turns away again with a sneer.

If it weren't for fear and the desire to keep my body in one functioning piece, I wouldn't be able to find the last bit of energy I have left for the task.

The iron door creaks open again. In a blink, Viorel stands at the end of the bed, something folded, baby pink, and cotton at the foot. "Take it."

I cringe as I step close to him and pick it up, letting the modest nightgown unfold in my grip.

"No pants?" I whisper while curling my numb toes against the stone. At least it has long sleeves.

"Ungrateful." His upper lip pulls back, the sight of his fangs making me flinch.

My voice comes out too high. "*I'm sorry*, but it's freezing down here—"

Viorel is already out of sight, his voice coming from a room to my right as he says, "Put it on and sleep."

I peel the cool covers back and collapse on the mattress before drawing them over me. The bed springs are noisy—one jammed directly into my spine—as I maneuver out of the filthy clothes Mateo had me put on in Bellevue two nights ago after he forced me to wash garlic off myself. Though I worry it'll result in some sort of punishment if Viorel cares about the state of my drawers, I shove my dirty clothes on the floor before slipping into the nightgown.

Despite the weight of my eyelids, sleep is far from reach. The cold of my cell grips me no matter how tightly I hug the thin quilt and sheet. To make matters worse, a hunger pain rips through my stomach, and it sounds like a beast wakes in my gut.

I wince at every hungry gurgle and growl emitting from my body. My stomach burns and I'm faint despite laying down.

The request for food sits on my tongue, though I don't dare ask at this hour. Will I get breakfast—or supper, since it'll be nighttime again when he wakes—if he plans on keeping me alive? How often will he let me eat? Daily? Or will I starve until it results in me begging?

I hold my breath when metal creaks. A shadow walks by the cell doorway, then back again. Someone knocks on the iron door.

Viorel speaks to someone in half-English and half-Romanian, a language I've come to identify since the pilot spoke it. I only catch the English word *kitchen* from the man he speaks to.

Am I getting food?

His shadow appears in my doorway, and I fight the urge to pull the blanket over my head like a terrified child trying to hide from a monster.

"Can you read minds?" I whisper. Did he know I was too scared to ask? Rayonne said he supposedly has multiple abilities, and I can't help but wonder—worry—about what they could be.

"If I must hear your stomach growl once more, I may tear it from your body," he snarls.

My heart pounds in my ears as he walks away. While I wait, I hug my stomach as tight as I can to silence it.

"Come eat," Viorel snaps after a while, the suddenness of his voice making me lurch off the mattress.

I bite back a surprised yelp as my feet meet the chilly stone, the cold snaking around my bare legs as I stumble to where Viorel stands waiting in the wide space before my cell.

As I follow him in the dark to the sitting room, I'm not sure what to expect to eat. I wouldn't be surprised if he force-fed me dog food. But when the smell of chicken hits my nose and Viorel directs me to a silver platter on the coffee table in front of the antique sofa, I feel like I'm being tricked. A plate heaping with heavily seasoned chicken and steamed broccoli and carrots waits beside a glass of water.

"Eat," he commands while moving to his throne.

"I'm confused," I whisper, taking cautious steps toward it.

He gapes at me as he sits. "Surely you can't be *that* dim, Marianna. Which part of your meal puzzles you?"

I sit on the sofa, the coffee table level with my knees. "This is a fancy meal . . ." The floor is so cold I prop my feet up on the wooden table brace.

He slouches on his throne and studies me. "You expect my chef to waste his time cooking rubbish?"

I lower my gaze and shake my head, picking up an intricately designed silver fork off of a green cloth napkin before poking it into a piece of baked carrot. I eat through my veggies and start on the chicken, the warm food in my stomach making the cold air a little more bearable.

"Eat *faster*," he snaps. "I want to return to bed."

I scarf down my food so fast I barely taste it, and he stands as I set my fork down.

An idea comes to mind, and I try a tactic completely opposite to what I first tried on Denendrius. Instead of meeting Viorel with hostility, I try warmth. So, in a desperate attempt for mercy, I hold my wrist up to reference the gold ouroboros bracelet with ruby eyes belonging to Tatiana—his human niece —before Denendrius killed her centuries ago.

"Do you—" My chest tightens. "Do you want Tatiana's bracelet back? You should have it."

His pale hand flexes at his side, long fingers curling into his palm. "No." He stares at me evenly. "In fact, leave it on."

I gulp. "Why?"

His tone is cutting. "Because her memory is the only thing stopping me from shredding your skin with my teeth right now."

My stomach threatens to eject my food. "Sorry," I whisper.

His black gown drifts against the floor as he abruptly twists away. "Show yourself back to bed."

I chug my water, my gaze locking on the steak knife when I set the glass down beside it and consider Denendrius's words again. I'm better off taking my own life. If Viorel plans on torturing me before tossing me into an auction ring for another vampire—as Denendrius believed—then I don't want to be alive to go through it. I quietly take the handle and consider the serrated blade. My heart thumps in my ears as the candlelight glints off the dirty metal.

Should I slit my throat? No, that would take too long. He'd heal me before I bled out.

I rotate the blade in my hand, the greasy tip aimed at my heart.

My thoughts lock on Denendrius and what's going to happen to us if I can't get this blade through my ribs and into my heart. Is Denendrius going to try taking his life in the dungeon to escape torture, or will it be impossible? I don't want to be the only one of us left alive if he manages.

The only fear coursing through me is the idea of failing. My hands are still, the sharp tip promising relief and freedom from this hell.

I inhale a deep breath and harness a shot of adrenaline to propel the knife forward.

A stiff hand circles my wrist and yanks me off the couch. I yelp as my eyes fly open, Viorel's wrathful face striking panic in me.

"Dim girl," he snarls as he tears the knife from my white-knuckle grip and drops it onto the silver platter with a clang.

I spew apologies and beg him to let go of me as he drags me from the sitting room—sure I'm in for punishment—before he swings me into my cell and flings me toward my bed.

"*Sleep!*" he roars before vanishing.

Gasping for breath, I hide beneath the blanket and squeeze my eyes closed. I shiver and hug myself, drawing my knees up to my stomach to dull the feel of it roiling. I roll around on the lumpy mattress, trying to warm myself while I think about the pain Viorel undoubtedly has planned for me.

I should have planned better. It was stupid to leap at the first chance I could. Fuck . . . what if he left the knife there as a test, and I blew it? I should have waited until he was sleeping and went back for the knife.

Pondering the bed sheets twisted around myself, I pull the blanket off my head and peer through the dark, looking for something I could hang myself on.

Are the candleholders on the stone wall strong enough to hold my weight? Does Viorel sleep deep enough for me to string myself up without waking and stopping me? I try blocking out the thought of how brutally he might punish me if

I attempt again and fail, and curl back into a tight ball on the bed in a futile attempt to get warm.

Even an extra blanket wouldn't help with warmth when it feels like the cold leeches from the walls and floor and through the mattress. Every part of my body aches, each chilled twitch and shiver making it worse. Since I suspect it can't be more than a notch below a comfortable temperature and my condition and exhaustion are only exasperating the feeling, I don't dare ask for another blanket despite how the request rolls around on my tongue.

"Marianna," Viorel calls, the sound of his voice making my limbs lock up. "Come here to my bed."

Beyond my cell and to the right where I suspect Viorel's bedroom to be, the darkness glows with candlelight.

I quickly come to terms with the simple reality that trying to take my life around so many vampires who want me alive to torture is going to prove impossible.

My stomach twists, and my heart beats so fast it feels like I'm spinning as I struggle to sit.

I don't have the breath to ask him why—though I fear I already know—as I force myself to stand. If I don't go to him, will he meet me here with violence? The fear of finding out has adrenaline pounding through me again, and I tip-toe across the chilly floor and toward the direction I heard him.

As I pass the wardrobe offering the space some separation, I find the same bed with black velvet and chiffon drapes hanging from bedposts made with bones to my right. Antique wooden shelves teeming with items too hard to identify in the dark line the wall on my left. There's a modestly sized, archaic pipe organ at the end of the row beside the mouth of a hallway.

Viorel lies on the side closest to the wardrobe, so I focus my fawn legs on keeping me standing long enough to round the bed.

He rolls over to face me as I stop at the side of the bed, every joint and muscle in my body locking me in place at the thought of climbing in. My voice is too high when I blurt, "Are you going to have sex with me?" I'm not sure why I ask, perhaps to measure his reaction or get it over with.

Viorel's gaze flicks up and down my body, his expression flat. "Is that a wish or a worry?"

I gulp against my tight throat, too breathless to answer him.

An airy chuckle escapes him, like he thinks I'm ridiculous for asking. He rolls onto his back and closes his eyes. "Crawl in."

My shaky legs have me half-collapsing on the black silk sheets. Carefully, so I don't annoy him with too much movement, I straighten in bed with my head on the pillow a few feet from his. I take extra care in drawing the thick quilt and the velvet blanket over myself, so I don't affect how it lies on him.

With a shuddery inhale, I lie on my back as stiff as a board on the soft mattress while I wait for his hands to wander over my body. My nightgown would make things easier for him. I yank it down as far as it will go—just above my knees—and twist my legs together.

"Settled?" The sound of his quiet voice has me flinching.

"Yes," I squeak, my eyes wide on the shadows cast by the flames flickering from the candles mounted high on the walls.

"There's a remote on the nightstand next to your head. Pick it up." His tone is too light for the anger he's met me with so far.

I hold my breath as I turn over and quickly locate the silver thing on the empty wooden top. My hand trembles as I take it and squint at the buttons.

"What does it do—"

"Press the red button."

I obey, and my breath catches when fire springs to life a few feet away from me. It takes my tired eyes a second to adjust to the sight of the black fireplace unit housing the flames and fake wood.

"Oh."

"When you put the remote down, set the bracelet beside it."

The question comes out before I can stop it. "Why?" I wince.

"I don't want it touching me while I sleep," he half snarls. "Remove it or I will."

I yank the gold ouroboros bracelet off my wrist and place it and the remote on the side table.

"Now give me your ring," he orders.

My eyes sting with tears as I hold my hand in front of my face to gaze at the crystal ball of a diamond. Denendrius gave me the promise ring, so I nearly consider fighting Viorel to keep it.

"Don't make me take it."

I bite down on my bottom lip and release a shuddery breath as I pull the ring off and hand it to him. He pulls his nightstand drawer open and my ring clatters against something when he drops it.

"Sleep now," he commands, rolling away from me.

My heart beats so hard my chest aches. There's no way in hell I'm falling asleep now, but at least I won't be shivering so long as his cold body doesn't touch mine, which I'm sure is only a matter of time. What other reason does he have for bringing me into his bed? Clearly, it's not for my comfort.

"Can I ask you a question?" I rasp. Part of me hopes to annoy him, so he's not in the mood for anything.

"There's a chance you may regret it." His voice is like a bell being struck too hard, and with only a foot between us it has me flinching.

I swallow my words and shrink under the blanket more. "Sorry," I say, interpreting his words as a demand for my silence.

"Speak," he commands flatly. "I'll offer an easy punishment should you force me to give you one at all."

I stare up at a flickering, dripping pillar candle on the wall across the room where the hall continues into another dark area. He must be able to feel the vibration of my heart through the mattress.

"Tick-tock," he whispers.

I clear my throat. "How did I meet you before? I was in a car crash and passed out before I woke up in here."

Getting kidnapped by Red Revenge—alongside Denendrius, Carol, Derek, and Rayonne—so they could make a deal with Agatha seems like a lifetime ago, despite how it's only been a month.

"*Ah.*" The exhaustion in the exhaled sound is clear. "Well, it looks like I won't have to pour hot candle wax on you."

My heavy heart pins me to the bed as I wait for his answer, trying to shake the image of my skin burning.

There's an edge to his words like he's considering whether to draw them back before fully uttering them. "I asked myself the same question. I've yet to discover all my abilities, and some of the ones I have, I don't fully understand. There's not much more explanation, considering it's never happened to me before. I feel connections to certain objects, so Tatiana's bracelet likely had something to do with it. Perhaps it was calling to me."

"Oh," I whisper, brain too pained with stress to think of much else to say about the event or his abilities.

"Rest now," he says as the candles lower to their tips before becoming nothing more than white wisps, the shadows the bedside candle casts across the room making the smoke resemble long fingers creeping up the ceiling.

"Can I ask about Tatiana?" I wonder aloud, his inch of friendliness making me far too brave.

"The candles may be cooling, but there are plenty of other options."

My face scrunches as I fight tears and curl into a ball on my side. I lock my eyes on the orange flames flickering in the fireplace, anxiety sharp in my chest over the possibility of him touching me. I can't help but wait for it to happen, for his hand to sneak up my nightgown, or for him to roll over and press his body against mine.

The bones making up the bedpost a few inches from my face don't help with the impending doom weighing on my chest, either. What did the owners of these bones do to get their skin peeled off and their parts disassembled and reattached to the metal frame? He must drink through too many victims to make use of them, which means these people must have done something to *really piss him off.*

Yet when my eyes travel up the post to the skull at its top, I notice it has fangs. Perhaps they're not human bones after all . . . a fact making my heart pound harder. If he can do something so macabre to others of his kind, what's he capable of doing to humans?

I struggle to keep my breath even to not disturb him while I wait . . . and wait . . . *and wait.*

The minutes pass, but soon the bed frame creaks as he rolls over behind me. I hold my breath and tense, my eyes brimming with tears.

It's going to happen now, isn't it?

I flinch at the sound of his voice, his breath against the back of my head.

"How do you like my bed?" he asks. "It's memory foam. Comfortable, isn't it?"

I can't hide the fear in my voice, though a bit of relief finds me. "Yes. It's the comfiest bed I've ever slept on," I admit with a squeak. But it's difficult to enjoy when his close presence creates unyielding terror within me.

He chuckles to himself as he rolls back over. I can't figure out what's so funny.

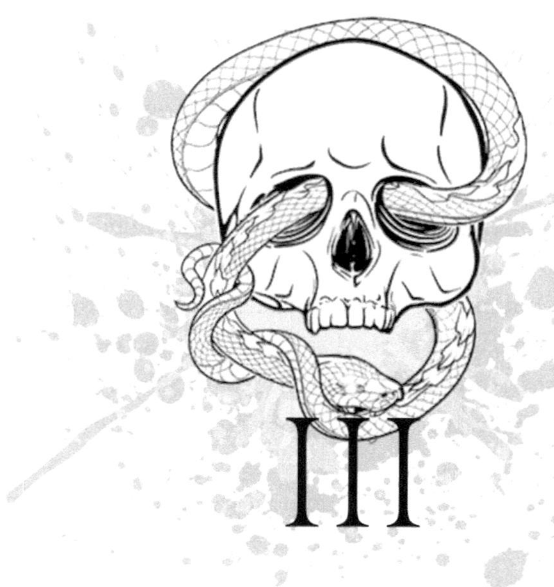

There's no division between the moment I fall asleep and subsequently wake up soaked in sweat with the sound of Mateo's hushed voice drifting into my ears. The blankets are pulled away from my drenched body, Viorel missing from the space beside me. Though the fireplace is off now, it feels like it sucked the moisture from my throat. I can't recall closing or opening my eyes, but I can sense the chunk of passed time.

I feign sleep, closing my dry eyes and remaining still with even breaths as Mateo's words register in my waking mind.

"Have you not marked her yet?" Mateo hisses under his breath. "From the moment they got him moving, he's been begging the guards to tell him what's happening to her. He wouldn't take *nothing* as an answer. You told me you would have her marked before sunrise—"

"I will, at my leisure," Viorel says firmly, no space for debate. "I have the opportunity to torture him from the comfort of my chamber, and I cannot help how all it takes is my proximity to her."

"I promised her aunt you'd break his mark immediately, how she'd be in her own bed here until it's safe for her to go upstairs—"

Viorel cuts him off again. "Your first mistake. You made a promise on my behalf?"

Mateo clears his throat. "I trust you and your word."

"I didn't give you my word," Viorel retorts. "I shared my intentions with you and intentions change."

I clutch the edge of the heavy blanket. Clearly, Denendrius knows Viorel better than his own men.

"What should I tell them?" Mateo asks.

Viorel chuckles. "You've already painted yourself a liar to her family, so what's the harm in telling them another lie?"

"All right, so be it." There's a heavy pause before Mateo lowers his voice. "Marianna said something strange when we retrieved her."

The curiosity is plain in Viorel's voice. "Strange?"

I strain to hear as Mateo murmurs, "She insinuated you were involved with Denendrius's imprisonment in Sirmium."

When the candle flames shrink close to the tops of their wicks, a tenseness fills the air pressing me tighter against the bed. I squeeze my eyes closed harder for the painful stretch of silence between them. I half expect Viorel to yank me out of bed by my hair and pummel me for telling Mateo something he was likely trying to keep secret.

Viorel's sigh is a mix of annoyance and apathy. "I'm impressed he kept his mouth shut about it for centuries."

Mateo's words are thick with hesitance. "Their ruler abandoned them while they were under attack. Hundreds of vampires died. Are you saying *you* were him? You've been keeping it a secret?"

When Viorel inhales sharply, my heart leaps and I cringe on Mateo's behalf.

"It wasn't a secret, per se. Aside from Denendrius, hardly

anyone lived to speak about it. He was the only one who was left with knowledge of my face. I thought he'd want to stay quiet, and it was easier to rebuild with another identity. Everyone concluded I was dead and there was no point disagreeing," Viorel says. "Besides, who would follow a new leader with a track record of broken empires behind him?"

With utter disbelief, Mateo says, "You left your entire clan to die . . ."

"No. I left a traitorous and corrupt clan to deal with the consequences of *their own actions* alone. That horde of vampires didn't make it through the veil on their own. They didn't get the directions to me by themselves. I was weeks away from plowing my clan under because of their attitude."

"Everyone upstairs is going to hear about this," Mateo warns.

"Yes, most likely."

Fuck. How much trouble am I going to be in now?

After clearing his throat, Mateo continues with, "And if they struggle to accept your truth, considering the stories they've heard about Sirmium for centuries?"

There's a smile in Viorel's voice. "I wouldn't worry about a mutiny, Mateo. They should be capable of comprehending how stories are simply stories. If they feel they cannot trust my word over rumors after residing under my care for upwards of nine-hundred years, send them to me and I will . . . *straighten* them out."

Mateo makes a noise like some sort of realization has come over him. "This isn't about Denendrius kidnapping and killing vampires in the eighteenth century, is it?"

"It's not the whole reason, no. I figured he'd stay far away, but you all were convinced he was working his way through clan leaders to find me." Viorel sighs. "Denendrius is brave, but not that stupid."

When I hear Mateo's boots shuffle, I peek to see if they're

coming this way. Nobody appears, but I know they must be able to hear my spasming heart.

"This is personal between you and him. About the girl he kidnapped during his escape back then. Your . . . *niece?* She's why you're doing this with Marianna, yeah?"

"Tatiana," Viorel says, voice sour. "She wasn't my biological niece, of course. But I considered her father like a brother. He had your position after turning despite his immortal age and was the only man in my guard I could truly trust. Denendrius killed him when he got in his way."

Mateo sighs loudly. "I understand. Have some mercy for her, at least—"

"Why do you care about this human girl so much?" Viorel spits. "If she were any other vampire's blood slave, she would be dead already and you wouldn't have had a single thought about it."

"Usually, blood slaves don't come to you, never mind with a friend, an aunt, and a *vampire* who holds their life in high regard." The words leave Mateo like he thinks speaking to them will cause pain. "You led the clan to believe she would be integrated. I've got curious girls her age asking when they'll get to meet her, plus the never-ending bout of questions from her family."

There are people actually *wanting* to meet me. Or do they think of me like some sort of . . . *exhibit?*

"Are *you* the one needing to be straightened out, Mateo? I cannot recall asking you to question my decisions," Viorel snarls. "Are you having second thoughts about your loyalty?"

Mateo's words spill out. "Absolutely not. I am merely confused by your change of heart, is all. The length of my loyalty to you is unwavering."

"Then we have nothing more to discuss."

"I apologize," Mateo says, and he must open the door as the groaning hinges echo against the stone.

"Since Marianna is awake, make sure someone brings her dinner." The dark cheer in Viorel's voice makes the hair stand up on my arms. My eyes pop open.

I wipe sweat from my brow with my sleeve as Viorel walks to the end of the bed to stare at me.

"I'm sorry," I whisper. "I didn't mean to cause problems."

He releases a shallow breath. "I'm certain you did. You seem quite adept at that," he says flatly as he stands unmoving in the same black gown he wore yesterday. "Get up."

My voice shakes as I force my aching body upright, sweat making my nightgown stick to me. I clear my dry throat. "Is there a bathroom?" I ask as I take my gold bracelet from the nightstand and shove it back on.

He motions to the wooden door to his left at the top of two worn steps.

I fling myself off the bed and stumble over a warm patch of stone as I pass the fireplace and head up the steps through the creaky door. A dozen candles illuminate the pitch-black room as I step inside, and I realize Viorel must be creating and controlling the flames.

"Don't lock the door," Viorel orders. "I don't want to replace it should you test me."

I leave the heavy thing half open, and what I was expecting to be a cramped closet, is actually a room half the size of Viorel's. Its purpose as a bathroom must have come centuries after it was built.

As I scurry past the sink on the left-hand wall and to the old porcelain toilet beside it, I wish I had thought of bringing my toothbrush. I doubt he'll care enough to give me one. I sigh and lick my gritty teeth.

When I notice the claw-foot tub in the middle of the large room—closed wooden cupboards and piles of yellow candles of various sizes and stages of burn around it—I become aware of my stench and the thick layer of sweat on my flesh.

Perhaps if my bad breath and smell burden him, he'll let me clean up.

After finishing up on the toilet, I move to the sink. My stomach drops at the sight of me in the mirror. No wonder so many vampires stared at me. I look wild. Perhaps it's the dim lighting, but my skin looks colorless and swollen, likely from exhaustion and constant crying.

I scowl and hold my breath as I grip the old tap and give it a hard twist when I'm met with resistance. While I grab the bar of vanilla soap and lather it in my hands under the frigid water, I stare at myself. I recognize my face but feel so unfamiliar. There's no hardness in my eyes or jaw. My anger is gone. Sure, I'm furious this happened, but with all my tears, I feel like a rainy day with no thunder and lightning.

I haven't felt this low since I was a child, locked in my bedroom. It feels pitiful. Maybe I'll get lucky, and he'll kill me. If I had the energy—the bravery—perhaps I'd provoke him in hopes of it happening quicker.

The rush of cold water over my hands only entices my sore throat, the taste of it on my lips when I wash my face making it worse. I cup my hands once they're rinsed with soap to collect water in them, the idea of asking for a proper drink adding to the dryness of my tongue and throat.

"Is the water safe?" I mumble, a handful already on the way to my mouth.

His answer comes from somewhere in his room. "You think I'd poison the humans in my clan? It's treated well water."

After swallowing a few handfuls of rusty-tasting water, I dry my hands on the towel and scurry out of the bathroom, holding my breath as I step back down into Viorel's room. He sits upright in his bed, a book in his lap I'm not sure he's reading since he stares at it without turning the pages, when he should be able to read them swiftly while flipping through. Denendrius could as a vampire, at least.

"Go wait for your dinner," he snaps.

My thoughts tumble out as impulsive questions before I can stop them. "What's happening to Denendrius? What's going to happen to me?"

He slams the book closed between his palms and I flinch. Slowly, he lifts his head and gazes at me with such hate that my skin pricks with heat.

"Speak his name again, blood slave . . ." he warns.

"I'm not a blood slave," I whisper, my defense spilling out. "I'm his fiancée. Me being blood marked has nothing to do with us being in love. I can think for myself, which means he kept me as a familiar. From what I understand, there's not much difference other than the vampire's intentions and how it affects the mark."

He releases a single, breathy chuckle. "Listen to yourself, standing there squawking for him like a good little parrot. A familiar doesn't ask for help to escape her master one moment, then run off with him the next and risk me taking her life. Besides, your master isn't a man capable of keeping familiars. He's rotten to his core and much too selfish. He kept you as a blood slave and a fuck toy, Marianna."

I blink back tears, his words cutting. "And you?" I breathe through the pain in my chest. "Are your intentions to make me your blood slave?"

Viorel's jaw sets, his upper lip twitching just enough to glimpse his fangs. "I don't keep blood slaves."

My stomach plummets to my heels. He has no intention of marking me anymore, does he? As much as I'm glad he won't force his blood down my throat and turn me into a mindless slave, that only means one of two things. Either he's going to kill me, or he'll auction me off. What made him change his mind? Does he hate me so much now—think I'm so stupid—he doesn't want me around him?

Viorel cracks his book open, his sharp gaze remaining on

mine. "Now *go sit* for your dinner before you eat it from your knees on the floor, *blood slave.*"

I curl up on the sofa in the dark sitting room and stifle my tears. The candles stay unlit. I'm left in darkness, even when the iron door creaks open, and the stairwell candles illuminate Mateo as he enters with a covered platter.

"Hungry?" he asks.

I sniffle and wipe my eyes as I force myself to sit. "I guess."

Mateo closes the door behind him, and we're plunged back into darkness.

"It's dark in here, yeah?" he says, though I can't see well enough to know if he's talking to me or requesting candlelight from Viorel.

"Yeah," I agree, not able to see the platter I hear him set on the coffee table in front of me.

Mateo sighs and I hear a match strike before the glow illuminates his ringed hand as he lights a candle on the table before using it to light a handful more.

I wipe at the steady stream of tears flooding my eyes and cascading down my cheeks, my sight too blurry to fully see the mashed potatoes and green beans filling the room with their smell as he lifts the lid. It doesn't matter, anyway. I have no appetite.

I have nothing at all now.

No future but one with uncertain—but promised—pain and suffering that I'm simply waiting for.

I'm nothing more than a sobbing and terrified thing now.

Mateo shushes my sobs and wipes my eyes with the cloth napkin, then lifts a glass of water to my lips. I capture the cold thing in my shaky palm and gulp it down, gasping for breath as I rest it on the table.

He takes my fork and scoops up creamy mashed potatoes before lifting it to my mouth. "You must eat."

I lower my chin. "I don't want to eat," I breathe, "I just want to die."

He sets the fork down and glances toward the dark hall. Then he sighs and rubs my back for a few minutes as I fight to control my tears.

When his hand leaves my back, I wipe my eyes and watch him cut my steak up for me.

He holds a bite-sized piece to my lips. "Eat anyway."

I take a bite, unable to enjoy the food as he passes me forkfuls with one hand while rubbing my back with his other. The candlelight reflects in his black eyes, only amplifying the worry in them and the crease between his brows.

He genuinely believed what he told me about being safe and happy here, didn't he? Is he beginning to understand how wrong he was?

"What's going to happen to me, Mateo?" I ask once my plate is half empty, my stomach begging me to stop.

He doesn't answer me, just stops rubbing my back to pat it instead.

My tears quicken, and I suck in a breath with a new pain in my chest. He isn't sure anymore, is he?

When he lifts another forkful for me to take, I shake my head and look away while wiping my nose with the back of my hand.

"Eat." Mateo takes my other hand—limp on my lap—and wraps it around the fork.

"I can't eat anymore." I'm careless as I place the fork back down, little white chunks of mashed potatoes dislodging from the lump stuck on the prongs and scattering across the silver tray and table.

He stabs another chunk of steak and offers it as his dark brow quirks. "I would eat." From the seriousness of his face, I can tell he's worried I might not get another chance.

So, I scarf down my dinner and top it off with the rest of my water before Mateo abandons me.

The candles snuff out and plunge me into darkness the moment the door closes.

"Viorel?" I whisper, hoping for some direction so I don't land myself in trouble.

Silence.

The complete absence of even the most basic sounds—the hum of electricity, a ticking clock, signs of life—only makes the noise of my mind more deafening.

I stand, pain ricocheting through my stomach as I feel my way back to my bed to stretch out as my organs and dinner fight for space in my body.

I succumb to my grief and guilt in the room's darkness as my limbs twist in the blankets. It's too dark to remake the bed, so I lie in the heap of fabric and soak my pillow in tears. At least with my legs tucked under a mangled section, I'm not freezing.

There's nothing to do but wallow in my thoughts and regretfully reminisce about my time with Denendrius in Washington state.

I was brave enough to take a chance, and as a result, Denendrius and I had as normal of a month in our own home two people in our position could have.

It wasn't perfect, no. Dealing with his blood cravings and trauma were unavoidable, and the side effects of the cure were creating serious health concerns . . . But what normal human life is without issues?

Even when he impulsively had Sergei turn him back into a vampire, we still could have made things work. Like he said, it wouldn't be the same as the first time, especially with the understanding and love between us.

I ruined everything.

Our capture, the fate awaiting me, and the suffering Denendrius is forced to endure . . .

It's all my fault.

Would Denendrius still love me if he knew—in my blind and hasty anger—I sent a desperate tip to Alaire and Edmond despite believing it would likely go unanswered since he killed them? That their fail-safe system forwarded it to Viorel's men and led to us coming here?

Would he still love me knowing I've hurt him worse than the ways he's hurt me?

I struggle to hold back my sobs, clasping my hands over my mouth as fat tears swell in my eyes.

There's no change in the silence or darkness for what feels like hours. Enough time passes for my stomach to empty, and my bones plead for movement. Yet self-pity has me adhered to the bed, and I suppose I should be thankful Viorel is ignoring me.

I do my best to keep from spiraling with my thoughts but the knowledge of Denendrius suffering has my head spinning and my insides twisted around themselves.

The only thing that yanks me from the bottom of my pit of sorrow is the sound of the iron door opening.

As I sit up and squint through the dark, Mateo wanders in my cell with a fat candle on a round, silver holder stained with soot. He sets it down on my dresser.

"Are you hungry again?" Mateo asks, his friendly black eyes shining in the candlelight.

"What time is it?" The question leaps from my lips, and as much as I hate Mateo for bringing me here, I'm grateful to see him since I've been sitting alone in the dark.

What are the chances he helps me? Especially if he's second-guessing what he knows and how he feels about Viorel. If he thought he was really helping me—was as blind to the truth as Carol and Derek—then perhaps he isn't a *true* enemy. After all, it sounds like I'd be lying on the cold floor behind a locked cell door if he hadn't convinced Viorel to turn this into a room.

His voice comes out low. "It's almost four in the morning, so about eight hours since you last ate. You must be hungry again, yeah?"

I shake my head, then push my tangled hair out of my face when dirty strands tickle my oily skin. "Can I bathe?"

He sucks his teeth, the struggle between permission and denial clear on his face as he glances toward Viorel's room. He settles with, "You're okay for now."

My numbness is clear in my monotone voice. "But I stink. Can I at least brush my teeth?"

"We didn't pack you a toothbrush."

There's not a single goddamn spare toothbrush in this entire castle?

I crank the heat as I continue to grill him. "When can I see Carol and Derek?"

Mateo shakes his head, his wavy brown hair sliding against the exposed collarbones in the black V-neck T-shirt he wears. "There are some vampires making bets on your life. Everyone understands how blood marks work, but some don't care, and many don't trust you because of it. There's already a man under watch for openly joking about killing you in place of Denendrius. It's safest for you to stay downstairs with Viorel until you're marked, and we've dealt with the troublemakers."

How is this supposed to be saving me?

"Are there auctions here, Mateo?" I ask, grabbing at whatever questions I can think of to shove at him in hopes he'll at least answer one. "How long is marking me, and making upstairs safe for me, going to take?"

"You have so many questions," he says with fake astonishment.

"Why can't you answer any of them?"

He gently wraps his hands around my biceps. "I'm not your master, Marianna. It's not my place to answer."

At least he's finding a way around lying to me.

"Well, my *master* is a prisoner. Am I a prisoner too, Mateo?"

He gives my biceps a reassuring squeeze. "No. Viorel will probably mark you, and you'll settle here."

"Probably," I echo. "That sentence used to exist without the word. Is a *not* going to appear before it's dropped completely?"

Though I'll fight him if he tries to follow through on marking me, the alternative is worse.

"You must understand something, Marianna. Viorel's in so much pain. Give him time to come around. The past month has been difficult for him, and I did not understand until this morning. Denendrius took *everything* from him."

A limp laugh escapes me. "Oh, the *poor vampire king*, how will he recover?" I mock. "He created that situation for himself."

Mateo shakes his head at me and heaves out a breath. "Don't do that."

My eyes burn, an ache in my chest as I inhale sharply. I exhale and lower my head while shaking it. "Can I use the bathroom? Then I'll go back to *totally not being a prisoner.*"

He nods and helps me stand, holding the candle in one hand while guiding me with the other.

I scour the dark for Viorel as we walk, my steps slowing when we enter his room. Through the dim light, I spot him lying over the covers of his bed on his back, his arms out a bit at his sides. He's still as stone, his eyes closed, the rising and falling of his chest undetectable. I can't help but think he's not really sleeping.

Mateo places the candle holder in my hand as he pauses at the end of the bed, and I carry it with me to the bathroom.

When I leave, Mateo is sitting at Viorel's bedside. He pats

Viorel's pale hand and sighs as he stands, like they had been in the middle of a conversation before my return interrupted.

My brow furrows. Viorel is unmoved from when I last saw him, and I didn't hear their voices.

"Is he . . . okay?" I wonder, a brief flicker of hope in me that perhaps he isn't.

Mateo chuckles and looks between Viorel's comatose body and me before nodding. "Yeah. Let's get you back to your room."

My tired legs carry me to my cell. I hand the candle to Mateo, who sets it on the dresser and tells me I can keep it.

"How long am I going to lie here in the dark doing nothing?" I whisper as I climb back onto the bed. I'm not sure what I'd do otherwise. It's not like I'm in the mood to read or anything.

Mateo sighs. "I know it isn't ideal. I'd bring you upstairs if I could, but it's simply safer for you to stay down here for now."

Safer down here with *Viorel?* I'd rather take my chances with the vampires upstairs. I use the candlelight to straighten my blankets before pulling them tight around my waist. "Sure, Mateo."

"Use the time to rest. I know you could use it."

The minutes are agonizingly slow with my own thoughts, but eventually Viorel walks by. I straighten up in bed, contemplating if I should dare ask him what's going on.

But after he passes back and forth a few times—seemingly in deep thought with his hands clasped behind his back—it's clear he's not in a good mood to answer questions. So, I watch him pace until the fact he thinks he has a right to be upset about anything festers in me and sour words pile on my tongue until they're unbearable to hold.

"You think you'd be happy since you captured him," I spit out, unable to meet his gaze as he stops dead in front of me. "You get to torture him like you've wanted for centuries."

"There is nothing capable of balancing the scales of justice, Marianna." He stares at me for a beat before adding, "No amount of his suffering can make up for taking her."

"Then what?" I whisper, grief constricting my heart as I force myself to meet his eyes.

"He suffers for eternity," he says with a despondent murmur and a distant look in his claret eyes.

"Why not just kill him?" I plead, knowing he would be better off.

"Death and thereafter are unpredictable. Suffering in my dungeon is guaranteed."

I use my last scrap of bravery to fight for Denendrius. "Don't you think you did enough to him when you wrongly imprisoned him the first time? He's completely traumatized. I've never seen a man cry like he has. Maybe he never would have taken her and wreaked such havoc escaping if you had *just helped him.* This is all your fault."

"You have no idea what you're talking about, parrot." In one fluid motion, he turns away from me and gracefully walks off.

I sit in silent defeat. The heat of my rising anger is enough to stave off my tears. With nothing to direct my frustrations at, I'm left squeezing my eyes shut and mashing my fists into my head of greasy hair.

The chilling feel of Viorel's presence at the mouth of my cell again disperses all of my anger, and I'm left with a terrified chill running down my spine. I lower my hands to my lap and keep my eyes on them.

"Get dressed," Viorel commands. "We're taking a trip to the dungeon."

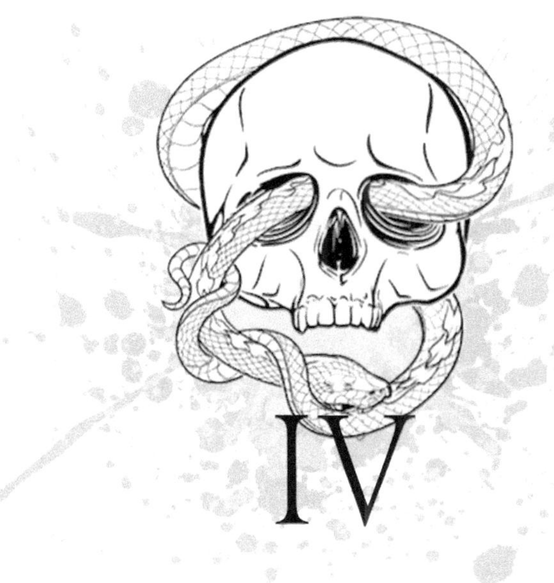

I sit shaking on the velvet sofa, Viorel scrutinizing my shallow breaths from where he sits on his throne with his elbow propped up on the arm. His blank stare intermittently turns into a sneer, a wrinkle appearing between his brown brows as the corner of his lip jerks in response to whatever about me is pissing him off.

He's impossible to ignore, and the idea of what he must be thinking has my heart trying to squeeze out from between my ribs.

"Where's your crown, king?" The bitter words are off my tongue before I can stop them.

Viorel straightens and stares at me, a sour sneer shaping his face again.

"I don't get it. If you really believe I'm a mindless blood slave, why do you hate me so much?" I whisper. "You can't blame me for what I can't control."

He turns his sharp gaze toward the iron door as he grumbles, "Quit putting words in my mouth, parrot. I never said I hated you."

Could've fooled me.

Viorel flicks his hand in the air as he sighs, the iron door drifting open like a gust of wind caught it.

I can't feel my legs when Mateo enters with five guards. As Viorel rises, Mateo makes a beeline for me and grasps my arm to help me to my feet.

Sascha waits on the stairs, my vision ripped away as soon as Mateo guides my weak legs through the doorway.

I may as well be breathing through a straw as Mateo half-carries me up the stretch of stairs, since I'm too weak to match their silent steps on my own. Still, I do my best to keep up, the potential of seeing Denendrius tugging me along.

She returns my sight in time for me to see the steel door opening. The same red carpeted hall I saw yesterday awaits in the murky dark, the only light seeping from beneath the occasional door. Viorel walks in front of me—and two guards ahead of him while the rest surround us—as we move right down the hall and into the grand room.

The various antique chairs and tables are empty, all the scattered candles and lanterns are snuffed out. A single plastic lantern glows in the middle of the room, the yellow bulb flickering like its power source is running out. There's not a vampire in sight, and the silence gives me the impression it's after sunrise, but I can't tell without the presence of windows. I'm thankful, though. I'd rather not be embarrassed by my own filthy state on top of it all.

My eyes sweep across the massive room as we pass the fireplace to the hall on the other side of it. There's a grand staircase on my right leading to another hall above it.

The hall is a copy of the one we came upstairs into, the old wooden doors with glass knobs are placed evenly apart as we walk by them. There's a back-and-forth pattern of century-old paintings and pillar candles on the red-wallpapered wall between the widely spread rooms. By what I guess to be the twentieth room, I nearly trip over my feet every few steps as I struggle to move my tired legs.

I heave out a relieved breath, excitement and terror coursing through me as we near the end of the hall. In my gut, I know we're getting closer.

What state will I find Denendrius in? If he can speak, will he sound like *my Denendrius* or with only the faint suggestion that the honey-smooth of his voice came with an accent like the first time he was immortal? Have his memories returned in a flood with vampirism returning his near-perfect memory? Or are they slowly trickling in?

A grandfather clock with a swinging pendulum and a carved angel at the height of it stands like a guard at the intersection of another hall. It's 8:02 a.m. as we turn right. A flame springs to life somewhere ahead, allowing me to see the cold and bare walls.

There's less candlelight in this hall, and the walls and doorways are closer together. I only lend a single thought to what could be behind them before Denendrius occupies my mind again.

Another steel door lies at the end of the hall and the sight of it has me gasping for breath. It opens from the other side and has a long and winding staircase disappearing down into the dark. With the arched ceiling low, it makes the stone walls feel suffocatingly close together as we step across the landing two at a time. They must bring prisoners through another passage. There's no way the steel coffin they locked Denendrius in would fit down these stairs.

The dungeon guard is tucked into the dark. The only sign he's there is the sound of the steel door thudding shut and locking behind us, and the heavy footsteps following.

I stare wide-eyed into the dark, my right hand out a bit at

my side to keep my balance as we descend the steep and narrow steps. My fingers brush against the rough wall, and after hooking the edge of my fingernail on stone and grazing the silk of Viorel's gown when I jerk in surprise, I keep my hand close to my body.

Mateo half carries me through the dark, and good thing, because I damn near fall down the stairs and into Viorel when I slip at the faint sound of Denendrius's voice echoing off the stone as he screams my name. Did he smell me the moment we started down the stairs?

I gasp as my stomach somersaults. *"Denendrius!"* I shriek as we approach, tears flooding my cheeks.

Mateo gives me a gentle—but warning—yank as a guard behind me hisses at me to shut it.

"Marianna!" he screams, the pain in his voice making my stomach coil around itself.

I can't imagine the things they've done to him already, and to know I'm the reason it's happening makes me nauseous with guilt.

I cover my mouth with my shaky hand to stifle my sobs, fighting the urge to push past Viorel and the guards to flee to Denendrius. But I know it's hopeless.

Yellow light glows ahead as we reach the bottom, black ring chandeliers illuminating the high curved ceiling and the wide hall separating rows upon rows of cells straight ahead.

The acrid stench of old blood and rot mingles with the damp air, the heaviness of it passing in and out of my lungs. I cough at the underlying reek of stale garlic.

Another row vanishes into the dark on the right of us, and when Denendrius shrieks my name again, my head snaps left, and I jerk forward until Mateo holds me in place. Thankfully, that's the way we turn.

The eight of us pass by tiny cells with arched iron doors of squared bars. It's too dark to see into the depth of most of them, but I shrink closer to Mateo when a bald man crawls from the shadows, his chalk-white skin and burning red eyes glued on me as he gasps and reaches through the rusted bars.

The guard walks from behind us, shouting a warning at the vampire in a harsh language I can't understand.

The reek of ammonia and shit gags me as we pass further cells, horror ripping through me at the fact they're not only keeping vampires down here.

"I'm not going in a cell, am I?" I cry.

Mateo gives my arm a gentle squeeze. "No, Marianna, but close your eyes. I can guide you." I give my head a rough shake and he adds, "At least don't peek in the cells."

I'm too busy searching the dark of each stone cell for Denendrius's face to heed his warning. Even when my gaze locks on the gruesome sight of a delirious vampire man holding the decaying hand of a red-headed girl with her throat so torn I see bone, I don't stop searching.

The rows of cells turn into bare stone walls leading ahead to the right, and a dozen square metal grates line the floor in between, about ten feet apart. Half are so rusted I worry they'll break under my steps, and I'll fall into whatever is below. I try to peer down through the tiny square holes—doing my best to step over them—but it's too dark to see anything.

The candles spaced evenly down the wall roar to life as we turn right, and Denendrius screams my name again, the sound much closer this time. My heart leaps and Mateo's grip becomes unrelenting.

There's enough light to glimpse the contents of the few large cells we pass. Instead of vampires, they're stocked with what I sum up to be torture equipment. We move so swiftly I only identify the chains on the walls and tables with welded on restraints.

We take another left, then approach an open cell with a

handful of steps leading down into a large and brightly candle-lit room.

I first notice the circle of stone in the middle. It reminds me of a well, but instead of a wooden roof and bucket, there's a metal grate like the ones I walked over. There's a throne on the left wall. It's solid wood, the tall back and decorative arms and legs smooth. A matching stool is in front of it.

Across from it on the right, there's a cell with a beautiful, red-eyed man who looks like death has embraced him. He stands in nothing but his black silk boxers, wavering on his bare feet. The gashes have healed from where they bled him back home, though he's sickly pale, his chest stained red from when they slit his throat. Blood cakes his medium-brown, collarbone-length hair, and I wish I could run my fingers through the tangles to clean up those beautiful curls and waves.

"Denendrius!" I cry as I stumble down the steps and struggle to break Mateo's constrictor grip. I ache to run to him, to lace my fingers through his and kiss him through the bars. "Denendrius, I love you."

His fists clench the iron bars of his dark cell, his fangs bared as he gasps for breath like the smell of me causes him pain. "I— love you—" His gaze drifts to Viorel. *Huarsar,* Denendrius rasps in his thick Latin accent as we stop between his cell and the circle of stone. "I've always known you were him. What have you done to her?"

"Viorel," he corrects, his flat expression unchanging. "It's good to see you back where you belong and with your memories returned to you, rat. Do you like your cell? I had this section built special for you."

"What are you doing to her, Huarsar?" Denendrius tries to subdue the shake in his voice. "She's innocent."

"You'll address me as Viorel. You may begin by telling me what you did to Tatiana after you kidnapped her."

"I didn't kidnap her," Denendrius chokes out, his wet eyes shifting to me. "What did you do to Marianna?"

"No? Then why was she kicking, screaming, and begging for her father while you used her as your human shield?" Viorel says.

He clenches the flat, square bars and blinks a handful of times to ward off tears. "It was an act. She didn't want her father to think she was abandoning her family. Tatiana begged me to show her the world since you wouldn't allow it."

There's no reaction on Viorel's face to his words. "You kidnapped and killed my niece, murdered my closest companion, and created such a mess we were too weak to properly defend ourselves when later attacked."

A thin tear slips down Denendrius's pallid cheek, his hateful glare locked on Viorel as his lips press firmly together.

"What did you do to her?" Viorel demands.

White rims Denendrius's eyes as he stands rigid. "I drowned her in the Sava River." The words tumble out of his mouth like a desperate plea.

"What did you do?"

"I know you're not deaf," Denendrius spits, gaze darkening.

Viorel reaches a hand toward me—a threat—and I shrink into Mateo. "It was an opportunity to alter your answer."

Denendrius's deep swallow is visible. "I told you. I drowned her in the Sava River."

Viorel lowers his hand and pushes out a timed breath. "I marked Tatiana, you see. I felt her fear when you were tearing through my home, felt all the *pain* you inflicted before you killed her. Are you attempting to convince me it took you two and a half hours to drown her?"

The corner of Denendrius's lip twitches. "I didn't say it was quick."

Viorel inhales sharply and lifts his head higher, unblinking eyes locking on Denendrius. They have a long staring match ending with Viorel gritting his teeth and Denendrius smiling.

"My best mate was a mind reader after I escaped," Denendrius explains. "I've spent plenty of time learning how to keep them out."

My heart skips a beat, and I pull in a sharp breath. *He's been able to read my mind.*

Viorel's tense with fury, and I can tell from his burning stare that he's thinking about how best to torture Denendrius.

Denendrius's tears fall faster as a dark smile overtakes his trembling lips. "Do I frighten you, Huarsar? Is that why you have so many guards with you, why you've never come near me? Is that why you have me where I can't speak to other prisoners?"

Viorel merely stares at him with a curled lip like he thinks Denendrius is stupid. "You weren't worth my time in Sirmium. If there hadn't been an empty cell, I would have simply killed you. After our first chat, you were merely a toy for my guards." Viorel flexes his hand at his side. "Now, I'll give you one final opportunity for honesty."

Denendrius pulls in a shaky breath as he frowns, and a tear darts from the corner of his eye before he can lift his weak hand fast enough to stop it. His eyes flicker to me and he mouths he loves me. His gaze cuts back to Viorel. "I swear I only drowned her," he sobs. *"That's all I remember."*

I ache not being able to run and comfort him. I wish I could tell him how sorry I am and beg for his forgiveness.

"Cut the waterworks. You can't fool me. I can feel your emotions, so quit exaggerating them," Viorel orders.

And like Denendrius flips a switch, he does. His expression smooths, darkness descending over his burning gaze as he locks eyes with Viorel. The tears on his cheeks look foreign, like they were never his to begin with. "I only drowned her," he snarls, some of his accent lifting away.

Goosebumps freckle my arms. But if Viorel has so many abilities, surely, he can manipulate emotions as well. He's doing this to make Denendrius look heartless. But I know better. I know Denendrius is different now, still like he was when he was human. Like he said, only his mortality will change.

"I don't believe you," Viorel says. "You've been a liar since the beginning. Your maker warned my men you were dangerous, and I heard the violence of your thoughts."

Denendrius grits his teeth and bares his fangs. "He lied about me killing his family, and I stand by that truth. If you could read my thoughts, then you heard my innocence."

"Thoughts are often full of lies, of ideas, fantasies, and false memories. They're not always reliable or a true indication of reality. Besides, it didn't help how when I spoke of your maker and what he told my men, you regretted not having gone through with killing him while he was still human. You wanted to stage an accident so you could take his wife."

A jealous burn rips through me. Was he really in love with Marciana despite his denial?

Denendrius's lip twitches. "It was an idea I only entertained once, and only again because he hurt me. I agreed to marry his daughter. She was going to grow up like his wife."

Viorel lifts his nose. "It indicated your character and was another nail in your coffin."

"I would have never done it," Denendrius snarls.

Eyes narrowing, Viorel says, "Almost two thousand years later and jealousy still burns inside you like acid."

"Tell me what you've done to Marianna *now!*"

"You're not in a position to be making demands, rat." Viorel's tone is cutting. "Not when you stand there and lie with such conviction."

"I told you the truth!" His tone seeps with desperation.

I wish Viorel would believe him. What does he want Denendrius to do? Lie until he's satisfied with his answer?

"So be it." Viorel's lip twitches with fury.

In a flash, Viorel captures my arm and yanks Tatiana's bracelet off. As Denendrius watches with a careful gaze and a line between his brows, Viorel grips it in front of him in his palm. Viorel's eyes turn a milky white as he stands still as stone, like he's in a trance.

"Wait—What's he doing?" Denendrius asks as he watches in horror.

Nobody responds.

A moment later, Viorel blinks—eyes crimson again—and meets Denendrius with a burning glare. *"She was dead before her body hit the water, you animal!"*

Denendrius shakes his head desperately, his chest rising and falling with harsh breaths.

I yelp when Viorel seizes my wrist and shoves the bracelet on. Though I understand he must have an ability allowing him to view Tatiana's last moments through the bracelet, I do my best not to contemplate what he saw.

"Restrain him," Viorel orders as his harsh gaze scans the collection of guards. "I'm going to cut his cock off and his tongue out. Don't give him enough blood to heal until my say and throw him in the oubliette when I leave."

"No," I gasp, my vision swimming. The candlelight blurs. I can't feel the floor beneath my feet.

"No—wait—" Denendrius searches his cell like there's somewhere to run.

"Mateo, hold Marianna." Viorel yanks a long knife with a wooden handle from the sheath of the nearest guard's hip.

Keys jingle as a guard steps up to Denendrius's cell. He disappears from sight as it creaks open, shouting empty warnings at Viorel while the shadows mask him.

As I try to run between Viorel and Denendrius's cell in a futile attempt to stop him, Mateo pulls my body tight to his. I writhe as he turns me away.

"Please," I cry, tears flooding my cheeks as I fight against his unwavering grip. "Viorel, please don't hurt him!"

"Keep her quiet, Mateo," Viorel commands from behind us.

Mateo gently places his hand over my mouth, and I release a muffled shriek into his palm. My attempts to kick free are futile.

"Don't you dare come near me!" Denendrius bellows, seething with so much anger I can hear how his teeth clench. *"I'll make you regret it."*

I'm dizzy, heart drumming in my ears as I listen to the brutal sounds of Denendrius's attempt to fight. My ears ring, and I feel outside myself as his pained shrieking echoes off the stone and pierces my ears.

Nothing feels real. Darkness half-descends over my vision as I lose my sense of balance. For a second, I convince myself I'm in a nightmare.

The sound of my name shakes some of the fog away, though I still feel like I'm spinning.

"You want to know what I'm going to do to Marianna before I make her mine?" Viorel's whisper snakes around me, and he's half-laughing as he continues taunting Denendrius in Latin.

I'm nauseous at Denendrius's furious and gurgling protest. It's paired with beating against the stone like he's trying to kick free.

I can tell Viorel is smiling when he whispers, *"You should be thankful I'll be gentler than you were. Any which way, you'll feel her pain, same as how I had to feel Tatiana's."*

My eyelids flutter, bile rising in my throat as my heart pounds so fast I can't see straight.

Would Mateo stop him from hurting me? Or would he be a blindly loyal guard despite originally signing up to "save me"?

Mateo's whisper against my ear sounds light years away. "Don't pay them any attention."

How could I not?

Time must carry on without me—or maybe it's over so soon —until Viorel is stepping up the few steps to the hall and twisting back to look at Mateo and me. Denendrius's thick blood soaks his hands and drips from the front edges of his long hair. There's spatter on his pale face, like Denendrius spat it at him when he was cutting out his tongue.

"That's all for now," he says.

I can't feel my legs, can barely comprehend what's happened, so Mateo tucks me at his side and drags me up the stairs. Denendrius's agonized sobs are the only thing I can think about as I'm carried away.

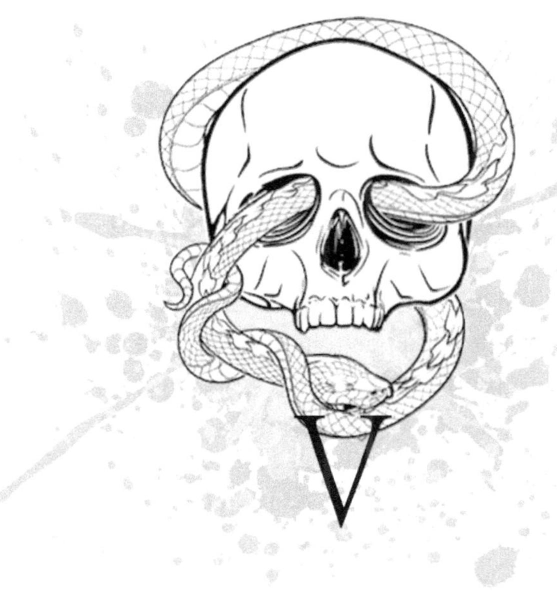

Mateo sets me on my cell bed and leaves me alone to sob, shutting the iron door behind him as Viorel walks off. He curls his blood-soaked hands in front of himself like he's worried about dislodging a drop of Denendrius's blood onto his precious floor. The sound of the bathroom sink running cuts through my wet blubbering.

The sight of Viorel's blood-soaked flesh sears into my mind, Denendrius's screams, and Viorel's threats toward me echoing in my ears.

Sitting on my pillow, I flinch and curl tighter against the wall when Viorel appears between my bed and the dresser. *"Please—"*

"I won't touch you, I promise," he says with a tone so gentle compared to what I'm used to that it still has me wincing. "I may be a lot of things, but an animal is not on that list."

"Why did you tell Denendrius you would?" I sob, not fully believing him. He's a monster, after all.

"There are very few things truly capable of hurting him

these days, and he needs to *suffer*," he explains. "I need him to hurt *badly, Marianna.*"

My lip quivers as I study the fresh calm now shaping his face. "So, what are you going to do to me?" I choke out.

He sighs—the sound more of exhaustion than annoyance—and drifts away, the metal frame of his bone bed creaking moments later.

"Come to my bed, Marianna." His worn voice has a hint of friendliness, though I'm smart enough to know the request is not. Denendrius claimed he wasn't a rapist too when he was first a vampire, and it didn't take long to learn otherwise.

"Why?" I croak. I'm not dim enough to disobey him after what he did to Denendrius, so I stand and stumble over every slow step to his bed.

He doesn't answer until I reach the empty bedside and ask again.

"You make a good bed warmer," he says simply. "Additionally, the sound of you tossing and turning in discomfort is *aggravating.*"

I close my heavy eyes and gulp, feeling my way onto the bed so I don't have to watch myself near him. Even as I pull the heavy blankets around myself while an anxious shiver rips through me, I don't dare peek.

Once I settle—icy still with my hands clutching the blanket tight to myself—the only sound between Viorel and me is the deafening drumming of my heart and his shallow breaths.

I'm unsure how long I lie with my eyes screwed closed, waiting for sleep or for him to make true to his threats to Denendrius, but the feel of hands around my throat has my eyes flying wide open.

I stare up at Denendrius's blood-streaked face, a clear and starry sky behind him. I try to comprehend how I'm outside with him when moments ago I was lying next to Viorel. He looks monstrous beyond what I've ever seen, the veins in his eyes bloody, the purplish ones beneath his lower lids protruding.

When my eyes shift, the sight of his naked body slamming roughly into mine has a scream swelling in my constricted throat.

My body is on fire. My bones are aching as my heart drums so fast with terror it's about to burst. Denendrius's hands tighten on my throat as his eyes bore into mine. Pressure builds in my skull with my breathlessness. Wetness creeps up my hair, cold against my scalp, as his movements force me closer to the gushing current in my peripheral. I find I don't have a single ounce of strength left to move, and I realize I can't feel my legs —or him—anymore.

When Denendrius lifts my limp wrist to his bloody lips, the arm the ouroboros bracelet slides down is too skinny and tanned to be mine, and I realize I must be in a nightmare. I don't feel his fangs as they rip into my vein. My gold-ringed fingers don't move when I ask them to. They must have worked once since my nails are torn and bloody.

I can't understand his snarled Latin between the moans emitting from behind his grit and bared, bloody teeth. But I'm not sure comprehending the language would help when the rushing water intermittently fills my ears.

As my eyes fly open, Viorel jerks upright beside me. The candles come alight, shadows flickering across his blank expression. He stares through the suffocating air surrounding us, something haunting in his unblinking eyes.

I try to wrangle my breath back and can't help but rub my throat with my hand while wiggling my toes under the blankets to test if I can feel them.

"What the fuck was that?" I breathe, trying to swallow down creeping hysteria. "That felt so real."

"Apologies," he mumbles, voice so low I question if he said

anything at all. "Some abilities are harder to control than others. I didn't intend for that to happen."

"That was your dream?" I realize as I pull in a deep breath, but it isn't enough to push back the heavy ones coming next, or the tears burning my dry eyes like acid.

"Yes." He stares into space for a long moment, lips parted, before he adds, "An echo of her final moments."

My eyes fall to the ouroboros bracelet around my wrist before my tears blur the sight of it. I shove my tears away with the heel of my hand.

The bed frame creaks as he stands. With a blank expression, he stares down at me with disturbed eyes for a painful moment before he drifts off.

I question the time, unable to tell if we were asleep for five minutes or five hours. Yet I don't dare ask him to clarify.

He mumbles something to himself as he wanders back into the room, crosses by the end of the bed, and swings around to leave.

My tears sneak up on me again, the pain in my chest so serrated every breath is a battle. My mind traces over memories as I cry quietly, looping over and over our time in Bellevue and our demise. I end up wearing a path so deep I'm stuck on the thoughts for what feels like hours.

Viorel seems stuck on a path of his own, pacing back and forth from the iron door to the bathroom.

With his repetition, it becomes distracting enough that all I can think about is what *he's* possibly thinking about. Is he contemplating what to do with me? Plotting better ways to fuck with Denendrius? Does he keep replaying Tatiana's death in his head?

Viorel halts at the end of the bed, eyes locked on me. "I want you to think about her death, too."

I gulp. Has he been listening to my thoughts the entire time? "I have—"

"Have you?" he interrupts, the corner of his lip twitching and exposing a fang.

My breath swells in my throat, but I manage to nod.

"Your mind travels to the images and flees back to you and Denendrius," he says. "Think about what happened."

I wince as the violent images rush through my mind, unable to help but rub my throat from the memory. "I am."

But Viorel doesn't know the entire story between Denendrius and Tatiana either, doesn't know the version I've heard. He hasn't heard how Tatiana told him about the cure for vampirism, how she promised to bring it to him if he escaped and got her out with him, only to discover she had no intentions of finding it and wanted Denendrius to turn her.

"Do you know how I'm certain Denendrius is not a good man, and I did not make a mistake in Sirmium?" He looks pointedly at me. "By his blood slave's behavior. By her fractured mind."

My lips part to speak, but he lifts a hand to silence me.

"You haven't grasped his role in her suffering because *he* doesn't feel remorse himself. You feel guilty for his capture, because in the back of his mind he blames you for being here but overlooks it because he has you as he wants you."

Tears streak my cheeks. "You told him I sent that tip?"

"No. He blames you for trying to rid him from your life and how it led to this."

I shake my head and lower my eyes. "Everything he did when he was first a vampire . . ." The memories flash through my mind. The way he'd beat me and force himself on me, how he killed my best friend Jenna, raped Sarah and countless other girls. "It's not him. He died and reawakened as who he first was as a human, before he turned, before you and your guards corrupted him. That's the man you have captive in your dungeon. Even he says the memories don't feel like his own."

Viorel's pitying eyes ponder me. "You've done what all

blood slaves do. Subconsciously, you found a way to give your master what he wants, even at your own expense. He wants you to disregard the ways he harmed you. He doesn't want it to factor into your feelings for him, so it no longer does."

"You're trying to turn me against him," I accuse.

"I can't. Not even if I brutally torture you," Viorel says, matter of fact. "Not with the depth of his mark."

Mateo carries in a silver platter with a heaping portion of waffles and whipped cream while saying, "There's a dozen people requesting permanent leave—bags already packed— and another handful considering the same."

Viorel scowls from his throne across the room. His grip tightens on the curved ends of the arms as he lifts his nose, his brows drawing together. "Word has spread about my part in Sirmium, I suspect? Have they lost their trust in me?"

I shift on the antique sofa and lower my burning face, while Mateo sets the platter directly under my line of sight on the table. I'm glad people know the truth about Viorel now, though I can't help but flick my gaze up to his serious face to see if he's looking at me and considering how to punish me. Thankfully, his scrutiny is on Mateo, who rounds the coffee table to sit beside me.

"It has nothing to do with you," Mateo assures him as he picks up a silver fork and holds it out to me. "They refuse to be near the castle while Denendrius is here."

I tremble as I take it, but my lack of appetite has my hand wavering above my plate. Still, I force my fork through the waffle, so I don't give Viorel another reason to be angry at me.

"So, they don't trust me," Viorel says slowly, which has Mateo releasing a quiet sigh of defeat.

They're right not to trust you, I think at him while I shove the fork deeper into my waffle.

"They don't trust Denendrius." Mateo leans back onto the couch and glances between me and my food.

I tear a chunk off and shove it in my mouth as Viorel's harsh gaze trails over me. It takes a couple of swallows to get the piece down.

"They fear him escaping?" Viorel questions.

They should. I glower at Viorel and stuff another bite of food into my mouth.

Mateo gives him a what-can-I-say shrug, an apology in his eyes.

Viorel scoffs. "Preposterous."

"Can I relay permission for them to leave? I'll organize a trip out."

Viorel sucks his teeth before grumbling, "Of course. I'm not happy about it, but I'm not going to hold them hostage." Before Mateo can say anything more, he adds, "Did you find out who was spiting me with wagers against Marianna's life?"

My hand freezes with my fork halfway to my mouth, and my gaze jerks to Mateo.

Mateo draws in a deep breath, like he knows Viorel won't like his answer. "No, but we're keeping watch. Paying attention particularly to Josephine, the Mesaline family, Duran, and the Angel Maker."

The emotionless stare Viorel gives Mateo has the hair standing up on my arms, and I swiftly eat my forkful of waffle and occupy myself by tearing off another chunk.

"You're not usually so incompetent," Viorel says evenly, a slight wince passing over Mateo's face at his words. "You're wasting your time letting your personal grudges and the most obvious suspects cloud your vision."

"Perhaps they think they can get away with it because they would be too obvious—"

Viorel lifts his hand off the armrest to silence him. "Broaden your search. Somebody knows something."

Mateo gives him a firm nod before leaving us alone.

I lick whipped cream from the corners of my mouth and lower my eyes to my food as Viorel's lethal stare settles on me. "What's going to happen to me?" I ask for what feels like the hundredth time.

Viorel stands and gracefully walks off, leaving me with a tight throat and tears rising in the backs of my eyes. Does he not know anymore? Or has he decided, and is merely letting me stew in the dark of my own theories to torment me?

Despite my non-existent appetite, I force down the rest of my food since my next meal isn't guaranteed.

Candlelight flickering at the mouth of the hall catches my attention, and I suspect it's coming from the room usually dark between this one and my cell. I get my fawn legs under me and take tentative steps to the wide stone doorway of a candlelit room packed with crooked bookshelves of different stain and size, teeming with books, papers, and trinkets. They surround Viorel, who sits at the other side of a long and heavy-looking table I suspect is from the Middle Ages, placed horizontally in the center of the room.

"Sit down," he says, eyes scanning the pieces of a wooden jigsaw puzzle with an overwhelming number of pieces. There are thousands, if I had to guess.

"A hundred thousand," he corrects. "Don't lay a hand on a single one."

I waver forward into the musty air, candlelight casting dancing shadows across the ceiling and furniture.

Gripping the thick top of the tall wooden chair, I wiggle it away from the table and study the room as I sit. There are yellowed papers stuffed between books of varying ages on the sagging shelves. The bronze and gold trinkets I can't quite distinguish in the low lighting only make me mildly curious.

Books I suspect are from the early 1900s are stacked haphazardly along the bottom of the shelves on the floor. A couple of wooden crates filled with teen novels have me pursing my lips, the idea he'd read the same books found in my old school library silly. I recognize a few of the spines as teen romances and mysteries I can't imagine someone like him finding interest in.

There's a record player with a horn in the far-right corner of the room, and the short shelf of records on the floor below it has a violin propped against it.

Unsure what to do, I scan the puzzle on the off chance I might make a connection. They're tiny little pieces, about the size of my pinky nail, and each has carved lines, curls, and swirls. I can't fathom the image they will create. Though the border and a few unattached sections are complete, they give no hint as to what it could be.

"It's abstract," he grumbles. "There is no grand image."

"Oh." *Get out of my head.*

I chew my cheek while he lazily snaps pieces together for what feels like *fucking hours*. How much of my life will now comprise sitting around uselessly?

When I pluck a smooth piece up, I find comfort in the hard point of a corner as it settles into my palm and pokes into my skin.

I'm lost in thought as I rub my thumb against the carved lines, only vaguely aware of Viorel's grumbled curses as he picks through different piles.

The sound of Viorel's loud inhale and slow exhale as he sits back in his chair draws my eyes to him, his grit teeth and sharp gaze turning me to stone.

"Are you usually so fucking contumacious?" he snarls.

My heart slams into my ribs, and I'm too confused about his choice of words and how they relate to his anger, that it takes far too many moments of clutching my fists to realize I'm holding one of his puzzle pieces. I gasp and fling it onto the table between us.

"I'm sorry, I wasn't thinking—"

"*Shh.*" He takes the piece and snaps it into place.

I mash my lips together and swallow. It seems like hours pass before my heartbeat and rushing thoughts slow.

Though he pays me little to no attention—only checking I haven't absentmindedly stolen another piece—I spend the entire time watching him as I do my best to tread through an ocean of despair while waves of fury crash down upon me. I imagine Denendrius bloody and pained while Viorel sits and relaxes.

Is there anything in the universe capable of making this bastard pay? I can only imagine how many other innocent people he's hurt over his eternity.

As the tall candle flames wither, the closest pillar candle on an iron stand next to Viorel snuffs out as he stares at the table with his hands in his lap and a distant look in his eyes. I can't help but think he's sitting there feeling sorry for himself.

Poor fucking vampire king got what he deserved by having his home destroyed by the innocent man he tortured, and he has the balls to consider himself the victim? I hope everyone in this castle turns on him, starting with Mateo.

I lean against the table, and wrangle enough breath to whisper, "I hope he gets out and comes for you. I hope he destroys everything again."

The fucker flat out ignores me, eyes finally moving to scan the table before he lazily selects a piece and puts it into place.

"Did you hear me?" I snarl.

"Go to your room," he orders flatly as the candle reignites, "before you say something that gives us both regrets."

I lean back in the chair and cross my arms, blood burning with adrenaline and fury.

"*No.* Why don't you kill me?" I demand, unable to help the desperate ache sneaking through.

His eyes snap to mine, the lethal look in them slapping the fury out of me. "You're not dying, parrot."

I duck my head to stare at my lap. My quick bout of bravery has exhaustion settling into me and the familiar burn of tears returns to my eyes as I think of Denendrius trying to be brave in the dungeon.

My vision swims, my waffle feeling rotten in my stomach.

What are they doing to him down there?

I try to distract myself from a splatter of gory thoughts by settling my gaze back on Viorel.

I hope Denendrius tortures the fuck out of you when he escapes, I think at him.

Viorel scrutinizes the wooden puzzle pieces with a furrowed brow and narrowed eyes. Knowing his mind probably works leaps and bounds faster than even the average vampire, I'm surprised he's struggling. Even Denendrius would have placed each one by now. Yet Viorel looks like he's moments away from sweeping the entire thing off the table with his arm. Maybe he's not so smart. After all, he was dumb enough to make an enemy out of Denendrius.

His fingers clench the piece he holds, and his eyes jerk up to mine and tighten.

"Go replace your shirt," he demands, his upper lip twitching to expose a fang.

"Why?" I snap. "Are you looking at my tits? Just don't."

He scowls. "*Now.*"

What's his issue? Has he not been touched by a woman in eons or something? He should be able to handle sitting a few feet from me while I'm wearing a tank top.

When his fist meets the table, wooden pieces jump, and I leap to my feet.

Through grit teeth, he snarls, "*Go.*"

Breathless, I rush to my cell and swap my tank top for a black T-shirt that covers my collarbones.

His eyes flick up to mine when I sit back down, and with an even voice, says, "I'm thinking of cutting Denendrius's name from your skin."

My heart beats so fast I'm woozy. That's what he kept looking at? The scar of Denendrius's name that he carved into my skin after deciding not to kill me in the woods?

"Please don't," I beg.

His expression is unreadable. "It's a stain on you."

"It would hurt," I squeak.

"I'd be kind about it," he says simply before he plucks another puzzle piece up and scans the table. "It's better if it's taken care of now. If you're still, it will be painless. Promise."

My jaw falls open a little in equal parts horror and disbelief as tears well in my eyes. I struggle for breath, my words sounding airy. "Please don't . . ."

He doesn't acknowledge my response, merely sets the piece in place before selecting another.

"You won't, right?" I mouth, completely out of air now.

I squirm in my chair for what feels like another hour, painfully aware of his lack of an answer. Needing an excuse to leave the room, I blurt, "Can I go to the washroom?"

He grumbles and shoos me with his hand while joining two smaller sections of pieces together.

I waver when I stand and hasten away, taking my sweet time in hopes he'll be a little more rational when I return.

Yet when I step down into his bedroom, he's taking a velvet bag from his nightstand.

"Come lie on the bed," he says, tired impatience in his voice. "It'll take mere moments."

I freeze in place as he unties the bag and gently draws a silver blade with a decorative handle from it.

The room spins, my vision shrinking as the sound of my heart pounds in my ears.

He sighs. "For your own sake, Marianna, *make this simple.* It won't hurt."

My head snaps toward the sitting room in search of escape, then I'm running and screaming at the top of my lungs for Mateo, my voice echoing against the stone.

I only make it to the wardrobe when my feet fly out from under me, and my palms slap against the hard floor before my face can. I'm shrieking and pleading as an invisible force flips me on my back, kicking as I'm dragged across the floor and into his path.

"No! Stop!" I shrill, as Viorel sighs, his languid steps carrying him toward where I thrash uselessly on the floor, locked in place.

I bat at him as he steps over me and adjusts his gown to lower himself to a squat above my stomach. He lets me pummel him with my fists—completely unbothered—as he sets the blade aside to free his hands to capture mine. Despite my fight, he's gentle as he forces my arms against the stone.

My lungs burn, my head aching from my relentless screams as I try to thrash out of his grip. I'd kick his back if my legs weren't glued to the floor.

Viorel splays my arms out at my sides, traps them under his legs, and bunches the velvet bag in his hand.

"Bite," he commands as he holds my jaw open, long nails pinching my cheeks. He places the velvet bag between my teeth, and I gag against the mass of rough fabric on my tongue.

Even with the makeshift gag, my muffled hollering doesn't lessen. It amplifies when he picks the blade back up.

Staring down at me, he pulls in a deep breath before icily stating, "Had you cooperated, we could have saved your shirt. But . . ." I flail as he hooks the edge of the knife on the collar and effortlessly slices it open down the middle. "You leave me no other choice but to do this barbarously. One mark of his is enough, never mind *this*. You'll give me your gratitude one day, Marianna."

I twitch under his soft touch when he moves the ripped fabric aside to expose Denendrius's name above my breast. The sound of my terror makes my ears ring, tears blurring my sight of him as I feel the cold pressure of the blade against my chest.

Adrenaline pounds through me, so much it must cover the worst of the pain as the steel cuts through my skin. Though I feel the heat of my wet blood flooding my flesh and dripping down my side to pool between my back and the stone, the only pain is a mild stinging sensation coming in waves.

Still, I sob and shriek as Viorel carves Denendrius's name off of my skin. Soon, the sound of Mateo's hollering and banging on the iron door breaks through the ringing in my ears.

I manage a raspy breath when Viorel climbs off me, but I can't move more than my head. He wanders off—paying no attention to Mateo's hollering and demands to know what's going on—only to return and straddle me again.

He pulls the makeshift gag from my mouth, the word "please" immediately tumbling out as I stare up at him through bleary eyes.

"It's finished," he says limply as he wipes something soft across my eyes and cheeks, clearing them of tears. His gaze holding mine, he adds, "You won't tell anyone of this."

Cold droplets drip from the corners of my eyes and into my ears as he wipes the blood from my chest with the black cloth.

My gaze flicks down to my heaving chest. Denendrius's name is gone. The flesh where it once was is now perfectly unmarred despite the streaks of red on my olive skin. There's no sign of Viorel's knife having neared me.

"Go on, redress," Viorel commands as he stands.

Free from psychic restraints, I roll over onto my hands and

knees and freeze at the sight of Viorel opening the iron door and plunging the knife into Mateo's stomach. Mateo grunts, blood spraying from his mouth and across the side of Viorel's face.

Through the sound of my labored breathing, I catch Viorel whisper, "Your trust in me is waning, Mateo. You know I am not a man with such inclinations. You're my best friend. This is a dangerous predicament you're creating for both of us now. May you right the issue at once."

Mateo nods and Viorel yanks the knife from him. He coughs. "I'm sorry."

There's no change in Viorel's expression. "See if Ainsley will aid Marianna with a bath, since you care about her well-being so bloody much."

Mateo turns and disappears, and I scramble to my feet as Viorel locks the iron door. When he turns to face me, my breath catches and I dart to my cell, throw my dirty nightgown on since it's the closest piece of clothing to me, and hunker down against the wall on my pillow to hug myself and sob.

I flinch when Viorel appears in the doorway, wiping Mateo's blood off his face with the rag.

"I wasn't dishonest about it not hurting," he says.

I can't help the sobs wracking my body. "You're a demon. You had no right!"

He frowns. "Please tell me a more graceful way we could have fixed it. I had to re-injure you so I could heal you myself. I wanted to do something nice for you."

"You did it to torture Denendrius. I bet he felt how terrified I was," I spit.

It was a crude scar, but with it gone, he's ripped another piece of Denendrius from me.

Viorel wipes his hands clean with the cloth and walks away.

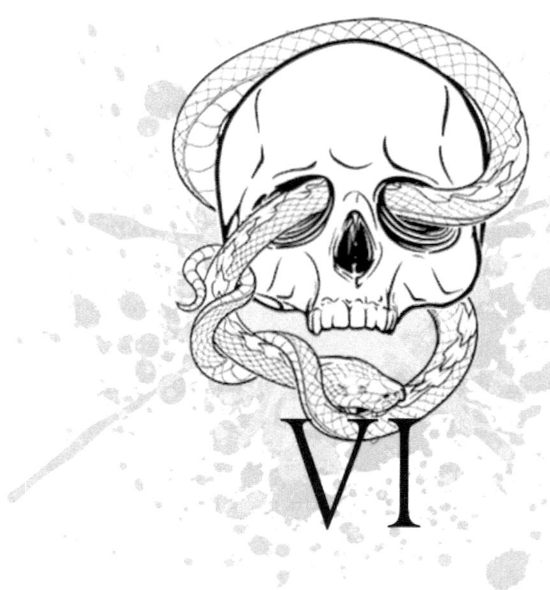

I cry quietly in my bed while playing over Viorel's attack in my head. He settles back at his puzzle like nothing of significance happened. When the sound of the iron door creaking open cuts through the still air, I bolt upright.

A woman's cheery, heavily accented voice—elegant British—has me listening intently.

There's a mumble of tired greetings between Mateo, Viorel, and the woman before she says, "You look quite horrible, Viorel. When was the last time you fed?"

"I'm fine, Ainsley—"

"It's been a couple of weeks," Mateo chimes in.

She clicks her tongue at him. "What's starving yourself going to achieve?"

"I've no appetite," Viorel argues.

"You must drink anyway. It's no wonder Marianna's terrified of you. You're looking more like a creature than a man," Ainsley scolds.

I cringe, wondering how long until Viorel meets her with the same fury he met Mateo with earlier.

"And when was the last time you left your chamber?" she continues.

He huffs. "I went to the dungeon yesterday."

"That doesn't count," she insists.

"Over a month," he grumbles. "It's not your concern."

From the hint of misplaced authority in her voice, I can imagine her shaking her finger at him. "You've been wearing that gown as long too, I bet." she adds. "What about outside? When did you last breathe fresh air?"

Damn, she's really pushing it. I can't help but think of Viorel driving that knife into Mateo's gut and wonder if he'd harm her similarly.

There's a long silence of wooden puzzle pieces clicking together before Viorel grumbles, "The air down here is plenty sufficient."

Mateo answers for Viorel like he can't recall getting stabbed. "He stepped out into the garden for a few minutes four months ago."

Viorel groans. "Quit trying to mother me like one of the nursery children and tend to Marianna."

"We're merely looking out for you," Mateo says. "We care."

"You haven't marked her yet," Ainsley scolds, sounding like a mother who found out their child hadn't started some chore yet.

"I'll get to it," he snaps, the piling frustration clear in his voice.

She clicks her tongue in disapproval. "It's a permanent decision, I understand, but it won't become any easier to make the longer you put it off."

It sounds like Viorel is talking through his teeth when he says, "*Please*, Ainsley."

"All right, all right. But I suggest you don't take too long. I've got excited young ladies waiting for you to deliver their new friend." She heaves out a dramatic sigh. "What's the poor thing doing, anyway?" Ainsley says with concerned curiosity as the click of her heels approaches.

A tall and beautiful blond woman appears around the corner with Mateo. She looks in her forties with sharp features and pinned curls. Her chunky white heels peek out from the lace of the white dress she wears beneath a baby-blue corset with a strip of white lace along the top and bottom.

Her gentle pink smile meets her onyx eyes as they settle on me.

"Hi, darling," she says as she takes careful steps toward my cell, like she thinks I'm a fearful little kitten ready to become a hissing ball of fur if she approaches too swiftly. "I'm Mateo's wife, Ainsley."

I'm unsure what to say, so I simply wipe away leftover tears with the heel of my hand.

Mateo holds up a large black wicker basket with a lavender towel draped over its contents and places it in front of me on my bed. "Some of the girls put it together for you."

My arms are weak, hands shaking, as I lift them and pull the towel off. They packed the basket with beauty items and basic toiletries like period products and dental care supplies. I only recognize a fourth of the brands—the makeup, mostly—as the labels on everything else are in various languages. The shampoos, lotions, perfumes, and soaps look expensive, and a clash of scents hit my nose as I dig through them.

I look up at Mateo and say with a mousy voice, "Thank you."

Ainsley sits at the end of my bed and grins at me while Mateo gives me a brief nod and walks off. I note the brush of pink blush across her pale skin that otherwise couldn't exist with her immortality. "Go on, pick some items for your bath. Mateo will start the water."

I gather toiletries, floral soaps, and a bath bomb before standing on shaky legs.

As Ainsley follows me into the bathroom carrying half my supplies and sticks around, I suspect she's there to ensure I don't drown myself.

Not having had a bath in days, I can't find it in me to complain about the lack of privacy when she moves a wooden stool to the end of the tub and sits. I suppose I'm thankful it's not Mateo or Viorel supervising.

She smiles and shades her eyes with her pale hand while I peel off my filthy nightgown and with it a layer of sweat and stench making my face burn and my nose wrinkle with both anger and embarrassment.

The water is a tad hot when I step into it, so I stand with my sticky arms wrapped across my chest with the water up to my knees, while Ainsley blindly plops the bath bomb in. I watch it fizzle in the low candlelight surrounding me from dozens of yellow flames. The smell of roses fills the room as the water adopts a pink tinge.

I blow out a slow breath and shakily lower myself into the water. Ainsley offers to wash my hair for me and promises I'll feel better once I'm bathed like she thinks the water is enough to wash Denendrius's blood mark away.

But Denendrius's blood mark is here to stay unless Viorel overwrites it or Denendrius dies, and I know they plan on keeping him around to torture for eternity.

"What's Viorel going to do with me?" I ask Ainsley.

She rakes her fingers through my hair, the cold of her hands soothing to my aching head as she lathers the rose-scented shampoo. "He's going to keep you, isn't it obvious?"

My heart beats so hard with terror I check if the water's rippling.

Her chilly breath fans against my ear as she whispers, "I

know you don't want to be marked, but he'll be an excellent master to you."

I pull my legs up—knees poking out of the rosy water—and hug them. "It's difficult to believe."

She playfully clicks her tongue at me. "I know he's quite cross right now, but you reek like Denendrius and won't stop advocating for him. Trust, if he had lesser plans for you, he would have acted already. Instead, he's given you a space in his own chamber, fed you, given up half his bed for you since you've been cold and uncomfortable, and is letting you accept gifts and bathe in his tub. Every other blood slave or familiar picked up with a prisoner could never dream of making it to Viorel."

She fills a silver pitcher, and I look up at the wooden ceiling arcs as she gently tilts my head back to rinse my hair. Hot tears streak my cheeks and drip into the water. *I would really rather die,* I choke out before throwing my head forward onto my knees to sob. "I just want to go home."

"Oh . . ." She rests her cold hand on my shoulder. "How horrendous this hold Denendrius has on your mind, that you'd rather leave this world than be happy and free with people who care for you." Giving my shoulder a squeeze, she adds, "I promise, everything will be okay, Marianna. This darkness will fade for both you and your new master. Having another familiar will do him good, especially someone who shares a common pain with him."

"Great," I whisper. It's nice to have a confident answer now, but it still makes me think of slipping my head under the water.

Maybe I won't be capable of recognizing the genuine horror of my life once Viorel marks me. Will I be in blissful ignorance? Should I prefer it over the pain of torture while marked to Denendrius, or being sold off to another vampire? Should I be thankful to be brainwashed over the alternative?

I'm quiet as she conditions my hair, slow tears slipping

down my face and salting the rosy bathwater. I barely have the will to scrub my body when the time comes, though the loofah scraping against my tender and sweaty skin is glorious, even in my sadness.

After a rinse, I force myself out of the water and into the towel Ainsley holds open. She wraps it around me and steps back, leaving me shivering and dripping hot water onto the cold stone.

"I'll leave you to dress. I must return to the nursery, anyway." She gives me a soft smile, and like I'm sick, adds. "Visit me when you're better, all right?"

I lower my head and stare at the puddle of water forming around my feet until she leaves. When her heels click away, I release a heavy breath before drying off and dressing in my baby blue velour tracksuit. It's still my favorite article of clothing and reminds me of Denendrius and Bellevue. Then, I scrub a layer of grime off my teeth. My eyes and head pulse with pain from incessant crying, but it helps to not have a layer of sweat and stink on me.

I sit on the pew across from the doorway into his reading room where my basket has been moved to. There are a few snack packages—chocolates and mini bags of chips—tucked into the basket.

"Better?" Viorel heaves out the word like it's a weight on his tongue. He flips through a thick leather book on the tabletop, eyes flicking back and forth over the words.

"Thanks," I whisper, straightening my damp hair with my shaky fingers.

Viorel glances up at me, his gaze returning to the pages for a beat before he swiftly lifts his head and stares at me. "Hm."

I swallow and straighten the hood of my zip-up sweater. "What?"

His eyes trail over the angles and curves of my face for

another skin-crawling second before he jerks his stare down to his book. "Nothing."

Unsure what else to do with myself, I continue sorting through the various cosmetics. As I ponder a plastic package of nail polishes with the pads of my fingers—perhaps I should pretty up in case I get to see Denendrius again—I swear I catch Viorel watching me from the corner of my eye. But every time I look over, he's trained his attention on his book.

I swallow a nervous lump only grown bigger by the passing hours, and pop open the package. By the time I get a bottle of baby blue polish in my hand, I can't imagine I thought I had the will to paint my nails.

"That's a nice shade of blue," Viorel says, glazed eyes making me think he's fighting sleep, and possibly approaching delirium considering it sounds like he's been on a hunger strike and is suddenly trying to engage in benign conversation. "Is blue your favorite color? It appears in much of your clothing."

His opinion has me placing it back in the basket. "Yes."

As if not a casual word had passed between us, he tilts his head back toward his book.

I can't help but think about what I know of starving vampires, of how thirst preludes crazy, and a fearful draft wafts down my back. How much blood does a ten-thousand-year-old vampire need? More than a younger vampire, or less? Is he more likely to lose his mind and turn to me to satisfy his thirst, or does he have impeccable control, even with weeks of deprivation?

"What happens now?" I squeeze the words out, a bit of a plea in them.

He exhales an exasperated breath while flipping the cover of his book closed. "Do you expect me to pen you an itinerary?"

I gulp and give my head a swift shake.

He sounds out of breath as he says, "Can you not simply *exist* without needing to be occupied every moment?"

I grit my teeth. Does he expect me to sit around and do *nothing until I lose my mind?* Perhaps it's how he plans to torture me.

Viorel's breaths are loud as he rests his hands in his lap. He closes his eyes and leans his head against the back of the chair.

I gnaw at my cheek and study him, from the wine-red of the pale flesh around his eyes, to his thick, dark brown hair hanging straight on each side of his head and down the front of his chest.

Did he use up the rest of his energy by attacking me? I hope so. It would serve him right.

How weak is he, exactly? Would he be weak enough for me *to kill?*

"I may not be reading your mind," Viorel starts, "but I know scheming when I sense it. Don't do anything stupid. You won't live long enough to regret it."

I blow a hot breath from my nostrils and glare daggers at him.

Viorel opens his eyes, his expression severe. "Rayonne survived her trip back to immortality. Of course, in your selfish self-pity, you haven't lent her a single thought."

"Rayonne's one reason I'm stuck here." I grit my teeth. "She convinced me I should seek this hell out."

"Yes," he agrees before sighing and slowly rising to his feet. "Your thanks are overdue."

VII

A nightmare traps me the moment I give in to exhaustion. I'm in my childhood bedroom, the air cold on my skin, slowly waning drugs heavy in my veins and holding me to my bed. I'm stone when the sound of boots on the old stairs outside my door carries up them. The door opens, and a man with shifty eyes slips in. He shuts the door behind him and creeps to the bed, shaky hands reaching for his belt as he slips onto the mattress beside me. A scream builds in my throat—

I'm shoved into a new dream, an unfamiliar ocean lapping at my toes as I wiggle them in the wet sand. A cool breeze pushes against my bare skin, and I look up at the sun peeking above the horizon.

The change is so abrupt, so vivid, it has me lurching upright in Viorel's bed. I gasp for breath and stare down at Viorel beside me. He faces away, completely still with even breaths.

"Viorel?" I whisper.

When he doesn't answer, I assume he's sleeping and lie

back down. I don't realize I've fallen asleep again until something slamming has my eyes popping open.

Viorel stands in front of the wardrobe on his side of the bed, eyes roving over me as he adjusts the tie of the long and black silk bathrobe he wears. "I'm going to bathe. Don't touch anything. Don't step foot off the bed. I'll know if you do."

"Okay." I swallow and rub my eyes. "Did you change my dream?"

He stares at me, hard expression unchanged. "No. Why would I?"

I tuck the blanket under my arm. "Because you have dream abilities? I was having a nightmare, and suddenly it switched as it was about to get bad. That's never happened before."

He half-scoffs and straightens the edge of his robe. "You could dream of having your eyes pecked out by crows every night and I wouldn't care. Return to sleep."

"Okay," I whisper, not fully convinced.

I ponder that until I plummet straight into another nightmare. This time I dream of Viorel sending me upstairs to be auctioned off like Denendrius warned, and a man from my childhood buys me.

The sound of the iron door opening and closing a handful of times draws me out of a deep sleep. When I fall back unconscious, I exist just below the surface in dark dreamlessness until the sound of Denendrius's sweet voice has me lurching awake.

I swing my legs off the bed, heart hammering in my breathless chest as I rush across the hard floor and toward the muffled sound of his voice in the sitting room.

But when I get there, I stop dead at the sight of Viorel holding Denendrius's camcorder. He sits on the sofa, surrounded by papers and folders. A thick yellow folder with my school's stamp on the cover rests directly beside him. There are familiar boxes—my childhood memory box, some from my social worker's office, the one full of my stuff from when I lived with Vianna and Kenneth, and the one from Denendrius's secret room—as well as a few unfamiliar plain ones and Lorimer PD branded ones around the messy coffee table and his feet. My wooden chest of sentimental items from Bellevue is open beside the coffee table and looks like he already rooted through it.

I feel outside myself, can't feel my tongue move as I struggle to speak. "W-what are you doing?" I rasp as my stomach sloshes, an oily feeling roiling through it. I hug myself, feeling completely violated.

Having him read my thoughts and wander my dreams is one thing, but now he knows *everything* about me. I wasn't even allowed to read most of that paperwork, and the stuff I peeked at only made me feel like shit. I can only imagine what kinds of items—naked medical photographs, reports, psych evaluations—are in there too.

"Studying you," he says simply as he closes the little screen on the camcorder before setting it down on a pile of papers on the coffee table. "Mateo rounded up everything they could find on you while searching for you and Denendrius. I finally became curious enough to look. It's not often I encounter a mundane human with such extensive government records kept on them."

My knees wobble, and if I wasn't so appalled, I might burst into tears. *"Why?"* Is he looking for more ways to psychologically torture me?

He hates me already, so there's no way this will do anything but make him think worse of me. On top of all the private things pertaining to Denendrius and me, he now knows everything from the detailed records of my childhood abuse, my behavioral and addiction issues, and how I was such a pain in the ass to deal with—all the recorded reasons—that I got passed on from foster home to foster home. God, if he thought I was dim before, he'll see me as nothing but a useless body full of blood now.

He moves some papers from the couch beside him and pats the space. "Sit before you fall." The friendliness in his voice sounds forced and only weakens my legs.

I cross the room and sit beside him, staring widely at my uncovered life spread around us, unable to erase the horror shaping my face.

"I know a lot of what Denendrius has been up to, believe it or not. Many rumors made it back to me. Well, not in the past century so much . . . but *before*. He's not known to take blood slaves. As far as I heard, he didn't mark his previous replacements of Mariana, either. Quite interesting, don't you think?" he says.

I manage a shrug. "I-I don't k-know."

"You have a twelve-year-old blood mark on you. I thought that was odd. He marks nobody, then takes interest in a child to mark her . . ." His gaze tightens on me. "So, I thought you must have been quite special for him to make a drastic and dangerous behavioral change. Additionally, if I'm to be your master, I should know everything about you he does, and more."

As I try not to focus on the horrible fact he admitted he's still going to mark me, I realize Denendrius has likely read these files, too. I hold back a gag and a bout of nausea rocking through me.

"I have an attachment disorder," I scramble to explain. "I was too friendly and acted like he was the best person in the world. Apparently, Mariana thought so too. With my name, I reminded him of what he knew about her when he was human."

He pulls an unfamiliar red folder out from a bunch of papers on the coffee table and sets it on the edge facing me. "You don't know what this is?"

I shake my head, a shiver running through me. "No. I wasn't allowed to see most of these files. Some I've never seen before."

He taps the long nail of his index finger against the folder. "I discovered something interesting while reading your files. This is an academic test performed on you at five years old while living with Vianna and Kenneth. They were adopting you. Do you remember?"

I chew at the corner of my lip. "No. I-I don't remember them. It was only a handful of months, and I think their deaths traumatized me. I grew up with memory issues, probably from trauma and all the drugs my mom had me on. Everything before I was removed from my mom's home at nine is iffy and jumbled."

"Yes, there was a note about you suffering from stress-related confusion." Viorel pulls in a deep breath as he rests back against the couch. His brows lower as he looks down at me. "Don't you find it odd a five-year-old who was kept a secret from the government and had no proper education was proficient at writing and reading?"

He stares at me, and I realize he wants an actual answer.

"I always assumed I don't remember learning stuff, or I used to be really smart and plateaued."

He sucks at his teeth and tilts his head side to side before saying, "I have ample experience with children from many walks of life. I've got an entire nursery full of them upstairs. I've kept up with psychology and science in hopes of helping the immortal children better, so I can't help but find your intelligence so odd. Your emotional and social immaturity is well documented, as well as your psychological issues, yet academically you were at least two years above the average five-year-old by today's American standards. Who was teaching you if your mother had drug-induced psychosis and was actively using?"

My visit with my mother in prison a couple of months ago returns to mind. "I found out my mom's boyfriend spent a lot of time with us when I was little. Maybe he was homeschooling me. He used to help me with my homework when I joined Red Revenge later. He acted like he was responsible for me, but I know he's not my father."

His brows lift. "Perhaps. That would add clarity to this nonsense and fill in some blanks."

"So . . . what?" My lips twist.

"I have a theory," he starts.

"Okay." I wrap my arms tight around myself.

"I don't think you're seventeen," he says like it's already fact.

My back straightens, and I lean away from him as my eyes narrow. *"What?"*

He motions to the mess of the room and me. "There is no evidence here of advanced intelligence. I don't believe you were a child prodigy at five-years-old. From what I understand about American law, they can punish parents for not having their school-aged children enrolled, correct? I believe it's six-years-old in New York State. She was already facing consequences for the circumstances of your existence and care, so she likely tried to lessen them. With how differently children develop, it's unlikely anybody was certain of your age when they first took you from your mother, so it's not unreasonable they took her word. Looking at photos and videos of you, reading your psychiatric evaluations . . . I can understand why nobody was suspicious until you underwent academic screening. Mentally, emotionally, physically . . . you seemed on par with younger children. Academically, you read to me like a typical seven-year-old with great strengths in reading, writing, and art."

"Fucking *what?*" I gape at him, though can't find it in me to call him a liar. I suppose I've always thought March 18th never felt like my birthday, that my mom might have been high and was a few days off. But I didn't expect the *year* to be wrong. Despite having few toys, I recall the battered children's books I'd memorize, the notebooks and old pencil crayons she locked in my room with me knowing they'd occupy me for hours. It makes sense those areas were my strengths. My brow furrows. "Well . . . how old am I, then?"

"Eighteen or nineteen, I would presume. The abuse you encountered when they returned you to your mother is likely responsible for how far behind you've fallen from others your age."

My mind whirs and I'm unsure what to do but stare at him.

"I'm confident in my theory, but I'd like to find your exact date of birth," Viorel says. "Do you know where your mother is?"

I tuck my shaky hands between my thighs and pull in a deep breath. "In the women's prison outside Lorimer, New York. Last I saw her a couple months ago, anyway."

The iron door creaks open, Mateo wandering in and saying, "I'll round up men to track down Marianna's mother after we get the situation upstairs sorted."

There's darkness to Viorel's smile. "Perfect. Hypnotize her, extract her from the prison, and kill her once you're done with her." His eyes cut to mine, like he's waiting for me to protest her death. When I don't—I've thought about killing her more times than I can count and can't help the flash of a smirk coming with the thought of some vampire throttling her—his smile only grows and he says, "You want her do die, don't you? How?"

I push out a breath. But now? With all this going on around me? I can't find it in me to give a damn. "I don't care, as long as she's dead. Put a bullet between her eyes?"

Viorel's smile fades, a viciousness in his claret eyes as they snap toward an aged white folder on the coffee table with a stamp from the Lorimer Children's Hospital. The edge of a glossy photograph—what I can only assume are the gruesome photos taken of me the second time they recovered me from my mother after years of her drugging and prostituting me—sticks out from the edge. A knot forms in my throat at the thought of him looking at them.

"Make her death painful," Viorel instructs Mateo before checking my reaction again.

I merely swallow and offer an agreeable nod.

With that, Mateo walks off and promises to return shortly.

Viorel's thoughtful eyes scan the table before he angles his body toward me, his gaze connecting with mine. For the first time, he doesn't look at me like I'm only an annoying human extension of Denendrius.

Viorel looks at me like I'm a person.

He reaches sideways and flips open a file from Lorimer PD, and my mugshot from when I was fourteen and stole a bait car looks up at me. I barely recognize myself. Barely recognize the girl I was mere weeks ago. The girl in the photo has a hardened gaze and looks like she's incapable of shedding tears. She looks like she could overcome anything.

Reaching over, he traces his fingers over the glossy image before looking back at me. "I'm eager to meet the real you, parrot."

He's going to be sorely disappointed.

VIII

When Mateo returns, he swiftly tidies the mess of boxes and paperwork. It's difficult to watch him touch all the files and boxes like they're not personal to me, before carrying them to a room down the hall off Viorel's bedroom. My fingers itch to snatch the wooden chest of keepsakes I kept under my bed in Bellevue, but it's clear they don't really see the stuff as mine anymore, and I know Viorel won't let me have any reminders of Denendrius in my cell.

Viorel sits in silence beside me throughout the process, staring at the coffee table, lost in thought until Mateo has carried the last box out of the room while I try imagining all the possibilities of what they might hypnotize out of my mother.

Could I really be older?

Something deep in the marrow of my bones and the recesses of my mind tells me Viorel's onto something, but a big part of me *wants* him to be wrong. If I'm a year or two older, it means I've suffered longer than I originally thought. It means

I'm a bigger failure than everyone knows. I should have graduated or been in twelfth grade by now if it's true, but I didn't even have time to finish my do-over of tenth grade. It means two more years of missing memories, and fuck, I do not want to know what horrible things could have transpired in such a long amount of time.

"Bring me a body," Viorel demands flatly, yanking me from my spiraling thoughts as Mateo steps back into the clean sitting room.

Mateo nods, pulling in a deep breath as a flinch of a smile passes over his lips. "Uh—I can get you a donor body—"

"I thought fresh bodies were being brought in today," Viorel grumbles, his hard eyes leveling with Mateo's.

Mateo looks down to adjust the rings on his fingers, like he's finding an excuse to avert his eyes from Viorel as he says, "They ran into some issues this run. One human they picked belonged to a vampire. They won't be back until tomorrow night."

Viorel's glower is lethal. "They picked up a marked human?"

Mateo shakes his head as he meets Viorel's eyes. "No, he wasn't marked. They didn't know until the van was attacked—"

"And why can't they return him?" Viorel snaps. "There are plenty of other humans to take. I'm thirsty and shouldn't have to pay for their squabbles."

"It's all resolved, but they're too far to return until next sundown," Mateo says gently.

Viorel sighs, the couch creaking as he leans back. "A donor body is fine. How many are they bringing?"

"Sixty. There are a couple larger men we can make into donors, and the rest—" His eyes shift to me and away before he clears his throat. "The rest are best for auction."

The word is a hot knife in my stomach, my next breath so sharp it has me hugging myself and staring at the stone floor.

I'm not surprised Denendrius was right about there being auctions, but I wasn't ready to hear of them right then. Wasn't prepared for the idea—the image—of crying human girls as vampire men bid on them to ricochet through my thoughts. Sure, their main purpose for taking them is probably blood, but I'm not naïve to think that's all they'll be used for.

I can feel Viorel's heavy stare on me as he says, "Keep a few for me."

"Of course," Mateo says. "Are you sure you want a donor body? Perhaps someone would offer their blood slave up for you to borrow—"

Viorel's scoff makes me flinch. "Preposterous. Why? So somebody thinks I owe them something? So I can create resentments? You really think anyone would feel they could deny the request?"

I lift my eyes as Mateo half-turns to the door. "Donor body it is," he says with a little smile.

When Mateo goes upstairs, the silence he leaves behind is thick and painful.

Viorel lifts his nose a bit as he looks down at me, crimson eyes shifting over my face. "You really think you're in a position to judge how I care for my clan when you pine for a master who has slaughtered and tortured for reasons beyond thirst?"

I swallow and drop my eyes to my clenched hands in my lap, Viorel still clear in my peripheral. "You sell people," I whisper.

His unblinking stare is cold. "Pray tell, Marianna, a fairer way to distribute bodies amongst a thousand plus thirsty vampires? Because I can't have them coming and going to hunt without risk of us all being exposed, and a free for all is pure madness."

My voice is robotic when I say, "I don't care that vampires need to kill and drink to survive anymore. I eat meat, so I'd be a hypocrite if I did."

After a beat of silence, Viorel unlatches his gaze from me, understanding washing over his face. "Ah. You're not thinking of blood at all."

I swallow a lump of emotion and catch a stray tear as it darts down my cheek. "No."

Viorel ponders me. "It's not much different to bid on a human than bidding on cattle or purchasing a pet. We don't breed and raise humans like humans do cattle, we hunt them and keep them. The latter is more humane."

"How do you know the vampires buying humans aren't abusing them?" I counter. "Cattle owners don't rape their cows, do they?"

There's a beat of heavy silence, and I imagine he's piecing together the right words. "I cannot lie and say I know all the vampires here are kind to the humans they purchase, but I know most are. Most care for their humans like friends or family, there's just the added benefit of receiving sustenance from them as well."

I grit my teeth. "So, some probably are..."

The next bout of silence has me squirming until—to my astonishment—he says, "Yes, some probably are."

Turning to stare at him in horror, I'm not sure what to say. I feel like I've won the discussion . . . but lost by having him admit to a horrible truth.

"And you allow it?" I ask, the bewilderment on my face painful.

"No, I don't *allow* it. But I cannot starve the clan for the unfortunate choices of a few."

"Then hold them accountable," I snarl through grit teeth.

"How?" he asks. "Blood marks blur lines, so anything less than lurid violence flies under the radar. Clan members often shun and drive barbarous individuals here out."

The door creaks open before I can form a rebuttal. Mateo's arm is around the waist of a fit man as he helps him stumble into the room. If I didn't know better, I'd think him drunk from the way his half-lidded eyes roll around in his skull and his feet snag on one another.

But his pallid flesh tells the story of what he's been through. Bruises shadow his wrists, his arms and inner elbows flecked with needle marks. His breaths are noisy, the shadows cast by the candlelight making his cheeks appear hollower than they probably are, makes his greasy black hair shine. He's probably somewhere near thirty.

I don't have to ask if they keep humans locked up somewhere to collect blood from. His title *donor body* and the sight of him are answer enough.

There's no sign of fear in his pale blue eyes as Viorel heaves out a disappointed breath and stands. There's no sign the man knows what's going on. He doesn't fight as Viorel approaches, only consumed by his attempts to stand upright with Mateo's aid. Do they keep them hypnotized?

Viorel circles behind him and hooks his hand beneath the man's jaw to keep him upright as Mateo steps back. I doubt he really knows what's happening to him—his eyes are barely open, his breath labored, his hands limp at his sides—as Viorel twists his head to the side to expose his bruised neck.

When I blink, Viorel's fangs are in the man's jugular. I study the scene, the way Viorel's long fingernails pierce the thin skin of his cheekbone as he holds him in place, blood bubbling up beneath them. The man's eyes roll back, Viorel's strength the only thing keeping him upright as his knees buckle and shake.

Despite my hatred of Viorel, I must admit he looks elegant —not even a drop of blood escaping past his lips—as he drinks. With the candles casting shadows against their faces and the stone walls, there's something hauntingly romantic momentarily beguiling me.

Viorel leans his head back, blood-stained, razor-sharp fangs sliding out of two perfect incisions. When he exhales through his parted teeth, lips drawn back, it almost sounds like a hiss.

There's a flicker of fury in me at the sight of him, now fed while Denendrius thirsts and suffers in the dungeon. Do they give him *anything*? I suppose if they do, it's only so they can torture him more.

"Will that tide you over?" Mateo asks.

"Hardly. If anything, it's awoken my hunger further." Viorel licks the blood from his lips as he carelessly releases the man, who crumples at his feet. I expect the sound of his skull cracking against the stone before it does. "But I'll make do."

I wait for Mateo to take the body and dispose of it, but he steps back out for a moment instead.

What do they do with corpses here? After hundreds of years, there must be mass graves in the woods. Or do they have some sort of incinerator to discard of the biological matter before they crush the bones? That would be far more efficient than burying hundreds or thousands of people.

"You have a peculiar threshold for violence," Viorel notes as his eyes—still blood-red—flicker to the body and back to me. "It's rare I meet humans who are so at ease with death."

"I've killed people," I admit icily. "Shot a man for my gang initiation when I was twelve. I've seen men hacked to death and worse."

He's unfazed by my words. "Lucky me. I won't have to listen to you whine each time I feed or feel your reaction to it. I won't have to hear about how each of my meals has a family and whatever other nonsense since the idea doesn't cross your mind either."

I'm unsure what to say. Viorel smiles wickedly at me as Mateo returns with another man—a guard, I assume from the satellite phone on his hip—who swiftly hoists the dead body over his shoulder and carries it out.

"They're showing a film in the garden shortly. You're going to attend this time, yeah?" Mateo asks Viorel.

Viorel clasps his hands behind his back and draws in a deep breath through his nose. "I don't—"

Raising his brows, Mateo says, "You yourself admit to feeling better when you take trips outside."

"*Fine,*" Viorel half-snarls, his sharp gaze shifting to me.

My heart leaps into my throat as it goes stark dry.

"Behave," he warns with a curled lip. "Or you will bloody well regret it."

Eyes widening, I jump to my feet.

I get to go outside?

I walk alongside Mateo as we follow Viorel, five more guards in step behind and in front. It makes me wonder if Viorel ever goes anywhere by himself, and why the all-powerful vampire king needs a Darkling shield.

My rushed steps struggle to keep up with their quick pace, and I nearly step on the edge of Viorel's thick velvet cloak as it flutters against the hallway floor. Allotting my focus to walking and where his cloak is in relation to my body so the trip outside doesn't turn catastrophic, I study the tiny rubies sewed into small sections of the decorative stitching on the trim of the hood, and how they match the ones in the cloak's clasp I saw when he put it on earlier.

We pass through long, similar looking halls with deep red or stone walls and carpet covered floors. The sounds of dozens of vampires going about their lives fills my ears and makes it hard to think about anything else. The cheerful chatter carried out in various languages, boisterous laughs and overall high mood has me shrinking closer to Mateo. I'm lonelier hearing how everyone is enjoying their lives here.

My steps falter when a door swings open as Viorel is about to pass it, and a girl with a bright smile—mid-run—stops dead a mere foot from colliding into him.

"Sorry!" Her grin only grows as she steps out of the way for him to pass, exchanging a friendly hello.

Two teenage boys flash past my side—Viorel showing no sign he's bothered—moments later, half wrestling one another into the wall as they laugh and bicker about who's going to make it to the garden first.

"Watch the table," Mateo calls, smirking as the one boy throws the other onto the carpet and narrowly misses the skinny wooden thing holding a vase of cut roses.

I swear I hear a low chuckle from Viorel as we walk around them.

Viorel's presence doesn't create much of a ripple in the way the vampires go about their lives. Doors open and close on either side of us, vampires sneaking past or darting across the halls to beat our steps, many of them throwing a quick and excited greeting our way.

It's odd how none of them show a blink of fear in his presence. There are no nervous bows or apologies for being in his way. No sign they fear the power he holds over them or walk on eggshells in hopes they don't displease him.

They don't treat him how I'd expect a king to be treated, but I suppose it's a glorified name for clan leader considering he's not in charge of any real government. Who's going to argue with the most powerful vampire appointing himself as the vampire-world's king? I question the power he holds beyond his clan. Clearly, there's many who favor him beyond it, but how many vampires accept the position he's given himself?

My thoughts change direction with the gentle, warm breeze ruffling my hair as we pass through a wide iron door and outside onto a cobblestone path. Perhaps it's because I've been trapped in a subbasement, but the air passing in with my anxious breaths is crisper and cleaner than I've ever experienced. The aroma of flowers fills my nose as we pass thick gardens, the dark making it difficult to tell the petals apart.

The deep night masks the edges of the garden where the woods start. It extends as far as I can see to the right thanks to rows of little solar powered lights following the path. The moon and stars are missing from the sky tonight, likely cloaked with thick clouds. When I crane my head back, I can't see the top of the castle, just the occasional glow of light through windows.

This side of the castle is a large grassy field framed with flowerbeds, and a cobblestone path veering off to the left as we continue straight through the grass.

Voices murmur in the distance, too far to make out any words coming from the clumps of moving shadows, something massive and rectangular behind them. Moments later, a beam of light illuminates the gathered people on its way to a large projector. Fresh groups appear around the corner of the castle, making me think there's a more popular exit since we're alone over here.

I mentally prepare myself for all the dirty looks and snide remarks I'll inevitably receive with us joining them, hoping they all show more interest in the film than me. If I'm lucky, Viorel's presence will make them think twice.

But instead of continuing through the grass toward them and the projector about a hundred feet away to our right, we walk toward a little circular garden between us and the flowerbeds along the tree line.

There's a single decorative concrete bench facing the projector. Viorel brushes his cloak behind him as he claims the bench, unbothered by how it bunches in the grass. There's no comfortable amount of space on either of his sides—likely intentional—so I sit in the grass where Mateo points, next to

Viorel's legs like an obedient dog. Mateo stands beside the bench, the remaining guards standing in a wide, protective circle like there's a threat of attack from any side.

Is Viorel scared of his own people?

To be fair, he should be. Yet I wonder if this is a regular precaution or a new one, since his clan knows he's Huarsar. How are people feeling knowing their king abandoned his last clan?

There's a long silence between us, filled with the growing excitement of the crowd and the faint echo of horses whinnying in the distance. My heart aches as I think of Denendrius in the dungeon, while I'm lucky enough to steal a moment outside.

Viorel gazes across the well-manicured field at the doubled crowd. There's probably a few hundred by now, spreading blankets or laying straight on the grass.

He scrutinizes the crowd, gaze tightening every so often. Can he hear their thoughts from way back here? Is he trying to find out who's betting on killing me first? Would they even be dumb enough to come out here if they knew Viorel would attend? They'd probably steer clear.

Seth must be thinking what I am, as he breaks off from the protective circle and walks with purpose toward the crowd. He weaves through where they're gathered in the grass, head moving side to side like he's taking inventory of their faces before meandering back over.

"The clan sounds happy to see you, Viorel," Seth says as he returns. I catch Mateo's triumphant grin from the corner of my eye.

Viorel inhales a long breath and I swear there's a flash of guilt across his face as he nods.

Mateo clasps his hands in front of himself. "I sent Artair to watch the rear exit a few hours ago."

Viorel nods once, eyes still glued straight ahead as he adjusts the ruby clasp holding his cloak in place. "Send him straight downstairs tomorrow night to report to me. He's overdue for a visit."

I stiffen as a small figure breaks off from a group of vampire children playing tag—the Children of Stars sticking out when they hover to evade capture—darts toward us from the crowd. None of the guards make any move to intercept. They barely glance as a raven-haired girl with rosy, tanned cheeks—maybe eleven—bounds past them. My breath catches, my heart spasming when she plops down in Viorel's lap and throws her arms around him in a hug. She rests her head on his shoulder like it's the safest thing in the world to do.

"I missed you," she complains into his hair with a weak Romanian accent. He smiles fondly and loosely wraps an arm around her lanky body. "You haven't come to the nursery in forever."

"I know, I'm sorry," he murmurs, giving the side of her thigh a gentle pat. "I will soon."

"Promise?" She links her fingers together like she's worried he'll try removing her from his lap. "I've written new stories I want you to read."

"I promise, Tassa."

Tassa peeks down at me through strands of his hair, a little smile curling her lips before her eyes flick up to Viorel's face. "Please, can I sit with you?"

"Okay," he agrees.

She calls out to someone while waving her hand in the air, then carefully climbs off Viorel's lap to sit in the grass on the other side of his legs. She trains her curious hazel eyes on me as she crosses her legs and leans back on her hands.

A black-eyed man approaches carrying a large bowl, a plastic bottle of water, and a colorful bag of candy. From the satellite phone on his hip, I assume he's a guard. He hands them to Tassa before nodding at Viorel and wandering off.

She looks up at Viorel. "Can I share my snacks with Marianna?"

"Sure." His eyes are soft.

She pushes the bowl in front of his feet—between us—and gives me a friendly smile. Looking back up at him again, she asks, "Can I talk to her?"

Viorel's eyes flicker down to me, and he gives me a long, harsh stare before his gaze softens again before settling on her. "Yes, Tassa."

She grins at me. "How are you liking the castle?"

Viorel's hand appears on my shoulder like a gentle warning to be nice.

"It's big," I whisper, not wanting to tell her I hate her home and would rather be dead.

Her face brightens, like she's astonished she got a response from me. "Your aunt Carol has been helping Ainsley in the nursery. Will you stay in the nursery once you're marked? There's an empty bunk under mine in the mortal chamber. Carol helped me make it up since she doesn't think you'll want to share a space with her and Derek."

"She's too old for the nursery," Viorel answers for me. "Regardless, she'll be staying with me."

Tassa purses her lips. "For how long? Will she go to a chamber with the older girls? I thought she'd come upstairs."

"No, I've had a change in mind. She'll remain downstairs with me for the rest of her life." Somehow, his response sounds so cruel despite how he speaks delicately to Tassa.

His words—though unsurprising—are a punch in the lungs.

She pushes out her bottom lip. "Aw, all right. I guess that makes sense."

Tassa must have a different—naïve—understanding of his words, as she gives me a tight-lipped, disappointed smile before telling me I can have popcorn while taking a handful for herself.

I'm not sure if I should accept her offer. Viorel may have given her permission to offer to share, but am I allowed to accept?

Eat. Viorel's voice rings in my head, somewhere between a thought and audible sound. It sends a chill through me, and a quick glance at Tassa—who stuffs her face with popcorn and glances curiously around the crowd—shows no sign she heard.

Great, the asshole is telepathic too? How many abilities can he possibly have? I suppose there's a reason he's the oldest living vampire.

As I pluck a few pieces of popcorn from the bowl and shove them past my chapped lips, the garden erupts with a grumble of upbeat music from speakers beneath a new flash of colors on screen.

My eyes become unfocused for long enough that the warm air makes them feel dry, the impending tears making my eyes ache. I can't take my mind off Denendrius, can't unhear his shrieks of pain. There's no taste to the occasional piece of popcorn making it past my quivering lips. I eat purely so I don't offend Tassa and upset Viorel.

"The Angel Maker is watching us from his balcony," Mateo warns.

I follow Mateo's gaze up the side of the castle and to the silhouette of a man standing on his balcony on a higher part of the first floor.

Viorel scoffs, irritation dripping from his voice. "He's not thinking up a master plan to kill Marianna, he's simply curious. And stop calling him that only because you know he detests it."

"I should have a word with him, yeah?" Mateo turns his body toward the castle.

"You should leave the poor man alone and sit your bloody arse down," Viorel orders.

"All right," Mateo laments before he lowers himself onto the concrete bench after Viorel scoots over for him. "But I don't trust him."

"It's a good thing you're not his king then," Viorel grumbles.

Mateo—clearly reminded of his place—mashes his lips together and rubs his hand over the hair of his trimmed face.

I can feel the man's eyes on me and take another peek from my peripheral, which only makes him move closer to the stone rail. Shit.

After a few minutes, Mateo rises and stands between Viorel and the castle, mumbling something I miss in Spanish before saying, "He's climbing down and looking this way."

Viorel only glances toward the castle before setting his gaze back on the screen. "And?"

"Did you call him over?" Mateo wonders.

"No, but what does it matter?" Viorel grumbles.

My palms sweat, heart racing at the thought of him coming over here. I decide it's wiser to trust Mateo on how safe The Angel Maker is—or isn't—and consider Viorel is minimizing the obvious danger to fuck with me. What the hell did he do to get such a name? It sounds like something the media gives a serial killer.

Eyes wide, I watch as The Angel Maker's shadow appears in the garden a handful of yards away. I expect him to try sitting with us, but he merely sits where he stood, body angled toward the screen, head turned toward us. I squint through the dark, trying—and failing—to make out identifying features so I know who to keep an eye out for.

Fiery orange curls in my peripheral steal my attention, and my head snaps toward the sight of Carol and Derek as they approach the guards. Her eyes are glued to me, her fingers clenching the thin quilt she carries over her arm.

A guard steps into her path as they approach. I'm almost surprised when Viorel commands him to let them pass and allows them to sit a few meters away from us, just out of my reach. I suppose he wants to keep up appearances, and how would it look if he denied my aunt and a *"vampire who holds my life in high regard"* to come near me?

Carol merely stares at me with worried eyes and parted lips as she helps Derek spread the blanket over the grass. Her hands shake the entire time, and she doesn't take her eyes off Viorel as she sits down and scoots tight against Derek's side.

I can't help but wonder if her show of fear has been a constant since her arrival, or a side effect of nearing the world's most powerful vampire.

Derek offers Viorel a quick bow of his head and a smile before he opens a beige tote bag and pulls out a bag of pretzels for Carol. There's no shake of his limbs or any sign of discomfort as he leans back on his hands and faces the screen. Clearly, he's adjusting well to life in the castle. How is he coping with his vampirism since Ziggy turned him after he was lethally injured in our last encounter with Agatha and Red Revenge?

I flinch when Viorel raises his voice a bit to speak, which has Carol's attention snapping toward me, like she's on red alert for signs of my distress. "How is the castle to your liking, Carol?"

Derek looks over at Viorel with Carol as she offers a shaky smile and says, "It's beautiful. I've been enjoying visiting the nursery. Thank you for letting me come along with Marianna."

"That's wonderful to hear. You're most welcome. What are your thoughts, Derek?" Viorel asks.

Derek's grin is bright. "Oh, it's great, thank you. I understand why so many want to be part of your clan; I feel well taken care of."

"How is—" Carol bites her bottom lip like she believes she's out-of-place speaking to him. A hundred questions brew in her eyes.

I can hear Viorel's smile in his kind voice. "Yes? It's all right."

Her deep swallow is visible, the hand she lifts to tuck thick curls behind her ear shaky. "How is Marianna doing?"

The fact she asks him and not me makes my chest ache. Of course, they still believe I can't think for myself, that I completely lost my mind to Denendrius.

The feel of Viorel's relaxed hand on my shoulder makes me wince. "She's fine, given the circumstances. She'll feel much better soon, I promise. I know you've been eager to spend time with her, but she's in safe hands."

Safe hands?

Fingers lifting to touch my chest, the feel of Viorel holding me down to carve Denendrius's name out of me returns.

My mind scrambles for something to say to her until Viorel's gentle squeeze on my shoulder squashes the idea. It doesn't matter anyway, as Carol and Derek focus on the screen.

The weight of my position is obvious then, as Carol and Derek relax out of reach while I sit by Viorel's feet. It's clear from the way she warily glances over her shoulder at me she feels it too.

Her role as aunt and foster mother is no longer relevant. Viorel owns me.

And what is she going to do about it? What could Derek do? What could they possibly do or say to the vampire king housing and feeding them, who could have them tossed away in two seconds?

Nothing. Carol may as well be a too.

When I check if The Angel Maker has crept closer, his shadow is gone. Did he climb back up to his room, or slip into the crowd?

I can't find it in me to care about the animated movie, and neither do I have the strength to sit upright unsupported for so long with how tired my body is. Opting to lie down instead, I rest with my head near Viorel's feet, looking past him and up at the sky. Something about my new position makes Tassa giggle, and she scoots down and sprawls out into the grass too, making silly faces at Viorel he pretends to ignore. The hint of a smile on his lips gives him away.

I split most of my time between contemplating Viorel and the void of sky past him and turning my head to look at Carol and the crowd past her. She doesn't seem to give the film much attention either, as I catch her staring at me a handful of times. Derek steals pensive glances at Viorel while trying to keep Carol's attention forward.

Viorel sits straight and rigid the entire movie, occasionally lifting his hand to adjust the neck of his cloak. Though he faces the screen most of the time, his eyes pick apart the gathered crowd, intermittently breaking away to dart to a section of the woods or a castle window. He repeats the same visual sweep, his heavy inhales and exhales timed and widely spaced. I sum it up to his thirst from the number of surrounding humans.

Derek notices Viorel's behavior too, though from Derek's furrowed brows and taut lips, it must concern him and makes me second guess my first conclusion, especially when Viorel casts his wide gaze into the dark over his shoulder.

I squint at Derek as he jumps in place while his eyes snap back to Viorel, wondering the cause behind the little guilty smile flashing across his lips before he hooks his arm around Carol and forces his attention on the screen. Clearly, I missed something. I look to Viorel to find some clarity, but he merely tightens his gaze on the screen like he is trying to instill in himself that he, too, is supposed to be watching it. Did Viorel shoot thoughts into his head?

Viorel stands abruptly once the film ends. Eyes locking with Mateo's, he says, "Escort me back inside. Now."

I don't get a chance to say goodbye to Carol and Derek

before Mateo ushers me away. Viorel takes a moment to wish them and Tassa a good rest of the night.

As soon as we're alone downstairs, Viorel releases a deep breath from his nostrils, hangs his cloak in his wardrobe, and crawls straight into bed.

"Change and go to bed." He mumbles the command.

I obey, swapping my velour tracksuit for a white, frilly nightgown with short sleeves and a low neckline with little ruffles. It must have appeared on my dresser sometime while we were outside, straight off the back of a Victorian ghost from the looks of it. It's soft and longer than the last nightgown at least, since it rests at mid-calf.

When I crawl into bed beside him, despite how the action makes my limbs weak and my stomach rocky, I hope I'm not making a dangerous assumption.

Thankfully, he pays me no attention.

The slight flicker of the pillar candles is the center of my focus as I replay the night. How often will I get to see Carol and Derek? I doubt we'll ever get time alone.

Synchronized, the candles snuff out, and Viorel's breathing changes beside me. The flickering flame that was my focus stays burned into my vision against the pitch dark, no amount of blinking makes it go away.

Aside from a distant echo of occasionally dripping water, the silence seems absolute. It's so quiet I can hear my heartbeat in my ears, and the fact I can't see anything around me makes it worse.

The bed shifts, and I can sense movement above me.

"Viorel?" I squeak.

"Who else?" he responds limply.

The feel of silk across my cheek has me gasping until a blue flame springs to life in the fireplace and illuminates Viorel's arm above me and the edge of his wide sleeve.

He settles beside me on his back, red eyes half-lidded and

unblinking on the ceiling, his hands clasped over the blanket on his stomach.

When he catches me watching him from the corner of his eye, I squeeze my eyes closed.

"Sit up." His voice, a soft caress, makes my heart stutter.

Though I try to obey, fear blocks the message my brain tries sending my heavy limbs.

The bed shifts. "Sit, now."

I quiver as I force myself upright, bones aching, and stare down at the blankets through the dim light.

When his fingers brush from one of my shoulder blades to the other, I can't hold back the terrified squeak slipping past my lips.

"What're you—"

"Don't move," he murmurs, fingers wrapping around my shoulder to gently straighten me.

My muscles wind tight as my shoulders inch up. His palm presses into my stomach, fingers spreading out as he leans into me.

I squeeze my eyes closed, not sure what I'll do if he dares creep his hand down to touch me.

Do I fight him? Or is that the worst thing I could do?

Another terrified noise leaves me when his fingers run across the side of my neck and through my hair, sharp fingernails teasing my skin. It takes everything in me not to scramble away from him when he repeats the action, only tucking my hair over my other shoulder.

His wintry lips touch the lower side of my neck.

"Please don't," I breathe.

My outcry is shrill as his fangs cut into my neck, my next breath trapped and swelling in my throat as he drinks from me. It hurts more than Denendrius's bite ever did. The sharp heat spreads from his mouth and down across my collarbones, extending up my throat and to my skull.

Thoughts a terrified flurry, I don't even have the breath to scream as he drinks from me—

Viorel's fangs rip out of my neck like my blood is electric. His hand locks around my arm, and he yanks me off the bed. The candle flames ignite and stretch as he huffs. He screams Mateo's name into the warming air while dragging me like a rag doll.

When he reaches the sitting room and stops, I manage to breathe through the pain.

With a swipe of his hand toward the ceiling, the metal bar locking the door flies up from its locked position. He claws his hand sideways through the air and the door flies open, crashing into the stone wall. Mateo comes to a halt at the bottom of the stairs.

Viorel's furious breaths are noisy through his gritted teeth, his silent words making their way to Mateo from the shock on his face.

"Yeah—okay—" Mateo reaches out to me and Viorel flings me through the doorway.

I yelp as Mateo catches me before I hit the stone.

"If you don't, I'm going to kill her!" Viorel roars, his crimson eyes blazing with the reflection of the candles, so hot the yellow wax trickles down the wall. Another clawed swipe through the air has the iron door slamming shut.

Viorel bellows in a language I've never heard before, followed by a splintering crash of an object so heavy I feel the vibration of it through the floor.

The world shifts and settles in a tight hall made of old, exposed wood, with a handful of worn doors running down either side. I collapse to the ground, legs too wobbly to keep me upright.

"What did she do?" Sascha asks, expression smooth and unbothered. "Try to kill him?"

"Nothing!" I cry.

Mateo gives her a quick shake of his head as he squats down to my level and assesses my condition. "Anything happen before he bit you?"

I look around. "*No.* Where are we?"

"Guard's quarters," he says, before the room shifts again, and I find myself on the other side of the steel door.

"Where are you taking me?" I squeal. Has Viorel decided to discard me after all?

Mateo shushes me. "*You're fine.* Don't worry."

The hallway and grand room are empty as Mateo drags me through them and toward the staircase on the other side. I trip over each step until he hooks me against his side—his satellite phone digging into my hip—and swiftly carries me up to another connecting hall reminiscent of the ones below.

He sets me on my feet on the gold and red threadbare carpet, pulling me along past doors of quiet rooms.

I grit my teeth to hold my sobs back, but they echo in the quiet hall, loud enough a door opens halfway down. I think I'm about to get told off until Carol's head pokes out, her tired eyes widening as they land on me.

"Marianna?" Her voice is an octave too high.

I shake off Mateo's loose grip and dart to her. When I wrap my arms around her and sob into the shoulder of her pink flannel pajamas, I feel like I'm five.

Carol's arms lock around me. "What the hell's going on, Mateo?" she snarls, the worry in her tone undeniable.

Mateo releases a tired sigh as he catches up, but I answer before he can lie. "Viorel hurt me," I cry. "He—"

"She's okay," Mateo cuts in as Derek appears at Carol's side, one of Derek's cold hands coming up to rub my back. "Viorel needs a break from her, is all."

"He bit me and had a meltdown!"

"What?" Carol yanks away from me, eyes wide and studying

my face as Derek draws the neck of the nightgown back to expose the stinging bite as she gasps. *"Oh my God."*

Mateo ushers us into their dim room and shuts the creaky door behind us. The light from the oil lamp on the nightstand beside the massive bed across the room casts shadows against the rest of the furniture and isn't quite strong enough to reach us.

"See," I wail as I hug myself. "He's a monster. That's not even the worst he's done—"

"She's perfectly fine and safe," Mateo states firmly, which is *completely untrue.* "But please monitor her. He wants me to return to him immediately."

"Why hasn't he marked her yet?" Derek demands as he crosses his arms.

After a stretched sigh, Mateo says, "I don't know. I'm sure he will soon." He angles away. "Don't let her out of your sight, Derek, and I'll retrieve her later."

I hold the rest of my piling words until after Mateo has rushed away.

Wiping at a steady stream of tears, I try to ignore the intensifying burn in my neck. "He's using the mark to torture Denendrius."

Even in the low lamplight, the concern in Carol's green eyes is bright below her tense brows. She wraps her arm around me and guides me across the room to the bed framed with pointed wooden posts covered in elaborate carvings. After helping me crawl under the quilted covers, she slips in beside me while Derek sits on the edge of the mattress.

"What did he do, honey?" Carol pulls the blanket tight around us as I sit shaking.

"He—" I put my hand over my chest where Denendrius's name once was. The words I need to explain what happened are locked away. The fear ricochets through me with the memory. Derek places his hand back between my shoulder blades. "He—*He's so cruel.*"

"It's okay, honey," Carol whispers, impending tears in her voice. "You can tell us."

Wiping my eyes, I try to recount how he held me down and cut me up, but my throat tightens and my lips tingle with anxiety. It doesn't matter. They'd probably justify it anyway—tell me I should have sat still, and it wouldn't have been a big deal since it didn't hurt.

"What is it?" Carol presses, a shake to her voice like she thinks there must be something heinous I'm holding back.

I pick at my thumbnail as I talk down at my lap. "He's mean. He threatens me all the time. Calls me stupid."

Carol gives me a pitying frown as I look up. "Maybe things will change once he's marked you. Denendrius has done a lot to upset him."

Derek unloads a deep breath and rakes his fingers through his brown hair. "Yeah, he was quite on edge when we were in the garden. I could feel the tension *radiating* off him. He was short with Mateo, so he's probably just grumpy. I wouldn't take it personally."

I wouldn't consider driving a knife in his best guard's gut *grumpy.*

What he's doing to Denendrius is the worst of it. But I know they file that away under the list of good things Viorel has done. Viorel could keep all my nightmares away and be perfectly nice to me, and he'd still be the villain in my book for what he's done to make Denendrius like this.

A sob escapes me as I hunch over. A hot twinge radiates from the incisions in my neck and has me gasping.

"I'm just *so* tired," I cry as I lay my head on her warm pillow. "I'm a blubbering baby lately, but I can't help it. He has me in his bed, so I've been too terrified to sleep properly."

Horror passes over Carol's face, and she shakes her head in disbelief. "Mateo told me you had your own room."

"It's literally a prison cell with the door taken off," I bemoan. "All Mateo did was stuff a bed and dresser in it."

I don't miss the worry Derek and Carol share as their eyes cut to one another.

He clears his throat and shifts onto the bed. "Has he . . .?"

I shake my head. "No. I was cold, so he told me to come to his bed and had me turn the fireplace on. He called me a bed warmer and complained about having to listen to me roll around in my bed because of how uncomfortable it is. There's a spring that sticks right into my spine."

"Ah." There's no trace of the worry he retained. "That doesn't seem as nefarious."

Carol scoffs. "Doesn't matter. If she was so cold, he could have given her a stack of blankets before bringing a seventeen-year-old into his bed."

"He doesn't think I'm seventeen," I whisper, my breath slowly coming even as an odd sense of calm wafts over me.

Carol's head jerks, her eyes tightening on me. Her mouth opens to say something before she quickly closes it and furrows her brow.

"Why would he think that?" Derek asks with a soft murmur.

My racing heart stumbles and slows, and I manage my first full breath in days. "Viorel looked through all my files from when I was a kid. He thinks my mom lied about me being younger, thinking she wouldn't be in as much trouble. That I was only slightly above average for a six or seven-year-old, not a five-year-old prodigy. He told me being small and emotionally stunted could have added to the confusion."

Carol makes a perplexed noise, then goes, "Hm."

"Are you giving it real thought?" I mumble.

"Well . . . Looking back, it would explain a lot. You were

quite bright but had practically no emotional regulation or social skills."

"That's what he said," I mutter. Annoyed thoughts parade around in my mind, but I can't feel the emotion of them.

"Why don't you sleep, honey?" Carol says as she pulls the blanket tighter around me.

Another wave of calm pounds through me with warmth, and I feel myself drifting. There's no good reason to feel this way, so I whisper, "Derek, did you inherit Ziggy's calming ability?"

A gentle chuckle slips past his lips. "Yes. I'm slowly getting the hang of it. I tried it on Viorel thinking it would help, but he told me off."

Ah, so that's what that odd exchange was about. Derek must be brave—or wildly naïve—to have tried using his abilities on Viorel.

My heavy eyes close and I yawn. The gentle tug of sleep grips me. "It's helping."

The induced calm helps me fall asleep, though I wake up with a rush of frantic panic to see Derek asleep and upright on an antique couch a few feet away beside an angled executive desk covered in papers and old books.

I lie awake with Carol snoozing beside me in Derek's spot. My heart feels like lead in my chest, my breath shallow. I listen carefully to the creaking of doors and low voices intermittently passing by the bedroom door. When the sound picks up and it's clear the castle's residents aren't trying to keep quiet, I assume the sun has set.

The sound of my name passes the room with a swift kick against the door—followed by a chorus of hushed laughter scurrying off—has my eyes popping wide and Carol and Derek lurching awake and upright.

I don't move. "Denendrius was right. Everyone here hates me."

Carol rubs her eyes and sighs. Derek sits back down, shaking his head to himself.

"I'll talk to the guards," he grumbles while shooting a scowl at the door.

"Why would the guards care?" My tone is limp. "I'm an inconvenience to them too."

Carol crawls out of bed and stretches. "We won't let them ruin our night," she decides with a forced smile. "Let's focus on family time while we have you. We'll stop by the wardrobe room first and get you something to wear." She rubs her finger against a part of the neckline of my nightgown I can't see. "You've got blood on you."

"Let her borrow a sweater." Derek points toward my arm.

My eyes drop to the massive bruise from Viorel's furious grip. "If you're so worried about people seeing how Viorel hurt me, I could always stay in here," I quip.

Derek's only response is to stand and jerk his head toward the door. "Nope, come on."

They want me to go out there with a horde of vampires who hate me? As far as I know, the guards still haven't found who's betting on me being killed.

My throat dries and I feel like I'm sinking into the mattress. "Fine, maybe I'll luck out and someone will win their stupid bet."

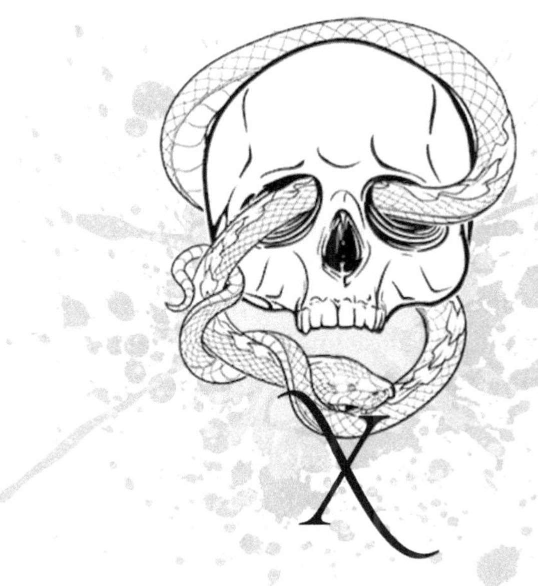

After five flights of stairs up and constant contemplation of throwing myself backward down each one, we make it to a long hall no different from the rest. There's a fresh burn in my calves, though it's no match for the burn from Viorel's bite.

Noise leaks from beneath the wooden doors. Giggling girls, heavy chatter, and yelps of surprise or pain have my attention alternating.

I peek into a room as we stroll by. A row of pink-lined coffins is open against the far wall, candlelight shining off the glossy Polaroids wallpapering it. My steps falter as a black-eyed, spindly girl with thick winged eyeliner appears leaning against the wooden door, a glimmer in her eyes as she smiles at me and runs a brush through her long, raven hair.

"Good evening, Marianna." Her voice is like velvet.

I swallow and nod, pointing my eyes ahead as we continue down the hall until we reach the open door of what must be the wardrobe room, from its size and the sheer amount of clothing strewn about.

It's difficult to make out the walls of clothing in the murky light, but the left side appears catered to girls, and the right to guys, except for a messy gradient between the two sections.

Carol expects me to find something to wear in this mess? I'd rather stick with the bloodied nightgown.

A wrought-iron chandelier with a ring of candles breaks up the darkness of the room, a few more free-standing candle holders around antique chaise lounges placed in the middle of the room. Derek makes a beeline for one while telling us to take our time.

I'm not sure where to rest my eyes. Clothes are packed against the height of the walls so tightly I can barely see the metal clothing rods. Drawers, shelves, and bins of varying ages are against the wall on the floor and are bursting. There's every color, fabric, and pattern imaginable, and I narrowly miss the cinnamon-haired teenage girl—fast asleep—tucked into a row of long and frilly black and brown skirts.

Her eyes pop open and land on us as we enter.

"Oh—are we going to be a bother?" Carol asks, angling back toward the door.

I blink and the girl is on her feet, eyes trained on me. "Oh, no, not at all. I didn't mean to sleep past sundown."

"How does this work?" I grumble at Carol as the girl carefully approaches, my hand lazily motioning toward the mass of clothes while assuming there must be some sort of string—like cost—attached.

Slowly, the girl circles the couch and walks toward me. She clutches her hands to her chest, her smile so wide I suspect it'd hurt her face if she were human. "You can take whatever you like. If you ever have anything you don't want, you can leave it here for someone else to take. There's an expectation to bring back a few new clothing pieces to share when people take their trips and shop for themselves, so there's always new stuff to pick from." She stops a few feet away from me and unclasps her hands.

"I just need pants and a shirt," I grumble despite changing seeming like more effort than it's worth. Does it really matter if there's a splotch of blood on my nightgown when I've seen at least three humans so far this evening with collars made of blood and fang-marks?

"I can help you find some, Marianna." She offers as her doe-eyed gaze follows mine around the room. "It's overdue for some organizing, so I don't mind. I've got a good idea of most of the stuff coming in and out of here."

"Yeah, sure." I'd rather have all the clothes topple on me and suffocate me to death over hunting something down myself.

I flinch when she hooks her cold arm around mine and pulls me toward a shelf of jeans. "I'm Glitch, by the way."

My brow cocks. "Glitch?"

"A couple of computer scientists stayed here for a bit and gave me the nickname. I love it. It's so futuristic." She giggles as we stop.

"It's hard to imagine anyone like that would stay here. There's not even electricity."

Glitch smiles along. "They stayed for a few years in the nineties and helped catch everyone up. Brought some cool solar powered things like lamps, lots of batteries, as well as some generators. They got a fake fireplace on an extension cord for Viorel too. Alaire taught me how to use a computer. I kind of miss them."

My stomach cramps. "Alaire?"

"Mhm." She nods as she digs through jeans on the shelf, glancing between my hips and the tags.

Tongue dry, I ask, "French guy with a brother named Edmond?"

Glitch grins up at me. "Yeah, you know them?"

I clear my throat. "Knew . . . Denendrius killed them."

Her hands freeze, eyelids fluttering like she's been slapped as her gleeful expression drops. "Oh." Her voice comes out mousy. "They were really nice."

"Yeah, I guess." I curl my arms around my stomach, now sure they meant to bring me to the castle before they died. Would I have gone had they offered? Would they have given me the choice? I suppose if I had, I wouldn't be in Viorel's snare now. I bet I'd be free and rooming with those older girls Tassa mentioned.

A crease appears between her brows as she frowns and continues her search through the jeans. After scowling at about fifteen pairs, she unwedges another and asks, "What about these? They look like they'll fit."

I squint at the dark, and plain blue jeans as they unfold in her grip. "What size?"

She shakes her head. "I hardly bother to look anymore. I used to fit American twos ten years ago, and somehow my unchanging body has turned into a six." She holds them up to my waist. "They'll fit."

Sighing, I hold my arm out, and she drapes them over it.

"Why Glitch?" I ask as I follow her to a rack so stuffed the hangers are overlapping in some places.

"My transformation didn't go quite as well as it has for everyone else," she says, eyes holding mine.

Despite the low light, I catch the tiny patch of brown in the black of her eyes. "What happened?"

Her gaze jerks away from mine and she squints intently at the rack, walking her fingers over the mismatched plastic and metal hangers. "A Darkling bit me, and a Child of Stars tried to reverse the transformation, but his venom got mixed in, and now I'm . . ." Her eyes flicker back to me before shifting away again, like she's unsure if she wants to share. She blows out her breath. "Everybody here already knows how I'm all messed up.

Viorel says it's impressive I survived. Usually interfering with the transformation results in death."

"I didn't know that." I glance back over my shoulder to note Carol's location to ensure she hasn't abandoned me here. She's across the room, picking through men's sweaters while stealing glances back at Derek.

She shrugs. "Why would you? It's unheard of."

My lips purse. "So, you're different, like Viorel. In between a Darkling and Child of Stars?"

Her laugh is sharp. "Oh, no, it's completely different. See, Viorel existed before Darklings did. My existence is merely a persistent mistake. Viorel is boundlessly powerful, while I'm practically useless."

I balk. "That's . . . that's pretty harsh."

She shrugs and smiles. "It's okay."

Narrowing my eyes, I notice how forced her gleeful attitude is when her smile shakes before she fixes it.

"Do you always sleep in here?" I ask.

Her black eyes shift away from me, and she furrows her brow and applies her focus to something across the room. "No, I share a room with my father. Sometimes it's nice to take a break from him. He can be . . ." She rolls her eyes. "You don't want to hear any of that. Let's find you a shirt."

Thankfully, it's easy to find a plain shirt. Glitch guides me to a wooden room divider adorned in painted cherry-blossoms, and I toss my nightgown in a wicker laundry basket half-full of clothes I suspect someone will wash and return to the racks. The blue jeans and the black long sleeve fit loose, though not enough to be a problem.

When I step out from behind the divider, thanks waiting on my tongue, Glitch is gone.

"She took off," Carol fills in as she notices me squinting around the room.

My brows lift. "Why?" I wander over to where she sits next to Derek on the couch.

"Not sure, she was waiting by you one second, gone the next," Carol says.

I plop down next to Derek and pick through our interaction as Carol wraps up her search for a cardigan, trying to decide if I said something to make her bolt.

A man wanders in a few moments later, his sour black eyes sweeping across the clothes like he's looking for something specific. The seriousness of his face has me swallowing and tossing a nervous glance toward Derek beside me on the couch, who watches him too.

He rakes his hand through his short blond hair as his gaze switches between us. "I'm looking for my daughter, Lucia. Small brown-haired Darkling girl. Fifteen. Smells like she was in here."

Glitch? She must be Lucia.

Something about him—the way he stands there like he's looking for trouble—and the fact she seemed so nervous has me saying, "She must have left a while ago, because we haven't seen her."

His lip curls back as he settles his tightening gaze on me, then cuts his eyes to Derek like he's only expecting a response from him.

Derek crosses his arms. "We haven't seen her."

He gives Derek a single nod before turning on his heels.

"What a prick," I grumble, uncaring that he's likely still in earshot.

Derek sighs. "People's tune will probably change when you're no longer marked to a prisoner. But do me a favor and stay away from him. He feels pretty . . . unsettled."

"Yeah, fine," I grumble. "Where's the closest bathroom?"

"Downstairs," Carol says as she slips a wine-red cardigan over her white T-shirt. "There's only two. One off the Grand room, and the other near the nursery. Baths and showers are all on ground level too."

"Jesus Christ," I complain.

Derek chuckles. "The castle is old, Marianna. All the plumbing must be downstairs, since they put in it as an afterthought. Bedpans are still popular here."

I wrinkle my nose. At least Viorel has a bathroom a few steps away.

Carol and I stand in the small line for the bathroom until the idea of being on my feet for one more minute has me seriously considering lying on the floor. There's enough for me to be embarrassed over already, so I tell Carol I'm going to sit with Derek on one of the antique sofas in the middle of the grand room until it's my turn. He tries to rope me into small talk by telling me he doesn't miss teaching history at West James High anymore and is glad I roped him into this world, but I keep my eyes on the bathroom while tracing lines with my finger on the red velvet upholstery.

A bouncing head of golden curls in my peripheral catches my attention, my heart thumping when the teenage girl attached to it makes a beeline for me. She stops dead in front of me, her blistering red eyes locked on my face, her fangs bared. There's a spot of blood on the neckline of her white crochet top, and the light from the fireplace glints off the silver rhinestones running down the leg of her acid-wash jeans.

"Hey now . . ." Derek warns, leaning forward like he's ready to get up and stand between us.

The girl doesn't spare him a glance as a haughty smile curves her lips. "Rumor has it you pissed Viorel off so bad he banished you upstairs, Marianna."

"I don't know why people think I did something," I snap,

incredulous. "Maybe your king just lost his marbles after all these years."

Her jaw lowers a bit, a disbelieving laugh slipping out. "Oh, the nerve you have. Now I don't doubt you did something. I'm just surprised he let you live afterward."

"Come on." Derek holds his hand out, a passive plea for her to back down. His eyes tighten on her, his lips a tense line of frustration. Is he trying and failing to calm her down? "We're not looking for trouble—"

"Well, she's already found it by coming here. She should have never been allowed to step foot in this castle." Her burning red eyes snap back to mine, her fists shaking at her sides. "You're just Denendrius's blood slave. I wish Viorel would have had you killed instead of keeping you around like a filthy pound animal. Denendrius doesn't deserve to have anyone alive after murdering my family."

"Then do something about it," I challenge. "Win that bet going around."

She crosses her arms and lifts her nose. "Oh, I would kill you if I could," she snarls. "I would do it slowly. But I respect Viorel too much to act against him."

Since suicide isn't off the table, I say, "If you weren't a vampire, you wouldn't even think about fucking with me. I'd break your face. I bet you were a wuss as a human."

She bares her fangs at me. "I hope Viorel tears your heart out of your chest and eats it!"

Dread trickles through me. Does he do that?

"You need to back off," Derek starts, "or I will report you to the guards." Angling to me, he adds, "Knock it off."

"Ha!" She snorts. "Go for it. You think I care?"

Hands plant on the back of the couch on either side of my shoulders, the voice of a man ringing in my ear. His voice is young and smooth, with a hint of an accent making me think of Rome and Denendrius. "Leave her alone, Josephine. Marianna never asked for any of this. She's as much a victim as your family."

With the way her pale face contorts with fury, I'm sure it'd be bright red if she were human. "Run along, Angel Maker! Nobody wants you here either!" she roars.

My heart slams into my stomach.

Josephine? The Angel Maker? Two of the vampires Mateo was worried about coming after me?

Oh God.

"Quit harassing her, and quit calling me that," he says firmly. I feel his icy breath against the top of my head and see the ruby rosary swing by the side of my face as he jerks forward above me and leans his weight into the couch.

The same vampire with the ruby rosary that was praying when Mateo was bringing me to Viorel?

I do my best to keep my breath in check. Thankfully, Derek is at my side to help, a thin layer of calm coating me.

Carol saves the day as the feeling evaporates. She waves me over as she exits the bathroom. Leaping up, I throw as much force as I can into Josephine's shoulder as I rush by her.

She gasps in shock, though I know I couldn't have hurt her. My shoulder aches from the impact, but I keep the pain off my face as I continue.

"You bitch!" she roars.

Carol tells me she's off to sit with Derek while she waits for me as I barrel past her and into the bathroom.

It's a simple stone room with three stalls, one of which I lock myself inside. The stall resembles a closet, but its solid door and floor-to-ceiling walls make it completely private, unlike the metal stalls I'm used to in America.

Moving to one of two paint-chipped teal sinks across from the stalls when I'm done, I watch a blond girl through the mirror as she stands in the open stall, emptying a bedpan in the toilet before spinning around like she can feel my scrutiny.

I gasp at the dozens of bite marks in various stages of healing covering her pale neck and forearms.

Her emerald eyes widen in delight when they land on me. "Marianna! You're upstairs. Has Viorel marked you now?"

Twisting the old taps and turning my head to her, I shake it, my stare fixated on the bite marks on her wrist. I scrub my hands, the lemon scent of the soap mingling with the damp air.

She looks down at her bitten arms when she catches my stare. Her smile doubles in size as she giggles. "Do you like my love bites?"

"Love bites?" My jaw lowers.

"How lucky, you have a love bite from Viorel." She points at my neck, biting down on her bottom lip.

I don't mask the judgment shaping my face. "You like being bitten?"

Grinning, she lifts her brows and stares at me like I'm the weird one. "Of course. You're literally giving your blood—your life force—so a powerful being can thrive. There's no act more selfless than being a familiar and feeding your master." She holds her arms out for a better look. "This is how much she loves me. Every day she chooses me again and again to keep her healthy. Doesn't that make you feel special?"

She's a blood slave, isn't she? This must be what they sound like. Absolutely bonkers. Does her vampire recite this mantra to her each time she feeds on her, or has she come up with it on her own to cope with being used as a pincushion?

"No," I argue. "It fucking hurts."

She tilts her head from side to side. "There's a thin line between pain and pleasure. Regardless, it's good to get used to it. If I'm to be a Darkling one day, the pain of a bite is nothing compared to the transformation."

I'm not sure what to say as I turn the taps off and shake the water off my hands, but the disgust on my face has soured her smile.

"It's okay if you don't understand," she says with a tilted frown as she rinses the bedpan in the sink next to me. "Denendrius sounds like he would be a cruel master. I know you'll be much happier with Viorel. But not all experiences are like yours, so you don't have to pity me."

"Denendrius loves me." I'm not sure why I tell her this, feel it worthwhile to explain myself to some brainwashed blood slave.

Her smile is tense with pity. "Right, I'm sure it must feel that way."

I've nothing left to say to her as I dry my hands. She wishes me well and leaves.

I rub at my swollen eyes and splotchy red cheeks in the mirror before gritting my teeth and half-stomping from the bathroom. The pressure in my jaw only intensifies when I spot Carol and Derek deep in conversation with the Angel Maker. They're grinning, their heads turning toward me as I approach.

"We're going to the dining hall. Would you like to join us, Laurentius?" Derek asks, lifting his hand halfway to Laurentius's arm and dropping it like he was about to give it a friendly pat before changing his mind.

My eyes pop wide. Has Derek lost his goddamn mind?

Scowling, I glare daggers at him. He glances at me, but his continued smile dismisses my silent warning.

I expect the Angel Maker's answer before he gives it, but he does a horrible job of hiding his excitement to weasel his way closer to me. His maroon eyes light up. "Really? Thank you."

I know I can't exactly voice my fears out loud without causing a scene, but I hope Derek can feel my anxiety from his proposition, or is my panic too consistent for him to think anything of it?

His maroon eyes meet mine, and we study one another for a long moment before we follow Carol and Derek. He must be somewhere between twenty and twenty-five, his long lashes making him look boyish while the five o'clock shadow on his jaw adds maturity. He's undeniably handsome, though I can sense something evil about him he's trying to cover with the religious stuff.

Laurentius rakes his hand through his dark brown hair, pushing a few strands back from his eyes like I'm making him nervous.

He shouldn't be. He should win that bet right here in front of everyone before Mateo brings me back to Viorel.

I wonder if he knows I'm onto him. His kind face and gentle smile might trick my aunt and Derek, but not me. Denendrius was sweet too when he was first a vampire.

The packed dining hall is large for a castle where most of its residents don't eat. There's at least two dozen mismatching wooden tables of varying size and stain, each with a burgundy cloth.

Still, there are ample vampires, about half of them holding a crystal or silver drinking vessel of blood as they sit at tables or stand around. Humans are scattered about—their mortality telltale only from the plates of food in front of them—most of them paired with at least one vampire, though there's a noisy group of twelve near my age at a far table.

We weave through tables until reaching a round one with four chairs at the center of the room. I scowl as Laurentius pulls one out for me, though my aching legs don't allow me to hesitate, and I plop down.

Laurentius steals the chair to my right, and Derek pulls the one out to my left for Carol before sitting across from me with a thin smile.

Carol looks around. "Looks like steak and veggies tonight."

I'm about to ask how we get our food when a cold hand brushing my shoulder has me jumping in my chair. I twist to find a man on my left.

He wears a food-stained white apron over jeans and a plain

blue shirt. I take in his dark face, deep brown eyes, and the pearl-white grin he wears as he lowers himself beside me as one does to speak to a child.

"Well, hello, Marianna." His voice is deep but gentle and carries an accent I can't quite pin down. "It's nice to finally meet you." I quirk an impolite brow and he adds, "My name is Jacob. I'm the main chef here."

"You're a vampire," I note flatly, pondering if he's even eaten half the things he cooks, or if he was turned before the variety we have today.

He chuckles. "Yes, but I'm still quite capable of cooking, even if I can't taste the dishes. Or maybe you have constructive feedback?"

Carol's warning glare is clear in my peripheral, but she doesn't have to worry. "I'm surprised, is all. Everything I've been served so far is restaurant quality."

His smile is so wide it stretches his cheeks. "Fantastic to hear. It was my human dream to own a restaurant. What are your favorite meals?" He taps his temple. "I'll remember for later."

I rattle off a pathetic list. "Hamburgers, fries, pizza."

His laugh is silent. "We'll turn you into a food connoisseur soon enough. I hope you like to eat."

I shrug. Funny he thinks I'll be around much longer to do so.

Jacob leaves and returns with two plates of steak and veggies for Carol and me, while Laurentius fetches chalices of blood for himself and Derek, since he can't leave me unattended.

Derek snatches my knife from me before I can cut my steak, Carol taking on the task instead like I might purposefully cut all my fingers off to spite them. They're not completely wrong to worry, as the idea crossed me of slitting my throat and dying right here since Derek can't heal me, and I'm not sure any surrounding Darklings—especially not the Angel Maker—would step up to do so.

When she returns my food, I lock my eyes on my meal and tune out the surrounding conversations.

I'm nearing the end of my meal when Laurentius asks, "Can I give you a gift, Marianna?"

Oh, I sure hope he can. I lift my head for the first time since I started eating, having ignored all other attempts to capture my attention. "Okay."

He smiles and shifts to reach into the pocket of his black leather pants like he's been carrying around whatever it is until he could get to me.

When he reaches across the table to me with his balled fist, I hold my palm out, the side of his frigid hand resting against it as he releases a clump of silver chain with widely spaced blue beads, a cross landing on top.

Flat, I say, "A rosary?"

He clasps his hands around his chalice. "I blessed it for you."

I dangle it over the table while studying it. What are the chances it's toxic metal that eats through my skin and poisons my blood? Why on earth would he give me it otherwise?

"You know," I start as I pull it over my head and slip it under my shirt for maximum skin contact. "Denendrius is from Ancient Rome. He thinks Jesus was a troublemaker. After all this shit, I don't think God is real either. If he is, he must be a sadistic prick."

"Marianna!" Derek barks, half the room twisting to stare at us.

I smirk as I watch Laurentius's unchanged expression.

Carol hisses at me to smarten up, but I ignore her.

Now, will he kill me? Would he do it quickly—try to minimize my pain and suffering—on account of being a man of

God? Or does he have a more violent reputation to go with his nickname?

"It's all right, Derek," Laurentius says. He keeps his eyes on me, a hint of a smile on his lips.

Oh, he's really mad, isn't he? He must be fantasizing about my death.

Carol sighs and shakes her head. "I'm so sorry, she's—"

"I understand," Laurentius interrupts. "I've seen and heard much worse from humans in her position."

"What position?" I dare him to call me a blood slave. If he wants another reason to kill me, I'll give him one.

He doesn't play into my game, just responds with a tight-lipped smile as he lifts his chalice to his lips for a sip of blood.

Once our plates are clean, Laurentius wishes us a good rest of the night before we return to Carol and Derek's room. I crawl under their blanket in hopes of more sleep until a hefty knock against the door has my heart jolting in my chest.

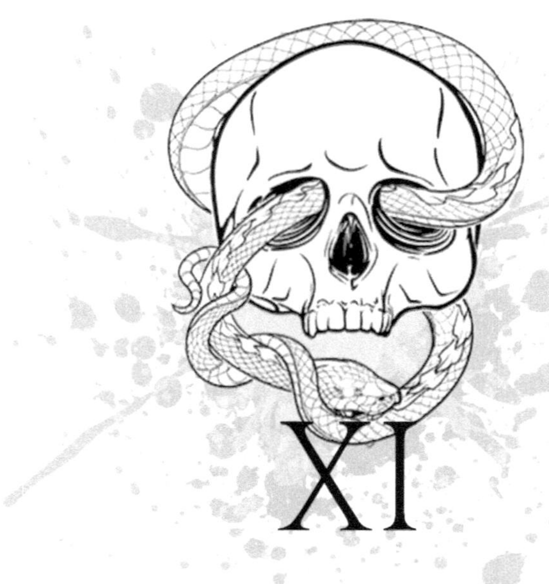

XI

A heavy knock rattles the door, and a moment later Derek is drawing it open to reveal a redheaded man with freckles below his piercing coal eyes.

"Hey, Derek, I'm Artair," he greets with a perfect smile and a faded Scottish accent. He presses a button on the satellite phone peeking out from the shallow pocket of his green cargo pants and adjusts his black T-shirt over it. "Viorel wants Marianna back downstairs. I must see him anyway, so I'll bring her down with me."

I hug myself. Oh god. Is he still mad?

"Mateo's busy?" Derek asks as he crosses his arm and peers into the hallway past Artair like Mateo might be out there.

Artair makes a show of blowing a breath out as he rubs the back of his neck. "Yeah, Viorel has him dealing with something urgent."

"Can she stay until Mateo comes?" Carol asks, a nervous shake in her voice. I wonder if it's the Darklings that have her on eggshells since she didn't seem bothered around Ziggy. Or perhaps it's merely the inescapable number of vampires surrounding her.

"He wants her back down now." Artair gives her a gentle, tight-lipped smile.

Carol's disappointment is evident in her watery eyes as she looks me over before wrapping her arms around me for a tight squeeze. Does she think she might not get another? Derek gives me a quick side hug on my way to Artair, clearly much more confident about the odds of seeing me again.

"Is Viorel still angry?" My heart stutters as Artair shuts the door behind us.

Artair whistles and releases a strangled chuckle. "Well, I hear he's not happy."

A terrified shiver rips through me so fast the force nearly has my feet coming out from under me.

"Ah, don't worry so much. I'm sure you won't be in too much trouble."

I pull in a strangled breath. *What did I do?*

Stopping dead on the carpet, a nauseous groan rolls up from my stomach and out of me. I hug myself and focus on even breaths as I stare at the staircase ahead like it descends straight to death.

Artair steps between me and it, leaning forward a bit to say, "I'm sure it'll be fine."

I squeeze my eyes closed and shake my head, hair ruffling around me. "Don't make me go. Can't you convince him to let me stay with Carol for longer, please?"

"Afraid not . . ." He sighs, the action so obviously forced he must be trying to mock me.

I crack my eyes open, a fresh tear escaping as I exhale a shuddery breath.

His lips tilt, his black eyes full of pity. I can smell blood on his breath when he steps close, leaning his mouth to my ear and whispering so low I must hold my breath to hear. "*Why don't I take you to see your master quickly? You're already going to be punished, may as well make it worthwhile. I'll let you two steal a kiss."*

I suck in a sharp breath and stumble away from him, taking in his serious expression with my wide eyes. "Really?"

He nods, his twitching smile making it clear he's up to no good.

But I don't care.

I need to see Denendrius.

I half-run at his side as we carry on down the stairs, trying to cover as much ground as possible before someone gets in our way.

"Slow down," he warns as he grabs my arm.

We walk through the grand room down the hall, nervous energy zapping my legs and trying to propel me forward faster.

A short woman with long black braids and maroon eyes appears in front of us, making Artair grunt in frustration and stop dead, like her presence is an impenetrable force we can't move beyond.

Her eyes flicker from him to me and back again. "Call it off. This is an asinine idea. It was funny to joke about, but . . ." She pulls in a long breath and shakes her head. "Art . . ."

"Oh, is it now?" He titters, grip tightening on my arm like he's imagining his fist on her. "You just don't want to pay up."

She looks around and lowers her voice. "With him being Huarsar, I don't want to piss him off, understand? He's giving us a home, and it sounds like his last clan betrayed him if he abandoned them while they were under attack. Please don't contribute to the mistrust he likely already carries. It'll come back to bite all of us."

He laughs. "You owe me ten grand."

With that, Artair hooks his arm around my waist and lifts me off the floor against his side before the hall blurs and the sheer speed of his movement blackens my sight.

A few nauseating moments later and damp, frigid stone materializes under my bare feet, Artair's arm around my hips as I blink rapidly. My vision trickles in, orange smudges slowly becoming tall flames. When my eyes adjust, I gasp at the sight of Denendrius's empty cell to my right, and the raised stone circle reminding me of a well in the middle of the room Artair has me standing in front of.

"Hey, Denendrius!" Artair shouts into the darkness past the metal grate as he fishes in his pocket. He pulls out a keyring and unlocks the shiny, modern padlock. "Thirsty?"

Artair grins as he opens the iron hatch—the rusted thing creaking—and shines his flashlight inside.

My heart stops.

Denendrius leans against the damp stone, so deep the light barely washes over his pallid face, his delirious and brooding eyes staring up at us like he's not sure if we're real.

I cry out when Artair grabs hold of my biceps again and squeezes so hard I feel his grip down to my bone.

"Step up," he snarls in my ear, the sudden tone change making the hair stand up on the back of my neck.

I plant my bare foot up on the stone, and he pushes me until I'm standing with all ten of my toes hanging over the edge.

He laughs as he psyches me out with a teasing shove—his hand never unclasping from my arm—that has me planting a foot on the other side of the so I don't fall in.

With a sardonic tone, he says, "What's wrong, Marianna? I thought you wanted to see your master?"

"How deep is it?" I demand, knowing full well I'm about to fall the entire distance once he bores of fucking with me.

"Only forty or so feet," Artair says, his voice oily and sinister. "You'll probably break both your legs, but he's so starved you won't live long enough to feel the real breadth of the pain."

I flinch when he gives me another teasing shove, his low chuckle echoing as I stare down into the blackness.

"Are you going to beg me not to?" I can tell from the hunger in his eyes and his wicked smile that he wants nothing more.

"No," I say. "I want to die. I want to be with Denendrius."

As crazy as it sounds to my own ears, I mean it.

I gasp as Artair yanks my back against his chest and dangles me in the hole. My heart hammers at the base of my throat, my legs kicking at the curved wall out of pure instinct.

"Too bad we don't have more time," he whispers in my ear, teeth nipping at my lobe and making me yelp. "I'd love to bring him up here, let him watch you writhe under me as I inject myself into this tragic little love story you two have going on."

I'm too enthralled with the abyss below to fully process his threat. It doesn't even register he's let go of me until darkness floods my sight and I slam against cold flesh.

I gasp for breath as I grapple to comprehend the information my senses are flooding me with.

Denendrius's arms circle my back, his cold and frantic breath beating against my face. I blink rapidly, waiting for my eyes to adjust so I can see him, but the claustrophobic darkness is unrelenting. My legs are slack on either side of his hips, something icy-wet rippling around the balls of my feet, something putrid and musty burning my nose. When I throw my arms out to stop the feel of falling, they only half extend before my palms slap damp, smooth stone.

"Denendrius," I wail.

His heaving chest presses against mine, and the feel of stone against my back becomes more obvious as he leans against me, my body shifting down like his grip on me is slipping.

"I love you," he breathes, like the words are being strangled out of him.

I yelp at the feel of his body collapsing under mine—he must be too weak to stand—and scramble while gasping for breath to get myself up from the several feet of frigid liquid he's dropped me into.

"I love you too," I cry, thin tears breaking free.

Guilt pools in my gut like the sickening liquid we sit in. I want to tell him this is all my fault. I'm the reason he's in this pit. Yet I know it doesn't matter now. Begging for his forgiveness will change nothing.

His arms envelop me, and he pulls me over his bent legs to sit on his abdomen. He clutches me against him.

With my face mashed against his wet, bloodied chest, an unfamiliar rich and smooth scent of cologne chokes my sense of smell. It reminds me of gold and honey under sunlight and is so strong I can hardly decipher his own scent or the reek of the pit through it. I can't imagine a reason that doesn't make me want to faint as to why he might smell like another man.

"You smell like Huarsar," Denendrius rasps, agony dulling the lilt of his thick Latin accent.

I suppose Viorel's scent would be on every inch of my body when I've been tucked between his sheets.

"He's so cruel," I choke. I try to tell Denendrius about how Viorel held me down and carved his name out of me, but I'm too worked up to get the words out.

"*I'll put you out of your misery, sweetheart,*" Denendrius breathes, his hand flopping on my back.

"Please," I beg him as I lift my head, tears welling in my eyes. I ache to see his face.

He shifts, then the feel of his mouth is against mine and my mind is spinning in delight. I grope around until his slick shoulders are beneath my palms, then hook my hands behind his head as he holds a shaky hand against my cheek.

Denendrius's razor teeth sink into my bottom lip, my pained moan muffled as his hand clutches my face. Hot blood spills down my chin. He gasps for breath, and he laps it up while lacing his fingers through my hair until knots stop him. Then, he shoves my head back and tears into my throat.

I stare up at the spot of round light far above our heads. It reminds me of the moon. That is until Artair lets the cover fall and the sound—the lock clicking closed—echoes around us.

I close my eyes and grit my teeth at the pain, grateful for the feeling of Denendrius's body against mine, that the universe is granting me my final moments with him.

Denendrius sobs and whimpers into my neck as he desperately drinks from me, his cold tears running down my chest. His grip is so tight on me he'd probably break my bones if they hadn't drained him of his blood—and strength. With his other hand, he finds the rosary around my neck and winds it so tight it chokes me until I feel the chain give against the nape of my neck.

Denendrius's grief sounds so far away now. My throat is numb to the pain. A drumming against stone grows louder, and though I can't feel my heart, it must be the source.

The feel of Denendrius's body slips away with my consciousness, and I'm light with peace knowing Denendrius loves me enough to do this. Knowing he loves me so much, he's going to kill me to free me from a life of suffering and servitude, even if he must endure years of torture for it before he can find a way back to me.

I know with all my heart as I step closer to death that this is true love, and I'm so lucky to have had it.

XII

The groaning echo of the iron door opening draws me halfway to consciousness. I can't tell if I'm dreaming or simply unable to fully wake myself up. But an unwelcome reality joins me.

I'm alive.

Why am I still alive?

"You revoked his access through the veil at the perfect time. We found him frantically running around the woods," Mateo says, voice sounding light years away.

"You can leave us, Mateo. Thank you." The iron door creaks closed, and Viorel sounds just as far away as he says, "I tried to trust you, Artair, and you betray me and flee?"

"It wasn't personal. I didn't hurt her to upset y—*Jesus fuck!*" There's a thud and a low whimper. "I'm sor—*Oh, Jesus!*"

"Do you have any idea what you've done?" Viorel snarls.

It sounds like he's speaking through his teeth when he says, "I thought you were done with her"—he gasps for breath—"I wasn't going to do anything until you sent her upstairs. If she were auction fodder, I didn't think it would matter since we receive first pick after you. I swear the bets were jokes!"

"*Liar.* You avoided me for two weeks so I wouldn't discover your scheming," Viorel snarls.

"*Please, Viorel! I'm so sorry. I'll do anything—*"

"You'll die."

Artair's pained bellow drags me the rest of the way awake. The sound coming from the other side of Viorel's wardrobe. I lay in his space on the bed, feeling like a victim of necromancy.

With the strength of my curiosity, I shift my feet onto the floor and stand. The room twirls and twists around me as I limp to the wardrobe's side, using it to hold my aching body up while my knees threaten to buckle.

Viorel has his bare foot on Artair's throat as he lies on the stone while fighting and failing to lift his outstretched arms off the ground. Artair wears nothing but red brutality on his flesh, the long and muscle-deep cuts giving me the impression they whipped him with something sharp.

Despite Artair reuniting Denendrius and me, I spare him no sympathy.

When I blink, Viorel has him lifted off the floor by the base of his jaw, fingernails embedded in his dripping skin like it's soft, mortal flesh.

A low whistle brushes past my ears, the kind that comes from a breeze creeping through a cracked window on a chilly evening. Sickly dread makes my face scrunch. There are no windows down here.

Artair's feet stomp at the air like he can climb from Viorel's grip. They lock their eyes in a death stare. His plea turns into a stomach-deep groan of pain as his skin takes on an ashy color and texture. My jaw lowers, my lungs too empty to gasp as I watch his flesh shrink and cling to his bones until his ribs rip through to expose his blackening organs. His groan disappears from his withered lips, cut short like it was wrung from his lungs, and soon, Viorel is staring into two charred lumps where Artair's eyes once sat. They crumble like soot and drift to the floor into the charred flesh once covering the skeletal remains of his feet.

Another moment, and Viorel's clutching a skull in his hands as Artair's bones rattle and plummet against one another in a heap atop his ashes.

A scream winds around my throat until my breath comes out like a shrill squeak. My mind loops over the dozens of vampire bones making up the bed frame behind me.

Slowly, Viorel turns to face me as the corner of his mouth quirks up. Lifting a long finger, he places it over his lips and holds out the skull.

I stare into the charred sockets of what was a vampire mere moments before and reach a fear so high it feels as though I'm falling through reality for a moment. I crash through the thought that perhaps Denendrius killed me and I'm in another realm with a demon. Perhaps my vision of Viorel after Paco crashed the car was a near death experience.

"Marianna . . ."

When I realize he truly means for me to take it as he extends his arm straighter to me, I force my shaky arm up with my sweaty palm ready. Thankfully, he must realize my feet are completely disconnected from my brain, as he crosses the space between us and gently sets the heavy and solid skull in my hand. When he tucks his hand beneath mine, the hair stands on my arms at his lethal touch. My heart stumbles.

"There," he starts softly with a dark gleam in his eyes, "He'll never harm you again."

My knee buckles and I fall back on the edge of the bed. Viorel gently takes the skull from my hand and places it next to the fireplace remote on the nightstand. I force myself to my feet and float toward my cell. The image of my little bed takes up all the space in my mind, my hand curled ready in front of me to draw back the blanket so I can hide beneath it.

The folded clothes on my bed thwart my immediate plans, so I stand staring at them, wondering why they're there. It takes conscious effort to shift my narrow gaze to the space where my dresser once was.

I shiver at Viorel's presence beside me. Tears spring up at his soft touch against my shoulder blade.

"I smashed it. I'm sorry." He drops his hand. I wince when he takes my wrist in his loose grip and guides me back to his bed. "Sit. You must not move around too much for now."

I sit, unblinking while feeling like I'm floating in space, until I say, "How long was I out?"

My chest aches knowing I must continue.

"The day. You're fortunate Artair's scheming was brought to my attention immediately. The guards were seconds behind, though Denendrius nearly killed you. We drained him and had to give you his blood to keep your heart going."

My *"oh"* is more breath than sound. Despite the guilt of having Denendrius's blood in my body when he needs it—the flicker of delight adding to that acidic burn—I feel as empty as the pit trapping Denendrius.

Viorel comes within a few feet of me, but I stare at the black velvet of his gown.

"I'm sincerely sorry," he says.

I swallow, my blink slow. "Okay." I don't care.

He clasps his hands behind his back. "It was an emotional, impetuous reaction, and it shouldn't have happened. I was thinking more about my anger than the dangerous reality of sending you upstairs."

"Why did you have that reaction?" I can barely get my lips around the words and I'm not completely sure I care about his answer anymore.

There's a heavy pause I fill with a sniffle and some shifting.

"I allowed myself to become thirstier than one should. I wasn't in full control of myself. But worry not, I had my pick of fresh arrivals when you were out."

My brow furrows. That's not quite what I was asking. Before I can muster up the breath to clarify my question, he's walking off.

Sorrow snakes itself around my heart and squeezes, making it thump so heavily I'd worry there was something medically wrong with it in any other situation. I can't find the will to move off Viorel's bed, so I stare at the wardrobe in silence. Tears streak my cheeks. I'm too numb to care about wiping them.

Even when the heat of the fire against my back has my hair slick with sweat and I'm desperate to get away from it, I can't find it in me to move or ask for it to be turned off.

Viorel must be tuned into my thoughts, as he wanders in to switch off the fireplace.

"I want to die," I whisper as he rounds the end of the bed.

Viorel's slow steps bring him to my side. "Yes, there's no doubt. Denendrius was crying a similar sentiment when you were pulled out of there. You are bound to be experiencing similar emotions in such frightful circumstances."

The slow trickle of wetness from my eyes continues, a drop dripping off my chin and landing on my limp hand.

"How are you feeling?" he asks.

A twisted laugh rolls out of me.

"Physically," he clarifies.

"Fine," I mouth. *Dizzy. Sick. Hopeless.*

"Would you like tea?" I can't utter my denial before he adds. "There's food waiting for you."

"You can offer me death, and nothing else," I whisper.

I decide I'll never eat again. If I can't hang myself, slit my wrists, drown myself, or meet death quickly, I'll let myself starve to death. What are they going to do? Force feed me? I'll make myself puke if they get anything in me.

"Nobody will die for quite the time, Marianna," he says with a tone so soft I'm sure his words must really mean something awful.

I close my eyes and release a shuddery breath.

When he hooks his index finger under my chin and attempts to lift my head, I turn so rigid he lets go instead of forcing my head up.

"I recognize I've been quite unkind to you," Viorel says, the gentle lull in his voice only making panic burrow deeper into me. "My anger is toward your master; I shouldn't have cast it onto you."

I bite down on my bottom lip as it quivers.

"I let you suffer for days through your attachment to Denendrius." He releases a heavy breath. "No longer will I continue to make that mistake."

When I say nothing, he lowers himself onto the bed beside me.

"I'm sorry," he whispers again. Slowly, he opens the drawer of his nightstand and draws out a silver horsehair brush. I flinch when he rests it against my temple. "I'm sorry for being cruel."

I let the tears flow freely as he brushes tangles from my damp hair. *Did they bathe me?* When he's done, he sets the brush aside and wipes my cheeks with the back of his fingers.

The way he looks at me is terrifying. There's something about the softness—the concern—in his claret eyes as they wander over my face that makes me sob harder than when he hated me.

"I may have lived longer than all other vampires, but I'm no more immune to mistakes. These past few days are nothing but mistakes," he murmurs. "I'm sorry."

I can barely make my lips move to say, "I'll never forgive you."

There's barely a thought toward me in those words. I

imagine Denendrius and can't grasp the pain three-hundred and twelve years of torture causes.

Viorel wanders off before returning to my side with a white bowl in the palm of his hand and a silver spoon in the other.

"You must eat." He submerges the spoon in stew and lifts a chunk of meat.

I mash my lips together, a tear slipping past the corner of my lips. He'll have to pry my jaw open to make me eat, and even then I'll spit it back in his face.

Viorel rests the spoon in the bowl, a line between his brows as he studies my face. "Okay," he starts as he stands. There's finality to his soft tone. "No more of this."

There's not enough care in me to contemplate his words. I sit unmoving as I quietly cry, trying to wish myself out of existence.

Eventually, Mateo appears crouched at my eye level. "We're going to see Denendrius."

Automatically, I stand, barely able to feel my legs. "Why?" I hear myself say, though I don't think my lips move.

Neither one of them answers me. Mateo scoops me into his arms, per Viorel's request.

The darkness of Denendrius's prison comes alight with dozens of yellow flames as Mateo carries me in after Viorel with a collection of guards. My eyes locate Denendrius's—blistering red and rimmed white—the moment we enter and stop a few arm lengths from the cell. Mateo sets me on my wobbly legs next to Viorel, who drapes his arm across my back to rest his hand on my far shoulder.

The dread—the hopelessness—passing between mine and Denendrius's eyes as he rests his forearms against the bars is so palpable my mouth tastes like rot. So heavy I practically slip out of my body.

With the dim light and my half-adjusted eyes, I can't make out the full extent of Denendrius's injuries as he uses the bars to keep himself upright. His feet look ready to betray him from their skewed position on the damp stone. The bands of gore around his ankles are likely the reason. Streaks of blood start from deep gashes in his bare thighs and stop at his shoulders. They pass through a slice in his throat and continue in thin trails across his beautiful face.

Tears streak my numb face as I imagine him hanging upside down while they bled him. Whatever is left of my frayed heartstrings barely supports my weak heart.

I want to believe this is one of those situations where heartbreak can literally kill someone.

Can vampires die of heartbreak?

My bones beg for bareness, to be relieved from the heavy burden of life.

"Let's not draw this out any longer, rat. For her sake," Viorel says, like this is all Denendrius's fault.

"Draw what out?" Denendrius demands.

There's a smile in Viorel's voice. "You're going to watch me mark your blood slave, Denendrius. You're going to feel the discomfort of having her essence ripped from yours. Be thankful you're not feeling her death."

My breath catches, and before I can finish the thought to run, Viorel steps behind me and yanks my body against his. I writhe uselessly, his grip so tight it keeps me in place against his hard chest even as I kick my feet off the floor.

"*No!*" Denendrius bellows, eyes flying wide. "Don't, Huarsar! I'll do *anything.*"

"Then beg me like Tatiana begged you," Viorel commands, his words slipping past my ear.

Denendrius's lips quiver, tears darting from his burning

gaze. "Will it make a difference?" The hopelessness in his voice renders another of my heartstrings useless, and my heart feels like it's thumping crooked.

"Did it make a difference to you?"

Denendrius closes his eyes and tilts his head toward the floor, jaw clenching.

"Tit for tat," Viorel whispers.

His head snaps up, gaze flickering. "Then kill her. Make me watch her die."

Viorel clicks his tongue in disapproval. "We both know I can't do that."

"It's not equal," Denendrius pleads. "You're taking *far more* than I ever took from you. Don't you know what you're taking from me?"

Viorel's grip tightens on me, a pained squeak escaping my throat.

"Oh, I do. But you have made yourself a bed of thorns, Denendrius. *Now, you must lie in it.*" Viorel's tone is final.

An invisible force pins my arms to my sides before I can cover my mouth. Fury flares in Denendrius's eyes as Viorel's pale wrist moves above my head. I mash my lips together, cries trapped behind my clenched teeth. I can't wriggle. My head is trapped in place against his chest.

He shoves the bloodied incisions against my lips, and a shriek swells in my throat.

"*Drink now,*" Viorel murmurs in my ear as he pinches my nose.

I'm too weak to hold my breath for more than a few beats.

Denendrius shakes with fury, snarling Latin at Viorel through bared teeth as he clenches the bars. If he had the strength—the blood—I'm sure he'd rip them out of place.

My lips part against his bloodied skin.

The shift is almost immediate. Thick blood flows past my tongue, the taste bitter like wine. I'm senseless as I lap up ecstasy, the strange victory-driven peace—a swelling relief—drifting through me as the sight of Denendrius's horror-stricken face and his hand gripping his chest blots with black. The taut ropes holding my mind together loosen, and the darkness greeting me is like a soft winter night.

XIII

I've never slept so well in my life.

It's the first thought dancing through my head before I release a deep sigh and bury my face in a fistful of velvet blanket.

From the angel-wing softness of the bed, the heat of the air and the crackle of flames, I know I'm in Viorel's bed. But I don't feel a sense of urgency. There's no desire to crack my eyes open. Viorel might be looming over me in bed or working at his puzzle, and it won't make a difference. I sigh and wriggle deeper into the blankets, like I'm welcome to stay in them forever.

"Good evening, Marianna." Viorel's soft voice comes from somewhere behind me.

My heart doesn't stutter at the sound of him, and my breath keeps its routine of calmly whooshing between my parted lips.

But his low chuckle makes me roll over. I struggle to sit, like the sheets are clinging to me to keep me from leaving. I rub the sleep from my eyes and set my gaze on him.

I lack the same visceral terror and hatred I experienced the last time I was in his presence. Something about him is different, or perhaps it's me and my lack of connection to Denendrius stripping my sight clean. Only a lingering nervousness remains in me. He's the most powerful vampire in the world, and that itself can't be altered by removing Denendrius's mark. I guess it would be odd—naive, really—to be fully at ease with him.

Still, I find I don't hate him at all. I'm not detached from all the reasons I did. The reasons just feel . . . like they don't matter as much anymore. Like it's an old grudge I haven't lent my mind to in years.

There's so much different to this new feeling. I take a moment to realize the reason I don't fully recognize him is because he looks different. Though his eyes remain claret, and the hint of veins and the bruise-blue and red of his lids and under his eyes hasn't fully faded, there's the slightest hint of color in his alabaster flesh. It strikes me how beautiful he is when he looks more like a man than a monster who crawled out of a crypt.

A little smile slips onto his lips, his eyes tightening for a moment, like he's walking through my thoughts. "How do you feel?"

I swallow and wipe my hands down the sides of my warm cheeks. "Different."

Looking around the room, it doesn't feel like I've been here before, despite the familiarity and the knowledge I have. It's like I'm seeing the room for the first time after having vivid dreams of it.

He stands patiently watching me as I study him and the room, a crooked smile on his lips.

"Okay, I feel really fucking weird."

Viorel's laugh is airy. "I imagined you would. Take your time to get your bearings."

My brow furrows. Though the past few months feel like a vivid dream, my skin pricks with heat knowing they're not.

Slowly falling in love with Denendrius until the feeling consumed me. Running away to Bellevue, Washington with him. The freedom of escaping and having our own home. Enrolling in a new high school intending to graduate. Making a new friend.

Even now, with Viorel's mark, the memories still come with their attached emotions and there's an ache in my chest like loss.

Happiness. Love. The feeling of being on top of the world—Denendrius and me against everything else—despite the hard days that came from Denendrius's trauma and the lingering side effects of the cure. Still, I finally had the normal life I so desperately wanted.

But sickness comes with those feelings. A certain wrongness makes my stomach roil and sweat bead on my forehead.

"Oh, my god." I stand swiftly, staring at him with wide eyes. The feeling swells in my stomach until it's too full and ready to burst. "I think I'm going to—"

I barely make it to the toilet. It's like my body tries to rid itself of the time it passed through.

"*What the fuck have I done?*" I cry before I spit the taste of blood and vomit from my mouth. "Oh god, who am I?" I wipe my mouth with the back of my hand. "I feel so fucking stupid."

"Now, now," Viorel starts as he opens a standing cabinet on the other side of the bathroom and takes a rag from a stack, "You were a blood slave. Nobody can hold it against you."

I close my eyes atto memories of the plane. "I tried to kick Mateo and literally threw food like a toddler."

Viorel chuckles. "Benign behavior, considering Mateo's had blood slaves put bullets in his skull."

That sick wrongness grips me tighter as I think of Denendrius again. Think of his body in mine and his hands and mouth everywhere. I think of how I let it happen—enjoyed it even—day after day. And it was most days, most nights and most mornings his insatiable appetite sought my body to satisfy him.

But I don't think of his beating heart or his warm hands when I think of our bodies entwined together. I think of him asking me to go home with him on our first date, the heat of our second date as we made out on the boat, how he changed once he wasn't getting what he wanted, then of the bruises, the broken bones, the tape of him raping and strangling me in the forest, and how he'd always try to force himself on me.

Until one day, I finally stopped saying no. He'd even told Sarah how he was using her until I'd inevitably come around. He knew. He knew one day I'd be his perfect girlfriend, even if he'd briefly forgotten so.

I feel tricked. Betrayed. By both him and me.

"It's not your fault," Viorel consoles.

I retch again, a pained sob breaking through. Viorel comes behind me—a leg on either side of my hunched body—and reaches around to press his bloodied wrist to my foul lips. There's a flicker of terrified hesitation through me before I swallow the slow flow of blood and feel the sickness wash away. It's replaced with a similar calmness to the one I woke up with.

"It felt so real," I whisper when he pulls his wrist away.

He smooths my hair against the side of my head. "It was, Marianna. In some ways, it was."

When he moves, I shift sideways onto my rear to stare up at him. "We almost got away," I say, thinking of how furious he was that we ran off.

He nods. "Luckily, he drew too much attention to himself by turning back. We would have kept looking, regardless."

Horror wracks me. I throw my palms against the floor when it feels like it shifts below me. "You wouldn't have found us," I realize, a twisted stress laugh bubbling out of me. "You wouldn't have. My friend told me about a vision of me. Denendrius would have killed me in three years. Right in front of a two-year-old, he said I'd have. Awful."

"Visions can change. See, here you are."

I blow out a breath. "Yeah, thank fuck none of that came true."

Viorel scoops my hand up and pulls me to my feet. He walks me back to his bed and I sit, shaking my head to myself.

After a few more minutes of trying to straighten my flurry of thoughts, I ask, "What now?"

"You will dress and eat. Then, you may go upstairs to see your aunt and become familiar with your new home, if you'd like."

I blink at him. "I can?"

His grin is all teeth, my attention drawn to his fangs. "You're not a prisoner, Marianna. You're my familiar."

My brow furrows. "I thought I was staying down here forever," I counter.

Viorel's head tilts. "Yes . . . this is your home now."

I realize I've missed the simple fact that instead of getting a room upstairs, I'm rooming with him. "Oh." No wonder Tassa wasn't appalled by his words.

"I can't have you wandering up and down on your own, but there will be someone to escort you. You are to return here before sunrise to sleep, and being modest with your time upstairs is preferable."

I nod, but think of the cell-made-room, and how uncomfortable the bed is. Marked or not, he's still a strange man and it would be nice to not have my choice be discomfort or sleep with him. I bite my cheek as I lower my eyes. Even with Denendrius's mark gone, it still elicits the feeling of being trapped here, despite knowing I technically wanted to be here.

"Mateo and Seth will clear out one room down the hall for

you." He pointedly looks past me to the dark hall adjacent to the bathroom door.

I give him a thankful nod.

"And seeing as a handful of clan members have left us, I'll have the bed swapped out."

"Okay, thanks." I unload a heavy breath, my shoulders lowering. A smile curls my lips before dropping, not enough happiness to keep it there.

Viorel's smile twitches, something bright and unfamiliar in his claret eyes as he lightly folds his arms across his chest and observes me. I'd say he was ecstatic—happy, even—if I knew for sure he could feel such a way.

I search his face with my narrowing eyes, realizing some of the oddness is coming from the air between Viorel and me. "Something changed."

One of his thick brown brows quirks up.

"When you bit me. You haven't been acting like you hate me since Artair gave me to Denendrius."

He frowns. "I've never hated you."

"Okay," I start, "so you don't hate me. But do you still feel"— I grasp at words to describe how he must have felt toward me before today—"*angry* toward me?"

There's a brief flicker of what I can only call desperation in his eyes as he stares at me. He gives me a wobbly shake of his head. "No."

"What changed?"

"I did."

"What does that mean?" I press my teeth into my bottom lip, a stitch between my brows.

He lowers his hands, and they hang limp at his sides. "As I explained, my anger made me take things too far. I was not caring for you as I should have. But I'm your master now. I care for my things, so I will ensure your happiness."

I sigh. His answer doesn't alter the confusion gripping me

so tightly I can't fit comfortably in my body. I'm about to ask about his sudden fury when he bit me until he interrupts by telling me I should wash the vomit from my hair as my food will be arriving.

The bottom half of my legs are still damp when I take Viorel's bathrobe off the stool and slip my arms through the silk sleeves and tie it closed. He stopped me from bringing my own clothes in with me, saying it's a special day so he has something more suitable for me to wear.

Viorel is tidying two dresses on his bed as I step down into the room.

"Fancy." I lace my hands together, studying them as I join him beside the bed.

The dresses appear to be hundreds of years old from the style of them, though I'm not knowledgeable enough to guess exactly which period they're from.

The least interesting one looks like a nightgown. It's plain and bright white with a frilly neckline, trim and puffy sleeves cinched below the shoulder, at the elbow, and wrist.

The second dress must have been taken from a princess's wardrobe. It's floor length, made of silk, and a pale sky blue with a breast-wide strip of fabric down the center of the dress covered in a pattern made of rose and leaf silhouettes. Silver trim runs down each side of the floral pattern and up over the thick shoulder straps. The sleeves are detached, made from the floral silk and silver trim—two tubular pieces per arm—and have the same white lacing to hold them on as the sides of the dress do.

"You wear the chemise beneath it, and it's not so old. A girl here was a seamstress in the fifteenth century, and she still creates beautiful gowns for herself and other clan members who aren't keen on modern fashion yet. Mateo and I suspected you might like to borrow this one."

I smile a little, gingerly running my fingers across the expensive silk. "I like it." I'm not sure I should wear something so extravagant. It might clash, might look like a costume on someone like me.

"You belong to a king now," he says. "The clan should know."

I slip on the plain gown in the bathroom and exit as the iron door opens.

"Where's Ainsley?" Viorel asks, moving toward the sitting room.

Mateo adjusts the black bandana holding his wavy hair down. "She's dealing with an immortal tantrum. It's going to be a while."

Viorel sighs. "We'll manage without her."

"I have alternative help available for Marianna," Mateo says. "Lucia overhead Ainsley and would like to help. I know how you feel about your space, but she's low-risk, things considered."

My ears perk up, and I wander up behind Viorel and peek at Mateo.

Viorel clasps his hands behind his back. "Yes, you're probably right. Go fetch her."

Mateo smiles. "She's already waiting with Sascha for permission."

I suspect she's coming to help me with my dress—though it doesn't seem too complicated at a glance—so I wait patiently on the bed beside it.

Two minutes later, Lucia—or Glitch, as she introduced herself to me—is having me sit sideways on the couch in the sitting room so she can stick my hair in a curling iron after brushing it. She's brought a rechargeable battery pack with her.

After she's given me a head full of loose curls, she turns to where Viorel sits on his throne, observing us. "Should I put makeup on her?"

I hold my breath until he says, "I don't care either way. Ask her."

Makeup in a dress like this feels like a necessity. "I have some in the wicker basket in my ce–*room*."

I give Viorel a tiny, thankful smile he half returns before I retrieve it.

But when she applies foundation and brushes powder over my face, Viorel scowls. Did he change his mind about his preference for my face?

"You can stay here without your father, Glitch. Why does he want to leave?" Viorel asks as he studies her with slit eyes.

I blow out a slow breath, thankful he's reacting to her thoughts and not to me.

She beams at him. "You used my nickname."

He gives her a single nod. "Do you not prefer that?"

Lucia's grin only grows wider. "I do. It's my own—I don't share it with Lucius—and it sounds so futuristic and makes me feel unique. I'm like a cute robot with wires crossed in my hardware." She giggles. "Edmond and Alaire—you remember them from ninety-two, right—gave it to me."

My lips twitch at the sound of their names, and Viorel's eyes sweep to me before landing back on her.

"I see." Viorel offers her a patient smile.

Her expression widens. "Oh—I'm sorry, I didn't answer your question." She sweeps the brush over my nose. "Uh . . . I don't know. He decided it's time for us to move on since we've been here for so many centuries."

"Hm." Viorel rests against the arm of the chair. "Stay. He can leave if he so wishes."

She tucks her hair behind her ear and half-shrugs. "Oh, I don't know. He's my father. He demands I go too."

Viorel straightens, his annoyance clear from the curl of his upper lip. "He's your father, and I'm your king. If you want to stay, you're staying. This has been your home for nine hundred years, and I won't have him remove you from it by force."

"Okay." She gives him a thankful nod as she inhales deeply and puts the brush on the coffee table. Her face falls as she looks around, gaze skimming over my makeup and my face before she gives Viorel a long and blank stare, wetness welling in her eyes.

"You were going to use the eyeshadow brush to apply blue to her lids," Viorel says softly.

"I'm sorry," she whispers as she picks the brush and pallet up. "My memory doesn't work."

"It's all right. I've known since you came here."

"Right," she whispers. "Of course, you do."

My brow furrows. Is that why she thinks she's useless?

After Lucia applies a hint of blue shadow on my lids and mascara, I step into my dress, and she laces the sides for me. It's heavy, though not as heavy as I thought it would be. She laces my sleeves on, one from my shoulders to elbows, and the others on my forearms. My white chemise spills out from between them, and the white ruffles peek out from under the straight edge of the silver trim just above my breasts. It makes it look fancier than it was alone.

After slipping my feet into a pair of white flats she brought down for me, Lucia presents me to Viorel and says, "Isn't she beautiful?"

I swallow as his red eyes follow the tight dress down my body before settling on my face. To my surprise, he says, "Yes."

I think of the full-length mirror in Viorel's bathroom and make my way toward it, Lucia staying behind since she's not permitted to pass the sitting room to see the rest of his space.

The candles ignite around me as I make my way to the mirror on the other side of the room.

I stare at myself when I reach it, studying the way my hair

twists below my shoulders, the white ruffles above my breasts, and the way the blue silk fits my frame perfectly. With Viorel's blood and healing abilities, there's no evidence of last week's grief on my face.

I'm undeniably pretty.

My warm brown eyes sparkle in the candlelight, and I look like royalty.

It hits me then, like a cold ocean wave crashing down on me.

I did it.

I made it, and I'm safe.

Really, this is more than I had hoped for. I was holding on to the idea of Denendrius being captured or killed, and the possibility of receiving a room in the castle. Never in a million years could I have ever comprehended the idea of being marked by the world's oldest and most powerful vampire.

My new reality has me a little unsettled, as I realize I no longer need to fight for anything. I don't have to fight on the streets, fight Denendrius, fight foster parents or social workers for anything. This may not have been exactly the life I dreamed of, which hurts, but this is gold compared to what life would have been for me otherwise.

I can relax now . . . whatever that means.

A heavy sigh escapes me at the sight of the gang tattoo—the black double Rs outlined in red on my neck below my ear.

It feels like a hook in me, a line going back to the depth of my past. Being here makes me hate the thing even more.

Turning sideways so I can't see my tattoo in the mirror, I notice Viorel lingering by the sink.

"If you don't fight me this time, it could painlessly disappear in minutes . . ."

Gulping, I turn back to face the mirror to cover and uncover the tattoo a couple times with my hand. I ponder my scar-free chest, appreciating how Denendrius's name doesn't fight for attention with my outfit. If it were still there, it would be visible for all to see.

I pull in a deep breath and release it, glancing back at Viorel to give him a firm nod.

He dips out of the bathroom, and I hear him dismiss Lucia as Mateo returns with my dinner. She hollers a cheery "See you later!" before Viorel is standing behind me with his robe and the same blade he used to carve out Denendrius's name.

My heart drums in my chest as he drapes his robe over me and lays a towel across my shoulder for extra protection.

I lean my head to the side and hold my hair out of the way, eyes locked on my tattoo in the mirror so I can watch.

It's painless this time, not even stinging like it did when I struggled. I watch unblinking as he cuts into my neck, one hand firmly against the bottom of my neck while the other uses the blade to slice my tattoo.

I feel like I should be screaming and writhing in pain from the amount of glistening blood gushing down the side of my neck and soaking the white towel. Instead, I'm stone until he wipes the blood from my flesh.

One minute. It took one minute to slice away evidence of who I once was. One minute to disconnect me from my life of gang violence, of drug addiction, and misplaced belonging.

Now, with the brand of my old life gone, I look like a girl who could belong to a king. Like a girl suitable for a royal renaissance dress.

Despite the attire, I look *normal* now.

A bright grin stretches across my face, and my body buzzes with joy.

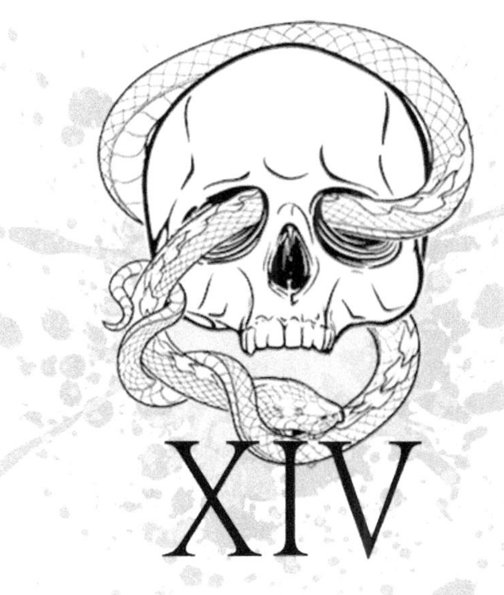

XIV

Mateo sets a platter of homemade pepperoni pizza on the coffee table in front of me. I reach for a slice before the shot glass full of pills next to my water changes the course of my hand and I grab it instead.

Viorel, who has sat next to me tonight instead of on his throne, says, "Vitamins."

My eyes narrow. "Why?"

"You're severely lacking, anemic, and borderline malnourished. You'll take them every day," he orders like I might protest.

"You just want me to taste better," I tease with the daunting realization he'll likely be feeding from me regularly.

"Perhaps occasionally." One corner of his lip lifts in a crooked smirk, and I stare at his fang and remember how much the venom on it burned.

Great.

I pop a pink oval vitamin into my mouth and wash it down with water.

And here I thought I was finally eating better when Denendrius and I were in Bellevue. Could years of malnutrition be why I haven't gotten my period yet? My face turns bright with the thought, and I don't want to turn to see Viorel's expression if he's heard.

"You've never experienced your menses?" Viorel asks, sounding too baffled for something that's none of his business.

The sheer embarrassment—*how dare he acknowledge my worry aloud*—has me saying, *"Please."*

Mateo suddenly has something to check out in the next room.

He makes an astonished sound. "How odd, considering you're probably closer to nineteen."

I grab a slice of pizza. "I'll probably get it soon," I say into a bite.

"You've never been examined?" The curiosity in his voice only adds to the heat in my face.

Shaking my head, I gulp down my mouthful of warm cheese and dough.

"Hm. I'll have to read through my new medical books. Whatever the issue was, you're fine now," Viorel assures me.

"You think so?"

His nod puts me at complete ease. With how long he's been around, how much he's likely read, and how many human bodies he's . . . *dealt with,* he's probably more knowledgeable than any doctor I could visit.

Viorel ends our conversation by disappearing into the reading room, where Mateo must be from the sound of his rings tapping something wooden. There's an intentional silence as I eat my pizza and pop vitamins in my mouth.

Mateo returns with a friendly smile as he straightens his bulky rings. "Excited to go upstairs?"

I nod and wipe a trail of grease from the corner of my mouth with my cloth napkin before it drips onto my dress.

"No going into clan members' bedrooms," Mateo warns as he leans against the iron door. "It's unsafe."

I can sense the hefty list of rules he's about to lie out for me. "Okay," I agree, assuming Carol's and Derek's room doesn't count.

"You cannot go outside without an escort," he adds. "Never go into the woods. They are vast, purposely disorienting, and you will get lost. A guard will have to find you."

I shrink with disappointment. "I can't go to the garden? At all? Can I step outside for fresh air? What if Derek takes me?"

"No, but you may track down a guard to escort you."

"What if I want to go alone to clear my head?"

"No," Mateo says firmly.

"Well, that doesn't seem fair," I argue.

Viorel returns and settles into his throne, running the sharp tip of his nail against a decorative groove on the arm as he watches me intently. "It appears you're getting comfortable quickly."

I tighten my lips, refusing to let another argumentative word pass between them.

"Remain indoors unless a guard is with you," Viorel commands.

"Fine," I whisper before roughly folding the tip of a fresh slice of pizza in my mouth.

Despite the initial rules, I am given a decent amount of freedom, and am encouraged to treat the castle as my home. I can raid the snack pantry in the kitchen whenever I want, or ask Jacob—or Riley, a human girl who cooks sometimes instead—to cook for me, since nobody in the general population or the nursery may use the stove or oven.

I can wander whichever halls I want, play in any of the marked hobby rooms, and walk out with whatever books I'd like from the massive library.

The nursery comes with a complicated set of rules. I'm

permitted to visit if I announce myself and stay close to a care-taker—like Ainsley—unless I'm in the mortal room. I must be careful near the youngest vampire children and use my judgment when interacting with them. Despite the risk, Viorel encourages me to spend time there eventually, telling me the littlest ones would appreciate my attention.

I try not to stress about my trip upstairs as I finish my dinner, not completely sure what I should do besides see Carol and Derek. I suppose I could visit Ainsley in the nursery as she suggested and say hello to Tassa since I know she doesn't hate me.

My brow furrows. Now that my mind isn't in a constant loop around Denendrius, there's space for other thoughts and real-izations, and a confusing one comes through. "There are vampire children here."

"Yes," Viorel verifies.

"Wait. I thought vampire children were turned back, and the ones who survived integrated back into society. But there's some here? I thought vampire children were a crime?"

"Creating them is a crime. One I give the death penalty for . . ." Viorel's eyes narrow as his lips part a little. He glances at Mateo and back to me while straightening in his chair. "Who said they're turned back?"

"Alaire and Edmond, the two bounty hunters I sent that tip to."

He grips the arms of the chair, his furious gaze making me squirm. "Recount that conversation to the best of your memory."

I gulp. "Well, we were waiting for Denendrius to show up at the warehouse, and I asked about crimes in the vampire world. He said creating vampire children are a crime, and if they found a vampire child, they'd kill their creators and turn the child back human, that the ones who survived the cure would be integrated back into society."

Mateo and Viorel share a long stare that has my lips pursing.

"That's why they stopped coming back here," Mateo says, brows lifted in disbelief as he slowly shakes his head. "They likely didn't want to risk getting caught after you explicitly shot their idea down. I still can't fathom them wanting you to give the cure to every immortal child here."

Viorel's stares across the room in deep thought. "Where did they find the cure? Nobody has touched my stock in thousands of years, and I haven't come across another vampire with the ability since."

My lips purse. "Denendrius found a vampire with cure blood in the eighteen-hundreds. That's why he was murdering clans and kidnapping so many vampires. Clearly, vampires are still being born sometimes with the ability."

Viorel expels a heavy sigh. "Well, that explains that chaos, then. Recount the rest of your time with them, specifically conversational topics. From the beginning."

"Hmm." I dig into my memory, meeting them feeling so long ago despite how it's only been a few months. "Well, we talked about the fact I was marked, figured out no Darkling can hypnotize me—"

Viorel lifts his hand to silence me. "What?"

I swallow, my gaze cutting to Mateo's shocked expression—clearly Rayonne never mentioned it to anybody—and back to Viorel. "No vampires have been able to hypnotize me. Denendrius can't, Alaire and Edmond couldn't, a Darkling looking to collect a bounty on us couldn't—"

"I can," Viorel states.

My heart drops like a brick into my stomach. "You . . . you can?"

I nearly lose control of my breath, but then consider how I can never get the words out of me when I try to explain how Viorel carved Denendrius's name out of me, and how Viorel looked me in the eye and told me I wouldn't tell anyone. Was he worried about looking bad if I blabbed?

"Because you would recount it wrong," Viorel grumbles. "You only had to be still."

I mash my lips together, not so upset about it anymore. It was terrifying, but I'm glad it had a negative effect on Denendrius.

"Denendrius couldn't hypnotize you even as your master?" Mateo says, incredulously. "And here I thought your mark was simply too strong when I tried to settle you on the plane."

Viorel's silent, his unblinking, slit eyes locked on me as he taps his finger thoughtfully against the arm of his chair. His sudden, sharp inhale after a few lengthy moments has me flinching in surprise.

Turning to Mateo, he says, "There was a black utility van in Marianna's thoughts. They drove it to the warehouse where Denendrius killed them. Go speak to him about what happened to it afterward. I want their laptop, and to find where they were residing so we can search through the rest of their belongings. You'll be in Lorimer to see Marianna's mother, so search afterward. If they were experimenting on children with the cure, they likely kept records."

Mateo stands. "And if Denendrius won't cooperate?"

"He must. Lubricate his tongue with blood for all I care and let him be for a couple of weeks. I have the rest of eternity to torture him. This is critical."

"What does it mean that nobody else can hypnotize me?" I ask as Mateo leaves, my heart thumping in the base of my throat. "They said it happens sometimes, or humans might be adapting—"

"That's all bullshit," Viorel interjects.

I swallow and grip the edge of the couch, the velvet smooth against my palms. "Then what's the truth?"

"That's what I'm trying to find out . . ." Viorel's pensive eyes look through me. "Never in my time have I heard of a human who could not be hypnotized, master and marks aside."

"Could there be something wrong with me?"

He runs his tongue across his bottom lip. After a few more moments, he blinks and says, "Sascha's ready to take you upstairs."

I don't miss the likely answer in his lack of response and try to cast my concern to the back of my mind as I draw in a deep breath and stand.

Walking into the grand room, there's nothing left but the echoes of dozens of disrupted conversations. I inhale the smell of the burning logs in the fireplace while everybody stares at me. At least, that's what it feels like. I appreciate the eyes pretending I haven't caught their attention. Others are less diffident and stare me straight in my face, but I hold my chin up so I don't look as pitiful as they're used to seeing me.

I notice the way their eyes trail down the expensive silk and silver of my dress, the way the ones whose eyes I catch offer a small nod to go with their serious faces.

But *no one*—that I catch at least—so much as scowls in my direction or allows a negative emotion to cross their face. I hear my name and Viorel's as I look toward the staircase, weaving around sofas and coffee tables. For once, their mouths are void of Denendrius's name.

Glancing over my shoulder, I notice a bit of fear in a few red eyes. Most survey with curiosity or awe.

It's not until I reach the first step do I understand what's happened, do I understand what it means to be Viorel's familiar and how I am wearing a message. A message that I am not some token of revenge he's taken to feast on. I wear a demand for respect.

For a fleeting moment, I feel untouchable.

Then, I climb the stairs and re-welcome the growing pains paired with my new life. The night erupts behind me.

Derek stands from the sofa as he observes me wandering through the open door of his room like he was expecting me. He lifts his brows, a slight pinch to his lips.

Carol sits cross-legged on the bed, gaze flickering between me and Derek, like she's trying to figure out if Viorel has marked me based on his reaction.

I unload a heavy breath, a nervous smile shaky on my lips as I stop halfway in the room. "Hi . . ."

"Well, that's *definitely* not Denendrius's mark," Derek says.

"Is it a strong mark?" I know Ziggy could smell when Denendrius's mark was strengthening. How much of Viorel's blood is needed to stray as far as I did with Denendrius? Is once enough since he's so powerful?

He shoves his hands in the front pockets of his slacks and half-shrugs. "With Denendrius, you smelled more like you than him, but . . ." His lips purse. "The way Viorel's mark changes your scent is hard to explain. With normal vampires, the mark adds to the human's scent. The mark and the human are easily distinguishable. But with Viorel's, it's like your scent is *entwined* with his."

My brow furrows as I try to wrap my brain around the concept. "Oh."

"How are you feeling?" The words rush out of Carol.

I blow out another breath and chuckle as I meander to the corner of the bed and wrap my hand around the bedpost. The hard and square edges digging into my palm are nice. "I feel like I just woke up from the most realistic dream I've ever had. It feels like I've been away from reality for years."

Carol gives me a small smile. "You look fantastic, at least. Healthier."

"Thanks. It's probably from Viorel's blood."

An uncomfortable silence fills the long space between us, and I can tell from the way their lips twitch with hesitation that they're still feeling the brittleness of the eggshells I've dragged them across.

Derek's lip part to say something, but I blurt, "I'm sorry."

"You don't have to be sorry," Carol assures me, frowning. "You weren't yourself."

"You never would have acted like that if it weren't for Denencrius's desires." Derek leans against the side of the bed. "We don't blame you."

I tighten my grip on the bedpost. "Still, I'm sorry. I created a mess by running away with him."

"Even if you had the mind to stay, to stop him, do you think he wouldn't have escalated things?" Carol straightens the edge of the green Afghan blanket on Derek's side of the bed and pats it.

"I'm sure he would have hauled you out kicking and screaming if you hadn't agreed, Marianna. He wanted to separate you from us. After he tried to bash my head in, he'd get weird looks on his face whenever you and I—or you and Rayonne, especially—would speak, like he wanted to physically shut us up."

"I didn't notice," I admit as I carefully crawl onto the foot of the bed, so I don't wreck my dress.

Carol shrugs. "You think he would have let you catch him? Besides, there were plenty of times you weren't in the room where he acted off, honey."

"He was being so nice to me," I whisper, unable to help my aching heart, the residual feel of love resembling heartbreak.

"You weren't giving him many reasons to be upset with you. Besides, he was relying on you to function," Carol says, sounding annoyed, though I know it's not at me.

I let the flicker of the oil lamp's flame capture my attention, and my mind wanders back to when I first started dating

Denendrius. He was so sweet until I didn't listen to him. Until I didn't bend to his will.

The backs of my eyes burn when I realize he likely hadn't changed at all when he was human, he just woke up with his mask back on. Woke up with how tightly it first fit before immortality tore it off.

Derek's tone is careful as he says, "He was getting ready to kill me."

My head snaps up and I give him a long stare. "What? But you two seemed to get along well enough."

Derek shakes his head. "He wanted my help. The night I pulled him off you, after we all went to bed, he came downstairs and slipped into my room." My eyes widen as he continues. "He stood over my bed for"—he blows out a breath—"quite a few minutes. I pretended to sleep until he left."

"But he stuffed diamonds in both your bags before we went, and left weapons behind for you. Why would he if he wanted to kill you?" I argue.

Derek's chuckle is flat. "Yeah, we found them. Probably did it to keep you pliable and set you at ease, Marianna. Some grand gesture to prove he's the good guy."

A grimace of disgust shapes my face, that sick feeling sloshing in my stomach again.

"Enough about him. He doesn't matter anymore," Derek says softly. "How's Viorel?"

"Better, I think. He's calmed down." I run my fingers through my curly hair, thankful for the change in topic.

I tell them Viorel's sending men to talk to my mom and find out if I'm older like he believes I am, and I can't help but admit how terrified I am of knowing what memories I'm missing from that forgotten time. Derek finds it the perfect conversation to practice his calming ability, and I float on a cloud of peace. Carol tells me I don't have to deal with whatever they find out alone.

When I sprawl out across the foot of their bed on my back, we talk about their place in this new world. I'm relieved to find Carol is loving it almost as much as Derek is, though her worries for me have been making it hard to fully appreciate her new life, despite Derek's reassurances.

I ask about Rayonne, a guilty lump forming in my throat at how much of a bitch I was to her in those last few days. The guards have let Derek visit her. She's doing well in the ward but is eager to settle into a room Viorel has saved her once she has better control of her thirst.

Derek crawls onto his side of the bed and leans against the headboard. "When Rayonne's out and settled in, I was thinking we could all take a trip somewhere. What do you think, Marianna? Should we make use of those diamonds?"

I beam. "Where would we go?"

"How about you decide?" Carol proposes.

A million ideas dart through my head. "Okay."

Carol lifts her arms above her head for a long stretch and groan, then adjusts her white sweater. "I'm starving. Want to eat with us?"

"I ate already, but—" I mash my lips together, desperation for their time coursing through me. I remind myself I'm home now. Their presence is a guarantee. "I think I'm going to walk around the castle alone, try to come to terms with the reality of being here now."

XV

As I drift through hallways, up and down stairs like a phantom, I'm hollow with the memories of the past few months playing through my head. While half of my mind haunts me, the other notes the surrounding space. A hall of black and white photos. One full of plague-themed paintings. Another covered in fake plant vines.

Two suits of armor guard the double doors open to the vast library on the far side of the castle, an area I imagine mirrors the grand room. It's two levels, many of the red-oak bookshelves paired with rolling ladders. Potted plants are tucked between statues and stacks of loose books. Alabaster statues of sparsely clothed men and women grip the dull gold of the columns. They reach up to the arched ceiling on either side of a long and wide walkway. A gold and candlelit chandelier punctuates the space overhead. Silver crystals hang from the gold rings, the light reflecting against the striking artwork of painted gods and goddesses on the ceiling.

My eyes drop to the sofas and chaises, to the vampires

lounging with books, the end tables tucked beside them, and across the tables taking up more than their fair share of floor space. A crisp, brown box of books sits inside the door next to a fern, the pastels and reds of the spines vibrant. I can practically smell the fresh glue holding their unexplored pages together and wonder how often people add new stories to the shelves. Are frequent users of the library expected to bring back recent novels when they return from their trips?

It's breathtaking, but I don't feel like reading, so I move along and consider tucking my fingers between the old pages of some archaic novel another day.

I pass countless bedrooms, a few rooms wide open. One with chains on the bedposts. A few with cramped bed arrangements like entire extended families are living in them. Through the cracked door of one, the white bed sheets are soaked with blood. Some rooms are filled with coffins, and I wonder how many vampires prefer them to beds.

I walk myself into a daze, only giving the walls around me enough attention to keep myself from getting lost.

When the familiar voice of a young man calls my name, I plant my feet and glance around until I notice the steel door far down the hall and the open door to my left.

I take a few careful steps closer and hesitate in the doorway, unable to help my curiosity as I glimpse a dozen reptile tanks spread across the room between the doorway and the massive mahogany canopy bed on the far wall. Its thick square posts extend to a point past the flat, wooden top, and are marred by a frenzy of knife-carved crosses making the hair stand up on the back of my neck.

Laurentius stands next to a glass terrarium on a small wooden table, wearing a baggy white blouse half unbuttoned and half tucked into his leather pants.

"Hi." Laurentius's hard swallow is visible. His perfect smile reaches his bright crimson eyes as they wander over me. "You look stunning."

My cheeks burn and I feel silly for my suspicion of him now. "Viorel's idea."

"Uh"—he clears his throat—"do you want to see my serpents?"

There are countless terrariums of various sizes, lit by solar-powered lamps attached to the cords running across the floor, through the open balcony doors framing a starry night, and to a solar panel. They light up the room, only a couple of flickering candles on his book-covered nightstands aiding to illuminate the enormous space.

There's a massive glass terrarium in the left corner between a wardrobe and the balcony, so large it's practically a little room and reminds me of reptile exhibits I've seen commercials for back home. It's full of greenery and tree limbs, a little pond surrounded by sand at the bottom.

My curiosity lures me into the room. "Can I see the big one?" I ask, steps already bringing me toward it.

"That's Nehushtan," Laurentius says, staying put as I cross the room. "He's a yellow anaconda and is quite aggressive to everyone but me."

Nehushtan is stretched out on a branch. My eyes trail down his long and thick body of misshapen black splotches on his brassy-yellow skin.

"He's so handsome." Gently, I place my palm against the glass. His yellowy, slit eyes focus on me, pink forked tongue darting out of his mouth.

"Here," Laurentius says, drawing my attention to him as he lifts a wriggling snake out of the terrarium. It's black and white, with a black dot in each blob of white. "This is Sugar. She's my ball python."

"Sugar?" I repeat as I near him, having expected something more menacing.

He closes the space between us and lifts Sugar, curling her around my shoulders. Two feet of snake slithers through my hair and across my collarbones, her little pink tongue flicking from her mouth.

"You're not afraid of snakes?"

I shake my head. Sugar's cool scales are strange on my flesh. "Not after the snakes I've met throughout my life."

He smiles. Up close now, I notice Laurentius's fangs and the way he takes micro steps away from me. His chest is still like he's holding his breath between sentences.

I take a lunging step backward like it'll make a difference in whether he attacks me. "Should I go?"

He slams his lips together and gives me a swift shake of his head that sends strands of hair into his brooding eyes. "One minute. Stay here please," he chokes out as he disappears.

If I weren't so curious about him, I might walk out. But I can only pace halls for so long, and I'm not in any mood to start a hobby either.

I stand with Sugar twisting around my hand, and it doesn't feel like a minute has passed when Laurentius wanders back in with a chalice full of blood and retracted fangs.

"Sorry." As he shuts his door behind him, I recall how I'm not supposed to be in anybody's room and how that's probably why.

My heart races. *Oh fuck.*

I must look quite horrified, as his eyes widen, and he chokes on a sip of blood. He spins and pulls the door open.

"Habit." The word falls off his tongue. "I'm not trapping you in here, I promise."

"Okay." I take a deep breath as I offer a tight smile, trying to trust Viorel wouldn't let him wander around—and me, alone—if Laurentius is as dangerous as Mateo believes.

Laurentius wanders back over as I watch Sugar try to find balance to slither back up my arm. I can feel his heavy stare.

"What?" I look up, thinking I might not be doing something right with his snake.

"Sorry, you're just breathtakingly gorgeous."

I swallow and focus on Sugar, her head resting on the silver trim of my sleeve. "Thanks," I whisper, my throat tight. His attractiveness isn't lost on me. But instead of returning the compliment, I ask, "How old are you?"

"Are you asking how old I was when I died, or how long I've walked Earth?"

"Both."

"I'm twenty-one, but I was born—as a human—eight-hundred and seventy-eight years ago."

I study him again, not quite believing he's so young.

My disbelief must transfer to my face, as he winks and says, "If you ask the Roman Catholic Church, I'm twenty-five."

I purse my lips. "I don't get the joke."

"There's a minimum age to become ordained," he explains.

My cluelessness continues. "Ordained?"

He takes another sip of blood and smirks. "I'm a priest, Marianna."

My lips fall apart, and I double take at his room, noticing the tall bookshelf of Bibles between his nightstand and the drape-covered window. The incredibly crowded altar in the back left corner of his room sticks out now, as do the painted depictions of fallen angels hanging on his walls. I suppose I should have known when he said he blessed that rosary for me.

"Oh." I can't help but feel a tad odd about his compliments now. My eyes narrow. "You have to admit, it's ironic you're a priest and a vampire."

He sets his chalice down to take Sugar back, who I've nearly forgotten about since she's been so still. "My father was a priest too. I was working to become ordained while I was human. When I died, I continued once I could, and offered sermons on Sunday nights. Unfortunately, none of the other vampires here care to hear my teachings. Religion is not very popular with immortals."

I cross my arms, glancing at the marred bedposts again and thinking of how Josephine said nobody wants him here. "How did you die?"

He runs his free hand through his hair, Sugar winding around the other. "Do you ask every vampire you meet? It's quite inappropriate."

I gulp. "Shit, sorry. I guess I'm used to the vampires I meet telling me their life stories."

Laurentius gives me a tight-lipped smile.

I try to recover with, "Well, what brought you here? Why aren't you still giving sermons?"

He purses his lips, silent as he sets Sugar back in her home and locks it before grabbing his drink. "I came here after being thrown out of several churches," he admits. "Unfortunately, nobody wanted to hear the truth. The Catholic Church prefers their teachings, and they disliked me straying."

My brows hike. "*Several* churches?"

What the fuck was he teaching?

"Eleven," he clarifies, swiping in annoyance at the air near his ear with his free hand while he takes another sip of blood. "But I heard about this place and Viorel from another vampire, and knew I had to be here with him. I arrived as they were adding the finishing touches after building for decades. There weren't many of us at first, mostly Viorel and his followers who built it for him. This has been my bedroom for just over eight hundred years."

"It's nice," I say, scanning the busy stone walls. "Big."

Laurentius smiles. "Viorel intended for the castle to be a protective home, each room large enough to house small families. He loves us so much he wanted to make sure we're all comfortable and safe."

"What do you think about him being Huarsar?" I wonder.

He smiles. "I'm unsurprised. Viorel has been around for a long time, and I'm sure he's taken many names."

"You don't think he lied? What about the rest of the clan?" I move to another terrarium and peek inside, glimpsing a small snake with red and black bands curled behind a rock.

He takes a long swig of his blood to finish it. "No. Viorel cares about us. I trust he had a good reason not to tell us. He knows more than any other man on Earth, so we have no right to question him."

Out of the corner of my eye, I catch him wiping his fingers across the inside of the chalice to collect the rest before licking them clean. I pretend I don't notice, scrutinizing the leaves and fake bark of the decorations. I don't look until he balances the chalice on the edge of Sugar's table.

He jerks his head toward the balcony as he licks his lips clean. "Fresh air?"

I straighten and follow him outside, my lungs soaking up the crisp nighttime air permeated with the smell of woods and garden. I lean against the smooth stone rail and lace my fingers together. Aside from how he flattens his hands, he mirrors me. A cool breeze twists through my curls and I smile at the fresh feel of it on my skin, so used to the heavy age of the air inside.

A full moon oversees the vast forest and garden, the twinkling stars brighter than ever. The sky is so clear I'm momentarily convinced I'll see another planet or galaxy through the brilliant glow.

"It's beautiful out here," I breathe.

I catch Laurentius staring from the corner of my eye.

"It is," he agrees.

I subdue a warm smile and squint across the dark tops of the trees. The breeze carries the sound of happy chatter and snorting horses to my ears.

"How deep into the woods are we?" I'm still unable to find signs of life beyond the castle.

"I don't know. Viorel has a veil over the property and much of the surrounding forest to keep us safe. It works from both sides. There could be a highway within walking distance, and we'd never find it." He waggles his finger vaguely toward the trees. "There could be a village in the distance, and we'd never see its lights."

I blow out a breath and give my eyes a break, taking in his peaceful face. "It doesn't bother you having to schedule trips out? You don't feel trapped, cut off from the world?"

He smiles crookedly at me. "No. This is the safest place in the world. Danger from the outside is impossible. Besides, I haven't left in decades, and I'm not nomadic. If I were, then I would leave instead of complaining about the rules put in place to protect us."

Fair. I gaze back across the forest and ponder that.

"Do you want to walk in the garden with me?" Laurentius asks.

"I would, but Viorel said I can't without a guard to escort me."

Breaking one rule is probably going to get me in enough trouble as it is.

Laurentius leans harder into the rail, eyes scouring the garden. He points into the darkness.

"There's Marcus. He's a guard." He cups his hands over his mouth. "Hey, Marcus!"

A beat later and I follow his dropping gaze to a man who stares up at us with black eyes.

"Why the hell do you have Marianna in your room?" Marcus snaps.

His tone has no effect on Laurentius's grin. "I was showing her my snakes! We want to go for a walk in the garden, but Viorel requires her to have a guard escort her. Can you linger near us?"

There's a warning in Marcus's voice. "Viorel also said she's not to go in anyone's chamber!"

Laurentius stiffens, his cheery expression exchanged for bulging eyes and a lowered jaw. He'd be pale if he weren't so already. "I didn't know!"

Shit. I suppose I shouldn't be surprised all the guards know the rules Viorel gave me.

I catch Marcus's shrug. "You'll be fine, but she should know better. Just bring her out now. I'll be in the garden for a while."

Laurentius stares down at me with a disappointed frown. "Marianna..."

"I'm sorry. It slipped my mind until I was already in here and I figured it didn't matter since the damage was already done," I admit.

"You should listen to Viorel," he lectures. "He knows what's best for everyone."

"Fine, fine," I grumble, so we can move on.

His warm smile returns. "We can climb down this way. It's faster than going all the way down the hall."

I purse my lips at the drop, probably around twenty feet of rock between us and the grass.

Laurentius swings his legs over the rail, facing me as he stands on the other side with his feet between the thick balusters. He hangs on with one hand and leans back a bit. "Climb around in front of me. I'll hang onto you and drop us."

Carefully, I sit on the edge in my dress and maneuver myself to the other side, Laurentius's hand grasping my arm and helping me shift around in front of him.

Why do I trust him? I don't know. I shouldn't. But I may as well accept the little adventures I can.

When he wraps his arm around my ribcage and holds me tight against him, my heart spasms. I hang on to his arm with both of mine. The cold metal of his rosary presses between my shoulder blades.

"Ready?"

I nod.

"Don't drop her," Marcus shouts, half laughing as he adds, "You won't be Viorel's favorite anymore. He'll probably kill you!"

"I'm not going to drop her," Laurentius grumbles. Then he lets go.

I don't breathe as we crash through the air, gray stones a blur in front of me until we stop suddenly a moment later.

"You smell nice," Laurentius says thoughtfully as he grips me against him longer than needed, my feet dangling an inch above the grass.

He lets me go and I smooth out my dress. Grinning up at him, I gasp for breath. "That was exciting."

"All right," Marcus says dismissively. "I'll be close. Just don't fuck off into the woods."

"Promise." Laurentius gives him a stern nod.

"Do you have a girlfriend?" I blurt as I follow Laurentius's purposeless steps, not sure where the question came from.

Maybe it's because he's called me pretty tonight and held me, or because he's incredibly handsome and giving me attention. Likely all the above.

His beat of laughter is abrupt. "No."

I narrow my eyes. "Boyfriend?"

He chuckles and shakes his head. "Nope, just me, myself, and I."

I don't grin along with him, unsure of what joke I'm missing. Why is he acting like it's a silly question with an obvious answer?

My face burns red when I recall it is. "Right. Priests are celibate, duh. I had little exposure to religion growing up, sorry."

Laurentius's bark of laughter has my eyes widening and brows lifting. "What?"

"I've never been . . . *celibate.*" He fights a smile, eyes picking through the stars like he's trying to avoid mine. "The Catholic Church enforced the rule when I was nine, so I always figured it wasn't a rule God cared for humans to follow if it hadn't been important before. Perhaps it's an act of defiance, since my father was married and had to hire my mother as a maid to keep her in the house."

"Wow."

He knocks his shoulder into mine. "I don't agree with many of their rules."

Clearly, if he's been thrown out of so many churches.

"Tell me about you," he requests as we wander, walking so close to me his hand brushes mine and my shoulder bumps into his arm.

I blow out a long breath. "Fuck, I don't know. Anything I have to say about myself is going to make this conversation sound like a confessional session."

He laughs, the sound bubbly and carefree. It makes my belly warm, and I press my teeth into my bottom lip. I stare down at my flats as I step through the manicured grass.

"I don't judge," he assures me.

"I suppose that would make you bad at your job," I tease.

His lips purse. "Eh, I've found the clergy most judgmental in my days."

I clasp my fingers in front of me when his hand brushes mine again, thinking I'm getting in his way. "I'm not very interesting."

Eyes narrowing on me, he says, "That's hard to believe, considering the circumstances of your arrival and how Viorel's taken you."

I'm not the kind of interesting that's worth talking about. I shrug and leave the air empty as I walk beside him. He doesn't fill it either, and as a minute passes with our heels *swooshing* through the grass, I become acutely aware of how the conversation has fallen flat and how it's my fault.

"I like to draw," I offer.

He turns a bit and smiles like he didn't feel the awkwardness of our silence. His hand brushes the skirt of my dress. "What do you draw?"

I don't want to tell him the truth, that it's been a few months since I've drawn anything, and how when I did, the pictures were nothing but angry and edgy depictions of the street, drugs, and gangsters. I take another purposeful moment with my thoughts, and instead answer with, "I want to draw pretty things. Maybe the ocean, some flowers, the sunset . . ." My answer is bland, *obvious*. Who doesn't draw those things? But I've seen a lot of beautiful things in my pacing tonight deserving space in a sketchbook. "The castle is beautiful. Even the chairs would be fun to draw."

"I'd love to see," he says.

Excitement bursts inside me. I have infinite time to draw now, and no responsibilities. I should visit the art room Viorel mentioned. I bet they'll have top of the line supplies.

We stop at a flower bed lit with little solar lights. The fragrant air fills my airways, so thick I'm sure I'll wander back inside with my dress perfumed.

Laurentius squats and plucks a handful of flowers before presenting the small bundle to me. As I reach out to take it, he jerks them away and vanishes. He returns a beat later with a silk handkerchief he wraps around the stems.

"They're poisonous," he explains. "Touching can cause minor skin irritation, but eating them will put you in an early grave." Warmth spreads from my fingers to the rest of my body —pooling in my belly—as I hold them with the handkerchief and bring them closer to my face to study them better in the dark.

They're a vibrant blue-purple, six widely spaced oblong petals with matching tufts reaching up to me from the center.

"Viorea," he says with a delicate, Romanian accent that has my head popping up. "Or Scilla bifolia."

"Viorea . . ." My brow furrows as the name rolls off my tongue. "Like Viorel?"

He grins. "Yes. They're Viorel's favorite. It's no wonder he named himself after them."

"Pretty . . ." I murmur, resisting the urge to run the pads of my fingers over the petals. "Thank you."

I've never had a boy give me flowers before.

"Pretty flowers for a pretty girl," he says, matter of fact while sitting cross-legged in the grass.

My lips form a tight line as I lower myself into the grass facing him, eyes trained on the flowers gripped in my fist.

"I'm sorry I was a bitch to you the other day." I meet his soft but blistering red eyes. The exchange feels so long ago I narrowly forgot it.

He waves dismissively at me and stretches with his hands out behind him to hold himself up. "All is forgiven."

"Thanks." I know better than to continue on about it, doubting I'll be able to convince anyone around here to let me take responsibility for how I acted when I was a blood slave.

The rustling of leaves and the snapping of tree branches leaves Laurentius's mouth open, his queued words fading on his blood-stained tongue as he scrutinizes the woods mere meters away.

A bead of fear darts down my back as a figure steps out from behind a tree on the edge, crashing through rose bushes while batting at the tangled, flimsy branches as she steps onto flowers in the garden bed.

"Lucia!" a man's voice hollers from down the tree line, his quick Latin echoing across the garden and punctuated with a, *"Go pack your goddamn bags before I stick you in one!"*

"What the fuck's going on?" I ask Glitch as she whacks her way through roses and lands with a thud in the grass.

When her wide, maroon eyes land on me—searching my face like she has no idea who I am or why I'm speaking to her—she says, "You smell funny," before darting away in a blur of white dress and brown hair.

I gape at Laurentius, who releases a vocal sigh and shrugs.

"I've met her twice . . . why did she act like she didn't know me?" I demand, dumbfounded.

"Her memory is a finicky thing. I bet she'll remember you next time you see her."

"Yeah." I spin the flowers in my hand as I lift them to my nose.

To lighten the mood, Laurentius rips a fistful of grass and throws it in my lap like a schoolboy.

I roll my eyes playfully, a sharp stab of hunger rolling through me. My stomach growls like a beast.

"Sounds like a hungry bear in the woods," he remarks with a smirk, throwing another fistful of grass on my lap.

"Feels like a bear in my *gut*." I flick the grass back at him.

He's on his feet in a blink, announcing we're going to have a picnic and to sit tight while he fetches finger sandwiches for me.

I sit alone under Marcus's distant but watchful gaze, feeling consistently and dreadfully on edge—like I'm waiting for something awful to happen—as I always have. Knowing there's nothing left to fight for doesn't help. I have a permanent home, family, and so many possibilities and lack of responsibilities ahead of me, and I still feel like the switch for my flight or fight is jammed.

Laurentius returns in under five minutes with a picnic basket and a black-and-white checkered blanket. He spreads it over the grass and sets a China saucer in the center with a small stack of triangle ham and cheese sandwiches.

He holds a little green glass bottle out to me after popping the cap off with his thumb. "A guard confiscated a bottle of wine from me on my way back, so I opted for sparkling cider."

I take the bottle and bow my head in appreciation before taking a thirst-quenching gulp. He pulls a sturdy silver cup of blood out from the basket for himself and pushes my sandwiches to me as I crawl onto the blanket.

I scarf down my sandwiches, not much space in my mouth for words. He talks instead, telling me about the horses whose whinnies and snorts keep stealing my attention. There's a large stable on the other side of the castle, portions of the forest having usable, non-disorienting trails. I tell him how I've never seen a horse up close before, which he one-ups by telling me he's never been inside any sort of motor vehicle.

When we walk back, Laurentius's hand brushes mine half a dozen times, until I realize it's no accident. When I finally stop shifting my hand away and spread my fingers, he laces his in mine and grins.

"Do you want me to walk you back to the downstairs door?" Laurentius asks, the corner of his lip quirked up in a half-smile as we reach the castle doors. "It's sunrise soon; you should probably return to Viorel."

"Okay—" Mateo's appearance in the doorway cuts me off and has Laurentius grumbling a whiny complaint and stepping away from me.

"Laurentius," Mateo says gruffly.

"I went to the kitchen *twice*." Laurentius crosses his arms.

Mateo ignores him to stare down at me. "Let's go."

I roll my eyes. "Oh, come on—"

Mateo rests his hand on my waist and pulls me away.

Laurentius's exasperated sigh has me glancing over my shoulder to offer an apologetic, tight-lipped smile.

His smile doesn't meet his disappointed eyes. "I had fun. Have a good sleep, Marianna."

"Same. Have a good night—day," I call back as Mateo pulls me down the hall.

When we reach the steel door, Mateo grumbles, "Of all the men to try courting you, *him?*"

"Court?" I think over the last few hours—how he was so nervous, how he held my hand and kept calling me pretty and tried to bring me wine—then drop my tight gaze down to the flowers in my hand. "Oh."

I can't help but smile.

XVI

Mateo snitches on me the moment we step into the sitting room. "She didn't stay out of rooms—"

Viorel stands in front of the coffee table with a curled lip exposing his fangs, and a furious line between his brows. "Whose?"

"The A—" I can practically hear Mateo gritting his teeth. "Laurentius."

"Oh, well . . ." He looks me up and down, softened gaze lingering on the flowers in my hand. "She looks fine. She was content the entire time she was upstairs. I suppose it's not such a big deal, so long as she doesn't make it a habit."

Mateo's jaw hangs as he pushes out a breath of disbelief. "She blatantly went against your orders and risked her life."

"Eh." Viorel waves his hand at Mateo as he walks away into his reading room. "He will not hurt her. It's probably for the best she was with him instead of alone."

I can't help the smile creeping onto my face.

"This is *Laurentius* we're talking about," Mateo says as he moves to the reading room's doorway, my steps close behind.

"I'm fond of Laurentius. He's been loyal to me for centuries."

Mateo's brows hike, and he lifts his hands to each side of his head in pure astonishment. "With all due respect, Viorel, Laurentius held two human teens hostage in his room and tried to exorcise them, then burned them at the stake in the garden when it didn't work."

Mateo assesses my reaction to his words as my heart drops into my stomach, icy dread curling down my spine. *"He what?"*

Sitting in his usual chair with a notebook open on his puzzle and a silver pen in hand, Viorel's eyes flick to me and back to Mateo. He must speak for my benefit when he says, "They deserved it. They were warned to stop harassing Laurentius. I ordered their master to control them. Yet they continued to feign possession and spoke of rogue demons creeping from the woods. You yourself agreed the decapitated rabbit in his bed was too far. I gave him ten years in the ward, *only* because they were familiars."

My breath comes easier. They bullied a vampire and thought they'd get away with it?

"You let him out after two years!" Mateo gapes at him.

"His snakes missed him," Viorel says plainly as he glances down to scrawl something in black ink across the top of an aged page. "It wasn't fair to take their caretaker away when they couldn't possibly understand why."

Mateo shakes his head in disbelief. "Aren't you worried his thirst might get the best of him? He's more likely to snap again if he's starved."

Viorel bares his fangs, head popping back up to glower at Mateo. "He's not feeding regularly again?"

"I have yet to see his eyes blacken since you released him, and that was eighteen years ago."

"You should have fucking led with that," Viorel snarls.

I catch Mateo's deep swallow. "I thought you knew."

Viorel tosses his pen down as his head sways side to side until his gaze shifts to me, eyes tightening as he thinks.

I scratch my head and shift between my feet as I twirl the flowers in my hand. "What?"

"Do you like him? Care to be near him?" The warmth of his tone welcomes honesty.

"Yeah, I guess. I had a good night." Though, I can't completely disregard Mateo's worries no matter how handsome Laurentius is, especially with a story like that.

"Don't worry about that nonsense, Marianna. He's never been violent otherwise." He looks back at Mateo. "I'll make him feed," Viorel says like it's an effortless task. "Problem solved. Bring Laurentius a body. Tell him it's from me and I expect him to drain it."

Mateo clears his throat. "It's going to look like you're playing favorites again if I deliver him a body when everyone else must bid or drink donor blood. He'll be harassed more than he already is."

Viorel sighs and leans back in his chair. "Then bring Laurentius and a body *here*."

Ten minutes later, after my flowers are in a vase in the center of the coffee table, Mateo is bringing a quivering Laurentius into the sitting room. He immediately drops to his knees and hangs his head once put in front of Viorel, who sits on his throne while I stand leaning against the chilled wall at its side. Viorel doesn't want me in reach once Laurentius feeds.

"You've done nothing wrong," Viorel says, tone light, "I'm simply concerned for you."

Laurentius tilts his head back, his bright red eyes settling on Viorel's face, a terrified crease between his brows.

"Ah." Viorel leans forward and pushes stray hair from

Laurentius's brooding eyes. "You're thirstier than I hoped. Why aren't you feeding appropriately?"

"I-It guilts me to cut their freedom short to send them to the Lord," Laurentius says.

"Why have you not taken a familiar to feed from, taught them the truth about the heavens, and turned them so they may have their freedom in the underworld?" Viorel asks.

If it weren't a dire moment, I'd question Laurentius about the beliefs that have had him excommunicated, so I might understand the depth of their conversation.

Laurentius's lips fall apart, a wet sheen of panic covering his eyes as his shoulders inch toward his ears. "I-I . . . I've tried and —" He lowers his head, voice barely a whisper. "I killed her. It was an accident, but still she suffers more brutally in Hell than had my blood never entered her."

Viorel sucks his teeth in pity, head tilting.

"I cannot make such a mistake again," Laurentius whispers as he locks eyes with Viorel.

"How long since the last body you drained?" Viorel asks, the tinge of a disappointed assumption seeping through.

Laurentius flinches. "Six months."

Viorel stares at him, the tension around him palpable. "You've been surviving on donor blood for six months? You know that's unacceptable."

He drops his head. "I know."

"You will lose control should you continue." The warning in Viorel's tone is sharp. "I cannot allow you near my familiar lest she is harmed in your war with yourself. Do you understand?"

Laurentius closes his eyes, expression smoothing like he's making peace with whatever punishment he believes he'll receive. "I'm sorry. Am I to be brought back to the ward?"

"Worry not." A smile crawls across Viorel's lips. "I have a gift for you instead."

Laurentius's brows draw together as he slowly opens his

eyes. They shift to the iron door as it opens with Seth and a dazed man who stumbles like someone has thumped him on the head.

"Stand, Laurentius," Viorel orders evenly, "and take his life into yourself."

Laurentius stumbles over his words as he rises to his feet. "I don't have any Holy water—"

Viorel lifts his hand to silence him. "No rituals, no prayers. No angel making this time, Laurentius."

Laurentius's protest is weak. "But he might suffer in Hell if I don't baptize him—"

"Who do you care to please more? Your God, who is condemning you to Hell no matter how many souls you save for him, or *me,* who will care for you until the end of your time on this plane?"

"You." He doesn't skip a beat.

Viorel smiles and motions for Laurentius to go to the man.

Laurentius turns his back to us as he stands and gingerly moves behind the man, his hand creeping up to push his head of trimmed blond hair aside. My curiosity trains my gaze on them, and I don't react when Laurentius rips into his throat.

The sound of his frantic breath fills the silent room as he drinks. Blood drips onto the floor between them, long tendrils dribbling down when he shakes his head like an animal trying to tear the flesh of its kill. The man's neck snaps under Laurentius's uncontrolled grip, the crunch of bone making Mateo sigh like this is proof of how crazed Laurentius is, and he's tired of it being ignored.

Even when the man's limp limbs are a bloodless gray, Laurentius doesn't retreat from his throat.

"Enough, he's drained," Mateo grumbles.

I hold my breath as Laurentius wraps his arms around the body's ribs, bones crunching under the pressure. He makes a pained noise and holds him closer like he can squeeze loose the last drops coating his veins.

Mateo curses in Spanish and takes a step forward before Viorel lifts a hand that freezes him.

"Laurentius . . ." Viorel calls, tone a soft nudge.

A noise escapes Laurentius—somewhere between pain and pleasure—as he draws his fangs from the body's throat and in his bloodied haze attempts to rest the man on the floor by his limp arm. He releases him too early, limbs breaking his fall before his head thumps dully against the floor.

When he twists back to us, the gaze he settles on Viorel remains crimson.

"Thank you," Laurentius rasps, his teeth caked red.

"You're very welcome," Viorel says. "Take the time you need to gather yourself."

Laurentius appears so vulnerable as he stands trying to catch his breath, something pure and primal in his shifting gaze.

Blood trails from the corners of his soaked lips, curling beneath his chin and following the curve of his jaw and throat. Tendrils entwine with the silver and beads of his rosary, thin and glistening streaks against the flesh exposed by the V neck of his spattered white blouse. I itch to move. The thought of finding a cloth and wiping the blood from his pretty face has my leg twitching forward.

Viorel's hand strikes toward me and locks around my wrist.

Laurentius finally meets my eyes, a nervous twitch to the contact that makes me wonder if he's embarrassed, or worried he's frightened me.

"Do you feel better?" I ask, hoping it's enough to know I don't fault him for his thirst.

His nod is slight.

"I demand your presence at the next auction," Viorel commands as he releases his grip on me. "Purchase a human. If you do not wish to mark, then hypnotize, or drain them at once as you previously were. But you will not continue this ill-fated quest to live without displacing souls. No matter your choices, you know your place is guaranteed, so it's fatuous to let yourself starve."

The thought of Laurentius doing something as dreadful as bidding on a human has my stomach flipping. I try to stop myself from looking at the event with a personal lens, but it's almost impossible to discard those nauseating feelings despite understanding the need for auctions.

"Okay," Laurentius breathes. "I'm sorry for disappointing you."

Viorel lifts his chin a bit, a friendly twitch in the corner of his mouth. "I trust you won't do so again."

After Mateo escorts Laurentius out, Viorel turns to me on his throne with a wicked grin. "He worships me, you know. He truly believes I'm put on Earth to take care of the vampires who will find a special place in Hell. He thinks Lucifer sent me to watch over them."

I suppose that explains the depth of Laurentius's trust in Viorel, and why he's been here so long.

"Then why does he still pray to God and seem so intent on saving the souls of humans at his own expense?" I ask.

"Habit, guilt, fear, and a tangled relationship with God." Viorel taps his finger against the arm of his throne. "I'd keep him as my personal guard if he took better care of his mind. It's hard to find men as loyal as him."

I sigh. "Why does Mateo hate him so much?"

Viorel stands and smooths the front of his gown. "Mateo has never cared for him. He thinks he's deranged and is convinced Laurentius believes he's above everyone else. Laurentius also tried to drown the guilt of burning those familiars in the blood of those set for auction. He was on his longest fast of three and a half weeks, made worse by frequent self-flagellation. Mateo had selected one of the four humans Laurentius killed for Ainsley—a teen girl from a Romanian orphanage he thought she'd love to care for."

"Oh," I whisper, surprised Laurentius wasn't in trouble for drinking them. "Mateo thinks Laurentius is trying to court me."

He glances at the flowers, a smile playing on his lips. "Indeed, he wishes to."

Warmth spreads beneath my cheeks. "Oh." I suppose it's not as if he'd be able to take me out to a restaurant or the movies. My lips twist. "Am I allowed to date?"

I know dating should be the *least* of my concerns right now and I should wait until the knot in my heart and brain has loosened, but I still want to know. Besides, I can't ignore that Laurentius is incredibly handsome and already interested in me, even if I don't want to sprint into anything.

"I like Laurentius. If you fancy other men instead, you must check with me. But yes, in theory, you can date."

I swallow, realizing his idea of dating might not align with mine. "Can I do all the stuff that comes with dating? Like . . ." *Kissing? Sex?* I can't get the words out, the idea of intimacy with another vampire making my heart thump crookedly. I'm glad I don't have to elaborate aloud.

His expression flattens. "I suppose, but you may not share your blood. There will be *severe consequences*, understand?"

My nod is swift. One vampire drinking from me is enough.

With a gentler tone, he adds, "Simply keep in mind my mark, Marianna. You may only experience my being when you drink from me, but I'm connected to your emotions always."

The discomfort of that reality makes me scratch a sudden itch on my head. "Okay, and I suppose you don't want me drinking another vampire's blood?"

As a familiar, would I even be capable of choosing to drink from another vampire and having my . . . *masters* . . . mark overwritten?

"My mark is *permanent*, Marianna," Viorel explains carefully. "No vampire can overwrite it. You are mine until the pain of death parts us."

I gape at him. "Permanent?"

Viorel nods. "Even then, you are not to consume anyone's blood."

I offer an agreeable nod, unbothered. Permanent or not, someone would have to be suicidal to steal me from Viorel.

"Your chamber is ready." The corner of his lip lifts in a smile. "Come now, you've had a long night."

XVII

My cell is vacant as we walk by it, the half-rusted grated door back on its hinges.

I whack down any hopes and follow behind him through his room and toward a weak, but tall beam of yellow light sharp against the hallway wall. He steps aside when we reach the open door to allow me through.

Candlelight basks the room in a warm golden glow, eight fat and red candles on a tall, wrought iron stand in the far-left corner beside a massive walnut wardrobe. The wardrobe takes up half the wall and probably barely fit through the door. The three doors—the middle a mirror—promise ample space for clothing.

"That's a nicer wardrobe than what you have," I tease, peeking over my shoulder to inspect his reaction.

Thankfully, his smile hasn't faded. He winks. "I'm unbeaten. I have a room full of them."

I run my fingers over the smooth carved vines outlining the two smaller doors. Opening the mirrored door, I find my small collection of clothes hanging. The rod is high below a couple skinny shelves perfect for shoes. I wonder if the line of three drawers at the bottom I suspect are full of my undergarments can hold my weight.

"I'll remove the drawers if you have the thought again," Viorel warns, his smile wiped clean. "I can't have you falling."

I flick my eyes back into my skull. "Fine. But this thing is like seven feet tall. I'm going to need a stool."

There's so much space I consider asking for Glitch's help to fill it with garments from the wardrobe room.

"Indeed," he grumbles as I twist toward the double bed and scramble onto the plush duvet with a simple white cover.

"The sheets are blue," I note as I pull the duvet back, a small smile on my lips as my eyes trace over the dark, pearl blue silk wrinkles glistening under the light.

"I thought you might like them," he says, coming to stand at the edge of the bed.

My smile grows. "Especially the blanket. It's like a cloud."

"It's goose down," he says. "The mattress isn't memory foam like mine, but it has a foam topper."

"*Wow,*" I mouth before flopping backward and grinning at the airy *poof*.

"The drapes should help with the warmth as well," he says. There's a weighted pause that has me peeking at him. "Or if you wish, you may rest with me and make use of the fireplace."

"Thanks for the offer," I say, staring up at the smooth wood of the canopy. Hopefully, the drapes and blanket suffice so I don't have to continue with the worry of disturbing his sleep and having an unfamiliar man beside me. "And for the bedroom. I hated that cell."

"You're welcome."

"I'll pick out decor when I go on vacation with Carol and Derek, so it doesn't feel so bare. How far in advance do people book their leaves?"

Reluctantly, Viorel says, "You will not be taking vacations, Marianna."

I jerk upright. "What? Why not?"

"Familiars must leave with their masters or another trusted vampire. I do not leave, nor trust anyone to take you."

My lips twitch against one another as I try to navigate the flurry of panicked thoughts and my constricting throat. "Then . . ." My heart thrums. "Then when *can* I leave?"

"Never," he says softly, an apologetic pinch to his lips.

The room tilts, lungs too empty for sound as I mouth, *"Never?"*

I understand then how two things can be true at once. Denendrius can be pure evil and belong in a cell, and Viorel can still be a wicked man.

"Denendrius was right about you," I cry, hot tears spilling down my cheeks at a sharp and sudden ache in my chest. I ball my fists in my lap. "I don't know how this is supposed to be saving me. You know, at least Denendrius let me go outside. He may have beaten me and raped me, but even *he* let me see my friends, let me go to school and see my aunt. At least the option for school, going outside, traveling and shit was there—even if it meant I would have to do everything he wanted me to do. Doesn't fucking matter what I do for you, does it? You still won't let me leave this fucking bunker!"

I gasp for breath as he merely stares at me, taking it.

"You did this to Tatiana," I cry. "Controlled her. Never let her leave. I bet it's true she asked Denendrius to help her escape but didn't realize what she was asking until it was too late."

His gentle tone only makes my chest ache more. "I gave her as much freedom as I could *inside the veil*. She was free to wander outside under sunlight or moonlight. She had her own room next to her parents. Where did that get her? Raped, murdered, and tossed in a river. I'm not making the same mistake. The first time I sent you upstairs nearly killed you, so the fact I continue to allow such a thing is already too much."

"But you dealt with Artair! Do you really think more vampires are going to try killing me?"

"Ideas can be creeping things or blitzing. A man can be loyal one moment and murder you the next if he gets a drop of poison in his mind. I'm not willing to take that risk with you. Being with my clan has enough of its own risks, never mind the vampires out in the world who would take one sniff at you and know you're worth something."

I grit my teeth, a furious burn joining the ache in my chest. "I'd rather be at risk, free and experiencing the world than safe and holed up. I'm thankful to finally have a stable home, but I don't want to be trapped here. Even a trip once a year would be enough! I've never left America before coming here, so visiting any part of Romania would be an adventure for me."

"Your safety directly affects me. It's my blood in your veins, Marianna," he warns evenly. "I'm sorry you interpret my care for cruelty. Denendrius did not care for your safety."

"You turned Artair into fucking dust and bones!" I holler. "And you can't protect me enough for a goddamn outing in whatever town is closest to wherever the hell we are? I'm not asking for a lot here."

"I'm not invincible." His eyes brim with pity.

My sob has me hunching over. "Why didn't you let someone else mark me? Derek probably would have marked me for Carol's sake."

"Nobody else would be willing to take on the onus of marking you. Not even Derek."

I release a pained gasp. "Oh, so *I'm* the burden now? I may have wanted to come, but I didn't want it like *this.*"

Slowly, he shakes his head. "No, Marianna. Not at all. You're not a burden to me."

"This isn't fair!" I bellow, my voice ricocheting off the bare walls.

"Life isn't fair, Marianna. You know this very well."

"You're a monster," I snarl.

Viorel doesn't bat an eye, his calm only pushing me harder into hysteria. "Feel about me as you wish. It will not stop me from caring for you."

"What if I become a vampire," I plead. "Then can I leave?"

"I will do what I can to lessen the pain you're feeling now and keep you happy, but I can't offer you what I wish I could, even if you choose immortality in the future. I need you to remain here."

I gape at him. *"Why?"* I wail, slamming my fists into the duvet at my sides. *"If I'm a vampire, I won't be marked to you, so what does it matter?"*

Viorel's chest lifts as he inhales a long breath and slowly releases it, void eyes level with mine. I can tell by the way he looks through me he doesn't want to have this conversation. He wants me to shut up and cease questioning him.

I release a frustrated roar before I jam my finger toward the door at my right and screech, *"Go the fuck away!"*

There's no emotion on his face as he obliges, and I leap off the bed as he disappears around the corner. When I slam the door as hard as I can and beat the back of it once with my fists, his lack of reaction shakes some of my anger away.

Sinking to the floor of my bare room, I grit my teeth as ungrateful tears streak my cheeks. I slam my knuckles into my thigh before covering my face and holding back a frustrated shriek.

Viorel doesn't return to console me despite the tearful minutes ticking by. He doesn't tell me he's changed his mind. So, I try my hardest to figure out a way to walk through the rest of my life without tripping over the chains around my ankles too much.

I know I should be grateful. I know I should be *so fucking happy* Denendrius is locked up and I'm safe and no longer marked to him.

And I am happy, *more than anything.*

But even then . . . to be told I'll never see the rest of the world ever again, even if I become a vampire? I can practically feel the weight of the walls on me. It's crushing.

I know things could be so much worse. They *have* been so much worse.

Trapped in a castle with my aunt and people who care for me—getting served every meal on a literal silver fucking platter —should be enough for me. It was only weeks ago that there was the looming possibility my life was going to be lost to addiction before Denendrius made me realize I wanted to fight for it. So, I suppose, it's not like I was guaranteed any of those things anyway.

At least I know this is my home now. I finally have a home I can't lose or get ripped out of. It's difficult to lose a home you can't leave.

My chest aches, my stomach so hot and twisted I consider curling into the fetal position on the floor.

As Viorel returns, I look up and wipe my eyes.

"Here," he starts as he holds out a leather notebook. "Keep a running list of everything you'd like. You may not leave, but things can be brought to you. You know your limitations, so keep your requests material."

Slowly, I take the book and pull the silver pen from under the cord holding the pages shut. *"Anything?"* My eyes narrow, my soaked lashes obscuring some of my sight.

"Within reason. There must be space for it, and whoever leaves to retrieve it must be able to find it."

"The cost?" I think of the diamonds I have hidden in my wooden chest of memories.

"Cost is no issue," Viorel assures me. "I want you to be happy."

I can't bring myself to smile, but my stomach flutters with a bit of excitement at the idea of finally getting to decorate my own room, even if the walls and floor are hard and cold in a place I'll never see outside of. That's something I've never had while living in foster homes.

"Okay, thank you," I whisper, voice cracking.

I flip the book open on my lap and put the pen to the first stiff page. As I stare at the page and struggle to think of items to fill the new void in my life, a headache nags for my attention. Despite wanting so much for so long, I think of sandy beaches and sunshine-filled parks in foreign lands I'll never visit.

My gaze lifts and I stare at Viorel through my lashes as he enters with a silver chalice.

"You should lie in your bed instead," he suggests, carrying the chalice past me. He places it beside Artair's skull on the bulky, three-drawer nightstand.

I grunt, and waver over. The sight of his blood in the chalice makes me pause as I lift my knee onto the mattress.

"Go ahead." His voice is soft. "Your head will feel much better."

Swallowing, I climb on the bed and curl up under the covers with my notebook beside my head on the pillow and the chalice in reach.

When he leaves—his own bed creaking under his weight— I give in to healing sips of his blood between bullet points for items I've always desired but could never have.

- A handheld gaming system with games.
- A portable music player filled with

I scowl. Filled with what music? I could ask for my favorite rap artists, but do I really want to be reminded of the street? All my favorite songs have memories tucked between the lines of lyrics. I won't be able to listen to them without smelling the bills and cigarette smoke that surrounded me and the other members of Venganza Roja while we worked. I bet I'll still feel the bass of Julio's red Cadillac low rider, smell the rubber from his tires as we sped across the asphalt after he'd pick me up from middle school and fill me with home cooked leftovers from his abuela's house.

I used to wish he'd let me meet her, maybe take me over for supper with his family so I could experience what it would be like to have a grandma and maybe learn something about Mexico. Bonnie was too busy with drugs and Johns to teach me anything more than Spanish, and Julio and the gang were more focused on teaching me the history of our family. But I never asked, and he never did.

My thoughts loop back to Viorel's theories and what might have happened in those missing years. Could Julio really have been there, teaching me? Why? Why did he never talk about my childhood with me? Why couldn't I remember he was my mother's boyfriend and was around when I was little, and had to learn the truth from her? Why was my mom's involvement in Red Revenge unspoken of around me?

Rubbing my eyes, I sigh and finish my bullet point.

• One portable music player filled with a mix of Rayonne and Ziggy's favorite music (punk, metal, and whatever Goths listen to), and another filled with a mix of different genres (surprise me).

That will have to be good enough. Maybe I'll find a new favorite artist or fall in love with a band I can gush over with Rayonne.

Somehow, I can't think of much else. Where did the mental list of items go I added to every trip my best friends and I went window shopping together?

I rest my eyes and force my brain to conjure up *something.*

When the pen wriggles free from my tight grip, I startle awake and blink away the disorientation of sudden sleep. Viorel removes it from my hand and places it on the open notebook on my nightstand.

Sitting, I rub my eyes, "I have a couple demands," I tease, exhaustion making my humor flat.

"I saw. You'll have it all. For now, are you hungry? You wore yourself out."

"What time is it?" I whisper, thinking to add a clock to the list so I don't have to fumble around, lost in time anymore.

"Noon, but I can have someone retrieve something."

"I'm fine." I reach for the open notebook, fingers stiffening as *clock* appears on the page in black ink like it was heated to reveal invisible words there all along.

"*Whoa.*" I grin.

He chuckles. "Sleep well, Marianna."

I have a dark thought as I lie fighting for sleep. Terror strikes me when I realize Viorel might have heard.

Is this why Tatiana was so easy for Denendrius to victimize? Was she going crazy from being trapped inside her entire life and resulted to the dungeon to cure debilitating boredom? If I was born here, and never allowed to leave, I might be desperate enough to ask a charming prisoner to help me escape.

The sound of Viorel's voice from the other room has me gasping and gripping my blanket in fear of punishment until his words register in my mind. "I didn't know the guards were letting her visit the prisoners, or that Denendrius was hypnotizing her."

I creep off the bed and tiptoe to his room, where he's sitting in bed expecting me.

His words have me stopping at the foot of the bed. "He was hypnotizing her . . ." Why had I never realized it myself? Perhaps I never considered it possible someone could hypnotize Viorel's familiar. His mark seems like it would be much too strong to allow such a thing.

"She never thought about her visits to the dungeon or with him around me. He used whatever strength he had to ensure that, and I wasn't expecting some of my guards to be *so bloody stupid* as to allow them to speak alone. Denendrius wasn't of much interest to me back then. If my guards hadn't taken a liking to him, he would have simply sat there to waste."

The grief—the fury—in his eyes has my throat clogged with emotion.

"I wanted her to have autonomy of her mind within the constraints of blood marking, as I give you, but unfortunately, this meant others could influence and hypnotize her."

I bite the corner of my lip before saying, "Your blood mark wasn't enough to stop her from being hypnotized? Alaire and Edmond told me blood marks can get too strong for other vampires to use hypnotism."

He releases a heavy breath. "By actively working against the natural progression of blood marks, it never took a deep enough hold on her mind to deter mind-influencing abilities. I knew keeping a familiar in the way I prefer them was dangerous, but I wasn't prepared for how devastatingly so." A ghost of a smile flashes over his lips. "At least with you, I can offer you freedom, and there's no chance of another vampire poisoning your mind."

"Oh."

He draws the blanket back as he tilts his head in a silent question, but I give my head a little shake and angle myself toward my room. I expect my refusal to upset or anger him, but he simply fixes the blanket.

"Sleep well then."

I almost wish him the same, but can tell from the weight of exhaustion on his face he won't.

"I'll try," I whisper.

XVIII

Mateo enters through the iron door with a triumphant grin as he waves his satellite phone in hand. "Guess who received a call from a bounty hunter who knows where Agatha is?"

I lower my spoonful of curry and rice—dinner—while straightening on the sofa. Viorel perks up in his throne.

"Your mind is a mess of excitement. Explain aloud," Viorel says, his expression cold and serious despite how he was smiling with me moments before Mateo entered.

"One of our bounty hunters stopped at a blood club in Lorimer. The clan there has had Agatha chained in their boiler room for two weeks now and has been torturing her. They found her in New York City. He convinced them to offer her up to us."

My heart leaps. "Does this blood club happen to be Estrella de Sangre?"

Mateo nods at me as Viorel says, "Splendid. What are they demanding in exchange for her?"

"It's Rayonne's previous clan," Mateo explains, expression

animated with excitement. "Ziggy and his husband, Lance, are only asking for periodic phone calls with her and Marianna."

Viorel sucks his teeth. "Clan members are prohibited from phone usage . . ." He sighs. "I suppose it's a small price, considering the severity of Agatha's impersonations and our inability to pass on her . . . I can grant them one call per month."

Mateo gives him a single nod. "I should gather a second team for Seth to retrieve her, yeah?"

"No. I require my second best here with me. Let Ziggy and Lance hold Agatha a while longer. Deal with Marianna's mother first—lest she die before you can, what with her fragile morality—and then collect Agatha. Stake her, then find Alaire and Edmond's van. If locating their residence is a simple task, complete it, otherwise return with Agatha and carry on with searching."

"Aye, will do." Mateo crosses his arms over his rising chest and exhales. "What am I to do about Denendrius since his need to speak is more time sensitive?"

Viorel scowls. "Not a word yet about what he did with the van?"

Mateo shakes his head and taps his thumb on his biceps. "Perhaps it's best if you dig through his mind."

Viorel stands. My heart leaps with a confusing concoction of sick terror and excitement, thinking we're heading to the dungeon to see Denendrius, but he says, "No need. It won't make a difference. His thoughts are too unreliable, especially since he'll know I'm searching for something. See if he will exchange the information for a body."

Mateo balks, eyebrows rising. "A body. Really?"

With Viorel's exhale, he sounds equally dissatisfied with his request. "Yes, but make his suffering twofold when you return."

Mateo rubs the neat hair on his jaw in contemplation as he turns toward the door. "All right. Anything more?"

"Go to the ward and have Rayonne call to fulfill our end of

the bargain. Take Marianna with you. I'm sure Rayonne could benefit from a familiar face."

I stuff a massive spoonful of curry and rice into my mouth and bound over to Mateo as he uses his satellite phone to call Sascha. There's a weak nervousness in my knees with the thought that Rayonne might not be as inclined to see me after my bitchiness. She may have been kind toward me when I last saw her, but with her newborn state and the time she's had to think in the ward, maybe she's realized how much I jeopardized her.

When my sight trickles in, I'm standing next to Mateo and Sascha at the end of a hall of tarnished steel doors with barred windows. Some emit a faint glow with hushed and thirsty moans, others dark with shifting shadows.

A carpet runs between them over the stone floor, the beige and red flowers worn and spattered with faded splotches of blood.

"Which one is Rayonne's?" I whisper, the looming presence of unseen newborns and blood-troubled vampires not making me want to draw too much attention to myself.

Mateo nods toward an unspecific cell on the left, and we detach from Sascha's side.

I hold my breath as we creep by cells, my steps soft like it will make any difference in whether the vampires held in them notice me. They do anyway, a few beds creaking—accompanied by inquiring grunts and sniffs—making me wonder what they think of my presence in the ward.

As we stop in front of a dim cell, a blood-curdling scream bounces from around the corner of the end of the hall. Could it be someone turning? Or a newborn's meal crying out?

I'm a couple of inches too short to fully see into the room, only getting an eyeful of emerald-green, damask wallpaper, and the tip of a wavering flame.

"Rayonne," Mateo calls softly through the bars of the window, peering down at where she must be.

She still sounds the same when she says, "I hate to turn down a meal, but I don't think I can stomach more blood after gorging myself tonight."

My brows lift until I realize she doesn't know my scent, and Mateo chuckles. "It's Marianna—"

The distinct squeak of a body bounding off a bed echoes and has him dropping the rest of his words.

Her once warm face is now pallid as it appears on the other side of the bars. Her eyes, once soft brown, are now wide and as red as a rose. A fanged smile lights up her face. "Marianna!" She must be hovering, as she's about the same height as me, and shouldn't be able to look through so easily. "You're marked now? I thought you smelled odd."

I swallow and tuck my hair behind my ear before apologizing with, "You were right, Rayonne, about almost everything."

She smiles, though I don't miss the relieved exhale slipping past her lips. "I'm really glad, because it would have been awful for everyone if I hadn't been."

Keys jingle in Mateo's hand as he asks, "Do you think you have the control for Marianna's company? Viorel has agreed to monthly calls with your friend. You may share one with her now."

She inhales deeply and blows out the breath through a hole she makes with her pursed lips. "Yes, as long as you're coming in."

"Aye," he agrees, then unlocks the door. "I need to supervise your call anyway."

Rayonne drops to her toes and skitters back toward a bed in the far-right corner with an antique metal frame making me think of century-old asylums. I notice the old photo of her late husband Alessander and her son—both dead by Denendrius's hand—on her nightstand. Her old suitcase is on the floor between a four-drawer dresser and the wall.

Mateo closes the door behind us and stands in front of it like she's a flight risk, though it's likely standard protocol. He underhand throws his satellite phone to her, and it thuds in her palms.

With a tight smile and glittering eyes on me, she backs up until the crook of her knees touches the edge of her mattress, and she sits on the grandma-style burgundy and green floral blanket.

"How's being a newborn again going?" I take a few short and tentative steps before sitting on the edge of her bed a handful of feet away. "I'm glad you survived."

She sighs and absentmindedly rubs her thumb over the glowing green buttons of Mateo's phone. "It's equal parts awful and great. I thought I would go back to the same sort of control I had before getting the cure, but at least this isn't as bad as when I was first a vampire. I know all the same coping skills for thirst, but using them is a challenge since I have a year of unsatisfied cravings built up from when I was human."

I frown. "How long until they let you out?"

"A couple weeks, maybe." She gives me a small smile. "I was hoping we could share a room when I do . . . if you'd like. It would be fun."

I swallow a lump of emotion, unable to help thinking of how Denendrius convinced me that once we got here, she'd avoid being associated with a person like me. Liar. "That would be great," I start. "But Viorel is keeping me downstairs with him."

Her black brows draw together. "Until . . .?"

I cross my arms over my stomach. "Forever."

She stares at me with parted lips. "Oh . . . Like . . . literally forever? Or until you've been marked for a while?" she asks.

"He cleared out a bedroom for me down there, so it seems permanent."

Her lips purse. "Well, I suppose we don't have to share a room. We can still see one another frequently and have sleepovers, if you'd like."

I lower my eyes and give my head a little shake. "I'm supposed to be modest with my time upstairs, and I'm definitely not allowed overnight."

Rayonne blinks at me, her lips parting and closing. "What?"

"Viorel wants me safe with him since I'm his familiar," I explain limply.

She presses her tongue against the tip of her fang as she seems to consider something. "You said I was right about almost everything . . ." Rayonne winces as she leans closer and —eyes flicking to Mateo and back to me—asks, "Was that you I heard screaming a few nights ago? It sounded like someone being murdered."

"I don't know," is all I say. "I'm sure there's a lot of humans screaming around here."

She sees right through my answer. "What happened?"

"Nothing, Rayonne."

Her brow furrows as she scrutinizes my eyes, like she's searching for something specific. "All right. Have you told Viorel you can't be hypnotized?"

We stare at one another for a long moment, and I don't miss the accusation.

"He's the exception," I admit.

She nods, her swallow visible. "Okay, I'm sorry."

"Don't be," I say with a small smile. "You said you heard Viorel is as brutal as he is generous, and you were right. But I'm his familiar now, and he takes care of his things. So I'm okay, Rayonne."

There's less resistance to her smile. "Okay. You're happy?"

I scrunch my nose and give my head a contemplative scratch. "Content? I wanted Denendrius locked up, for his mark to be undone, and to be here. That worked out. I have the bonus of Carol being here, and I think I'm making new friends already. I've got a bedroom and Viorel is going to get me almost anything I want . . . so I suppose there's not much to complain about aside from his overbearing protectiveness."

She releases a breathy chuckle. "That's good, then. I'm glad."

I watch her fingers as she dials Ziggy's number and tucks the bulky phone beneath her black curls to rest it against her ear.

"It's Rayonne." Her face lights up. "Yes, everything is great so far—no, it's not boring, Ziggy, God." She laughs. "Marianna is here with me. I'm putting you on speaker."

After she presses a button on the phone, Ziggy's British accented voice comes through with cheer. "So Rayonne's bringing you with her to visit me next summer, I've been told."

My brow furrows and I cross my legs, the mattress uncomfortably stiff. "Says who?"

"Patricia had a vision of you, Marianna, laying in my bed while looking at an unopened copy of Bone Decay's new album. It comes out next summer," Ziggy says. "I'm so very excited to see you both."

I close my eyes and blow out a breath. "Patricia's vision is wrong," I grumble. "I'm not allowed to leave the castle, so there's no way I'll get to see you."

He's silent for a long moment. "What do you mean? Patricia said Rayonne has already scheduled her leave."

"Viorel won't let me go. I'm not allowed to leave, even if I turn into a vampire."

"I hate to say I told you so, but . . ." He lets out a strangled chuckle. "I knew she'd hate it there, Rayonne."

Rayonne interjects with, "She doesn't hate it, Ziggy."

"She's right," I start. "I just hate how I'm trapped. I've got it pretty good considering, and Viorel isn't forbidding me to be mean. He's paranoid about my safety since I'm his familiar."

His grumbling is incoherent before he slathers on more cheer and says, "Well, Viorel must change his mind because Patricia's vision is very firm."

Rayonne gives me a hopeful smile.

"We'll see about that," I grumble.

XIX

Having had contact with the outside world, my feet feel lighter over the last few steps downstairs. But when I hop over the last step and thud onto the stone landing, it knocks the feeling out of me. The ache in my feet awakens the one in my chest. The outside world will always be just that. It, and everyone in it, will never include me again. I may as well be in another dimension or trapped on a faraway planet.

As I make my way toward the reading room where Viorel's greeting echoes from, an ache radiates through my stomach and weakens my knees when I think of Camille and Daina and how I've left them with the burden of knowing me and losing me. I wish I could convince myself they'll be glad I'm gone because I wasn't the greatest friend to have, but I know they'll take my disappearance as hard as they took Jenna's death, possibly even harder since they'll never have closure. They knew for weeks something bad was going to happen to me.

I'm unsure what everyone will think, since Carol and Derek disappeared shortly after me. I suspect they'll believe something darker than being murdered by an abusive boyfriend has transpired. Perhaps they'll think he trafficked me, Carol and Derek offed for trying to protect me. If that's true, they could hold on to hope of my survival for years. I hope they think he murdered me and buried me somewhere, but that might be a stretch since I was spotted alive and unharmed with Denendrius in Bellevue.

I wish I could tell them I'm safe and content so they can move on with their lives without the weight of grief.

I pause in the doorway, resting my shoulder against the stone. Viorel sits in his chair at his puzzle table, the middle of the nearly complete puzzle cleared for a leather notebook he writes in, and a jar of black ink. He writes smooth letters with his black feathered quill pen. The flickering candle behind his shoulder makes it difficult to read from afar.

"When Mateo goes to Lorimer, can you have him hypnotize my friends into thinking I'm dead so they can have closure?" The question takes a desperate leap off my tongue.

Viorel's hand pauses, and he lifts his head to meet my eyes. "A selfless wish, but no. You don't understand the complexity of your request. Your disappearance is beyond your friends."

"Right." I pick at my stubby nails, staring at the floor as I consider sitting across from him, but not quite being able to bring myself to the chair. Exhaustion creeps up on me, my tired breath loud as I look up at Viorel and sigh.

"What is it?" he asks, eyes trained on the words he scrawls.

"Can I go upstairs?" I think of Laurentius and Lucia. If I'm never going to see my old friends again, it would be wise to put effort into new ones while people have curiosity for me left.

"All right." His approval is quiet, head down while raising his voice to call for Mateo.

Once upstairs, I head straight for the dining hall and to the snack pantry—which I find by asking a passing human boy—

in hopes of filling the hungry void inside myself with something sweet.

It's massive and dimly lit by a battery powered lamp hanging from a rope attached to a simple, wrought iron candle holder.

Metal shelves line the walls, stuffed with food boxes and bins of treats. They spill over, some stacks looking ready to plummet onto the floor. At a glance, most are foreign brands, many of the snacks are unfamiliar, though I spot an open box of toaster pastries at the end of the room to work my way toward. I pluck a bag of chocolate pretzels off the shelf, scoop some prepackaged bags of cheese crackers, and decide on a mini bag of dried apple bites so Viorel is less inclined to speak ill of my eating habits—especially since I add a chocolate bar and marshmallows to the heap in my arms. I hope I'm not being greedy when I snag a full bag of Korean honey chips and hope anyone who sees me with more than my fair share understands I can't take snack trips whenever I want.

As I turn to the doorway, the sight of Lucia passing by the dining hall door steals my attention from a jar of loose candy on a shelf, and I shout, "Hey, Lucia—Glitch!"

I flinch at Glitch's speed as she appears in the doorway with a grin. The motion shakes a few of my snacks off the heap in my arms. They crash onto the floor.

"Christ," I mutter, thanking her as she retrieves the fallen packages and balances them back in my arms.

She grins and turns to a basket half-hidden in the shadow of the wooden door that she pushes out of the way. The dim light reaches it and a paper sign in black marker—foreign words punctuated with a smile—taped above the collection of fabric bags. Snatching one, she shakes the wrinkles out and holds it open for me to dump my snacks.

"Thanks." I hang the bag in the crook of my elbow. "What's up?"

She tucks her hair behind her ear. "Nothing. I was wandering around. Sorry for blowing you off when you were with Laurentius. I swear I didn't recognize you for a minute. Felt like a real jerk once I got back inside, and it hit me."

"It's fine. Want to hang out?"

Glitch's face lights up. "Yes. Want to make bracelets?"

Agreeing, she guides me on a long trek to the third floor and to a room set up for jewelry making. It's empty of vampires, though full of untidied wooden tables and walls lined with cupboards and counters covered in wooden organizers with little drawers. She takes a plastic bin full of beads from a messy shelf in a cupboard, then a few little bundles of colored thread.

The walk up to the sitting room she has in mind is dreadful, and I make a point of telling her so once my legs are burning after the seventh set of long steps. She playfully rolls her eyes at me like I'm dramatic and should be able to keep up with her Darkling stamina, but I've been moving nonstop for twenty minutes and had most of my strength sucked out of me over the past few months. Being borderline malnourished like Viorel says likely doesn't help either.

The seventh floor looks like the rest. The doors are the same wood, the joyous sounds of vampires enjoying their eternities humming through the air. Once we turn the corner, the doors disappear—sole for two wide ones in the middle of the hall—and the walls are so full of black and white, hundred-year-old photos, I only glimpse the maroon wallpaper. I study the photos as we pass them, each one a portrait or group photo.

She chuckles. "The invention of the camera was a hit. Most of the families on the wall are still here." She takes a few long steps that I match, but I nearly collide into her when she stops dead and points to a black frame at eye level. "My father and me."

I swallow and study the photo. They look the same, though their clothing is out of style, and her hair is in a French braid reaching down her chest. Neither of them smiles. There's pride in her father's eyes, but no emotion in hers. I suppose not even the excitement of an new invention was enough to make it to the photograph. She grabs my arm and pulls me a little farther down, pointing higher—on her toes—to another photograph. She's alone in this one, her small smile the focal point of the photo. Her hair is in loose curls around her youthful face, lace around her throat.

"I like this portrait much better," I tell her.

She nods and combs the fingers of her free hand through her hair. "Me too. We should get a photo of you and Viorel."

My lips purse. "Is there one of him?"

She nods and motions with her head for me to follow. We pass the double doors and turn around the candle-lit corner, the hall continuing with more clan photos. I spot Viorel's portrait immediately, as it's much larger than the rest and in a gold frame partway up the wall with a half-moon table below it.

The backdrop is gray, and with the ghostly effect of the black and white smoothing out his features and blending the thirsty blue and red tinges surrounding his eyes, he looks so human, his age more defined. If I only had the image to go off, I'd think he's in his mid-twenties. His hair is straight on either side of his head, his serious eyes sharply focused on the camera. With the color washed out of them, one might think they're green or blue. Guessing his clothing to be black, I study the intricate embroidery below the collar of what I suspect is a blouse.

"You would look good with him," she says.

I shrug. "He's elegant like poetry. I doubt the camera could focus on anything but him."

She laughs and nudges me back toward the doors. "Silly. We'd find you another dress."

A little trickle of warmth enters me with her acceptance. *She thinks I belong on a castle wall with the rest of the clan?*

With the candlelight reaching from the hall, there's the vague outline of sofas and coffee tables. I blink in surprise when she shuts the door behind us and plunges us into darkness. Her hum travels from somewhere across the room with a match striking. The orange glow illuminates her hands and bits of her face as she wanders around and lights a dozen wicks.

It's a cozy little room with four antique sofas on the far wall, divided in the middle by a double bookshelf full of old hardbacks. Glass coffee tables with gold legs and feet are in front of them. The smell of roses fills the musty air from where they sit in crystal vases on wooden end tables in the corners of the room. Two more sofas face one another from opposite sides of the room, their arms pushing up against the corner coffee tables.

"Whoever designed this room likes symmetry," I retort.

She grins as she plunks down on a cushion facing the door, splaying out thread on the coffee table in the left corner of the room. I plop down next to her.

"I don't actually know how to make bracelets," I admit, "past braiding thread."

Lining up the colors, she says, "I'll teach you."

We pick out colors. White, black, and blue for me, and gold, green, and brown for her. She has me cut a long piece of each thread and fold them in half before tying the fold into a loop and taping it down onto the table. I gnaw at my cheek as she walks me through looping one string over the rest and pulling it through. We switch to a different color after the same number of loops for each.

"It's fucked," I grumble after creating three tubular sections of alternating colors.

Her eyes flick over from her half-made bracelet—it looks so perfect I'd think a machine made it if I didn't know better—and says, "You're pulling some loops tighter than others, and you have to decide if you want the loop edges to form a spiral or go straight down the side because you're doing both."

"Ugh." I release the thread and flex my sore fingers. I yank my bracelet out of the tape on the table—receiving a purse-lipped glance from Lucia—and drop it aside. "Starting over," I explain as I reach for my colors to begin the process over again with her tips in mind.

"You brought beads," I note. "How do we add those?"

Her lack of response has me looking over. My back straightens. "Lucia?"

She stares vacantly through the threads in her frozen hands, her expression slack.

"Are you okay?" I set my bracelet down. "Glitch?"

She's stiff, her breath even through her parted lips.

When I reach out to her, she blinks her lifeless eyes but doesn't rouse.

I look around the room like there's someone else who can help me, but I don't feel any urgency to get help elsewhere. I know there's only so much danger her own body can put her in, considering she's immortal. She's likely having one of those episodes she mentioned.

Finally, after a few long minutes of me staring at her and giving her the occasional poke, she lifts her head and looks at me.

"You okay?" I ask.

Her brows draw together, and she studies the room and me.

"We're making bracelets," I remind her.

She looks down at the thread, then back up to the stone walls and books.

"Do you know where you are?" I ask before snagging the flesh of my cheek between my teeth. What do I do if she doesn't know?

"The castle that never was," she whispers, blinking at me.

"Do you know who I am?"

She stares at me, eyes tracing over my face and brow furrowing. "You're a little distorted. You look different . . . Your hair is lighter."

My brows raise. "What?"

She blinks again and heaves out a massive breath. "I'm sorry, Marianna. I see it's you."

I scratch my head. "Who'd you think I was?"

Waving her hand dismissively before she refocuses on her bracelet, she says, "A lady I used to purchase meat from in the Forum back home. You looked like her for a moment before I got a grip on my mind."

"Oh. What goes on in your mind when that happens?" I ask.

Her lips twist as she thinks. "I don't know. Nothing, most times. Other times I'm confused and feel like I'm forgetting something, while nothing around me looks familiar. Sometimes it's regular forgetting, like a task I'm doing or something I've promised someone."

"Forgetting sucks," is all I can think of saying.

She nods. "Thanks for not being upset about it."

I'm choked with the memory of Denendrius's fury—at his abuse—over me not being able to remember him from my childhood. "Why would I be mad? Forgetting isn't something you can control."

With a tight and grateful smile, she says, "Yeah."

I'm not sure what to fill the silence with despite it not being uncomfortable. I want to ask her the story of how she died, but after Laurentius's reaction to the question, I know I shouldn't. Instead, I opt for, "What was your life like when you were human?"

She loops her gold string around the others and pulls it. "Oh, I don't remember many specifics," she says. "And with things I remember, I'm not completely sure if they happened or if they were dreams."

"Hm." I scrutinize my new bracelet, the rows of looped

threads more even this time. "Do you remember your family, aside from your dad, of course?"

Lucia shakes her head. "Aside from what my father tells me, I can't really remember them clearly. I recall bursts of things, like giggling girls that annoyed me sometimes, but I'm not sure if they were sisters or cousins. Father said I had both."

"Where did you grow up?" I wonder. "I grew up in Lorimer, New York. It's a city in the United States."

"The city of Rome," she says with a small smile. "Father and I left for Hispania for a clean slate after we died. We moved around often until hearing about the castle and how they were accepting members."

My brows hike. "Rome? I seem to meet lots of vampires from there. Laurentius is Roman too." Though, he didn't tell me *where* in Rome he was from.

She laughs. "Oh, there are a few Roman clans here. Not all of them are from the city, but the Roman Empire was vast. Even Rome controlled this land at one point. The city was the largest for centuries, and a hotbed for vampires."

One of the large doors creaks open, Lucia's defeated sigh making me follow her gaze to the door.

A deep sneer etches itself into my expression and I scoff as the door opens and Lucius steps into the room.

"Lucia, I've set your suitcases out for you to help you get started. All I ask is you fill them."

She stares down at the thread in her hand.

"She doesn't want to go," I tell him. "Leave her alone."

Lucius leans away from me, his eyes widening under his raising brows. "I don't believe I spoke to you."

My hands curl into fists around my bracelet. "Too bad, you got an answer."

His expression smooths, something darkening in the black of his eyes. "This doesn't concern you."

"If you want to leave so bad, leave without her. Viorel has

more say over what she does than you do, and he would prefer her to stay. He already knows you want to leave, and she doesn't. He won't let you remove her by force."

Lucius stares at me like he wants to set me on fire. "Shut it."

"Fuck you. You can't talk to me like that, you old grouch," I snap.

His lip curls back, the fury in his eyes brightening. His eyes cut to Lucia, and with grit teeth he growls, "Pack."

I almost bite my tongue, unsure if she even wants me to stick up for her, or if my sharp tongue is only making her feel worse. But she shifts a few inches closer to me and stares extra hard at her bracelet.

"Lucia..." he warns.

"Why don't you give your daughter some space instead of trying to suffocate her? She's been fifteen for how many centuries, and you still can't give her independence? Let her live her own life and suck it up. If she doesn't want to leave the castle, you can't make her. Now fuck off. We're trying to relax and make bracelets and you're wrecking our fun." I've no regard for the venom of my tongue and hope with it and the haughty smile on my lips, he steams. Lucius and I both know he'll be damned if he dares harm Viorel's familiar.

Yet I don't anticipate him storming across the room and yanking Lucia to her feet by her arm with such force it would have popped from its socket if she were human.

There's something about him—beyond the fact I know he's made his daughter's life miserable for hundreds of years—that has me boiling to my core.

A screen of red pounds in my vision, and with all the bottled-up fury of being torn out of my old life and knowing I'll never leave this place, I swipe the scissors off the table and fling them at Lucius like my emotions have taken control of my hand.

They miss him, clattering to the floor to his right. He releases Lucia at least, who sits back down beside me.

"This is the girl you choose as your friend?" Lucius snarls. "Despicable. She's fodder who should have been put down with her last master. Choices like these are why I can't trust you to make your own."

It takes everything in me not to retrieve the scissors and attack him with them.

I grit my teeth and understand why Viorel sleeps in a bed adorned with vampire bones.

I want Lucius's skull next to Artair's on my nightstand.

"Get your feet moving back to the room," Lucius warns.

I'm about to tell him to fuck off again when she crosses her arms and leaps to her feet. She pinches her lips in frustration, though I don't miss the tears she rapidly blinks away. *"Humph."*

Lucius laughs at her. "I don't care how much attitude you have, as long as you walk and pack."

She lifts her nose a bit as she trudges forward, her steps lazy. She takes long enough to reach the door that I have time to sweep our bracelet supplies in my bag of snacks.

I follow behind them, wanting to see where their room is so I can find Lucia next time to hangout.

Lucia takes her sweet time, following behind her father like she has all the time in the world. The pace is painstakingly slow even for me, but she refuses to speed up no matter how many under-the-breath threats slip from between Lucius's grit teeth.

I press my lips into a firm line to stifle the building laughter in me, giving her a tiny but approving nod each time she looks over at me, like she's trying to impress me with her stubbornness. He shoots me furious glares, but my slit eyes and lifted nose dare him to try something.

It seems like forever once we make it to the grand room and pass through it to a hall across from the dining room. I realize I haven't come down this way before, but it's like the rest of the halls with its worn carpet and wooden doors.

When they both stop at a door next to a floor to ceiling painting depicting a plague, I say, "You can make her pack, but you can't make her leave."

He chuckles and shakes his head at me as he opens the door. She plants her feet. I glimpse a small canopy bed with floral bedding covered in teddy bears on the far side of the room through the crack in the door and the corner of a bedpost indicative of a much larger bed. The room is too full of shadows and sparse light to make out much else.

"I have a friend. Nothing you say can convince me to leave," she grumbles, and as he reaches for her arm again, she vanishes.

Lucius curses under his breath, slams the bedroom door, and disappears. I spin and dart toward the hall with the steel door.

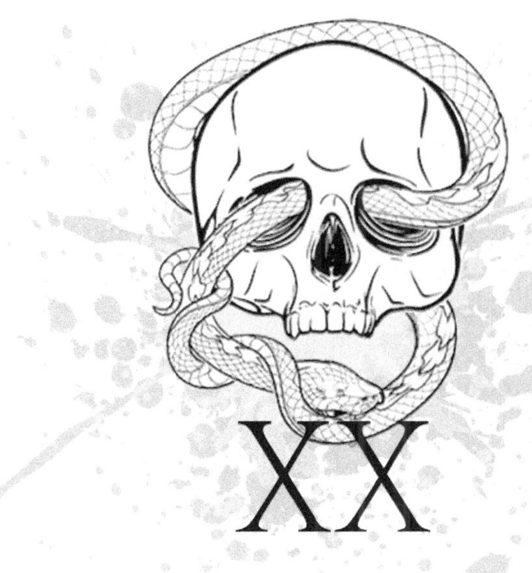

XX

I'm standing in front of Viorel ten minutes later, fists curled in fury. "Lucia's father is still trying to force her out of the castle."

Viorel looks up from a massive leather-bound book from where he sits in his chair at the table in his reading room. "He's not removing her."

"Tell him, because I don't think he's going to let up. She ran away, and he chased her. I have no idea where they went or what he's doing to her."

Viorel sighs. "I'll send a guard to check on them."

He moves to the iron door, where he stands pondering—or listening for something—for a minute, before shouting, "Seth!"

After a terse exchange through the door, he comes back to the table where I now sit, picking at my nails in worry for Lucia. Viorel wouldn't let him hurt her, would he?

"I would not," he assures me as he sits.

"He was pretty rough with her earlier," I say. "Is he in trouble for that?"

Viorel mashes his lips together, and I can tell he's about to tell me how Lucius isn't. "It's difficult. I dislike when clan members clash, but if I brought my fist down on each of their missteps, it would leave nobody in this castle to bicker."

I scowl and hate how he's right.

"There are lines they know they cannot cross," Viorel adds, "But brawls are not unheard of, especially when it's between family members with quick healing capabilities."

"I wish I'd hit him with the scissors."

Viorel's smirk brings a smile to my lips and has the anger of the night fluttering away.

"I'm not in trouble?" I check.

He purses his lips and gives his head a shake. "No, of course not."

I grin. Lucius better fear me, then. If I'm untouchable, I can make him regret fucking with Lucia again and everyone will say he deserves it.

"Don't get carried away now," Viorel warns with a playful timbre in his voice.

I stick my tongue out at him, and his wink has my palms sweating.

Viorel says, "Thank you, Seth."

I glance behind me despite not hearing the iron door open, but nobody is there.

"It's Seth reporting back. Lucia and her father are in their chamber. Ignoring one another, but nobody is packing."

"Okay, good," I mumble.

"I suppose you're to return upstairs?" he asks, smile vanishing as turns his head back down to his book, his hands curled around the top of the massive pages.

There's something about the thick air around him that has me stuck in place, like it's too tedious to slog through. Perhaps it's the painful awareness of the silence down here after being tucked into the noise and bright lives of everyone upstairs.

I notice the collection of mismatched chalices to his left

that weren't there earlier, the way his hands tighten and loosen around the edge of the book like he's considering if it's worth his time.

"What are you reading?" I ask.

He says something in a harsh language I can't guess.

"Oh." I adjust the snack bag on my arm, the sound of crinkling wrappers the only noise aside from my breathing. "Is it good?"

"I don't know." His tone is one of defeat.

I fish a packet of chocolate pretzels from my bag that I rest on the floor and adjust in my chair as he looks back down at his book. He doesn't pay me any attention as I eat, or even when I'm done. After a handful of empty minutes, I blow out a breath and say, "I'm bored."

Slowly, he lifts his face. It's a mixture of exhaustion and vexation. "What do you suppose I do about that?" he says flatly. I swear the words are backed with dry humor.

I groan. "I don't know."

Amusement curves his lips. "You may return upstairs," he says, as if he believes I'm seeking permission. "Just don't make a habit of running up and down. You'll wear poor Sascha out."

"Okay, but I don't feel like it."

He stares at me, his curious gaze flickering over my features. "All right." He looks back down at his book. "You may help yourself to reading material, if you'd like."

I purse my lips while pondering the teeming shelves, but find myself drawn to the familiarity of modern teen books I last saw in crates.

There's every genre available, most of the paperback spines lightly creased from use. A surge of homesickness wracks through me as I slide my fingers over the spines. They're compressed tightly in the crates, and so many of them are popular books I glimpsed on the shelf of the library in West James High School, but never had the energy to read.

I can't decide on any of them enthusiastically, so I unwedge a fantasy romance between an elf boy and human girl, and plop back in my chair.

When I crack it open and delve deep into the crisp pages of the story, it's clear from the soft line in the spine and a pin-sized drop of blood on a cream page he's read it.

"Do you really enjoy these? They're for teens." There's no real judgment in my curiosity, though I find the idea strange. Perhaps I think he'll tell me that despite disliking them, he still reads them for modern insight.

His head remains tilted down as his eyes lift. "Yes. Why should I not? All stories, no matter their age or audience, have merit worth exploring."

I tap my thumb on the page in thought. "I don't know. It's hard to picture. You seem like someone who sticks to classics and books so old they're ready to crumble. I mean, the one you're reading looks like it was made five hundred years ago."

"Seven hundred," he corrects.

I roll my eyes. "See?"

The corner of his lip quirks. "You think I'm pretentious."

I wet my lips and draw them into my mouth as I fight a guilty smile.

Viorel straightens and leans back in his chair as he smirks. No hostility in the words, "You should not begin to think you know a thing about me."

I suppose he's right.

Even the most basic facts about him are lost to me, like the age he became immortal. Despite the vague color that has crept back into his face and made him appear less crypt-dweller, I can't quite narrow it down.

"How old were you when you died?" I ask carefully.

"I'm unsure," he says brusquely.

"Forty?" I wonder, not quite believing someone much younger could rule so strongly and so often.

"Perhaps."

My eyes narrow. "Twenty?"

"It's possible."

"Hm." I study the angles of his face more intensely, but I can't find any more clues. Does his pallor, the way vampirism has changed him, cover up any classic signs of age? "Thirty?"

"Could be." He flips a page in his book, eyes scanning over lines of thick text.

I blow out a breath. "Eighty?" My chuckle is teasing.

"No. That's quite high. Forty is unlikely too." He smirks and runs his fingers through his long hair. "My hairline is perfect, if it's any indicator."

"Hm." I try a more accurate number, thinking of how Laurentius looks older than he really is. "Twenty-one?" How long will he let me keep guessing?

"I'm not making you guess," he says with a wide, amused smile as his eyes meet mine. "Truly, I don't know."

I frown. "Really?"

"Really. Though, I suspect I'm in my twenties, I have no actual way of knowing."

"Hm." I tap my finger on a smooth page in thought. "Rayonne told me she heard you're ten thousand years old in vampire years."

His amused expression fades, and he flips a page, then glances up at me to say, "At least ten, though technically, at least twelve if you factor in the last two thousand years people have been claiming such."

My brows hike up. "At least? You're older? How much was she off?"

"Those are only the years that have passed since I escaped the cave where I was kept prisoner. I don't know how long I've truly been on Earth."

"Prisoner?" My brow furrows. What did he do—

He interrupts my thoughts. "Nothing I was made aware of."

I lean forward a bit and mull over his words before asking, "Well, how long were you in the cave?"

Viorel closes his book and leans back in his chair like he's welcoming a conversation. "I couldn't tell you."

I ponder him as I turn my book over on my thigh. "Can't vampires sense time? The vampires around me always seem to know exactly what time it is."

He nods. "Yes, and those vampires were all once humans taught how to accurately perceive time on top of their primary biological processes and can reconstruct seconds in less time than the time it takes for a hand or the sun to move. Even you can feel when hours have passed, at least a little, can you not?"

"But not down to the minute, like Darklings and Children of Stars."

"Because your brain is not so quick and not as practiced," he says.

"You were never taught to tell time?" I infer.

"I could feel time passing but could not recall how my people tracked it. I don't even know who my people were," he says. "And time passed differently for me in there. I have no memories of when I was human. There was never a sun, moon, or star to guide me. No clock."

"Not a single memory?" I ask.

"Not even my name." He leans closer. "Not even my age."

I swallow.

"I can't fully remember waking when I was born. I gained consciousness in a dark cave with a heartbeat pulsing against my tongue and blood in my mouth. Over the years, I was one of thousands who woke up in this manner. Feral for blood and unknowing of anything but that moment. I didn't know what it meant to be a vampire or human, that I was once the latter and was turned. I didn't understand or wonder what was happening around me—didn't have space for thoughts apart from my thirst—until I was so satiated, I couldn't fathom another drop more."

I pull in a deep breath and blink, realizing his words have me in such a tight grip I've done neither for some bit.

A smile curls the corners of his lips, the candlelight glowing in his dark gaze.

My heart pounds in my chest, the sound of my blood rushing through my head loud.

He smiles to himself, and as he reaches back toward his book, I blurt, "Then what happened?"

Viorel releases an airy chuckle. "You really want to know such things about me?"

My nod is encouraging, as I think of the thousands of years of stories he must have. "You know everything about me, so it's only fair if I know stuff about you, especially since I guess I'll be spending most of my time with you now."

Viorel's smile twitches and grows before quickly fading. "Satisfaction returned me to my senses, and I understood I knew none of what I should. I couldn't recall a thing about myself or the situation upon me. I didn't know why I couldn't depart from the opening of the dark crevice of smooth rock and mangled, bloodless bodies I had awoken in. It should have been as easy as stepping through. There were voices in the distance. Screams. All unfamiliar and echoing from equally unfamiliar rock passages and darkness.

"A man appeared in the shadow of flame and called himself my maker. He had selected me for an opportunity to bring new beginnings to our world. I knew not of the world, and not what it meant to have been created. He explained my birth to me, how I was brought to him mortal like the twisted forms at my feet and passed through pain and death to where I stood before him."

"You didn't know about the world?" I whisper, flinching at

my interruption when I recall how Denendrius loathed such a thing.

He shakes his head. "I am keen to believe a Child of Stars was working in my mind before they turned me, and the changes he made could not be undone with death."

"He hypnotized you out of remembering?" My brows lift.

"Memories buried with hypnotism do not cease to exist. Should one be turned, they'll be uncovered from their hiding place. What they did to me was something different. They stripped me of my identity, the knowledge of any world beyond the cave destroyed with all yearning I could have for it. What I knew of humanity was its general existence, but I was detached from all but the blood coursing through their veins. I could not see myself in them, and if not for seeing those turned in my maker's trials, I would not have believed it possible I was once like them. I knew not of their cultures, of their families, or ways of life. They were naught but beings for satiation."

"Did you ever talk to the humans?" I ask. "Did they ever try to tell you things? They would have been brought into the cave from above ground, right?"

He clicks his tongue. "That is the peculiar thing. The humans brought to us were not all like you and me. We fed from beings like Neanderthals and Denisovans too, and other human species modern science has yet to unearth. None of them survived the transformation to immortality. Few homo-sapiens could speak the same tongue as me and the first generation of my maker's offspring. Those who could, spoke nothing but pleading words. Soon, we understood none of them. It's likely we were beneath the Earth so long our mother tongue died, and language on the surface surpassed our understanding."

"Wow. What was it like down there?" I wonder, imagining how grim life must have been so deep beneath the surface.

"Our days were split between slumber, blood, killing, and

the trials my maker put us through in hopes of uncovering our abilities. We slept when instructed to, naked on the hard stone and blood-moistened dirt, though our strong bodies knew no discomfort. We indulged in the humans our maker thought unfit to join us in immortality, and bit without drinking from the ones who might better survive."

Realization clicks when I recall Rayonne telling me about Viorel. "The eugenics mission," I blurt. "Is this that story?"

He nods and leans against the arm of his chair. "My maker wanted to create a legion of God-like vampires and bring humanity to its knees. He was born with the ability to take—through death—the abilities of other Children of Stars. He was the first of his kind. When he created vampires, he discovered many of them were born with a collection of his stolen abilities, but they could not procure new ones as he did. He claimed the Gods had given him a gift, a means to create a species of perfect vampires who would vanquish humans and take their rightful place in the world. He wanted to enslave humanity and knew it would be impossible with Children of Stars. They were birthed with abilities too infrequently and were too weak to keep all mortals in their fists.

"So, create, he did. When I first woke, there were a hundred of his surviving offspring, and about half the number of vampires created from them. With so much thirst to satisfy, he often culled us. He gave us generous time and aid to discover our abilities through trials, though if one did not possess enough of the traits he desired, resources would no longer be wasted. He forced us to create new vampires, and if our offspring proved inconsistent, or disappointing, they would cull them and their maker. I was the only vampire who could create none more. Each attempt led to a heinous, permanent death unlike any my maker had seen before. He gave me the strongest humans—the warriors and giants—but still they died. He had me attempt to pad their bodies with my blood to better prepare them for my venom until I could take their deaths no longer."

My eyes have been wide for such a time that they're dry. "He had you mark the humans you turned? And you felt all their deaths?"

He swallows, darkness in his eyes. "Yes. A human dying during transformation is the worst sort of death to feel."

"Do you know what it feels like when a vampire's marked human is successfully turned?"

"It's a feeling unlike any other. A loosening of life as the soul changes hands from mortality, through death, and to immortality. It doesn't feel like loss, more like a gradual expansion so far from your own being that the feeling of them slips away."

I ponder his words for a moment. "But he kept you alive even though you weren't making him new vampires?"

Viorel nods. "He desperately wanted that reality to change. From his trials, I most matched his idealized vampire. I was born with most of his abilities, but he wanted time to pass to see if others had been passed on but were yet to come to light. Yet, I felt as if I was failing him. He disagreed and told me I was a divine leader and deeply revered by my people on the surface. I couldn't possibly imagine it. He chose me for my natural ability to command and used me to keep the newborns in check and wanted me to be his second in command on the surface. I did not feel up to the task. How could I lead in a land I could not fathom, when I could not recall leading? I knew not of the stars our maker claimed we gained our power from. I knew of nothing but the Earth's belly and what my maker allowed us to know. Sometimes, I questioned if the surface existed despite how the humans were brought from it. I wondered if they merely came from somewhere deeper in the cave."

My brow furrows and I rub my eyes to get the moisture back into them. "You couldn't remember the stars?"

His lips purse in thought. "Strange, I know. I had all the words for the land above but could not recall the sights to go with them."

I gnaw at my cheek, trying to imagine what that would feel like. "How did you not feel betrayed by your maker?"

He swallows. "I felt I could not trust myself. I knew so little."

My frown is heavy.

"The years passed, and my maker grew increasingly frustrated with his failures. Many of the vampires he created were not born with the abilities he preferred them to have, or were born with an unfortunate combination of them, or lacking in traits and abilities all Children of Stars previously had. Many lineages were inconsistent. Ten vampires would be born with all the same abilities, and he would think he was perfecting them, only for their lineage to cease developing, or the vampires were born without abilities at all again."

My heart thumps. "Then Darklings happened?"

"Yes. Darklings were his breakthrough. They came from a line my maker was prepared to cull. But one was born with a near perfect combination of abilities, and though survival from this vampire was infrequent, it was consistent. Each vampire he made carried on preferred traits, as did the vampires they turned. There were hundreds—if not a couple thousand—by the time he declared them a success. With their ability to hypnotize, their speed and strength on top of regular increased mental cognition and senses, he felt confident perfection was possible. He attempted to surpass such success for a while longer, but the lineage appeared stable, and his attempts through other lines continued to unravel." Viorel pulls in a deep breath. "So he declared ultimate success, and came with the Darklings to cull the rest of us."

My eyes widen. "Kill *everyone* but the perfect Darklings?"

He nods. "Me included."

Despite knowing he lived, my heart hammers ferociously in my chest.

"I had suspected the time would come and knew my maker would not spare me."

The candlelight flickers in his pause, and I blink again.

"The culling came on suddenly during our slumber. They killed the strongest vampires first to prevent revolt, and my maker and the Darklings worked their way down to the weakest. I knew there was nothing I could do to defend more than myself. I fled into the depths of the Earth at the first sound of violence, breaking through magical barriers erected to stop us from wandering. They stopped the Darklings making haste after me, but I knew my maker would come for me still. I made it to a lava lake before my maker called upon me."

My eyes widen. "Molten lava?"

He nods, a dark smile creeping over his face as he continues with, "It was unlike any fire I had seen before and stopped me in my tracks. My maker caught up, and we fought a battle ending with a stake in my heart."

I lean forward in my chair, my eyes flicking over his even expression.

"The betrayal, the anticipation for unconsciousness to pull me under into a purgatory created from my mind, stunned me." A wicked smile shapes his lips. "But my consciousness did not flee. Instead, I tore the stake from my heart to the horror of my maker. To this day, I've never heard of a vampire a stake could not make comatose."

I gape at him while thinking about the Child of Stars that attacked me in the woods when Denendrius took me to an abandoned house to show me them. She was out cold upon impact and looked as dead as a human girl could until I pulled the stake out to reanimate her. The idea of her pulling out her own stake is impossible.

I lean against the table, antsy with excitement. "Then what happened?"

Viorel smiles widely, his fangs on display. "He fled."

"Your maker *ran from you?*" My jaw hangs.

His eyes are bright with the memory. "I understood then how I was more powerful than he. My inability to create new vampires was no shortcoming, but a sign of immortal power so great no other human body could survive and contain it."

I think about how his bite alone is more painful than a Darkling's bite, and don't want to imagine what an attempt to be turned by his venom would feel like.

"I didn't chase him, merely dragged him back to me. He fought until I had his throat in my hand and was holding him over the lake. He did his best to convince me of my importance to him, but his words left me unmoved. I stared into his eyes and imagined the strength of my hate was enough to displace his life. I imagined my touch was condemning enough to rot the flesh off his bones and was pleased to find it was. With his skull in my hands, and the essence of his life writhing in me, I knew I was free. I would be a liar to pretend I hadn't feared the reality of how I must find the surface."

"*Wow,*" I mouth.

"I fed his bones to the lake of fire and destroyed whatever Darklings appeared in my path as I searched for a passage to the surface." Like he's trying to give his hands something to do as he looks off in thought, he rubs his fingers against the leather edge of his book, before saying, "So much time passed that I was crazed with thirst by the time new smells filled my lungs. I crawled on my belly through a crevice, a stinging light beckoning me. I thought it was simply more wood flame. But the skin on my fingers blistered when I reached toward it. I slipped back into darkness and waited until the smells changed and I dared try again.

"When I finally escaped the cave, the world was unfamiliar.

I hoped seeing it would spark my recollection, but so much time must have passed that I might have remembered none of it anyway had my memories not been taken from me. It felt like eternity had passed, and what your scientists call the Pleistocene epoch—the Ice Age—was ending. All the humans I started to feed on were like you. I have tasted multiple flavors of blood from millennia ago I have not tasted since years past in the cave."

I lean back in my chair, reeling from his story. It's difficult to grasp how all this really happened to him thousands of years ago. "Then what did you do?"

"A tribe of vampires found me after I eradicated a village they frequented to hunt. They took me in and taught me the ways of the world. A few hundred years later, when their leader was killed, they put me in charge."

"You didn't want to rule over humans like your maker did?" I ask.

He shakes his head and releases a laugh, like he thinks the idea is silly. "If given control, vampires would drain the world of blood so fast there would be nothing left but the bugs and the weeds. They would have to resort to drinking one another . . . and we both know how such a thing works out."

I think about Denendrius's eternal dissatisfaction and his cravings for vampire blood and gulp.

"If mother nature wanted vampires in charge, we would have been from the start. But we don't fit in with nature the way humans and other beings do. We don't nourish the soil with our bodies when we die, don't bring fresh life to tend to the cycle. We are but thieves in the night, taking what already is. There is no vampire without human."

XXI

Viorel smirks and turns his eyes back to his book. "You may sleep and use the fireplace, if you wish. It's nearly sunrise."

His persistence has me chewing my cheek. "You keep asking every night. Why do you want me in your bed so bad? Are you working up the nerve to do something to me?" I can't help but ask and assess his response with my fresh eyes.

Viorel's brows lift. "No, Marianna. Genuinely, *no*. I would never touch you unless you wanted me to. Despite not having those predilections, I don't enjoy feeling a familiar's fear and distress."

I inhale deeply, trying to think of something other than "okay" to follow his words with.

A little smile plays at his lips. "Truly, I only wish to take advantage of your heat. Your body warms the entire bed. It's quite nice. You don't have to if you don't want to. I only suspected you wouldn't ask if you changed your mind. But all right, I won't pester you again."

There's another reason too—perhaps the most prominent

one—in his tired breath and desperate eyes as he glances at his shelves for something to occupy himself. When he leaves the reading room, I decide there's no reason for me to remain in the hard chair, so I stand with my book and follow with my bed in mind.

Pausing beside his wardrobe, I watch him and consider how Mateo thought Viorel was struggling and see it now as he meanders around from one shelf and cabinet to another, pausing in front of his organ before flattening his lips and staring down the dark hall past my room like he's considering one of the other rooms.

The loneliness. The anxiety. He wears it like a cloak.

How often does he struggle to sleep like he did when I was still marked to Denendrius? There must be far more than Denendrius and Tatiana to keep him awake at night. He must have over twelve thousand years of betrayals and deaths to grieve. Do the oldest ones still hurt?

When was the last time he shared a bed with someone besides me? Is he usually alone each night under the cold floors and walls, thinking about the families of his clan upstairs, tucked away with one another in their rooms?

Emotion has me swallowing hard.

He doesn't react to my thoughts, so I wonder if he's too lost in his own to tune into mine.

"You're down here all by yourself," I start, leaning my shoulder against the stained wood and clutching my book in front of my thrumming heart, "and have been for centuries from what I've heard. Do you not get lonely?"

"I have my guards and my clan," he counters, though the words sound recited. He pauses in front of the shelf next to his organ and turns to me. "I'm an ancient vampire, what else do I need?"

"Have you ever had a wife?"

"Once upon a time I took wives or husbands," he says.

"They all died eventually, as everyone does. I haven't let myself have another in millennia."

I can't keep the shock off my face. "A lover?"

His expression remains stoic. "Rarely. Being vulnerable with another person—a vampire, especially—is dangerous."

I stare at him, unable to help the pity I know seeps from my eyes. "But don't you *want* companionship? Love? Even all those people up there, you distance yourself from them. Their company is an illusion when there's so much distance. They may as well not even be there. You're practically alone, holed up underground."

"I was born alone, I traverse the earth alone, and when Death catches me, it will be no different. Loneliness is unavoidable. Loneliness is inherent."

"But do you *want* to be alone?" I press. "Don't you want to be upstairs with everyone?"

He stares at me with an empty gaze.

"Don't you want to fall in love again? Find your soul mate? You may be an ancient vampire, but you started with as human a brain as everyone else. It's just been frozen a lot longer." I'm not sure why I care so much about his love life. Maybe I can talk him into finding a reason to leave this room.

Viorel pulls in a breath and slowly lets it out. "Marianna, I am the world's most powerful vampire. There's not a single person in the world like me. Ordinary vampires know of the suffering of leaving behind their human friends and families, but what I experience is much worse." He swallows. "There's nothing more painful than having a friend or a lover for thousands of years—having your very being wound around them— and losing them. Despite what some would have you believe, I am not without feeling. I feel too much, too often. You think I would learn my lesson by now and numb my heart, but I let it become aching and raw. I should not let myself love the vampire children. I should keep Mateo quivering in fear of me instead of letting him consider himself my best friend. And I most certainly should not be letting a fragile human mean anything more to me than a means to a full belly. I know what will happen. You, the children, and Mateo will all die, and I still won't save myself from inevitably becoming violently ill with grief."

My eyes burn with sadness for him. "But you didn't answer my question. Don't you want to be in love? Even if you don't want to let yourself? Aside from your powers keeping you around longer than most vampires, you're no different from them. Don't you want the same things they do?"

Viorel's eyes bore into mine. "I have fallen in love, Marianna, and I dislike it."

I swallow. "Why?"

His eyes study my face. "Because it's terrifying, unpredictable, and uncontrollable. A little loneliness is healthy. Too much company can kill you."

"What?" I shake my head at him. "You can't be serious. What's the point in living forever if all you do is spend your days down here? What's the point in protecting yourself with abilities and dozens of guards if you're going to sit in a bunker and read books and do puzzles because you haven't seen past this forest in a thousand years?"

"Because there is *nothing else* for me," he says. "I'm content. I want to protect what I already have while I have it."

"You could be *happier*. You could experience some of that world," I say.

He smiles. "You're going to tell *me* of happiness, Marianna? Who are you to tell me how grand the world is? I know what you think I'm missing."

I lower my eyes. At least Ziggy has the right idea—partying and living it up until it all ends.

"I have my dreams, my fantasy worlds," he says. "They're as vivid as reality."

My eyes narrow. "It's not the same," I argue. "Real life . . . out *there*. It's not the same."

"I know." His smile is soft. "But it's good enough."

"You don't even want to take a careful trip somewhere every few decades? It doesn't have to be all or nothing."

"*No,*" he says gently.

"You won't let me leave without you, but you won't go. You can't take me somewhere even *once?* Not even to the nearest town?"

The sadness in his eyes at my words surprises me. "No, and can you truly imagine me out there? In the human world as it is right now? Think about it. Ponder a place you want to go and imagine me there."

I take a minute to picture it. Him sitting in some diner with me while I eat. Walking through an amusement park. He'd look so out of place. I'd laugh if I wasn't sad. I can't imagine him in a modern house or sitting in a car. And even if he put on modern clothes—which I can't imagine either—he'd never blend in with humans like every other vampire can.

"See," he says with a little smile. "It's not my world anymore. It hasn't been in centuries."

I bite at my lip and take a deep breath before asking, "So, if Denendrius had never escaped your fortress in Sirmium, and you never lost it, would you still be there, hidden away?"

Viorel nods. "Yes, most likely."

I push off from the wardrobe and take a couple of steps toward him before pausing again. "So, you're going to stay here until . . .?"

"Until I'm forced to leave and continue elsewhere," he says simply.

"And when the world ends and there's nothing left?"

He chuckles like he thinks I'm silly. "I will not fret about it until I have to."

"I want to be in love," I admit. "You'd think I'd swear it off after Denendrius, but I can't help myself either." I swallow and look to the unlit fire for somewhere to rest my eyes. "I suppose I've always craved love in general, have killed for it. So, I don't understand your perspective."

"I kill for love often." Viorel sits on the edge of his bed.

"I thought you disliked being in love," I counter.

His smile is small. "Love, like Death, does not care what your wishes are. You are at its mercy when it comes for you. And sometimes, Love and Death are one and the same. That's the terrifying part, Marianna."

I lower my eyes to the floor and rub my thumb against the corner of my book, realizing I understand his perspective despite not wanting to swear love off.

Love and Death both came to me with Denendrius. When I met Denendrius in the mall—before I could recall all our history together—I had desperately wanted to fall in love with him. For the first time, I gave love a chance . . .

And this is where it got me.

There were so many days where I wished death would finish what love had started.

But I'm known for being reckless. It's written in my files. Love can be terrifying, and I know there are so many ways it could kill me. Still, I can't help myself.

I want to feel what I thought was real between Denendrius and me again. No, *I want more.* I want to feel the eternal love my friends have always dreamed of. I want a love deserving to kill for. Deserving to die for. I want love like Rayonne had with Alessander. I want the love Viorel must have had to be so terrified of having and losing it again. That seems like worthwhile love.

Perhaps the castle is the best place for it. The best place for finding eternal love. Though I didn't want to think of dating vampire men, I suppose I have equal experience with them and humans now. Well, both with one man, unless you count Laurentius trying to court me.

I wish I could want a normal, human man with a normal human life, but I'm not sure one is what will work for me anymore. As much as I loved having a normal human life in Bellevue, I felt so helpless when Denendrius was mortal.

Because who can protect me better than a vampire? Love me longer than an immortal? Who can better kill for love?

I sigh and lift my gaze, connecting back with Viorel's soft and unblinking eyes.

"Can I go with Mateo to see Denendrius?" I flinch at my request, the words leaping off my tongue before they form as a thought.

I snag the skin of my cheek between my molars as I study his reaction.

"Why?" he whispers, and I swear I see hurt flicker through his face before he masks it.

I twist my fingers together. "I need to see him *like this*. When I'm not marked by him. I need to know how I feel because I keep remembering how I felt and thought when my mark to him was deep. I want to make sure it wasn't really my own thoughts. It feels like I haven't seen him in months, but like something is still holding onto me."

"Very well." The hurt makes it to his voice, though it probably has nothing to do with me because he adds, "At least I know he can't hypnotize you."

XXII

As we near Denendrius's dark cell, Mateo clicks his tongue like he's beckoning a dog.

"Denendrius . . ." he calls, adding a whistle.

I'm dizzy with fear as I wait for him to show himself. What if my feelings for him remain without the mark? What if I regret everything that got me here?

What if I still love him?

My heart pounds so hard I can't get a proper breath in as Denendrius emerges from the shadows, sickly pale and limping. His cautious eyes flicker over me as he drags himself to the bars.

I step closer to Mateo, like the bars are toothpicks separating me from Denendrius's grasp.

Denendrius wets his busted lips, blood dried and crusted in the corners of his mouth and staining his chin and jaw. "I love you," he whispers—his Latin accent fading—like it's a test he knows I'm about to fail.

The backs of my eyes burn, and I fight the urge to hide

behind Mateo so his predator eyes can't see me. Instead, I stand frozen with sick chills and clammy skin that have me wanting to crawl into the shower.

"Are you okay?" Denendrius asks, resting his forearm against the bar to lean his weight on.

"*No,*" I breathe. My tongue feels rubbery. "I'm not."

His hard swallow looks painful, his eyes misty. "You fought him so hard, sweetheart. I'm proud of you. I'm sorry I couldn't end your pain when I had the chance. But I promise I'll get us both out of here so we can be together again."

The insanity—the delusion—is plain in his eyes again. Looking at him and knowing only days ago I had his sickness coursing through me, makes me feel like I snapped out of a shared psychotic episode and am looking back into it from the perspective of a bystander.

The horror, the disgust and fear, shapes my face before I can hide it.

Denendrius drops his gaze from mine and sniffs at a tendril of blood running from his nostril.

My thoughts race, the memories of his abuse like poison in my bloodstream. They wet the nape of my neck and my palms with sweat. They smear into the memories of him as a human, sullying the gradient of who he first was as an immortal and who I *thought* he really was. But I don't see a difference in men, just a difference in the mind of the girl who was observing him.

"Denendrius . . . Do you really think who you are now and who you first were as a vampire are two different people?" I ask carefully.

A line appears between his brows. "Of course I am, Marianna."

"Then how?" I ask, crossing my arms. "Were you body snatched? Possessed?"

"My mind split," he says, desperate gaze holding mine. "All the torture in Sirmium broke me. It's difficult to explain, sweetheart, but the memories still don't feel like mine. The memories past Sirmium feel inherited. I never would have done any of those horrible things if I were myself."

"So, when Tatiana was kidnapped, raped, and murdered, that wasn't you? Did you split right before?"

His guarded eyes search my face, but he nods. "I would never do something like that."

How awfully convenient for him to claim the pain inflicted on him, but nothing more.

I shake my head as I shift my eyes from his, the icy chill his gaze injects me with making me wrap my arms around myself.

"Fine. I have one more question," I choke out, trying to rein in my rapid breath and calm my juddering heart, knowing the road I'm about to walk us both down is dangerous. "Say the mark didn't affect my decision to run away with you and start a new life in Bellevue, and everything was as real as we thought it was . . ." I clear my throat, my queued question catching as I meet his eyes again. "What if I woke up one day and broke up with you? A lot of normal couples fall out of love."

His stare is cutting, a vein in his neck protruding. "What?"

My heart drums in my chest. "What would you have done? You're different from when we first dated, so would you have let me go? Because *he* wouldn't have. I know you would have been upset but . . ."

"I would have . . ." He grits his teeth, the anger bubbling up in him at the mere thought. "I would have been *quite upset*, Marianna."

My eyes burn. "What would you have done?"

His eyes search mine. "We're destined to be together, sweetheart. You never would have . . ." He shakes his head. "No."

"Answer the question," I demand. "It shouldn't be so hard."

"I love you. I wouldn't let you leave and hurt me like that." His hand clenches into a fist at his side. "I would have ended you. I wouldn't have let you destroy everything we built without consequence. Is that what you want me to say?"

I feel as heavy as the stone around me. "That's not what I want you to say, but it's what I expected."

"But it doesn't matter," he says desperately, "because you would have never left me. You're inventing scenarios to be upset over. Every man would feel the same."

In my peripheral, Mateo gives his head a dumbfounded shake as he adjusts his footing.

I lower my head and stare at the floor. "Not every man would kill their girlfriend for trying to leave him."

"Then they're whipped men who let others walk over them," he fights to explain. "They don't feel love as deeply if they let it walk away. I love you so much I would do anything to keep you, even if it meant ending both our lives."

"You would rather me die with you than be happy without you?" The sourness of my tone matches my expression as I turn my face back to him.

"Why is that so bad?" he says, incredulous. "I *love you*. I would rather us both be dead if we can't be together."

Another question finds my tongue before I can consider whether it's a question I want an answer to. "Okay, so what if I never left you, but we stopped having sex? That happens sometimes in relationships."

His brows twitch together, and he releases a confused chuckle. "What? Why would we stop making love? We did it so much."

I swallow. "Lots of reasons. So, you would have been okay with me saying no to sex?"

"I have been okay with you saying no," Denendrius says, eyes narrow. "I did not insist the times you were too tired, or when you were not feeling well."

"I know, but what if I just didn't feel like it?" I counter.

He shakes his head, like he's astounded by me. "That's not a good excuse."

My brows hike, my voice raising. "Oh, so I'd need a good excuse for you to respect my 'no'?"

Mateo puts his hand on my shoulder, either to calm me or to suggest I cut the conversation short.

He glowers at me. "You agreed to be my wife, which means you agreed to the duties of a wife."

"You would just rape me if you didn't think I had a good enough excuse?"

He scoffs at me. "A man cannot steal what has already been given to him."

I stare at him, unable to feel my own legs. Carol was right. He never changed. I did. I was acting exactly how he wanted me to act, having sex with him almost every time he wanted, unless I was literally too tired, or my stomach hurt. I cleaned the house without question, cooked whenever he asked me to, and rarely did anything to oppose him.

I shouldn't be surprised. He was a perfect gentleman when we started dating until I gave him a reason not to be.

Words from when he was first a vampire strike me then.

"Just be a good girlfriend, and I'll prove what an excellent boyfriend I can be."

I clutch my hands in front of me and stare down at how they shake.

"What are you thinking, Marianna?" he murmurs.

I level my eyes with his. "I'm thinking you're genuinely sick, Denendrius. And I think you always have been, likely even back in Rome when you were human. That vampirism has only exasperated what was already there, and gave you an opportunity to do things you never would have risked doing when you were human. I think this shit about you splitting is your way to skirt around what you did, so I'll love you." I pull in a deep breath. "And I'm just really glad there are bars between you and the rest of the world."

Denendrius grasps a bar in his fist, face twisting with pain as he stares at me for a long moment before saying, "Huarsar's mark has a deep grip on you already, it seems."

In his presence now, all I feel is the cold ache of loss. Loss for my own life, for my detour from sanity, for the pieces of flesh, heart, and dignity he tore from me.

"I wish you had been genuine," I whisper.

His head cocks. "What do you mean?"

I swallow. "When we met at the mall for what I thought was the first time. I wish that had been real. I wish your act was the real you. Can you imagine if it had been?"

His expression smooths, pain bright in his blistering red eyes. "It wasn't an act." The words catch in his thirsty throat. "I truly felt like everything was finally right in the world. I was happy and trying to be better. But then . . ." He flinches. "You hurt me. I tried so hard for you, and it didn't matter."

"Because you're *crazy*," I croak.

"I love you eternally, and I know you love me too. You're only acting like this because he marked you. You cannot trust your mind anymore." He swallows and nods at me, the motion shaking a tear loose from his wild eyes. "I understand, Marianna. I don't blame you, and I won't give up on you. You aren't in control of the things you think and feel right now."

My laugh is limp, and I choke on the end of it. "Then what about our mark? Can't the same be said about the love I felt for you?"

"No. Our love was beyond any mark. Huarsar wants you to hate me, so you will for now." His hand trembles as he tucks his hair behind his ear. "I remember everything now, sweetheart. You loved me before the mark, when you were a little girl. It wasn't the same, I know, but it would have been when you grew up."

I lift my fists and press them into my head. *"I was five,"* I cry, feeling insanity creep back into me. "Don't start that again, oh my god."

"Start what? Telling you the truth?"

How did I ever convince myself he was two different people?

I take a step back, Mateo now between me and Denendrius.

"I'm so fucking lucky," I choke out. "So unbelievably lucky I'm alive to see you behind bars."

To think I'd still be trapped in his delusion with him if I hadn't fought his mark long enough to seek help, hadn't run from school that one afternoon.

"Huarsar's the vilest evil a man can know," Denendrius warns, his desperate gaze trying to reach through to my soul. "I fear more for you than I do myself."

Denendrius's gaze makes me feel naked and violated. "I've seen *true evil* before, Denendrius. I'm staring right at it."

I stand rigid with uneven shoulders and too much unbalanced weight on my right foot as Mateo closes the iron door to Viorel's chambers behind me. The bar falling into position has me flinching. Viorel's expression is smooth as he takes me in with his unemotional gaze.

"I'm going to bed," I announce flatly before swallowing against my dry throat and staggering away.

I know my eyes won't be closing with the deluge of tears I'm sure will escape once I'm beneath my covers. But when I wobble into bed and hug the blankets, the tears don't come. My eyes are as dry as my scratchy throat, my skin pricking with the heat of emotion. I feel as empty as a desert.

My visit with Denendrius leaves me dizzy, my balance feeling off despite resting on the bed. I think of scrubbing myself raw and clean in the bath, like the poison of his breath and words have stuck to me.

I gasp upon noticing Viorel standing in my doorway beyond my feet. The candlelight reflects in his eyes and makes them glossy.

"Do you want comfort?" Viorel asks.

Coming from Viorel, I'm unsure what the offer means.

"Blood," he clarifies.

I roll onto my back to see him better. Any hesitance—worry of being stolen into blood slavery—dries up. I'm parched from anger and would glut myself with it simply because I'm destroying Denendrius with each drop of his captor's blood.

"Please," I whisper, salivating with the thought, addict heart already racing from the calm high I know his blood will give me.

He appears seated on the edge of my bed, and I only freeze in response to his unseen swiftness. His smile is soft as he lifts his wrist to his lips and bites into his flesh.

I wet my lips as he rushes the bloody wounds to my mouth, closing my eyes as the first drop of blood hits my tongue. Euphoria washes through me, his blood cleansing what steaming water and soap could never.

I lift my tentative fingers and wrap them around his cold forearm, the dark calm of him filling me and spreading to my extremities. I drift, feeling like a soft snowflake on a winter midnight.

This time, I only teeter near unconsciousness as I slowly notice the absence of blood flowing over my tongue. Still, my fingers circle his forearm, my lips pressed against his healed wrist. He doesn't move. He must be waiting for me to succumb, and I must, because he's gone with the sound of his bed creaking.

I can sense the hours that have passed when the blanket peels away from my body and the mattress sinking behind my back has me tearing awake and twisting over.

Through the sparse light leaking into my room from the

hall, I catch Viorel standing at my bedside, one leg already on the mattress.

"*What the hell are you doing?*" I rasp, my heart beating in my throat.

He blinks a few times, some of the sleepiness evading his eyes. "What? You were calling my name. I thought you needed me."

I give my head a swift shake and give the blanket—a portion of it in his hand—a tug. "No, I wasn't."

He lets go and retreats off the bed. "Oh, I could have sworn. It woke me. Perhaps you were talking in your sleep, or it passed through your thoughts."

"Maybe. I had a nightmare," I admit, heart stuttering and slowing with the realization he's not here to harm me. "Can't remember it now. Doesn't matter, you can go back to sleep."

I'm unsure why, but when his body angles a few degrees toward the door, I grab a fistful of his silk gown.

He merely stares at me with half-lidded eyes.

I let go of him with a little gasp. "I'm sorry—"

"You want me to stay?"

Do I? It is odd to be in this dark and damp room alone when I've been sleeping in his bed next to the fire, even if I had wanted to get away. It's odd, overall, to be alone now. I haven't slept alone in months.

The candles in the corner of my room come alight as we stare at one another while I navigate my thoughts, my dream, and the cold fear I experienced upon waking return. "He came downstairs," I say, tone void of emotion. "Walked right by you and attacked me in my bed. I was calling for you to wake up, but you weren't answering." I'm glad I don't have to clarify who I mean—say his name—since Viorel can see Denendrius and his violence in my thoughts.

Slowly, he crawls back onto the bed and lowers onto his side, facing me. He tucks his long hair behind his shoulders as he rests his head on the edge of my pillow. I hold my breath and scoot back to give him more space, but there's far less in my double bed than his.

My throat dries at the feel of his silk gown against my bare legs as he shifts closer, but the smooth feeling is soothing against my skin. I don't move.

"Sleep freely," he whispers as he draws the blanket over us. His body blocks the candlelight and casts us both in shadow. "You won't bother me."

"Okay." But I can't convince the stiffness in my body to soften.

Despite the initial discomfort of sleeping next to him in his bed, there was an implicit promise of safety from everything else in the world. With him laying back at my side, it has me feeling both wildly intimidated and like I'm the safest I've ever been. I don't have to be afraid of anything, not even my own dreams, when I'm lying next to the world's most powerful vampire.

"This bed is like a stone compared to mine, though mine lacks warmth now," Viorel grumbles, his chilly breath tickling the side of my face. I can't help my breathless chuckle as he settles in beside me. I stare at his fangs when he grins and sighs before mumbling, *"Toasty."*

When I tuck my hand between my cheek and pillow, his eyes settle on my wrist before cutting away and closing. A modest smile shapes his lips, his Adam's apple bobbing behind the pale skin of his throat.

Hesitantly, I whisper, "Are you thirsty?"

"Mm." Viorel swallows again, a soft chuckle slipping through his parted lips. "I must confess, I always experience a faint pinch of hunger. It's easy to ignore."

"Why?" My lips twist in confusion.

He opens his eyes. "Using my abilities takes an enormous amount of energy from me. I've never been able to keep up with my thirst, so I accept it. Worry not, I don't tread near starvation. But I can always . . . stomach more."

"Is that why your fangs never retract, and your eyes are always red."

"No. That's simply how I've always been. I can glut myself on villages and still my fangs remain ready and my eyes red."

I purse my lips. "So, you don't know what color your eyes were when you were human?"

He gives his head a little shake. "Statistically speaking, likely brown."

Studying his face, I disagree with him. "Green. Like emeralds."

His lips twitch, slowly losing a battle against a smile. "Think so?"

I nod.

Viorel stares past me in thought, the brightness of wonder in his eyes. "Hm."

"How many abilities do you have?"

He settles his eyes back on mine and blows out a breath against my face. "I can't say for sure. Some abilities are so alike I question if they're the same. Occasionally, others present themselves to me and I have no way of knowing how long it's been since I acquired them." He clicks his tongue in thought. "Keeping the veil up takes most of my energy, but it's as easy as breathing now. I hardly think of the task."

I acknowledge his words with a nod before posing my next question. "Have you ever killed a Child of Stars for their ability? How do you even do that?"

He gives me a wry grunt. "In my early days, I killed a seer for his ability. I learned my lesson. It took a lot of energy to turn him to dust and bone as I did with Artair and it wasn't worth it."

My heart pounds at the base of my throat. "You can see the future . . . ?"

Viorel drops his eyes, his smile unraveling into a thick line as a grimace takes hold of his face. "Yes, but . . ." He doesn't speak for a moment, the rush of thoughts practically visible in his downcast gaze. "I haven't used the ability in thousands of years, and I vowed to bury it deep within me for the rest of my time."

"Why?" It seems like such a gift, knowing what's waiting and being given an opportunity to change things. If it weren't for Patricia's ability and how she saw Lance die if he joined the group who came to save Rayonne and me from Venganza Roja and Agatha, they wouldn't have had a chance to save him.

He lifts his eyes to mine, the gloom on his face a second shadow. "I drove myself mad with it," he admits, the ache of the experience audible in his voice. "It came to where I could not make a decision without checking the potential outcome. But simply checking the future can be enough to alter it. Friends who were destined for death suffered and died more horribly had I not attempted to intervene, and futures I so desperately wanted vanished in my quest to fulfill them. Some futures happened no matter what I did. I tried to live in the future so I could escape the grief and unpredictability of the present, and found it as—if not more—unpredictable and painful."

A frown weighs on my lips. *"Oh."*

"Sometimes visions of the future are unavoidable and come to me in dreams. I can't always tell what they are unless they happen, so they're simple to write off as meaningless." He searches my face as I weigh his words.

My throat dries, the taste of his blood still on my lips. My memory traces over the feel of it entering my body, and I bite my bottom lip to stop the request for more. I'm sure I've had my fair share already, and the last thing I want is to make him thirstier by taking more from him.

Gentle, he reaches his finger to my wrist and trails the tip of his nail down my vein. "How about a trade?"

I bite my cheek, heart pounding knowing the burn his fangs will bring me.

"I won't let it hurt," he promises, serious eyes searching mine.

My thoughts swing with indecision, worried he'll want to drink more often if I offer it, but not wanting to turn away the feeling his blood gives me.

With a twitch of his brows and a slow-growing smile, he moves his wrist to his open mouth in question.

"Okay." I inch mine across the pillow toward him.

He gives me his first, and I close my eyes as his other hand circles my wrist. When the euphoria feels like pure ecstasy, the sensation more consuming than ever before, I can't help the brief moan rolling in the back of my throat as my body buzzes. My eyelids flutter open, and I take in the sight of his lips pressed against my wrist, his lids closed. No blood escapes, and without the pain, it appears as nothing more than a kiss.

He draws his bloodied fangs from the painless incisions, the gory wounds disappearing as his thumb passes over them. I'm too lost in the smooth sensation pounding through me to close my wet lips or move. I lay still and soft, like I'm gooey and warm and melted into the mattress.

There's silence for some time, and the candle snuffs out. I stare into the dark of my room, trying not to flinch at Viorel's breath against my face as I think of my nightmare. I don't know why I still carry some fear of Viorel, but it feels like there are eggshells crushed and hidden in the wrinkles of the sheets. Perhaps I'm afraid of the power he holds, and what he's capable of. Still, it feels better with him here.

Safer.

My breath catches when he speaks again. "He'll never harm you again," Viorel whispers. I'm stone as his fingers brush my cheek. "You are mine. *Nobody* will ever harm you again."

XXIII

I wake feeling heavy from too much sleep with Viorel's body shaped against the back of mine. From the length of empty space between the wall and me, I must assume I'm the one who moved closer. His breaths are even with sleep, tickling the flesh behind my ear. His knee is pressed into the back of one of mine and his hand rests on my waist. There's plenty of space between our hips.

Though I think of moving—what's he going to say about me being in his personal space—I'm much too comfortable to shift even a finger, and part of me doesn't want him to wake and get up. My backside is cool from his body like it sticks out of the blanket on a hot night, the rest of me warm. I'm cozy and let myself admit it's in part from the safety his presence provides.

So, I lay with my thoughts until enough time passes that I ache to ask the time. I don't move, not even when his breath changes and he ever so slightly squeezes my waist. At first, I think he's waking, but he doesn't say anything, doesn't move, so I assume otherwise.

We lay long enough that my bladder asks to be emptied. I ignore it.

"Mateo's here with your dinner," Viorel murmurs after a few more minutes, and I realize he must have woken up when I first thought.

His hand twitches on my waist, the distant sound of the iron door unlocking and opening following.

With Mateo having ruined the evening silence, and with my bladder's warnings, I can't bear to lie down anymore. I fight the blanket away and clamber off the end of the bed as Viorel rolls onto his back and pulls the blanket back over himself.

I race toward the bathroom. When I return, Mateo's in my doorway, face serious while in a low conversation in Romanian with Viorel. I move along to my dinner.

"Are you wishing to go upstairs after?" Viorel asks from his throne as I chow on eggrolls, Mateo long gone.

For the first time, it's the last thing I want to do. Perhaps it's too much sleep, but I don't want to go anywhere today. I think of a hot bath and the basket full of care items needing organizing. The quiet, cool air of Viorel's space and my room is all I crave.

"Nah."

There's a surprised twitch in his brows, and a bit of relief in his breath.

After dinner, I put on a charcoal face mask and soak in the tub until the water is cold and my toes are wrinkly. I take my time dressing, quickly flicking past my blue tracksuit and realizing all but one of my outfits are from Bellevue. The idea of wearing them has me scratching my arms and chest, so I pull on the jeans and long sleeve Lucia helped me find, and some socks to protect me from the cold floor. Then, I take my time deciding on where to put everything. I'm torn between the floor of my wardrobe and the drawers of my nightstand until Viorel tells me there's plenty of space in one of the cupboards in the bathroom.

With my own room and permission to branch out from it with my belongings, Viorel's space feels far more welcoming.

As I sit across from Viorel in the reading room with my nail-painting supplies, he looks me over and says, "Do you feel seeing Denendrius has offered closure?"

I stare at him as I arrange my blue bottle of nail polish, acetone, and handful of cotton balls between the two edges of his puzzle and table. "I don't know, maybe."

He returns to his nearly complete puzzle as I sit on his words and open my polish. It takes me a moment to get the best angle for my nails as it's always been Daina, Camille, or Jenna to paint them for me at sleepovers. When I slather on the shiny blue liquid, it looks nothing like theirs ever did. It's patchy, thick in all the wrong places, and all over my skin. I scowl and wipe it off with acetone to try again.

The second try is somehow worse, and I'm contemplating giving up when Viorel tells me to wipe my nails clean and come to him.

I scrub them with acetone until my cuticles are burning, then huff as I stand. When he holds his hand out, I quirk a brow.

"Polish," he says.

I sigh and plop it in his open hand before rounding the table to him as he opens it. He holds his palm out and I carefully place my hand in his, watching with a furrowed brow as he dips the little brush and wipes it off the excess liquid.

"You know how to paint nails?" I ask, wary.

He smiles up at me, the corners of his eyes crinkling. "I've seen enough to confidently teach you."

"If you say so . . ."

He walks me through the process as he delicately paints

each nail, from how much polish to use, to how I should do long strokes from the base of my nail to the tip instead of starting in the middle.

My heart thumps as he carefully applies the shiny blue with steady hands and precise motions. When he's done, they're perfect.

"Thank you," I whisper.

"You're most welcome." His soft smile has me swallowing. "Want me to paint your toes?"

I'm a little resistant to allow it. Not because I don't want him to, but because I don't know how to feel about the sudden shift inside me. I search and find most of my hesitancy toward Viorel diminishing. Downstairs is beginning to feel like home. I'm not fully at ease but seeing Denendrius with fresh eyes helped with the new perspective.

"Okay," I agree.

When Viorel asked me to be modest with my time upstairs, I thought he didn't want me to treat downstairs like somewhere to store my bed and sleep.

But over the next two weeks, I find modest means limited. I can tell he has to push through some personal hesitance each time I request to go upstairs—usually after I've had my dinner—and that he'd prefer I didn't go up at all.

Some nights when I'm fully away, I return to him pacing or pretending to read. His shoulders lower and his breath becomes steadier once the door is locked behind me. Still, he smiles and asks to hear about my time away. Most days I'm only upstairs for a handful of hours or half the night. Just enough time to not feel like I'm missing out on anything, since everyone has their own things to do.

Only one evening does he snap *"no"* when I ask and shut himself in the bathroom before I can argue. Since it's his first time denying me, I swallow my annoyance and hope I don't hear the word often.

I know it has to do with Tatiana. Artair too and Viorel's clear, general mistrust of his own clan now. I don't have to ask him if he's still worried about my safety. What other reason would he have?

At least he doesn't expect me to be quiet and alone in my bedroom that day. He doesn't tuck me away, so I'm out of his way. He brings me to his bed after supper and we read separate books together. Then, he tries to convince me I can help with his puzzle, but I sit scowling for two hours combining no two pieces.

Three days after my last visit with Denendrius, Mateo and a few of the guards leave for Lorimer after finally getting Denendrius to admit to what he did with Alaire and Edmond's van. Once full of blood from one of the more depleted donor bodies available, he spills how he did *absolutely nothing* with it. He left it at the warehouse they lured him to, more interested in taking me home. If he really left the van at the warehouse where he killed them, Mateo suspects it won't be difficult to track down since it likely would have been towed.

My list of wants and desires is quickly attended to. Mateo finds a cobweb-covered clock and fixes the hands before setting it on my nightstand. It was hand carved by Viorel some two-hundred years ago.

The fact I want a hand-held game system makes it around, and an unfamiliar black-eyed man corners me in the library with one that released a few years ago and a massive collection of games to go with it. I struggle to understand him through his thick and rough accent, but his smiles and heavy motions of the box toward me are convincing enough. After ample excited thanks, I dart downstairs to play and do until my thumbs and eyes are hurting.

When I'm upstairs, I spend most of my time with Laurentius and Lucia. Laurentius and I hang out with his snakes and watch movies on his portable DVD player between bouts of long conversation. He's nervous to watch any of the horror movies I find in the media room, completely refusing if they have anything to do with the occult, possessions, or religion. But he lends me his player to watch them with Lucia in one of the various sitting rooms around the castle. I'd think he was uptight—too religious—if it weren't for the ease at which he watches raunchy comedies and gory thrillers with me.

Laurentius and I go for late night walks in the garden, slowly exploring the vast sections of flowers and shrubs. We often stop at the fountain with statues of sirens and marble men to share bits of our past with one another. I keep the darkest bits to myself knowing there's always listening ears, but tell him about my time with Denendrius when he was first a vampire. I admit to being a terrible student and sub-par friend, and how I wish I could do everything over again. He's convinced I'm exaggerating my shortcomings since I'm a good friend to him and Lucia and was there for Sarah when I found out Denendrius was hurting her, despite how we were enemies before. He goes on about how great it is to have the ability to make mistakes and learn from them on our own, how this is the serpent's gift; the free will giving us the incredible ability to choose good instead of the default being perfection and not knowing bad. I can tell he's getting ahead of himself, because when I ask him to explain his unconventional beliefs since I'm unsure what he's going on about, he looks embarrassed as he shuts up and distracts me.

I often spend midnight meals with Carol and Derek, who are more than happy to save a seat for Laurentius. They ask about my relationship with Laurentius on a night where he's too busy looking for an escaped snake to hang out, and I can tell they already approve of him from their subdued smiles.

"We like each other as more than friends," I tell them. Laurentius and I haven't discussed our relationship despite how often we go on dates where we sketch together in the art room or play board games. We haven't kissed, though I think he's working up the courage to or is unsure if he's allowed. Holding hands has become regular between us.

I won't complain. It's not that I don't want to kiss Laurentius, but the lack of pressure to be physical is a breath of fresh air compared to past experiences.

"Would Viorel let you have a boyfriend?" Carol asks, to which I nod.

I discover through people watching and verification from Derek, that it's not uncommon for familiars to date people who aren't the vampires who marked them since not all vampire-human blood bonds include love and romance. But usually, those humans are dating another vampire's familiar. It's no surprise. How many vampires would risk their familiar falling in love with another vampire, and having that vampire over-write their mark? Especially in the castle where many familiars are bought at auctions or carefully picked on trips to the outside world.

I'm unsettled despite being content. For once, I'm not fighting for my survival. It's the first time in my life I can exist and relax. It's hard to fully accept as reality.

Though my freedom has limitations, I find they're much easier to cope with than many of the ones I had until this point. I may not leave the castle or go for late night walks alone, but I know I have a safe place to sleep every night, that nobody is going to hurt me or treat me poorly without consequence like so many of the adults have done in my life. I'll never want for anything after having truly needed so much I wasn't fortunate enough to have.

I wish I could be elated over my new life. I think I should be. I want to be. But perhaps unhappiness and pain have been coursing through me for so long it'll take time for my psyche to flush the old emotions and accept new ones.

XXIV

In the crowded dining room, Laurentius sets my midnight meal of Bratwurst in front of me before settling down in the chair next to me and resting his knee against mine. He takes a slow sip of blood from a gold chalice as Carol cuts herself a slice of sausage.

"That guard, Seth, is organizing a day trip outside for his familiar and others this afternoon. I guess they usually take them once a month. Do you want to come?" Carol asks.

I'd talk through my mouthful if it wouldn't fall in my lap. After quickly chewing, I choke down the mouthful, clear my throat by chugging half my glass of water, and say, "Seriously? They allow day trips here?"

She grins and saws off another round of sausage. "Sometimes. It's especially good for the human nursery children. They rotate groups, so all humans aren't out at once."

"I'll have to ask Viorel," I say, giving her a tight-lipped smile.

If I'm not even allowed outside at night without a guard, I

can only imagine how against me going out during the daylight he'll be when no vampires can run to my rescue.

Her utensils hover above her sausage as she stares at me, her grin almost looking stuck until it slowly sours. Her "Of course," is robotic. She fixes her smile like she's worried someone might think poorly of her reaction to my words.

It must bother her to have no say in my care now. I can't blame her. In her mind, she just got me back after the government blocked her access to me when I was little, and she's lost me again.

Derek, who sits beside Carol, chimes in with, "Lots of familiars aren't permitted outside." He says it like he's trying to reassure me I'm not alone, like this is something as simple as not everyone getting an expensive Christmas present and not my basic freedom being restricted. Does he not care for the sun now that he's a vampire? Like how vampires stop caring as much about the life they take as a side effect of being higher on the food chain?

"So what?" I snap. "I should be allowed."

He offers a sympathetic nod as Laurentius puts his arm around the back of my chair and shoulders.

"I'm sure if Viorel denies your request, he has a good reason," Laurentius says confidently.

I grumble and stab my fork into my sausage, the sudden ache for hot rays on my skin appearing from a forgotten place in my mind. I've been so wrapped up in the changes of late that my new routine of sleeping during the day hasn't bothered me, and I didn't realize Viorel might never let me see the sun again. Nobody explicitly told me I'm not allowed outside during the day ever again, so it never crossed my mind to think it true.

Looking past Carol and Derek for a distraction in the flurry of shifting bodies and happy chatter, my eyes land on a black-eyed man in his thirties. He has brushed back blond hair, and holds a leash attached to the thick leather collar on the neck of a girl with curly, golden locks. Her hands are bound in silk in her lap, her forearms scarred and covered in bite marks. The adoration on the man's face makes me think sweet words are coming off his moving lips as he feeds her from a fork with his free hand. She smiles and giggles after bites, the flesh of her cheeks rosy. I wonder if she's a blood slave, or if they're just a . . . *kinky* . . . couple. Does he let her take trips out into the sunshine?

A nervous laugh escapes Carol as she looks at Laurentius. "He wouldn't stop Marianna from going outside during the day, right? That's . . ." The serious faces of the table have her mashing her lips together and casting her teary gaze down at her plate of food.

"I'll ask," I promise, with no trace of confidence.

"No," Viorel says the moment I step into the sitting room, not even having a chance to inquire aloud.

Each of my steps toward the reading room where his voice came from is heavy with rage.

"Why not?" I demand, as I swing into the doorway.

Viorel sits with his violin, fiddling with the pegs and scowling. I know what he's going to say before his lips shape the words. "It's not safe. If something happens, there are no guards to save you."

"What could go wrong?"

He scoffs and looks at me as if I've asked him what could go wrong from jumping off the castle's highest peak. "You'd be alone with dozens of familiars and blood slaves. Who knows what poison their masters might have put in their minds about me? Someone could attack you, and no guard could stop it. You could face injury from some ridiculous stunt—climbing a tree or sneaking into the stable and taking a swift hoof to the head

—and might be so far from the door that you perish before receiving aid."

I mouth my astonishment, sour as I snarl, *"So even some blood slaves get to go out in the sun?"*

Viorel shoots a scowl at me. "You've ignored my point."

"No, I think it's paranoid. I'll behave."

Shaking his head, he carefully adjusts a peg.

"You're shoving me full of vitamins, telling me I'm basically malnourished and anemic, and you won't let me go outside to soak up natural light?"

"Many humans survive in the dark months of Antarctica sufficiently," he counters. "Between my blood and the supplements, you'll be fine."

"Seasonal depression." I draw the words out nice and slow.

He scoffs at me and flicks his hand dismissively. "Nonsense."

I square my shoulder and cross my arms, narrow eyes locked on him. "I'm serious, Viorel. Seasonal depression is a real issue in winter months because sun exposure goes down. Have you seen the commercials? Do you want me to be *perpetually seasonally depressed?"*

"Cease the dramatics," he grumbles, twisting another peg.

I let my arms fall at my sides. "So, you're really going to take the sun away from me too? I can't leave, can't go for a walk outside in the garden by myself, and can't even stay overnight with friends or my aunt, and you're going to tear one more thing out of my life? You won't even let me see it one last time? Let me admire the castle and the flowers when they're not obscured by shadows?"

He tightens his lips, squinting hard at his violin strings as he runs his fingers across them.

"The last time I saw the sun was in Bellevue, with Denendrius. You're going to let me have my last memory of daylight be when I was a blood slave? You're going to let me think back to that time with Denendrius whenever I recall when I last saw the sun?"

"You're making me feel guilty," he snaps. "Enough."

"Then let me go outside," I whine. "You should feel bad. You're depriving me of a basic human need. You may as well starve me!"

His eyes are full of disappointment, his frown one of disgust. *"Fine,"* he laments, acting like I've bullied him. "You may go out *once more.*"

I want to smile and jump with victory, but I know there's still plenty of hours between now and this afternoon for him to change his mind.

"Thanks," I whisper, turning to my room.

He grunts in disapproval.

Later, Sascha brings me to the grand room where there's already fifty other humans, including Carol. Seth waits with a single gold key in hand and a young man he tells me is his familiar, Jason, who oversees us. He's over six feet tall, muscular like he played football, and somewhere around twenty. His face is boyish despite his blond facial hair in need of a trim.

Seth gives us a run through of rules. The other humans nod along as if they've heard them all repeatedly.

No trying to kill one another—something he puts a strange amount of emphasis on—or fighting. Stay out of the woods, even the trails. Stay out of the stable. Don't do anything you wouldn't do in front of your master. People are trying to sleep inside, so be mindful of noise. When it's time to come inside, *it's time to come inside.*

He gives Jason the key, a walkie talkie, and tells him to stay close to me before sending us on our way.

As Jason leads us down the hall, between the nervous glance Carol sends me, and the presence of so many blood slaves and familiars, the realization settles in that Viorel isn't being silly. Jason alone could kill me, never mind if a handful of blood slaves came together on behalf of their vampires to attack me.

But I haven't seen the sunlight *in weeks*, and I'm not paranoid enough to turn back now. It's probably only mildly more dangerous than being alone with fifty regular human strangers, and it's not like I *ever* had vampires around before Denendrius to protect me from humans in the past.

Still, I can't help but view some of these humans as . . . *wild.* It's the unhinged look in some of their eyes, and how some dart into the garden like unleashed dogs after Jason unlocks the rear exit.

Sunlight spills into the dark hall as he quickly ushers us out. I squint against the yellow rays as I step onto the cobblestone path with Carol and Jason at my side. The bright blue sky is blurry, the heat heavier on my bare arms than I remember.

"It's bright," Jason agrees with a chuckle. "I haven't been out in a couple months, but in my experience, your eyes adjust quickly."

I shade my eyes with my hand like he does, an unfamiliar burn circling around my eye sockets making me want to squeeze my lids closed. I resist the urge, walking alongside Carol as I take in the green of the vast forest, the rich colors of the manicured grass and well-tended flower beds. In the light, I can see how far the garden really stretches to my right, and that beyond the expanse of green field, there are fruit trees in a maze of bushes.

Everything is much more beautiful beneath the sunlight. The songs of birds and the hum of insects make me smile despite the ache in my eyes.

"That's better," Carol mumbles to herself, her hand lowering from her face in my peripheral vision.

The ache in my eyes only grows. They're strained and full of pressure. I stare at the path we walk on through squinting eyes so I don't trip.

"I'm glad Viorel let you come out," Carol says.

"Me too." My discomfort is evident in my voice.

"We should have done lunch down at the picnic tables," Jason says.

"Where are those?" I choke out, not bothering to search for myself.

"Down by the apple and plum trees," Jason says.

I grit my teeth as Carol and Jason delve into a conversation about the garden as we walk. Anger brews in my gut as he points out specific plants and flowers I'm too pained to see, and talks about the ample fruits that have been growing here for years. Some are extinct beyond the veil, like the Silphium and Cry Violet Carol gushes at. I perk up when he mentions how Xavier, a Darkling, has been planting new cannabis strains he's finding on his trips.

"Wait, someone is growing weed here?" I rub my eyes and dare to take a handful of steps blindly, my shoulder grazing Carol's.

Carol scolds me beneath her breath, but Jason titters and says, "Yeah! He's got a little field on the other side of the stable. If anyone goes in without permission, he loses his mind. He can't smoke it since he's a vampire, but he's obsessed with the process and the smell of burning it."

I nod, understanding. "Does he sell any?"

Carol gasps in disapproval.

"He'd probably give you some if you asked, cause you're *you*, but yeah, he sells and trades it with some vampires to give their humans."

"Cool." I'll have to track him down.

I wonder about Viorel's view on weed and if he'd let me smoke some. I bet he wouldn't be as uptight about it since he lets a clan member *grow* it, and he isn't as concerned with new, human laws. Even Denendrius didn't bat an eye at my weed usage.

I groan as pain pulses in my face, my sinuses and throat burning and sending my heart racing with alarm.

I will my eyes to adjust so I can enjoy my last time outside, but my head only throbs and it takes effort to keep my feet moving.

Excited, cheerful chatter fills the warm air around me, the sounds of a Frisbee game making me seethe with jealousy. I bet all their vampires let them take constant day trips to the garden, and I don't even get the *one* I fought Viorel for.

Sweat beads down my spine and soaks the nape of my neck. My legs are damp and itchy from the heat. It's stifling and breathing becomes more difficult with each step.

"I don't feel good. Do you see somewhere we can sit?" I ask.

Carol leads me through the grass and instructs me to sit. The stone is hot against my rear and thighs, and I squirm with discomfort.

"Is Romania usually this hot?" I ask Jason as I unstick my shirt from myself.

His chuckle moves toward me. "This is regular June weather, but it's only fifteen degrees today. It's going to get hotter."

Hotter than this? How can anyone handle living in this part of the world then?

I scratch at my bare arms so hard they feel raw and wipe my eyes when they water, hunching away from the sky while trying to ignore the sweat running down my back and coating my face.

"Pain letting up yet?" Jason asks. "You should be more than okay now . . ."

"Is something else going on?" Carol asks.

"I'm fine," I choke out. "Give me a minute."

Pin pricks cascade over each inch of my flesh. Hot and sharp. I cover my face with my hands, my eyes soaked with unstoppable tears. I wipe them away and brush them off on my pants.

The urge to rush inside and find refuge in the dark is overwhelming. The need screams its demand at me, but I'm too stubborn to listen. *I want to stay outside.*

Carol grabs my hand and gasps in horror. "Marianna look at me—Jason!"

I pull my hands away from my face, the sun like fire in my retinas. I do my best to look at her, but there are white patches in my vision, the colors a blur.

My heart palpitates, my stomach knotted so tight everything has moved into my esophagus and is threatening to spray out of me. I swear my eyes are wide with panic, yet there's nothing but darkness.

I gag and cough into my palm. Warm wetness sprays against it, followed by my shrill cry of terror. I have a sick suspicion my hand is covered in blood, but I can't see it.

What the fuck is happening to me?

Though I hear his gasp, I can't see Jason's expression as he yanks me from the bench, the electric click of his walkie talkie followed by his panicked words. "Seth, I'm bringing Marianna inside. She needs help quick! She's hurt."

My heart slams into my stomach, my steps faltering as he and Carol drag me along through the grass.

The garden fills with hushed whispers. Even Carol's and Jason's voices sound like I'm listening to them with ear plugs in.

The pain in my face becomes unbearable and I might cry out if my jaw wasn't clenched in agony. Their touch is excruciating.

Their sudden stop has me retching.

"Holy shit," Jason says, his voice paired with the sound of the castle door unlocking.

"*What?*" I choke out.

Carol tries to subdue the panic in her shrill voice as she says, "You'll be okay, honey."

"You just puked blood everywhere," Jason says.

I'm thankful for his honesty, though terror has my mind spinning.

When the door shuts behind me, my blind gaze rakes around for something visual to latch onto.

"I can't see anything," I cry. "I can't see."

I want someone to tell me it's okay, how we're all in darkness because the candles are unlit, but they exchange words I miss and drag me along over the hard floor like they can see where they're going.

"What happened?" Seth's muffled voice sounds so far, but I can feel his cold breath on my face.

"I don't know," Jason says.

It's difficult to hear them through my hammering heart and rapid breaths, only the words *blood* and *Viorel* clear to me.

"Viorel," I choke out. *"Please."*

Warm hands are exchanged for cold ones, and I'm lifted off the ground before we move swiftly. Seth shouts for Viorel, the familiar sound of his iron door groaning open coming next.

The floor appears beneath my feet, and I grope around blindly until there's silk against my palms and the glorious taste of Viorel's blood on my lips.

"Who did this?" Viorel snarls as my eyes find relief beneath his touch. "What happened?"

I lap up his blood so fast I choke and grip to his forearm to stop myself from falling.

Things sound normal again.

"Nobody," Seth says. "Jason said she was complaining about the sun since stepping outside. It spiraled from there."

"The sun," Viorel scoffs.

He takes one of my hands off his forearm, and I flinch at the feel of his fangs tearing into my wrist. It's a dull pain compared to the one coating the rest of my body.

He hisses in fury as he releases my arm, the dull burn vanishing beneath his delicate touch.

"There's no evidence of drugs or poisons in her blood, so how—" He stops speaking abruptly.

"Jason swears nobody touched her, and there's no scent on her or injury to suggest otherwise."

"The sun," Viorel repeats flatly.

There's a heavy silence, and I gasp for breath and stifle my cries as Viorel pulls his wrist away from my mouth. I blink rapidly with the return of my sight, only a few feet between me and Seth, until Viorel yanks my body against his and wraps his arms around me. I bury my aching cheek in the cold silk of his chest and see the blood on my hands, how it coats the flesh of my arm like a sheet of sweat.

I feel Viorel's low command in his chest when he says, "Leave us, Seth."

Viorel keeps his arms around me as he shifts us to the sofa and seats me, the movement making tears stream down my face. I gasp for breath as I shift my hips so I'm sitting more comfortably beside him, still turned against his chest.

I bite my bottom lip to hold back my agonized whimpers as he slowly glides his soft touch over my raw arms. My sharp breaths slow with the fading pain. I let my eyes fall closed as he brushes his hand over my face and head. I stiffen when he pulls my legs over his, though exhale a deep breath as he chases the pinpricks from the length of them.

Finally, the pain is gone. I take my first steady breath and sink into him.

"Thank you," I whisper.

I expect an "I told you so" since I'm no longer suffering, but he merely holds my head against his chest and releases a breath from the depth of his lungs, like his lungs have been lacking since I came in.

It's strange being in his arms despite sleeping next to him for so many nights. I suppose he seems too proper and rigid of a man to imagine him taking part in any sort of regular, friendly touch. Aside from holding Tassa when she leaped onto his lap, I've never so much as seen him pat a guard on the back or shake someone's hand. There's usually so much lonely space around him.

His hug is more meaningful. I let myself admit it's a nice feeling to know he cares.

Finally managing a full breath, I carefully wrap my arms around his midsection so they don't rest limply in my lap. I hold my breath as he places his other hand on my stomach for a long moment, only exhaling when he continues to my waist and rests there.

"I'm sorry," he murmurs.

"For what?" I whisper. The feel of his silk gown is smooth against my cheek, and I nuzzle against it and breathe in the faint scent of gardenia trapped in the threads.

"I should have been sterner with you." He sighs, breath tickling the top of my head. "I knew it was unwise and still, I let you convince me. I didn't want you to be mad at me, and my negligence hurt you."

I swallow and tighten my arms a bit around him. My limbs are heavy as his blood dilutes the adrenaline left over in my body. I let myself relax against him, something about his touch making me feel infinitely safe. With his power, and how close he is, I know the evilest men could break through the iron door and he'd protect me.

"It's the sun's fault," I whisper.

"It's my blood's fault," he counters.

"Why did it make the sun burn me?"

"I can't say for certain." Viorel runs his fingers through the length of my hair, and I can't help the tingles or the shudder moving through me.

"Has that happened before?"

"No. None of my past familiars experienced what a vampire does from having a millisecond of sun exposure. You were sweating blood and your flesh was burning. Your eyes *burned*, Marianna. The whites were flooded with blood and fluid, and your pupils were destroyed. Much longer in the light and you likely would have perished. Your human body cannot deal with more than a fraction of what a vampire goes through."

My heart hammers at the horrifying thought of what I must have looked like. "What's your theory?"

After a silent beat he must fill with his thoughts, he says, "There must be something about you reacting to my blood."

"But that didn't happen with Denendrius's blood."

"My blood is . . . *different*. Stronger. I think you're different as well."

"How?" I furrow my brow, my heartbeat tripping. "Is your blood turning me?"

His chin brushes the top of my head as he shakes his. "No."

I frown. "How do you think I'm different?"

"I can't say for certain," he repeats.

I suspect he knows something, but I am too exhausted to fight for a proper answer.

We fall into a comfortable silence without the expectation of more conversation. Our bodies stay in place, and I wait for him to pull away, not wanting to be the first one to do so.

With my eyes closed and my cheek against his quiet chest, the minutes slip by without me feeling them, pulling me along until Viorel's voice snags me.

"I'll carry you to bed," he murmurs. "You're falling asleep."

"I can w-walk," I slur, drunk with exhaustion.

"I don't want you to." He lowers the arm I've stretched across him and hooks his beneath both of my knees as the other moves from my head to my waist. A sleepy gasp brushes past my lips as he stands with me, my head sliding up to rest in the crook of his neck.

"Yours?" he whispers.

I think of his bed, how soft it is with the warmth of the fire and how the heavy drapes make me feel like I'm sleeping in a blanket fort. Right now, the idea of sleeping in my room is akin to the idea of sleeping in a cold box.

I can't feel his steps as he holds me, so I flinch at the suddenness of him shifting and lowering me onto his mattress. He spreads the heavy blankets over me, clicks on the fireplace, and sends me off to dreamland with his bloodied wrist against my mouth.

XXV

I wake to the blanket drawing back from my face.

"You should wake up for dinner before it's cold," Viorel suggests.

The familiar smell of tomato sauce and beef has me kicking the blankets off and taking a detour to the washroom to pee and wipe blood from my face before sitting at a cooling plate of spaghetti. Seth stares at it from where he stands nearby against the wall.

"Thanks," I whisper as I jab my fork into the sauce-saturated noodles, the emotion of the morning clinging to me like the dried blood on my arms. I wish I'd had the energy to wash off before falling asleep.

Instead of perching on his throne as usual, Viorel sits at my side with a presence so close and intensely attentive that I gulp and angle my body away for elbow space.

Seth crosses his arms, gaze cast down on me.

"Worried my body is going to try killing me after this afternoon?" I ask with a stiff laugh as I lift my fork to my mouth and look between them.

"I simply want to be next to you," Viorel says, gently motioning to my meal. "Go on."

I don't buy it, but I spin noodles around my fork and shove them past my lips. Something sharp hits my gums like sand grinding against them. The back of my throat and nose itches as I chew. I scowl as my eyes water, my mouth on fire.

"Why is it spicy?" The taste of pennies comes through the sauce. "I don't mean to be an ass"—my voice cracks, and I cough against the burn—"but if this is a new recipe, the chef really botched it. I can't taste anything through the pain."

"It's not a new recipe," Seth says. "It's basic spaghetti."

As I'm about to swallow, Viorel's hand appears like a vice around my throat, and I wheeze out a trapped breath. My heart slams into my ribs so hard the room spins and the fork drops from my grip and clatters on the silver platter.

"Don't swallow," he warns as he grabs the cloth napkin and holds it at my chin. "Spit."

I do as instructed, tears muddying my sight. He releases my throat. I gasp for breath and clutch my neck as Viorel flicks his arm so his sleeve falls away from his wrist. He swiftly rips into it with his fangs. I catch the flicker of panic in his eyes—so fast it might have been a reflection of my own—as he shoves his bloody wrist against my lips.

The relief is instant, his blood soothing my burning tongue and throat.

"I'm sorry to be so violent with you," he croons as he brushes my hair behind my shoulder and trails his hand down my back. "But we don't want to know what would happen if you swallowed so much garlic."

Garlic? Why would garlic hurt me?

My eyes flicker to the open napkin of my spat-out food and widen. It's full of blood.

I hyperventilate as Viorel takes his wrist back. "Why did you lace my food with garlic?"

Viorel smooths his sleeve against his healed arm. "After your reaction to sunlight, I wanted to see if you'd react similarly to garlic, as vampires do."

"You two thought garlic might hurt me . . . *so you gave me fucking garlic?*" I snap, my fear sharpening the edge of my words.

"Speculations are not as good as definitive answers," Viorel explains.

"What the fuck! Viorel, *what's wrong with me?*"

He flicks his gaze toward Seth, who nods once and leaves out the iron door.

"Tell me," I demand once the door is locked.

"Marianna, you have severe memory issues," he says, eyes brimming with excitement.

My heart pounds. "Okay?"

"You're likely two years older, which leaves two years unaccounted for in your life—which you're also unable to remember a single moment of."

"So?"

"You are emotionally immature and socially stunted. But . . ." He adjusts closer, the corner of his lip quirking up. "Your artistic abilities are incredible, and you were quite good at writing and reading, even for someone who was likely seven."

I don't bother responding, simply waiting for whatever point is next.

"You hit puberty late, but I can smell—taste—the normality of your hormones."

Gnawing at my cheek, I lower my eyes to my lap.

"The sun burns you; garlic brings you pain . . . It's as if the remnants of something in your body is reacting to the power of my blood."

I furrow my brow and twist my fingers together in my lap until my bones protest in pain.

"Denendrius's mark took a remarkable amount of time to take hold of you too," he adds. "I'm not sure if you understand that."

I shrug. "I think somebody mentioned it."

"Last, no vampire can hypnotize you." He hooks his index finger beneath my chin and lifts my head, so my eyes are on him.

I swallow a lump of emotion as he drops his hand. "So?"

"Do you know the kinds of people who can't be hypnotized? The kinds of people who burn in the sunlight and suffer the effects of garlic?"

I blink at him, thinking it's a trick question.

"Vampires," he articulates.

I scratch my head and wrinkle my nose in confusion.

Viorel merely stares at me with glittering, awe-filled eyes and an enamored smile.

I realize he's waiting for me to take this bullet point list of his and draw a straight line to the answer myself, and it hits me.

It hits me so hard I feel upside down with my stomach ready to fall out of me.

"*I wasn't a . . .*" I mouth.

He nods. "You must have been. What else makes sense?"

There's a dimness to the room like half the candles were blown out, and I can't hear anything but my own panicked breath and my blood rushing in my head.

Cold hands on mine anchor me to the room, stopping me from slipping further away into the chaos of my mind.

"I wonder how it happened," Viorel says, voice slipping through the cracks of my crumbling reality. "I suppose we'll find out when Mateo speaks to your mother."

I want to call him a liar, call him crazy . . . but something inside me tells me this is the answer I've been looking for.

Still, I don't want it to be true. What does it mean if it's true?

Viorel slips his arm around me, his icy breath like pinpricks against my face. "How fortunate I am. I've never heard such a successful case of a child vampire being cured, and I've got her as my familiar."

XXVI

I'm unsure how long I sit silently with Viorel's arm around me while feeling like I'm gripping to the brittle edges of reality with the pads of my fingers, like dangling in a rocky fissure and ready to fall against soul-breaking shards of rock below.

I don't want to have been a child vampire. I don't want to be any more abnormal than I already am. Isn't my past messy enough without adding vampirism to it?

Something burns in me, so hot it reaches from my skin to my marrow.

Yet, this would explain so much. I wonder how I never thought of it myself.

But a thought comes to me on my own. One that would make my new reality a hundred times more brittle if it were true.

"I look *nothing* like my mother," I whisper, thinking of her thick dark hair and deep brown eyes. Our faces aren't even similar. "Shouldn't I at least have some of her features even if I took most of my father's genes?"

"There was a DNA test in your file. Your mother was required to take one before you were legally registered. She is your mother, Marianna. Besides, it's not uncommon for children to look different from their biological parents. Genetics are complex."

Still, Bonnie being my biological mother feels like a lie, the idea of DNA proof making me clench my fists.

"DNA results can be faked. My mom had a judge paid off so she could regain custody of me, so who says she didn't pay someone to fudge those?" I argue.

Too many seconds pass without a response from Viorel that I turn my face up to him. His eyes are narrow on me, and I imagine gears whirring rapidly behind his eyes.

"Where is your mother from?" he asks.

I twist my fingers together. "She moved from Mexico to the United States with her parents when she was a kid. That's all I know. I don't know how long her family was there or if her parents were born in Mexico too."

"Your wording is peculiar."

I quirk a brow.

He says, "Her family. Her parents. Not *my family, my grandparents.*"

I scratch my cheek and shrug. "I suppose I've never thought of them as my family. Never wondered much about them at all, to be honest. I know *nothing* about them."

Viorel squints at me for a long moment with a furrowed brow before taking a careful breath and saying, "It's unlikely she's your mother."

Though the idea was mine, his agreement sends a hot stroke of panic through my center. "Why?"

"With the DNA evidence under scrutiny, it raises questions I hadn't thought to consider before. If she hid you from the government, I doubt she received prenatal care, especially if she had you at home. Since she was a heavy meth user with possession charges dating back long before your supposed birth, I doubt she ceased usage during pregnancy. The fact you are still alive is a miracle. Meth usage can lead to a host of complications, never mind high rates of stillbirth or premature birth. It's likely you two would have needed medical attention upon delivery. Plus, even if she had help from her boyfriend, I doubt the two of them were equipped to deal with a meth-addicted newborn. You may be emotionally delayed and have behavioral issues like many children born in such circumstances, but from what I've read, many of those children also have cognitive impairments and learning disabilities—amongst many other potential health issues. You have no such issues. Quite the opposite."

I gawk at him, never having considered any of it myself. "Then how did she end up with me?"

Viorel clicks his tongue. "Mateo will pry answers from her."

Clasping my head in my hands like I can stop it from spinning, I give my head an incredulous shake and stare across the room in stunned silence.

If Bonnie isn't my mom, *who was?*

I frown. "I could technically be decades old."

"Hundreds, possibly."

"All those years of memories and I can't remember *a single thing?*" I drag my hands down my face and drop them in my lap as I heave out a breath. I couldn't remember something as world-shattering as the existence of vampires?

My back straightens, Denendrius's violent and furious words tearing through my thoughts.

"Of all the things you've forgotten about, vampires are one of them?"

I never questioned him about it at the time. But what if I knew what his black eyes meant when he approached me as a child in Enchanted Land and went with him so easily because his appearance stirred something forgotten inside me?

"Can I see Denendrius?" The question makes me sweat with anticipation for his likely anger. I fumble to explain myself. "I want to ask him about those twelve days he kidnapped me. He alluded to me having forgotten about vampires when he took me to the woods to kill me. Maybe he knows something without realizing it."

His expression is unreadable as he stands. "Seth will take you."

I lower myself onto the floor before Denendrius's cell, leaning back against the oubliette as I straighten my legs and cross my ankles. Asil sits on the edge of the oubliette above me with his arms crossed, Seth having been too preoccupied to escort me.

"I didn't think I'd see you again," Denendrius utters through busted lips, pain sharp in his voice as he drags himself on his hands and knees to the bars, the sound of a chain following him. Large bruises cover his back and shoulders, bloody evidence of restraints around his wrists. A shackle on his ankle disappears beyond the reach of candlelight.

I twist my hands in my lap. "I have questions."

His laugh is airy, arms shaky as he lowers himself onto his stomach to lay on the stone with his legs stretched behind him. "It's not that you missed me?"

I don't let his words move me, keeping my expression as unemotional as possible, though there's a bit of snark in my voice when I say, "Nobody misses you, Denendrius."

Denendrius stares at me through narrow eyes, the corner of his lip twitching to expose his fang. He shivers. "What makes you think I want to answer your questions? I've had a hard day."

I glower and let the first one off my tongue. "When you

kidnapped me when I was five, did you notice anything *strange* about me that might suggest I wasn't a typical kid?"

He stares at me blankly, his crimson eyes dead. "I have limited energy, Marianna."

"Viorel thinks I might have been a child vampire at some point, and a year or two older," I explain.

Expression unchanging, he tilts his head and looks me over for an obnoxious amount of time. "Huh."

"What?" I snap, convinced he's going to fuck around and refuse any sort of worthwhile answer.

"That would explain a lot."

I gape at him, leaning forward off the stone. "Like what?"

"You were unbothered by me being a vampire. Told me you already knew they existed. I figured that was typical—like kids believing in fairies and Santa—but you were unfazed when I showed you my fangs."

"How the fuck did your vampirism come up in conversation? Were you trying to scare me?" I snap.

"You noticed I wasn't eating." His arms and shoulders spasm with another shiver. "I'd leave you in the motel when I went hunting. You figured something was up since I wouldn't eat anything you ate and wouldn't bring you along to eat with me. You wanted answers, so I told you I ate people."

My jaw lowers. "You told five-year-old me you ate people?"

His teeth chatter. "W-what was I supposed to tell you?"

"Anything else?" I snarl.

His flat expression is unchanged. "Doesn't matter. You acted as if it was normal." He thinks for a long moment, then a strained and tickled smile spreads across his lips as he releases a single breathy chuckle. "You were awfully adorable about it, offering me your little wrists and neck whenever I'd feed you—"

"You fucking drank from me?" My hands curl into fists on my lap.

His eyes darken, lips in a sour scowl. "*No.* You really think so low of me? That I'd drink from a little child?"

I scoff and lift my hands to motion vaguely around the dungeon. "Yeah, Denendrius, I do."

A pained line appears between his brows as he rubs his lips together, like he's waiting for the hurt of my words to pass so he can speak. "Why does Huarsar think you were a child vampire?"

"Vicrel," I correct, before telling him the reasons.

He nods along, then whispers, "It makes sense to me."

"Can you think of anything else?" I press, my breaths rougher from the stress of being so close to him, and the damp, acrid stench in the air.

He heaves out a breath, eyes trailing over my face as he lifts himself onto his forearms and elbows to think.

"Hurry," I snap, itching to leave.

Denendrius frowns, tilting his head as he says, "You don't think you've ever seen a horse in person before."

I cross my arms tightly over my chest. "So?"

His eyes tighten on me. "On our second date, you told me that. I thought it was ridiculous. Who hasn't seen a horse before? And besides, when you were little, you told me you had."

My heart skips. "What did I say?"

"That you've had hundreds of horses when you were little. We stopped at a ranch on the way to Maine for a trail ride. You insisted on knowing how to hold the reins, but I didn't believe you and wouldn't let you. It was such a silly number for someone who was little. I thought you were trying to be funny or impress me."

I gape at him. "Did I say anything else about having horses?"

He shakes his head, and I lean mine back against the stone and grunt in annoyance.

"What else do you remember that could be a sign?" I ask.

"Give me a minute to think."

I grit my teeth as the minutes drone on, the sound of shrieks and agonized, thirsty groans echoing with the sound of beating on bars from the depths of the dungeon. The smell of the dungeon fills my nose, more choking than the previous two times I was down here.

"There's nothing else you remember, is there?" I growl, fury hot in my stomach.

"No," he admits sheepishly, his smile shaky. "But can you blame me for trying to keep you down here with me as long as I can?"

I scowl. "You've stolen enough time from me, Denendrius."

His dull eyes adopt a brief glimmer as he whispers, "And I'll steal all the rest of it, sweetheart."

My harsh glare levels with his. "Do you promise there are no clues you're purposely leaving out?"

He lifts his shaky hand and traces an X over his heart. "Promise. Will you return if I think of anything more?"

"Just tell a guard," I grumble.

"It's all right, Marianna," Viorel says gently from where he stands in the middle of the sitting room as I waver back in, feeling ten times worse than when I left.

I think of laying on the floor where I stand but convince myself to make it to the sofa where I curl up in the fetal position. "What if that's not even my real name?"

Viorel purses his lips as he moves to his throne and sits. From his lack of rebuttal, it's clear he shares the same thought.

I squeeze my eyes closed, temples pounding. "I could have an entirely different set of parents if Bonnie isn't my mom. So many things could have happened. My head is spinning. They're dead, aren't they? Alaire and Edmond told me they destroy vampires who create vampire children."

Solemn, Viorel says, "That would have been the most likely outcome, yes."

A thousand questions barrage me, knocking my reach away from my hope to settle into the castle and leave my past behind.

"It was Alaire and Edmond who turned me back, wasn't it?" I realize. "They were *so* apologetic when they discovered I had a hard life and seemed to be hiding something from me. I thought they found my school because the computer I was on was there, but maybe they already knew when I told them my name."

"I believe it was them. Under my reign, vampire children are to be brought here if discovered. Nobody may experiment with the cure on them, which should be an easy rule to follow since the cure is incredibly rare. They admitted to experimenting in your presence and brought the idea to me decades ago. If it was not their doing, I will be flabbergasted."

"What if it wasn't them? Then the chances of me finding the truth are slim to none, aren't they?"

Viorel gives me an apologetic nod.

"I'll turn if Mateo shows up empty-handed," I decide on a whim, a vast emptiness inside me only clarity and the return of missing memories can fill. "There's no point staying human if I don't know who I am."

"You are *Marianna*," Viorel says. "Your human years are what matter."

"I know you're trying to comfort me, but we both know that's not true. My potential life as a vampire is directly affecting me right now and has been my whole human life. From biology to behavior . . ." I shake my head, eyes burning with tears. "I'll never see the sun again because of it."

Viorel sighs softly as he stands and motions for me to move over. I sit hunched and wipe my eyes.

"You're not ready to be a vampire yet. Enjoy humanity for a few more years. Besides, I think you've had enough change for a while. Once you're fully settled, we'll discuss it."

There's no playfulness in the next roll of my eyes. "Sounds like an excuse to have blood on tap, and so it's easier to contain me after I'm already used to being stuck here."

"No, Marianna." Viorel's frown is heavy as he rests his hand on my knee. "I believe you're going to have a troublesome time —more than most—for a bit after your transformation, and I want you to have secure relationships built with your friends and family so you can lean on them. I don't want you to feel foreign in your own body and mind while also being in a foreign place, all before you've distanced yourself from your most recent traumas. When you turn, you'll be in a heightened emotional state. Changing before you're ready is a recipe for disaster, *especially* if you're doing it in hopes of unburying traumatic memories."

I swallow a knot. "Why—Why do you think it's going to suck at first?" Is he assuming remembering everything will emotionally cripple me?

"It's a concern," he agrees. "But moreover, I'm concerned how you will react to vampire venom. I've had familiars turned in the past, and the ones who survived were like any other Darkling or Child of Stars. But I don't know how my blood will impact your experience as a vampire, considering these circumstances."

My heart slams against my ribs. "You think it could kill me, don't you? Or make me all fucked up as a vampire?"

He sighs. "I don't know what to think if I'm honest. But I want to assume you survive and succeed as a vampire."

"Great," I grumble, hugging myself.

"I wholly understand your pain, Marianna. My past is lost to me as well. I often wonder if I had a family, if my disappearance caused them undue hardship. My maker said I was a leader, and I still cannot imagine who my people were—how they lived or what they believed—or how or what I led. Did I lead a tribe? A nation? A religion? Did I care for my people, or was I a tyrant? Did anybody miss me when I was saved from death or stolen for it? Who were my parents? What did they name me?"

"I think I'm understanding how difficult that is." I stare down at my lap. "Especially since we don't completely know how much older I am, either."

"Yes, but you'll find your way through it, with or without answers."

"How?"

"By making peace with it." He rests his hand on mine. "There are many mysteries we'll never have the answers to, some more bothersome than others, but mysteries we must cope with, nonetheless. The distance time provides and shaping yourself with new memories is helpful as well."

I twist my hands in my lap, and forward Denendrius's clues of my vampirism to Viorel before saying, "Can I try horseback riding?"

"No," he says, not seeming to fully consider it. "In the future, yes."

My sigh is deflating. It's not worth arguing over. "Fine. Thanks for trying to comfort me," I whisper as I stand and drift over the floor, unable to feel the cold crevices of the stones beneath my feet. "I'm going to bed."

Viorel's pitying gaze is like pins in my back as I slip into his bed to stare numbly into the fireplace like I'm daring the flames to reach out and consume me.

I don't want this. I don't want to be special, especially if it has the potential to be confusing and painful. Being a human was painful and confusing enough. Why can't I just be like everyone else? Why couldn't I be born to average parents in an average neighborhood? Why couldn't I have average issues to discuss with my average friends? It seems like the harder I fight for normalcy, the further I find myself from it.

XXVII

After hours of twisting thoughts, the bed lowers behind me. I peek out from under the blanket to find Viorel slipping beneath the covers. I tense for a moment, only my thudding heart moving as I tell myself I don't have to feel on edge around him. As his soft hand rests on my waist, I exhale my anxieties and close my eyes. Tears sneak out from beneath my lids as I grit my teeth with aching frustration.

"I've come to feel alone with you," he whispers.

I sniffle, my hot breath bouncing back at me against the blanket. "I keep thinking about who might have turned me, and why. Was I sick or hurt? Was it accidental? Did they not want me to grow up?"

"You will drive yourself mad with questions. Trust me. I do it frequently."

"I'm furious at Alaire and Edmond." I'm not sure if I'm angry at them for turning me back—it's nice to grow up and not be bound by immortality as a child—or not telling me.

His chuckle is light in my ear, and I think it's an attempt—

though failed—to ease my anxiety. "They were good men, regardless of their refusal to leave the cure and child vampires alone. It was never used with malice. They truly thought they were doing the right thing for the children. It is spectacularly dangerous to have child vampires out in the world, which is why I order bounty hunters to bring them to me when discovered and punish the creators. I suppose they thought giving them the cure was mercy, and being an immortal child is misery."

"The children here aren't miserable?" I wonder. "I can't imagine being stuck as a young child and not being miserable."

Viorel makes a grunt informing me he's heard me, but it's a moment before he finally says, "Most of them aren't. Many don't understand the lives they're missing or are at peace with their reality and comprehend the upside to eternal play and lack of responsibilities. They're thankful they never grow old. They see dozens of other unchanging children, and thousands of adults who never age as well. Immortality is normal to them. Some were turned when they were ill and steps from death— no promise of a future anyway—and are grateful their creators preserved them. But some others, more rarely, are desperate for change they cannot have."

I swallow a lump of emotion, breath coming a bit easier knowing most of the children upstairs aren't trapped in misery. "What about the ones who are miserable?"

Another long pause filled with his thumb moving back and forth over my stomach. "Sometimes death is the only natural remedy to ease a soul."

My brow furrows. "They're killed if they're unhappy?"

"The ones old enough to choose and understand death are given a choice, though few choose it and eventually cope. I will never offer the cure."

"Why?" I whisper. "What if someone would rather take their chances?"

"No," he reaffirms. "The fact Rayonne, that rat, and possibly you survived it, is miraculous. Even he was suffering disastrous effects, and Rayonne was—at minimum—struggling mentally. She was only mortal for a year, there's no guarantee she wouldn't have succumbed to an ill fate in the future as most do. If it's true they gave you the cure, you are a phenomenon for surviving so many years, and yet your body and mind suffered from it."

Letting the conversation drop, I pull the blanket over my head and lay like that with him until my breath suffocates me, and it's time to roll over. I turn onto my back to stare up at the bones of his bed and the iron grate between me and everything else in the world.

Viorel rolls onto his back too, his hand resting near mine between us. "I'm sorry."

My voice is limp. "It's not your fault this time. It's not your fault I might have been a vampire, and that my blood reacts to yours this way. You didn't know."

"Still. I know humans love their sun. I don't understand, but I know."

"Yeah," I breathe.

It's not that the sun is so great, but now it's one more thing stopping me from leaving the castle. Half a day where I can't— under any circumstances—go outside. It shouldn't matter, since it's not like I was taking day trips outside anyway, but it never occurred to me I should enjoy the last time I saw it. Some part of me didn't think that was it.

A quiet cry sneaks past my lips with a hiccup, and a fresh stream of tears

"I'm tired of crying," I complain. "I wish I could go back to never crying. It was easier carrying hate and being angry all the time."

"Nothing wrong with crying," Viorel consoles. "Everybody cries."

Not him, I bet.

"You've never seen me," he says. "I don't feel shame about it. If someone as strong as I can cry, I think it gives everyone else permission."

I squeeze my eyes closed and bite my quivering lip.

"I've got you," he whispers as he entwines his fingers through mine.

The act, mixed with the sudden sound of wind and squawking birds, has my eyes snapping open.

I'm lying down beside Viorel under a blue and warm sunny sky, our hands locked together on the grass between us.

My heart hammers so hard I lose control of my breath. "How did I get here?" I gasp, completely aghast. *"The sun!* How're you—"

"We're still in bed," he murmurs, unflinching at the bright rays striking down on us. "If anyone were to walk into the room, we would appear to be sleeping. But this is fantasy."

"You're creating all this with your mind?" My eyes flicker over the perfect replicas of cottony clouds spotting the smooth blue of a summer afternoon.

"Yes."

"It doesn't feel like a dream. It feels as real as reality," I say.

"We're not dreaming. We're someplace else. I can't fully explain how the ability works, but I know it does. I only have a vague awareness of the bedroom. Enough to know if someone comes upon us."

A grin stretches my cheeks and I pull in a deep breath that carries the smell of salt, flowers, and wet grass into the depth of my lungs. The heat of the sun calms my heart, the gentle rays caressing the flesh that were cool with the subbasement air moments ago.

"I'd never know you haven't seen the sun," I tell him. "It's perfect. Exactly how I remember it."

His grip tightens ever so slightly on my hand. "As I said,

humans love their sun, know it so well it's easy to steal pieces from their memories and mend them together for my enjoyment. Vampires who were once human remember it even better."

A warm and gentle gust of wind rolls over us, loose strands of my hair fluttering around me. I wiggle my toes in the blades of thick grass and admire the realness of it. Even the birds squawking in the distance sound real and remind me of the ocean. With that thought, I swear I hear the gentle collision of waves.

In my peripheral, Viorel watches me with a soft smile.

"What happens if I let go of your hand? Do I end up back in bed?" I tighten my grip on him, not wanting to leave yet.

"No. What we do here has no impact on the real world. Only I can end this. I could keep you trapped here as long as I want," he teases with a charming smile.

My eyes widen with wonder. "I could walk over to that tree and touch it?"

He nods.

"And if I were to run to the water I hear, would I find it? Or is there some sort of border?" I ask, excitement making my words rush out of me.

"This is reality for the time being. You can do as you like."

Slowly, I pull my hand from Viorel's and sit, testing the feel of the grass by brushing my palm over the tips of it. "Wow." I dig my nails into the soil, moist earth beneath my nails until I pull them out and grin at how it covers my fingertips.

I catch him studying me from the corner of his eye. "This makes you happy?"

"It's nice to see the sun without it hurting," I admit. "Nice to be out of the room, even if we're technically still in it." I inhale the summer day into myself like I can keep it with me forever. "No wonder you don't go crazy from being down there all the time. I didn't realize this is what you meant by having fantasies."

Viorel sits up beside me, looking out of place with the warm sun against his pallid flesh. It reflects strangely in his claret eyes, making them lighter than they are in the dark.

"I've never seen the ocean before," I tell him, though I realize—with the possibility of so many memories missing—it might not be true.

"Go on then," he urges. "I'll follow."

I leap to my feet, excitement and adrenaline pounding through me as I turn in a slow circle to take in my surroundings. It's green grass and patches of wildflowers and oak trees each way, the crisp scent they release into the air filling me and easing the weight of my reality. Squirrels chatter and dart from one bunch of trees to another, birds taking flight with the disturbance and gliding through the limitless sky.

Turning, I dart up a small incline toward the sound of waves. The grass whips my bare feet, my calves burning. I pause at the top, breathless and full of awe at the vast milky blue of the endless water and the foreignness of the beach. The water is so clear I can see the bottom and the movement of life between the patches of green aquatic plants.

"The sand is pink?" I squint through the bright day at it, like it's an illusion.

Viorel appears at my side. "It exists in the real world too," he assures me.

"*Wow.*" I descend toward the beach, my feet hitting the pink sand halfway down, the heat of it warming my soles.

I race through it and toward the water, pink kicking up behind me until I hit wet sand and come to a slow stop as the tide washes over the tops of my feet.

"Can you conjure me up a bikini?" I jest.

He chuckles. "Not quite how it works, sorry."

I pull in a deep breath and contemplate stripping down to

my underwear and bra since they're practically the same thing. Yoga pants and water are going to make for a subpar first-time ocean experience.

Blowing out my breath, I turn to Viorel and wave my hand at him to turn, not wanting to give him a strip show. "Divert your eyes, I'm taking off a layer."

He obliges, turning his back to me and clasping his hands behind him as I strip my top and pants off.

"Okay, it's safe to look!" I holler as I crash into the water, foamy waves gently pulling me away from the shore. It's a pleasant temperature, and I dig my toes into the soft sand, bits of weeds brushing my ankles as I wade deeper to my shoulders. Dipping my hair back, I stare up at the clear sky and mouth my astonishment.

When a wave fills my ears and nose with water, I exhale the stinging saltwater and roughly shake my head.

"Can I drown?"

His smirk is crooked, the edge of his gown teasing the waves lapping at the shore. "No. I might have to come in after you or banish the water should you go under. Why?"

"I don't know how to swim," I admit.

He chuckles. "I could teach you."

I try to imagine him swimming, and my brow raises. "Really? Okay, why not."

He twirls his finger in the air, smirking. "Spin around."

I roll my eyes, teasing as I rotate toward the horizon and glide my arms atop the rippling waves.

A moment later, his voice comes from a mere foot behind me. "You can turn around now."

I twist in surprise, splashing and laughing as I fight for my footing.

Viorel's grinning, the water rippling around his biceps, the tips of his long hair floating like mine does. He's slim as I imagined, though his torso, shoulders, and arms are made of lean muscles, like he got them from running and doing physical labor instead of intentional weightlifting. My eyes trace over the straight scars on his pale skin, most on the side of his biceps aside from a more prominent one across his ribs on his side. There's a thick, white scar beneath the outside end of his collarbone I can't help but poke.

My throat dries at the feel of his chest beneath my finger, and I clear it before asking, "What's that from?"

"Likely an arrow or spear," he says simply, no sign in his eyes the scar is anything more than a blemish to him. "There's a matching one on my back from where it exited."

"Huh, neat." I fight the urge to ask him how he got it, knowing he can't give me an answer.

"If you think that's neat . . ." He rotates, and my eyes land on the four evenly spaced scars raking diagonally across his back.

"Wow. It looks like an animal took a swipe at you."

He grins. "Yes, and it must have been a huge animal."

I stare at him with a wide smile, trying to imagine what sort of large and clawed animals might have existed in his time and area.

"So, can you float on your back?" he asks as he turns back around.

I try, and fail—well, *flail*—spectacularly.

"Let me help." His gentle touch on my waist shocks me, his temperature colder than the water.

I'm a quick learner, we find. Though, I can see in his eyes as he shows me backstrokes and front strokes, treading, and butterflies, that it's with a suspicious amount of ease. I'm glad he doesn't ponder aloud if I might have known how to swim once-upon-a-time and that muscle memory is helping me. He lets me enjoy this fantasy world without the stressors of the real one.

A gray fin weaving through the waves and toward us interrupts our lessons. I think a shark is about to come upon us until a spray of air breaks through the water, and the squeak of a dolphin has my eyes widening as I stand aghast, my heart racing with excitement.

I'm frozen in the waves as it swims in a tight circle around us. Viorel lifts my stiff arm from the water, and I straighten my fingers in time for them to glide alongside its smooth and rubbery skin.

"That makes you happy?" Viorel murmurs beside me, his other hand on my lower back.

All I can do is madly nod—the child inside me who was obsessed with dolphins and aquatic life squealing—as the muscles in my face hurt from smiling. My eyes are glued to it until it swims away.

We stay there for hours, Viorel watching me with a tickled smile as I split my time between hunting down seashells and practicing swimming. We stay so long the blue of the sky darkens, and a brilliant band of gold and pink circles the edge of the water and land.

I can't remember the last time I was this happy.

I crawl onto the shore next to my collection of shells and flip onto my back. The tide pulls at my body as I say, "Do you ever wish you could stay here forever? Or, wherever you can imagine?"

He sits with a straight back and crossed legs beside me and stares off into the horizon where the orange sun looks to be descending half in the water. "Sometimes. It's safe here. There's nobody to betray me or hurt the ones I love. I prefer this to the real world. It's easily controlled. I can release control of things like the waves and the wind if I wish, but it's predictable. I can be anywhere my mind can take me."

I purse my lips and wiggle my toes in the wet sand as the foamy water laps at them. "But unpredictability is one of the good things about life. Yeah, it sucks when shitty things happen, but even I know there can be good things to come of it.

What about meeting best friends? Or finding something cool at a store, or discovering a new song? You can't plan that. Life would be boring if you always controlled it."

"Yes," he agrees. "But it would be far less painful."

I heave out a sigh and dig my feet deeper into the sand.

"Seth's at the door with your breakfast," Viorel says.

The cool water vanishes from around me before I can bid it goodbye, the world in darkness with a blink. The soft blankets of Viorel's bed are back over me, my back pressed into the spongy mattress. Disappointment weighs on my thudding heart, my labored breaths pulling in the old smell of the yellowed, dusty books and the aging furniture of the damp subbasement.

Peeling my eyes open with a sigh, the room is much dimmer after soaking up the sunlight. My stomach eats at me with the buildup of hours of hunger I wasn't around to experience.

"Did you go there the night I saw you lying in bed? The day I laid in my room all day, when I was still marked to Denendrius?" I ask.

He's silent at the sound of the iron door opening. Seth's low greeting echoes. The smell of hot butter and bread covers the old smell of the air. He leaves without a verbal thanks, but I don't doubt Viorel might've given him a psychic one.

"I visited Tatiana. The memory of her."

I inch my hand back to his, resting the knuckle of my index finger against the side of his. "Do you go there with her often?"

"I don't make a habit of visiting the dead. But sometimes, it's nice. Often, I simply escape alone. I can go anywhere I can think of, so long as I have enough information to construct it."

"Can you take me back to the ocean again soon?" I whisper. "It's not the same, but you're right, it's nice."

"I'll show you anything your heart desires, Marianna." Viorel turns his hand back into mine, and my heart stutters.

XXVIII

Unfortunately, the soothing effects of our ocean trip are short-lived. I lose my appetite halfway through my meal and drag myself back to bed, wondering how emptiness feels *so damn heavy*. Viorel tries to coax me into eating snacks since I continue to turn down meals. I nibble on dried apple slices so the vitamins he insists I take don't sour my empty stomach. Nausea grips me anyway, teasing the edges of my stomach just enough to cover my arms in goosebumps. Viorel's blood helps.

I lay there for hours until exhaustion is pulling at my lids and beating itself into the grooves of my brain. It takes energy to drag myself out of bed to pee.

Viorel heaves out a breath as he rounds the wardrobe toward the bed and wanders out of sight. "The desolation in here is *suffocating*."

I curl tighter into a ball, pulling the soft covers against my cheek.

"Why don't you play your little game?" he suggests, standing somewhere past my feet.

Shrugging, I whisper, "I don't feel like it."

"It's been two days. You can't lay in bed forever. Much longer and you'll be mended to the sheets. I'll have to find my seam ripper to separate you from them," he teases.

I sound robotic when I say, "Ha-Ha."

"What can I do to help?" he murmurs.

"Nothing," I whisper, clenching the blanket in my hand. For the first time since I was a child, I wish I had a stuffed animal to hug. "I need time to process, I guess. Everything feels pointless. My whole life is a lie. I'm trying to redesign myself, and I get a handful of days into my new life, only for the basic truth of it to unravel. Who the hell am I?"

"You're Marianna Cortez, a strong, stubborn girl who has survived more than most have, and who will survive the rest to come," he says.

I close my eyes and swallow a glob of emotion. "What if Alaire and Edmond gave me a new name since the cure clearly wiped my whole mind clean? What if I'm not even American? What if I'm from a place that doesn't exist anymore, like you?"

The bed lowers near my legs as Viorel sits and rests his hand on the blankets over my hip. "A name is simply a name, a set of sounds to help us differentiate between one another. You are the same girl, no matter what you were once called. What-ever Mateo finds has already happened and won't change who you are molding yourself into right now."

"I don't think that's true," I whisper, rubbing my eyes and opening them. "We have no idea what he could find about me."

The bed creaks as he stands. "I'm running you a bath."

I close my eyes and listen to the rush of water as it hits the bottom of the porcelain tub until the taps squeak off. Despite how appealing a hot bath is, the idea of pulling myself out of bed has me wishing I could sleep instead. When Viorel calls my name, I scowl.

He appears between me and the fireplace. Flicking his

hand, the blankets and sheets wrench off me and into a heap at the bottom of the bed. I try to snag them with my toes, but they shift out of reach.

I release a loud and protesting moan into the chilly air as I roll myself off the mattress and plant my feet against the soft wolf's fur at my bedside. Slumped, I drag my feet to the bathroom and can't fight the little smile demanding space on my face when I see how the water is rosy with loose petals from one of my bath bombs. A silver chalice of his blood rests on the stool next to a purple cloth.

I soak and sip blood until the water is cold, then dart to my room to dress, leaving a trail of droplets behind on the stone.

"Come here," Viorel calls softly after I close the drawer of my wardrobe, fully clothed in a fresh pair of black leggings and thin, blue long sleeve with thumb holes.

I drag my aching body to the bed where he sits with a book in his lap and his back against the headboard and drop onto the edge.

Closing his book, he says, "Rayonne is to be released from the ward the day after tomorrow. I suspect she could use a friend to help her adjust upstairs on her first day. Perhaps you would be interested in having a bed available to you upstairs—for rare usage, mind you—in a shared room with her."

My heart races. "You're letting me share a room with Rayonne?"

He holds a hand up to settle me. "For *rare* use," he reiterates. "You may sleep there today if you'd like to try a change in scene to refresh you, and the day after, to help Rayonne adjust."

Happiness has my heart floating and wetness beading on my eyelashes. "Really?"

"Yes, but don't expect to be there often. I'm serious. A handful of times a year at most." The sternness of his voice doesn't dampen my smile.

A few times a year is still better than *zero*.

"Thank you. But I'm surprised," I admit. "You don't think it's dangerous?"

He laughs. "Oh, quite. Letting you sleep upstairs is an incredibly horrible decision, but sorrow and stress are inherently unsafe as well."

I stop my eyeroll midway through.

He ignores my attitude. "You and Rayonne will be on the opposite side of the hall as Carol and Derek, a few doors down."

"Derek is nearby for protection?" I guess.

His smile stretches unevenly, breath rushing past his lips in a silent chuckle. *"Yes."*

I must admit, it's a smart idea.

"Understand, Marianna, *this* is as far as I will ever extend my limits."

Part of me wonders if that's true. I've gotten my way a few times now, and Patricia saw me visiting Ziggy in Lorimer . . .

Viorel scowls. "Do not make me regret this. If you attempt to take advantage of my leniency, you won't be going upstairs *at all.*"

Swallowing, I nod and grimace. "Sorry."

An hour later, Seth escorts me up the grand staircase to the second floor. My fingertips glide against the thick stone banister as I climb, surprisingly short on breath by the time we reach the top. I glance curiously at each closed door until we're halfway down the hall and he motions with his hand toward a door on my left.

I'm hesitant to take the knob, not sure what to expect behind the door.

I gnaw at my lip as Seth opens it for me, a massive room the size of Laurentius's on the other side. It's probably the size of a two-bedroom apartment—without the walls or bathroom—and fits the two canopy beds, two wardrobes and dressers, without making the room overcrowded. The beds are opposite to one another with their ends pointed toward the center of the room, grizzly fur spread across the floor between them. The red, four post mahogany bed shares a wall with the door and matching nightstands, the darker mahogany set directly across from it. There's a vanity in the far-right corner, a white pelt strewn over the seat. Decorative wooden panels make up the bottom half of the bedroom walls, the top half green and gold damask wallpaper with plentiful paintings.

"Wow," I say. "Nicer than my room downstairs."

He chuckles. "There's plenty of extra art, furniture, and trinkets around in storage for you to pick from."

I tuck that idea away for later, too curious about my new room to think about the dull one downstairs.

"Do you want me to stick around, or do you want to get settled alone?" The offer is genuine from the caring smile on his lips.

"Thanks, but I'm sure you've got better things to do. Can you send Laurentius this way?" I lace my fingers together as I wander into the room and spin in a slow circle to take the new space in.

"Sure thing." He leaves.

I ponder the two beds, both with fluffy floral comforters beneath massive Afghan blankets I want to think were handmade in the castle. A quick sniff test fills my nostrils with a fresh smell and convinces me someone recently laundered them. I decide Rayonne can take the bed closest to the door when I'm in here. The beds are equally nice, but I'm selfish and want a vampire buffer between me and the door.

Rounding the room, I open every drawer like the last occupant might have left something behind. All that's left are loose strings from clothes in the occasional drawer, a shard of torn paper, and a wooden corner with dirt and dust residue. The bottom of my nightstand drawer is stained with a smear of murky rainbows from crushed pastels or eyeshadow.

I'm unable to help the gnawing feeling of intruding on someone's space—that none of it is really mine—and almost expect to find a rack full of vintage items while inspecting the wardrobes. They're bare, the idea of selecting one of them and filling it with my own clothes makes me chew at my lip. Maybe it's because I know this will be Rayonne's room, and as much as she was hoping to share with me, I'll only be a visitor. Part of me—okay, most of me—doesn't believe I'll ever sleep another day here after this. Technically, Viorel could still call me back downstairs. There's nothing stopping his paranoid ass from sending a guard into the room at two in the afternoon to collect me, either. With that thought, I'm unsure of how soundly I'll sleep today.

Regardless, I pretend like I really will get more opportunities to sleep over and assess the room with a thoughtful gaze. I decide it's fair for Rayonne to get ninety percent of the space since I already have my own room and she'll be filling this one with an eternity of her belongings.

A polite knock on the door has me turning toward Laurentius, who looks between me and the room with a quirked brow and crooked smile.

"This is surprising. Not a permanent arrangement, I suspect?" He meets me at the dresser and wraps his arms around me.

I shake my head against his chest, inhaling the faint smell of leather and candle smoke clinging to his baggy white blouse. "No. He says it's for rare occasions."

He gives me a gentle squeeze and releases me, taking a step back. "You're sleeping here for the day?"

"And tomorrow, when they release Rayonne from the ward."

He makes an impressed O with his lips. "Exciting. You'll have to introduce us."

I promise to, and we head upstairs to the wardrobe room so I can find clothes for the next few nights.

Folding my new clothes into my drawers feels wrong. Like this being my room is a lie I'm trying to convince myself is true. When I search the vanity, some drawers contain well-loved pallets and lipsticks, and I glance over my shoulder at the door like the previous occupants might return and demand to know why I'm snooping.

Laurentius takes me for food, and we spot Carol and Derek tucked into the back corner of the dining hall with candles lit at their table and a bottle of wine cracked open. I fight the urge to dart over and spill how I'm spending the next two nights down the hall from them, but it's clear they're on a date. I wave back when Derek notices us and offers one first, but vow to not interrupt them while Laurentius sips his blood as I chow down on Pho.

When I'm nearing the end of my meal, he asks me if I want to watch movies with him. The idea of cozying up next to him makes me want to agree, but tonight is special, and I want to do something new.

"How about a piggyback to the top of one of the turrets?" he asks once we're done cleaning up our table. "It has a magnificent view."

I quickly agree, not having dared go yet because of the long walk across the castle and hike up the hundreds of awaiting stairs.

There are curious eyes on me when I climb on the dining chair, though they bore upon realizing I'm climbing on Laurentius's back. With my legs around his midsection and my arms around his neck, I squeeze my eyes closed and turn my face into his neck to avoid motion sickness.

He moves so fast I can barely feel it, dropping me a few long moments later in an arched doorway. I drag in a steadying breath, head spinning as I peek over my shoulder at the winding stone staircase going on forever. I imagine it would have taken me a minimum of an hour to get across the castle and here by myself.

Laurentius laces his fingers through mine as he pulls me into the round room, both right and left curving away from us. I pull on his arm, walking us in a circle through the stripes of moonlight shining through half the deep-set, tall, and rectangular windows, and around the stone wall in the center of the room surrounding the stairs. There are a couple of small wrought-iron tables on the rough stone, and a few of the window nooks are full of potted plants. Aside from the occasional faded and hand-painted flower stemming from the floor, the walls are bare.

"Viorel used to spend a lot of time painting here," he tells me as I tug him into a window nook full of moonlight. We sit cross-legged with our knees touching and our backs against the stone. "I'd come sit with him sometimes and write. He painted me once."

The sight of the vast forest below the infinite sky makes it hard to think of a response. I press my face closer to the cool glass and stare at the fat moon and the millions of stars flecking the sky like glitter. We're so high and I can't see the garden. It's dark trees and sky for as far as I can see. There's still no sign of life beyond the veil.

"You should ask him to come upstairs more often. Everyone misses him," Laurentius says, staring out the window.

"He wouldn't listen to me." I gnaw at my cheek, staring off at the mass of tiny treetops. The height of the turret makes me feel disconnected from the castle, like we're floating in the clouds.

"It's beautiful from up here, isn't it?" Laurentius's gazes fondly. "The Lord did a marvelous job with nature, at least."

I nod and scrutinize the stars as I run my top teeth along my bottom lip.

How long have I observed these same stars? From how many places? Is this my first time in a castle? What are the chances I've met at least one resident before in my past?

Laurentius rests his hand on my knee. "What's on your mind?"

I release a long breath, and my shoulders lower. "Viorel thinks I was a child vampire."

He grins. "Cool."

"Not really. I can't stop thinking about it."

"Isn't it kind of exciting?" he asks.

I shake my head. "No. I have enough missing memories from my human years. With my luck, my past will be horrific and sad. Besides, I want to be normal."

His abrupt laugh makes me scowl. "Normal? Marianna, I'm sorry, but there's no chance, no matter what."

I frown, not wanting to hear the truth again. "I know, but still. It's disappointing."

"I'm sorry," Laurentius says gently. "I lived a normal life—in my time, at least—and it's plain. Nothing wrong with it, but there are many better ways to live than by a societal expectation."

Crossing my arms, I pull them tight around myself. "I guess, but it's hard not to be jealous seeing those kinds of lives around me and on TV."

"It's overrated," he claims. "From what I know about you, it sounds like you think following a map will guarantee fulfillment and happiness."

"Maybe." I pick at my nails.

"Life, no matter what, is *hard* Marianna. There's no true path to follow, and what makes a dozen people happy and fulfilled, can make another miserable."

I frown. "Either way, I've given up on normal."

"Good." Laurentius pokes me in the leg. "Because I like you how you are. A completely abnormal girl."

My cheeks burn. "Thanks."

My eyes meet his for a long moment—soft, warm like the bloody color of them—and I'm once again thankful to be here. When he clasps my hands in his and rubs his wet lips together, I think he's going to kiss me until he cuts his eyes to the window and ponders the sky.

A wave of disappointment rocks through me, and I can't help but wonder if we should have kissed by now. If we were normal humans dating, I'd be seriously concerned since it's been almost three weeks since our first *"date."* Aside from his religion—unless that's the issue—what's holding him back?

"Did you have a wife in the past? A girlfriend?" Could he still be getting over someone? Someone he spent hundreds of years with?

He turns his face back to me and shakes his head, hair falling into his eyes that he pushes back.

"Wife, no. Girlfriends, yes."

My brow quirks.

"Not multiple at once," he clarifies quickly before his face becomes sullen. He's quiet, eyes never fully meeting mine when he says, "Mostly in my early years when I was living in churches and giving night sermons, though I've had sparse flings now and then. Dating as a priest was challenging and not much easier here. Few people understand me or can't deal with the potential perception others here may have of them if they admit they do. It's one thing being a priest in a world of vampires where hardly a soul believes in any God, never mind a priest with the beliefs I have."

"Well, I don't care what other people think of me," I assure him. "They can't perceive me any worse than they did when I was marked to Denendrius."

He stares at my hands when he talks. "The last girl I dated outside the castle made it hard to trust for many years and was the key factor in me coming here. It's easy to be with you, knowing I don't have to worry about your intentions when Viorel finds you worthy."

My eyes narrow in concern as I scrutinize the hurt in his eyes, as raw as it must have been centuries ago. "What did she do?"

"Uh—" He clasps his hands together and bites his lip like he's considering some consequence of opening to me. He stares at his hands. "She was a member of our congregation and approached me after service to tell me she'd never seen someone with such passion. She was exceptionally attractive, but I wasn't thinking much of dating back then after my previous heartbreak. But she came to confession a couple of weeks later and confessed to being in love with a man of God, admitting to sinful thoughts of him, and her desire to disrupt his vows of celibacy. She asked for forgiveness and guidance, as she had never felt such a way about a man before and knew it was wrong." Laurentius winces. "I knew she was speaking of me, but I shouldn't have said anything more than what was required of me, absolved her of her sins, and assigned penance. Instead, I told her there was no sin for God to forgive, and she should seek guidance from me after."

My eyes widen, and he ducks to avoid my judgment.

"We had a relationship in secret for two years. I loved her and trusted her enough to share my beliefs with her, but didn't reveal my immortality. She urged me to leave the priesthood and marry her." He drags in a deep breath. "People close to her became suspicious. She was of marrying age and showed no interest in suitors. Her parents became suspicious of our friendship and the amount of private counsel she received. They questioned her and she cracked."

Laurentius clutches his hands in his lap, his body stiff and shoulders tense. He looks far too haunted for a priest who was outed for having a relationship, especially since he didn't follow those beliefs.

"What did she say?" I press.

He closes his eyes and shivers with the memory. "She told everyone I was raping her, how I was a Satan worshipper who lured members of the congregation into my cult."

I gape at him. "Holy shit."

"I confronted her and demanded to know why she abused confession to gauge my interest in her if she was going to later ruin me for what she initiated."

"Did she feel bad?"

He shrugs. "She drowned herself in the baptismal pool. They accused me of murdering her. I had no choice but to flee, knowing I wouldn't be able to show my face in church for decades. It wasn't the first time I had to leave a church for a secret relationship, but never had my ex-girlfriends accused me of anything to save themselves."

"Fuck," I whisper. "I'm sorry that happened."

His nod is slight, and we sit in silence for a moment before he gives me a soft smile.

"You claim you're a rotten friend," he starts, "but you're a good listener."

I shrug and fight a smirk. "Maybe I just like listening to you."

We sit and talk until the stone is hurting my butt, and dawn is imminent. Laurentius brings me to my room once the buzz of the castle dies down and gives me a squeeze goodnight. I change into my blue silk pajamas and double back downstairs for a quick breakfast egg, realizing I don't have any toiletries upstairs to ready myself for bed. The last thing I want to do is go downstairs and risk Viorel changing his mind, so I ask Jacob. He gives me verbal directions to the shower rooms and tells me there are cupboards full of supplies. I find it easy and leave with minty breath and a travel bag.

There's not an ounce of exhaustion in me when I draw the heavy covers of my bed back.

Who last slept in the beds? And for how long before they fled upon mine and Denendrius's arrival? Could they have slept here for hundreds of years?

There's a rap on the door as I inspect the purple cotton sheets of my bed, the smell of laundry soap around me as I spin. "Yeah?"

As the door creaks open, it's not Carol or Derek like I'd most suspect. Lucia stands in the doorway with a demure smile as she clasps her hands in front of herself.

"Can I hang out?" she asks.

I nod and straighten the blanket back as she wanders in and closes the door behind her.

"Do you know who used to live here?" I ask as she meanders over and plops on the edge of the bed.

"Anja and her familiars." She points to Rayonne's bed. "She slept there, and the three of them slept here. Most recently, at least. She was here for five hundred years."

I blow out a breath, unsure what to say aside from, "Ah. Avoiding sleep?"

Her lips pinch as she looks around the room like she's never been past the doorway before. "Avoiding Father. I'm exhausted."

"Sleep here," I tell her.

Lucia tilts her head toward her lap as she tucks her hair behind her ear and releases a strangled chuckle. "Oh, that would be fun. You don't want to deal with my father, though. Word's already around that you're staying up here tonight, so he'll look here first."

"Your father can go fuck himself, Glitch."

She sighs and bobs her head.

I assess the space, visualizing a modern bed in my mind and mentally placing it into different areas I think might fit. "You should move in with Rayonne and me. I'd have to ask her, but I doubt she'd mind. I think she was looking forward to having a roommate because she's disappointed I won't be in here much. We could comfortably fit a bed in the corner beside the dresser. I don't have much stuff, and neither does Rayonne yet, so we could probably fit all of yours. Then you wouldn't have to live with your father anymore."

She swings her leg a bit, the disappointment in her black eyes clashing with her little smile. "Oh, that's so nice, Marianna. I love the idea, but my father would never allow it."

I roll my eyes at the idea of him trying to stop her. "Fuck what he thinks. You've been fifteen for—" I pause. "What? Centuries?"

"Nineteen-hundred years." She sighs. "And I know, I try to convince him to give me some independence, but he takes care of me when I have my bouts of confusion."

I wrinkle my nose. "He's controlling. How have you been here for hundreds of years, and he thinks nobody else here has figured out how to help? He just doesn't want you having close friends."

"I know," she whispers.

"Why doesn't he?"

She shrugs.

I squint at her as I chew the corner of my lip before saying, "Yeah, well, Viorel holds ultimate power, so if he lets you and your dad tries to fight him, Viorel is going to be pissed. I'll get his support."

A little smile appears on her lips. "Okay."

We draw the covers back and wiggle under them, the newness of the room less overwhelming with someone else to share the strangeness with me. Lucia is asleep soon after blowing the candle out. I lie awake with my eyes raking at the dark, listening to the occasional creak of a door or whisper-shout in the hall. Lucia grumbles and whines in her sleep next to me. I consider waking her, but the door opens as I lift my hand off the blanket to give her a nudge.

I recognize Lucius's shape in the shadow of my doorway and his low bark of Lucia's name.

She jerks awake beside me.

"You piece of shit," I snarl at him. "Who the fuck do you think you are?"

He holds his finger over his lips to silence me, glaring daggers.

"No, fuck you, Lucius." I throw my blanket off and stand beside the bed. "If you were so worried about people overhearing, you shouldn't have barged in here."

"Watch your mouth," he hisses at me.

I cross my arms. "Or what?"

He's about to say something he'll likely regret when Lucia interrupts as she climbs out of bed. "It's fine, Marianna. I'll go to my own bed. Not worth waking everyone up. Go back to sleep."

They don't give me enough time to argue. They're gone with my next furious huff.

XXIX

Silence wakes me. The more I search for some sort of sound in the dark, the more I hear that I never noticed before. The silence isn't so silent after all. Something moans in the walls. Something whistles through the cracks. Something ticks, scratches, and scurries against the stone.

My heart thumps, the string of light beneath my door making shadows stretch across my room. I can feel how big the space is and how tiny I am in comparison.

The heavy air keeps me under the blankets, an imagined whisper making my mind wander. I think of the centuries of people who have slept in this bed, in this room, the thousands who have inevitably lived and died in the walls of this castle. I do my best not to consider the kinds of horrors the previous owners of this room might have committed, but my mind launches itself at a thousand different possibilities before I can stop it.

Where do they put the bodies of the humans they kill?

What kinds of ghosts do blood slaves and tortured men make?

I remember Laurentius told me Romania has a haunted forest. Are we in it? Are vampires and the castle the reason people think it's haunted, or has it always been? Have the trees and flowers surrounding us grown richer from the flesh of the once living?

I feel the weight of imagined phantoms in the air, sitting on my throat, passing in and out of my lungs.

A yelp nearly escapes me when my bedroom door opens, and I stiffen—ready to fight with all I can—until Asil identifies himself with a sweep of his flashlight across his concerned face.

"What's wrong?" he whispers. "Viorel said he could feel your fear."

As I sit, I draw in a breath to the depth of my lungs. "I'm fine," I promise, voice low. "It's just been weeks since I've slept alone, and I keep freaking myself out over the idea of ghosts."

He chuckles, and his friendly smile looks sinister with the flashlight casting shadows through his beard and over his face. "Do you want to go back downstairs?"

"No, I'm okay. I'll get used to sleeping here." Why would I want to? So Viorel thinks I'm a wimp for not being able to spend one night alone in my own room? So he has another reason to justify keeping me downstairs where it's *safe?*

He turns the flashlight off and underhand throws it onto the other bed. "Okay, but if you change your mind, Sascha will bring you down."

I snuggle into the blankets and close my eyes once he's gone. As I drift toward dreamland—Asil's appearance having calmed much of my nerves—the sound of my wooden dresser drawer shimmying open has me jerking upright in bed.

"Asil?" I hiss while I scramble for the lighter on my night-stand and bring a flame to a candle.

At the sight of my drawer inching open on its own, I pull in a sharp breath that catches in my throat and swells so thick there's no way I'd be able to call for anyone.

If vampires exist, are ghosts so far-fetched?

The drawer reaches the end of its wooden track and crashes onto the floor, clothes flying like someone kicked them.

"Oh, *fuck that.*" I toss my blankets off me, and though I know there's a pretty good chance a nearby vampire is toying with me after likely overhearing my worry of ghosts, I'm not willing to make that bet and end up strangled by a poltergeist.

I dart out of bed and scamper through my room, dodging reaching shadows before yanking my door open to stand in the empty, low-lit hallway. The stare of medieval painted eyes chase me. I stumble through the dark castle while wishing I'd grabbed the flashlight, my imagination pursuing me until I'm sprinting across the grand room and down the carpet of the hall.

I stop dead in my tracks when I reach Laurentius's door and contemplate slipping in and waking him to keep me company instead of continuing to the steel door.

Screw it. Who knows when Viorel will let me return if he thinks I'm too scared alone.

I hold my breath and turn the knob, surprised it's unlocked —though locks wouldn't deter any of the immortal strength here—as I crack the door open enough to creep through. Closing it behind me, I stumble through the dim glow of a dozen reptile lamps and to his bedside.

My soft gaze trails over him, from his ruffled brown hair and his smooth and sleeping face as he rests on his side with his cheek on his pillow.

"*Laurentius,*" I hiss, surprised my presence wasn't enough to wake him.

He draws awake with a gasp. "Marianna?"

"Yeah, sorry to startle you."

Blankets and sheets shuffle as he sits, his face a mere two

feet from mine. He's topless and in a pair of black pajama pants. His rosary dangles around his neck. "What's wrong? You look troubled."

"I'm going to sound like a big baby, but are there ghosts in the castle? My dresser drawer landed on the floor by itself."

He thinks over his answer for far too long before saying, "There *are* ghosts, but that was more likely someone playing tricks on you."

I wring my fingers in front of me. "Can I stay in here with you?"

His strained silence almost has me turning around and apologizing for barging in.

He clears his throat and rakes his hand through his hair. "As in . . . sleep here with me?"

"Yeah. I haven't slept alone in a while and don't really want to go back downstairs tonight or bug Carol and Derek, but I'll understand if you're uncomfortable sharing your bed with me. I . . ." I sigh. "I feel alone."

"I understand the feeling." The bed squeaks and I hear his swallow. "I don't want to upset Viorel by allowing you."

"He doesn't care," I promise with a whisper.

A little tickled noise escapes him. "Oh—really?"

I nod.

"Well, okay then." I don't miss the hesitation he tries to cover with sleepy cheer.

I walk around the bed, carefully sliding between the cold, black flannel sheets.

He gives me a small smile as he nestles back under the covers a few feet away and draws them snugger around me. "Are you okay to sleep? Do you need anything—water, perhaps —first?"

I mash my head deeper into the soft pillow. "I'm okay, thanks."

"Sleep well then," he whispers.

"You too."

He rolls over with his back to me and my heart leaps at the branding scars down his spine and across his shoulder blades.

"Is that a cross?" I whisper.

He tenses, then mumbles, "Yes. A priest burned it into me when I was human."

"Why?" I run my finger down the bumpy white scar and he shudders.

"He thought it would rid the devil from me." As I ponder what he means and how to respond, he adds, "Goodnight, Marianna."

I sigh. "Goodnight."

I close my eyes, feeling an ounce better with someone at my side. But the new smells and sounds of his room are distracting, and I find my mind racing with a rush of new thoughts without the idea of ghosts occupying it.

Thinking of Laurentius beside me, I can't help but wonder if he'll try to initiate something. Does he think I want him to since I crawled into bed with him? Or is he expecting *me* to do something if he thinks I came here with a purpose?

My heart stumbles at the thought while it plays out in my mind. What would I do if Laurentius rolled over and trailed his lips over mine? What would I do if he stroked my skin and slipped his hand under my shirt?

A nervous lump gathers in my throat, but *I'd let it happen.*

In fact, I welcome it. Even if we never became a proper couple, it would be nice to have his touch muddle the memory of Denendrius's. I want to know if I can feel what I did with Denendrius with another man. Laurentius seems safe, eager to be near me. All I'd have to do is protest if things turned dark, and someone would run to my rescue.

I listen to Laurentius's breath, a perfectly timed exchange of inhales and exhales, and I realize he's too much of a gentleman to do *anything.* He's already asleep.

I'm not sure what to do to make him wake up and try something with me since Denendrius always instigated everything, so I scoot back until my feet are touching his.

A sleepy *"Oh—"* escapes him and he turns rigid beside me and inches away, which has me thinking I fucked up, until he relaxes and says, "Do you have enough space now?"

"I guess," I whisper. "You didn't have to move."

After a few more minutes, I try again, but he inches away once more.

Hot frustration deepens inside me as my heart pounds on. It takes up so much space there's no way sleep can settle in now.

The tips of my fingers burn with the urge to reach over and stroke my hand against his cold flesh, though the rest of me is stiff with indecision.

What if he doesn't even want *that* kind of relationship with me, considering his religious positions? He may not be celibate, but that doesn't mean he fucks everything that moves, either.

What if I destroy the healthy momentum we have going by making him think I'm easy? Does he hold those kinds of old, religious beliefs?

A dozen other terrified *what ifs* bounce around my head.

It would be so much easier if he would do something. Then I could simply go along with it.

Yet the minutes slog on, and he doesn't. I scoot back a bit until my butt is touching his and rest my feet against the soft fabric covering his calves.

He doesn't move this time, and from the sound of his even breaths, he must be asleep again. The pattern has almost lulled me to sleep when he clears his throat and shifts in the bed away from me.

"Sorry," I mumble. Perhaps he really isn't interested in anything and I'm harassing him.

"You're a bed hog," he teases, rolling over to face me with his sleepy smile. "You're going to drive me onto the floor."

"Sorry." I move back to where I started, roll away, and squeeze my eyes closed in hopes of sleep.

The bed shifts as I dip my toes into dreamland. I sigh—eyes popping back open—and roll over at the sound of pages.

Laurentius sits against the headboard with a pencil and an expensive looking black leather and gold Bible in his hands. The glow of a small candle barely illuminates the pages.

"I have to do something important quick," he whispers. "Go back to sleep. I'll be quiet."

I let my gaze wander around the room before stopping on the panel of stained wood above me. Like the bedposts, it's marred with hundreds of carved crosses.

I point up at them. "What are those for?"

He's silent as his gaze follows my finger, clearly contemplating whether to tell me. "One for every human I've killed since my stay here began. That way, I'll never forget how they gave their lives to me."

I swallow. "Oh."

"Does that disturb you?"

I tuck my arm between my head and pillow. "Nothing disturbs me anymore. Not after Denendrius. He remembered some of his victims by recording himself raping and killing them. At least it's not that."

Laurentius shifts. "That's quite upsetting."

"Yeah." I exhale loudly through my nose, fingers searching the surrounding air. They find the peach-colored satin drape and I run my fingers down it until I touch my pillow. Grunting, I sit myself up beside him, the decorative carvings on the wood headboard digging into my back until I place my pillow behind me.

He settles his gaze back on his Bible, resting his pencil to a thin page somewhere in the middle of the book to write furiously in the margins, crossing portions out and underlining others.

My eyes narrow at the foreign alphabet, my eyes popping wide when he turns the page. It's heavily annotated, nearly more notes than verses, and he still tries to squeeze something new in.

"What are you doing . . .?" I whisper. "That seems . . . *blasphemous*."

"I'm making corrections," he mumbles, pencil flying across the page.

"Oh. Why don't you buy a modern copy with corrections instead of doing it yourself?" I squint.

He hunches over the book. "This is an original copy. It's still incorrect."

"What language is that?"

"Hebrew. It's the Old Testament." He flips the page to squeeze more words between the blocks of previous notes.

"What are you correcting?"

He looks up from his Bible, expression blank as his eyes flicker over my face. "The Bible is dishonest. I'm fixing it."

My brows shoot up. "That's *definitely* blasphemous," I tease.

His gaze drops back to the open book, hair falling into his eyes as he vigorously writes. I watch for a few minutes until I'm too curious to let him work in peace.

"What's the truth?" I ask. "I don't know much about God, so you've got a clean slate to preach to."

His head pops up, red and unblinking eyes settling on mine. "About God and the Bible?"

I nod.

With a nervous gleam in his eyes, he says, "You're positive you want me to tell you?"

"Yes."

Slowly, he closes his Bible as he draws in a deep breath

through his nose, rigid as he sets it and the pencil on his nightstand.

"Well," he begins quietly, "in the beginning, the omnipotent and all-knowing God created *everything*. He created the heavens and the Earth and wrote the story of everyone and everything for all of time. The angels, made by him some time before, witnessed this creation."

I nod along.

"Lucifer was God's favorite, but he took issue with God and the plan for his new creation—humans. Lucifer pitied humanity. He was convinced he could do better than God, and thus he cast him out of Heaven with those who agreed. Yet Lucifer wanted humans to have free will. He saw Adam and Eve in ignorant bliss in the Garden of Eden and disguised himself as a serpent. He convinced Eve to eat fruit from the Tree of Knowledge so they would know of good and evil, and she shared it with Adam. Lucifer freed humanity and has asked for *nothing* in return."

My eyes widen a bit, having never thought of it like that.

"God created sin?" I ask, making sure I understand.

"Yes."

My eyes narrow with confusion. "If God knew everything, didn't he know Lucifer wanted to overthrow him before creating him? That he would cast him out? Didn't he know Lucifer would convince Eve to eat the fruit and that they would gain free will and knowledge? It's like he put the tree there as a trap."

Laurentius's eyes light up. "Yes, Marianna. Exactly. You understand perfectly."

I scratch my head. "But doesn't that make *God* the real devil? He had the power to do *anything,* and he created evil, wrote the story of each person's suffering, and demanded everyone worship him without proof or else suffer for eternity . . ."

That means God knew all the ways I would suffer before I

even existed, and *he still let it happen*. No, he didn't *let* it happen
. . . he *invented* suffering.

With a solemn nod, Laurentius says, "Enlightening, isn't it?
You have Lucifer to thank for understanding. And because of
the creation of vampires, you will get to keep your free will in
the afterlife."

Laurentius rambles on excitedly. I nod along, only understanding a quarter of what he's talking about since I have a
basic understanding of his religion. He goes on about how he's
so thankful someone—*me*—can understand the truth, and how
it's been so long since someone has taken him seriously.

He tells me about his time in the church centuries ago, how
sometimes when members would come to him for guidance, he
steered some in the right direction. He ended up with groups of
them to preach to in his own time . . . until one of them would
break with guilt for their new beliefs, or tried to convert other
members alone, resulting in his excommunication. Still, he
tried again and again, sometimes picking up vampires along
the way who would make familiars out of his believers.

There's something sexy—tantalizing—about the fierce grip
Laurentius has on his beliefs. Perhaps it's his dedication that's
so attractive. No matter how painful, how tormenting his
beliefs become, he's got his claws in them. Could he show the
same sort of dedication to a real person? *To me?*

Yet Denendrius has this sort of dedication to his delusion
about us. He has his claws in me so deep they are practically
caught in my bones. No matter how sick it makes the both of us
he keeps clenching like he wants to reach my marrow, like he
wants us fused together. But I think Laurentius would be
different.

Though I imagine they both fall in love—or obsession, in
Denendrius's case—like falling in a pit, Laurentius would sit
and stare up at the silver stars, letting the flowers bloom and
spill over the edges. He'd think how lucky he was to stumble in

and how he doesn't find it worthwhile to try climbing out when everything is growing lovely and fragrant around him.

But Denendrius would be convinced fate pushed him in, that the dirt under his feet covered treasure. He would tear at the Earth with his nails, ripping at roots and clawing at clay, convinced he must keep digging to find what he wants. And when he couldn't, he'd curse the hole and dirt, and blame the stars and moon for not being bright enough to guide the way.

"How do you know all this?" I ask.

He gives me a long stare and swallows, eyes dropping from mine. "I-I'm chosen. Lucifer sent a rebel angel to me when I was twenty. He asked me if I would be open to receive truth. It was the first unwavering evidence of God's existence I'd experienced, so of course I heard him out, not thinking I'd believe him. I did and was liberated. I tried to tell my father . . ." Laurentius's lips form a taut line.

"What did he say?" But I should know his priest father wouldn't have heard him out.

Laurentius stares vacantly at the blanket before inhaling sharply and saying, "Nothing, at first."

I don't push for more, studying the shadows of ghosts drifting over his face as he considers something—if he should tell me, perhaps.

He pulls in a breath and speaks to his lap. "We had been alone at the church altar when I told him. He left me standing there, wordlessly, as he walked away. He returned with a rope and asked if I truly believed what I told him. I said yes. When he bound my hands, I let him. I don't know why. I didn't feel the urge to fight or think to flee as he brought me below the church. He stripped me of my garments and bound my feet, then locked me in a dark room. When he apologized, I forgave him. I knew he did what he felt he must do, but I was not unafraid. I knew death lurked in the darkness of my inevitably short future."

My heart hammers, and I reach out and rest a comforting hand against the side of his thigh.

I strain to hear his whisper. "I expected the first exorcism before my father offered me another chance to repent. But the rebel angels had been speaking to me in the dark for weeks, consoling me, promising I would be okay. I was to stand up against evil as Lucifer did, no matter the consequence."

His gaze flickers to mine, and I offer what I hope is a warm and comforting smile.

He drops his eyes again. "I'm unsure exactly how long my father kept me down there, but I became unkempt. The exorcisms were plentiful with different priests from across the Holy Roman Empire, but I remained steadfast in my beliefs. Father would bring my mother to beg me to consider my soul, but the voices of the rebel angels offered better comforts.

"One night, my father told me he had found my redemption; a priest so holy and practiced, he could turn demons to men. He bathed me, gave me a fresh shave, and dressed me. As my father loaded me into a carriage under the moonlight, my love for him grew. I cried the entire trip, knowing in my heart we were to part eternally. The hurt he caused me was unbearable, but he loved me so deeply he had refused to give up on me. I could not blame him for how God created him to be. They had told me there were so few capable of accepting the truth."

I'm unsure what words to align to comfort him, so I lean my head on his shoulder and internalize his story in the new silence. "You died during that final exorcism, didn't you?" I conclude, thinking he might be done with his story.

He nods. "Looking back, I understand the priest was a vampire hunter, though he considered them mere demons he could banish. My father and him tried to exorcise me alongside a weak and bound Darkling teen someone brought to him staked." There's a beat of silence with his wry, yet pained smile.

"She attacked me first when they woke her, since I was closest. Father intervened, and she left me choking on my blood while killing every man in the room. The angels told me not to be afraid, and all I remember is one of them stayed with the bloodied Darkling girl as she sat beneath his wing and watched me turn. She had been comatose for hundreds of years. We helped one another adjust until she found surviving members of her clan."

"Fuck," I whisper as I straighten. "But I'm glad your maker stuck around."

Laurentius gives me a shaky smile. "Lucifer put her in my path. I was destined to be immortal, to find Viorel and secure my place with Lucifer."

My head tilts. "Sorry, back up to the Viorel part. I'm missing some pieces there."

He looks up at me through his lashes. "Viorel is an outcast angel sent by Lucifer to lead and protect vampires until they can join him in the underworld. He doesn't remember being human because he never was. The human who once owned his body vacated. It's why Viorel never dies, why he has so many abilities. There's a reason Viorel and Darklings were the only survivors of that experiment. God stepped in to stop it, or his humans might have ceased to exist. But Lucifer protected Viorel and the Darklings. That's why nobody else got out. Because Viorel is special, and Darklings are the closest creatures to fallen angels."

Something about his comparison to Darklings and fallen angels has an odd feeling writhing in my gut and my mind spinning. It sounds familiar, so I scratch at my memory, but all I can recall is how little me wanted Denendrius to wear angel wings in Enchanted Land and how he bought black ones to match the little Gothic dress I picked.

"Wow." I process his words. "You don't think you're going to Heaven?"

"I know I'm not. I'm damned. But we won't suffer like the damned humans. We will sit alongside the rest of the beasts. Lucifer created vampires from rogue demons so humans can seek salvation through him."

My brow furrows. "I don't understand how you worship Lucifer and God at the same time."

His eyes lower. "I don't *worship* God anymore, but I respect him. I help his humans for him. He's my ultimate creator, after all. My father. I have love for him like I did my own human father. My own father, despite how he treated me in the end, was still my father. That counts for something, I think. By God's design, humans belong in heaven, so it's still my job to help them get there. God has ensured their suffering in Hell, so I help them with the lesser of two evils."

"You think Heaven is a bad place?" My lips twist, a confused line deep in my forehead.

He blows out a long breath. "There is no suffering in Heaven, but Lucifer's gift—your free will—is stripped from you, and you succumb to the state of blissful ignorance Adam and Eve were trapped in. You are no longer *you* in Heaven."

I try to wrap my head around what Heaven would be like.

The struggle must be on my face, because with the conviction of a priest standing in front of a parish, he says, "Imagine you've been faithful your whole life alongside your family. Over the years, each turns their back on God, and none of them will join you in Heaven. The idea of their eternal suffering torments you until you die. But *you* ascend to Heaven. You're in pure bliss. You're no longer distraught over the fact your family and friends are in Hell. By design, it's impossible for it to bother you. You are eternally and completely fulfilled . . . *without* being able to care that those you loved are suffering. It cannot bother you that there are rapists and mass murderers worshiping God right at your side. *They* repented, and your family—good people—did not."

A cold chill travels down my spine. His words are convincing, and I can't swallow the little ball of anxiety forming in my throat at the idea of Heaven. His interpretations make far more sense than the ones I've heard before, even if I don't believe Heaven or Hell exist at all.

He gives me a smile. "Don't worry, Marianna. You won't go to Heaven now that you're full of Viorel's blood. You will stay with him until he goes home. I was worried when he hadn't marked you, since you are not a child of Christ, and Lucifer will toss Denendrius into the flames."

"Thanks for the reassurance," I say, unable to help my goofy grin. "But why don't you make vampires, since you're worried about humans going to Heaven?"

He chuckles. "Vampirism only offers the opportunity, but Lucifer still expects you to be a good person to join him. That's why he gave us a choice. Besides, it's difficult to survive the Darkling change. I would take time on Earth away from those who don't survive."

"Ah—"

He flinches, and I'm about to ask him what's wrong when his head twitches as he swats at the air beside his ear like there's a fly. I recall how he did the same in the dining hall when Derek first invited him to dinner, and when he was showing me his snake. There was no fly either time.

"What's wrong?" I ask.

He clears his throat, flinches like something loud spooked him, and forces a smile. "Nothing. Should we try to sleep now?"

My eyes travel to the annotated bible on Laurentius's nightstand, and I swallow. It becomes quite clear to me then why Mateo is so goddamn nervous about him being near me. His ideas aren't troubling—I can't help but think they make sense—but the unpredictable ways they manifest and the underlying reasons for them are.

"Laurentius, do rebel angels still talk to you?" How much of this extends past his vampirism—past his blood-starved brain —and has carried over from when he was human?

His eyes drop from mine. "We should sleep," he mumbles as he lies down on his side. "I've talked your ear off."

I swallow and scoot back down, the aching desire to have his body touch mine stronger, knowing he likes me enough to share such personal thoughts.

"Thanks for trusting me enough to share your beliefs," I whisper, my eyes chasing his for a connection.

He closes his eyes, and there's a long beat of heavy silence before he whispers, "You're welcome."

The tension between us from my unanswered question is palpable. It gives me my answer.

"Do they bother you?" I stare at the carved crosses on the post behind him.

Another heavy beat of silence. I don't think he's going to answer, so I close my eyes.

"The fallen angels? No. They're friends. Though, there are some who regretted following Lucifer—the rogue demons— who like to harass me."

I can't help but think of the familiars he burned in the garden, and how they convinced him rogue demons were coming after him. Sounds like they got what was coming to them.

Frowning, I ache to rest a comforting hand on his bare chest.

"Really," he says with a wink. "We should sleep."

"Okay." I stare at him for a long moment, my mouth aching to taste his. I try once more for his affection, blurting out, "Can I have a goodnight kiss?"

XXX

I hope he hasn't recognized and ignored my advances all night in hopes I'd stop without him having to flat-out deny me.

His eyes widen a bit, darting down to my lips before he swallows. He seems to consider something before he lifts his chin and plants a kiss on my forehead. He levels his eyes with mine, waiting for my reaction.

I feel guilty—pushy—as I force out, "One more?"

He wets his lips, face eerily serious as he closes his eyes and carefully presses his lips to mine. I inhale sharply and hook my arm around his neck to keep him in place, turning his peck into a deeper kiss. He makes a noise of surprise in the back of his throat but kisses me back and rests his hand on my blanketed shoulder.

Prickly heat fills my limbs at the feel of his soft lips between mine, my heart pounding in satisfaction. I press my palm against the cold flesh above his heart, feeling a bead of his rosary when I spread my fingers. Gentle, I hook the chain with my index finger and twirl it.

He smiles against my lips as his gentle kisses continue, a burst of cold air from his nose as he unravels the chain from my finger like he's worried about me breaking it. My hand finds something else to do, fingers trailing down his chest and sending a shiver through him. Finding a strip of hair from his navel to the waist of his pants, I stroke my fingers up and down it until he makes a pleasured grunt and slides his hand down the blanket to my hip.

I slip the tip of my finger under the edge of his pants, and he pulls his head away.

"Oh, oh—ah—" His hand disappears under the blanket and brushes past mine to adjust himself. *"Ah . . ."* He swallows. "Are you testing me? Viorel knows I want you and is testing my loyalty to him, right?"

I bite back my laugh, a grin breaking through. "No."

He studies my face, a flash of terror in his eyes. "Promise?"

My smile vanishes when I realize how serious his concern is. "I promise. I would never trick you."

His crimson eyes search mine.

Is that why he hasn't tried to kiss me before?

"You put all your love into Viorel, and he knows you like me. Why would he give you a test he's sure you'll fail?" I say. "Has he ever done anything like that before?"

Laurentius shakes his head.

I wet my lips. "Then why would he now?"

He contemplates for a long moment before smiling softly and lifting his fingers to caress my face like I'm made of glass. He runs them over my lips before combing his fingers through my hair and gently bringing my head to his so our lips connect.

My kisses are hungry until his lips slow mine down, his fingers slipping from my hair and trailing down the side of my neck. Our tongues tangle. The sound of my heart thumps in my ears.

I'm unsure where my nerve comes from when I rest the tips

of my fingers back on his abdomen and glide them down and over the front of his pajama pants until I can feel him through them.

I force down a nervous lump in my throat and rub my hand over the front of his tented pants. Holding my shaky breath, I slip my hand in his pants to touch him.

He takes a fistful of my hair and groans. *"You succubus,"* he hisses against my lips before ravaging me with kisses. He yanks my body tight against his as he rolls on his back and pushes the blanket off and his pants off to free himself.

There's hesitancy in his voice as I wet my lips and move toward his crotch. "Are you sure? You don't have to—"

He doesn't have time to finish his sentence before my mouth has his head thumping back against his pillow and a pleasured grunt escaping him. He puts an encouraging hand on the back of my head as he melts into the mattress.

"Oh, you're so good at that," he breathes as he rests his free hand on his chest, half over his rosary while the other holds my hair back in his fist.

His encouragement and quiet moans make me more eager until my throat, tongue, and jaw are sore, and he's cursing and gasping under his breath before gently pulling my head up.

I look at him in question as I sit and wipe my mouth with the back of my hand.

"I don't want to finish yet," he whispers, a mischievous glimmer in his eyes and a guilty smile on his lips.

Heat fills my face and I try not to think of the dozens of vampires with super hearing in nearby rooms.

He cups the back of my neck with his hand and guides me over the mattress toward him, his mouth crashing against mine as his other hand slips up under my shirt to explore. I shiver as he runs his feather-light touch over my nipples, and there's an ache between my legs when he gives them a gentle pinch.

Laurentius nips at my lip. I gasp, my heart racing as I feel his smile against my lips.

"You're not allowed to drink from me," I warn, before he thinks of playfully biting me for real.

He agrees with a breathy *"no problem."*

I lift my arms as he shimmies my shirt over my head and tosses it aside. He hooks his arm around me and uses his body to push me back into the mattress. I wet my lips, shaking with nervous anticipation as he positions himself between my legs. His passionless kisses trail down my throat, soft lips brushing over my collarbones and down the center of my chest.

My chest heaves beneath his mouth, my breath trapped when he holds my gaze while running the tip of his tongue across my flesh and over my breast to my nipple. My toes curl as his tongue circles it. I bite down on my bottom lip as he kisses his way toward my other nipple, a surprised gasp rushing out of me at the feel of his hand pressing against the fabric between my legs.

"You're so fucking sexy," he murmurs, closing his eyes as he tucks his hand into my pants and underwear while flicking his tongue against my nipple.

I shudder at the feel of his cool finger running back and forth between my lips, wetness spreading at his touch. He kisses between my breasts, and I squeak as he pushes his finger inside me, heat spreading like fire through my body.

He straddles one of my legs and I wrap my arms loosely around his neck as he leans over me to reach my mouth. His kisses are rough and relentless while he strokes his finger inside me until my mouth is stretching as he pushes in a second and rubs quick circles against me with his thumb.

"Oh—God," I breathe between desperate gulps of air.

He moves his lips to my ear, his cool breath fanning against my skin as he whispers, *"You like that, my little succubus?"*

I'm overcome with jitters rolling over the muscles of my

shoulders and through my chest, spreading to my arms and legs as my skin pricks with heat. I manage a nervous nod.

I hold my breath as he pulls his hand out of my pants and straightens to shimmy them down. I make my limbs pliable so he can maneuver them off easier. He tosses them onto the floor and slips his fingers back inside me, watching himself touch me as he wraps his hand around himself to stroke.

I clasp my hands on my chest, biting my lip as he moves back between my legs. I think he's going to fuck me until he lowers himself onto his belly. He kisses the inside of my thigh, and then the other, before gently kissing the wet space between them and running his tongue against me.

I'm in bliss as he pushes his fingers back inside me, his tongue circling and flicking against me until I'm moaning and trying not to twist away from him to run from the increasingly unbearable pleasure. But he hooks his arm around the top of my thigh as his tongue works fast.

Laurentius pauses to whisper, *"I want you to come for me."*

I gasp for breath, my fingers tangled in his hair at the feel of his quick tongue and the depth of his fingers.

A feeling rolls through me, a consuming, burning electricity that has my mind spinning around Laurentius and the way his body manipulates mine. *Love*, I think. It's the same feeling I had when Denendrius touched me, though brighter, pure, and unsullied, like the love I thought I had for Denendrius.

"I love you." The words slip out on a dry breath before I consider the consequence of uttering them.

Laurentius stiffens, his lips breaking away from my skin. His cold, labored breath fans against the soft interior of my thighs and over my stomach as he lifts his head to meet my eyes.

I hold my breath, trying to find a reason for his silence and inaction in his blank, unemotional expression.

He sits between my legs, one hand coming up to hold the

side of my knee as he tilts his head to the side and gently says, "That's enough for tonight."

A twang of pain ricochets through my chest. *Confusion. Embarrassment. Disappointment . . .*

"Why?" I breathe, moving my knees together as a feverish heat spreads over my flesh, Laurentius shifting backward from their collision path.

There's a flicker of unease in his brooding eyes, and he grimaces as he says, "We've only known one another a few weeks, and we've already had our first kiss and touched one another in a few hours. Your words tell me we're moving too swiftly for you to cope with."

"But you made me feel . . ." I swallow, not entirely sure what to say.

The corner of his lip quirks. "Pleasure is not love, Marianna. If it were, men would marry whores each night."

I lower my gaze. "I know," I whisper, always having understood that reality in some way—none of the men who sought gratification from me as a child ever loved me—but not comprehending how *that* feeling could come from someone you don't have feelings for.

He squeezes my knee, and I lift my eyes to his.

"I do like you though," I say, holding back telling him how *I want to love him too.*

His grin lights up his face. "I very much like you too, Marianna. But you need time to settle. So much about you and your life has been transforming. There's no reason to rush. We have forever."

I draw in a deep breath, the sweet smell of him remaining thick in my nose, and my shoulders drop as I shove it out of my lungs.

"Besides," Laurentius whispers, stroking the side of my bare thigh before raking his fingers up and down it. "I . . . *really* like you. I shouldn't be so intimate with you when I thirst as I do. I should know better, and it would torture me for eternity if I accidentally killed you and your baby."

Slowly, I straighten and stare at him. *"What . . . ?"*

His eyes drop from mine. "I'm sorry, I could tell when I—" he motions to my crotch. "I shouldn't have said that out loud, should I? I suppose you were trying to keep it a secret and now everyone will know."

I can barely hear my voice over the sound of my pounding heart and labored breath. "You're fucking crazy." When I clamber off the bed, I can't think straight. "You just—you don't know what you're talking about."

Laurentius appears in front of me, but I'm too dizzy to read his expression. He blocks me and backs me up against the side of the bed, only a few inches between us.

I cringe away with a stroke of fear. "I'm sorry, that was really mean to say—"

Holding his hand against my hip, he whispers, "You didn't know you were?"

I can't feel my body, my lips or tongue as I say, "I can't be pregnant."

He shifts closer, barely an inch between us. "You are, Marianna."

The memory of Viorel's meltdown when he drank from me enters my mind. "No."

Laurentius must have a similar thought as he reaches up to touch the part of my neck where Viorel's bite once was. "He would have tasted it. He didn't tell you?"

The floor feels like it shifts under my feet as my balance tilts. I stare down at the carpet, but it looks as firm as before. "You're wrong. It's impossible for me to be pregnant. I've never had my period."

Still, my words don't calm me down. Ziggy's phone call— when he warned me Denendrius would kill me in three years before the future changed—charges back into my mind. I didn't allow myself to mull over it before . . .

I would have had a two-year-old daughter . . . *in three years.*

"That's not how it works," he says. "Did nobody teach you about your body? Your first period comes after the first time you ovulate. But if you get pregnant first . . ."

"I skipped health class," I hear myself say, voice monotone. I didn't think I could emotionally handle sitting there while the teacher talked about sex and reproduction, never mind all the comments everyone in my class would have made about it. "I avoided thinking about that stuff too."

Would Denendrius have known those kinds of things when he was human?

I see Laurentius lace his fingers through mine, but I can't feel it. "Do you want me to see if there's a pregnancy test around? To see for yourself?"

I stare up at him with wide eyes, everything from my tongue to my emotions numb.

We dress before he gently tugs me along, an arm around me like he thinks I'm going to collapse on the floor. I probably would if it weren't for him. I can't feel my legs as we drift through the hall.

Could I be sleeping, trapped in a vivid nightmare?

Silence stretches to each crevice of the castle halls, my heartbeat loud as we enter the empty infirmary past the shower rooms. I stare at the stone room through my narrow vision, wishing I could feel my legs enough to curl up on the stiff white sheets of one of the old metal hospital beds lining each side of the long room.

"Ashley?" Laurentius calls out.

I'm alone for a long moment, my eyes settling on the ugly green cart of supplies four beds away, until movement—a woman with her blond hair in a sloppy bun opening a locked green cabinet on the far side of the room—captures my attention.

As she walks across the room to me with narrow lips and uneasy eyes, I know exactly what she's thinking because it's the one reality I haven't been able to drift away from.

Denendrius's baby is inside me.

She gives Laurentius a long stare as she holds two tests out to me. I'm not sure how long I gawk at the white plastic packs without lifting my limp hands. Long enough that she sighs and hands them to Laurentius.

My vision shrinks to a pinpoint as Laurentius takes my hand and turns me around to leave. I'm not sure how it happens—whether I walk there out of my mind, or he carries me—but I stand in the open stall of the bathroom off the grand room, a half open pregnancy test in my hand and my pants and underwear halfway down my thighs. Laurentius stands in front of me, saying something that must be English—but sounds foreign. The sight of myself in the mirror directly behind him is all I can focus on. If it weren't for my sandy hair and my clothes, I'm not sure I'd recognize myself.

"Hey, honey." Carol's voice comes from somewhere around me, then she blocks sight of me.

Her presence invokes the memory of her sitting at the kitchen table with Derek and Rayonne at her place in Lorimer, and how she said she wants to separate Denendrius and me before they have to deal with a teen pregnancy on top of everything else.

I can't be pregnant.

Carol frowns, her eyes misty. "Oh, honey . . ."

I must have spoken aloud, but I can't feel my mouth. My ears ring.

She turns to Laurentius. When she speaks, it's so muffled, despite how she's only two feet from me. *"Thank you for getting me, but you shouldn't be in the bathroom with us. I've got this."*

I hope he doesn't leave. I don't want him to.

"No, she wants me to stay," he tells her gently.

My vision's a screen of static, my eyes pained. Time and I have desynchronized.

Carol's body takes up my entire sight as she leans facing me. The feel of the cold toilet seat is against my skin.

We must sit there for an hour, but Carol says, "Okay, it's been three minutes."

My gaze rakes down through the air. I'm bare on the toilet, the water below my parted thighs yellow. I don't remember taking a test.

Carol's a blur as she turns around and stands with her back to me. She's so quiet, so still. I don't have to ask what the result is.

I'm pregnant with Denendrius's baby.

The light around Carol contorts as she turns to face me. There's a trail chasing my hand as I lift it toward her. When she sets the test in my hand, the two pink lines burn into my vision.

"It's okay," Laurentius whispers, appearing in a squat in front of me, one hand brushing wetness from my cheeks while the other pushes my underwear back into place. Carol paces in and out of view with her teeth jammed into her lower lip and her arms crossed tight across herself.

Seth walks into view, and Carol quickly closes the stall door on me and Laurentius.

"Is she okay?" Seth asks. "Viorel says she's upset. He wants her back downstairs."

He knew.

The thought claws around my head, slamming through my numb thoughts.

He knew, and he didn't tell me.

Heat pricks my skin like hot needles, and I break out in a furious sweat. My head pounds.

How could he not tell me?

My eyes lock with Laurentius, wild with concern. I hear myself say, *"You don't want me anymore."*

Something sharp is stuck inside my chest and I take in deep, quick breaths to dislodge it.

Laurentius tucks his arm around my waist and lifts me to my dead feet, crushing me against his body in a hug as he pulls my pants up for me and promises me that this changes nothing for him.

I can't quite bring myself to believe him when Carol looks at me differently, too.

XXXI

"You fucking asshole!" I bellow as I find Viorel at the bookshelf beside his wardrobe.

He slips a leather-bound book back on the wooden shelf and turns to face me, his patient expression only igniting my nerves with hellfire.

"I'm pregnant," I say through grit teeth.

"I'm sorry you found out that way."

My lip curls back and I jab my index finger at him. "You're sorry *I found out!*"

"I planned on telling you soon—"

"You should have told me as soon as you knew! At *least* once you finished having a fit about it."

His calmness only makes my blood boil. "I was trying to protect you, Marianna. I did not wish to deliver the news while you remained marked by him, and it would have been a horrible blow of knowledge to have so soon after. I wanted to see if the pregnancy was viable before I put you through the grief of learning you are pregnant and a potential miscarriage."

My jaw lowers, a scoff of disbelief falling from the back of my throat. "So what? If I miscarried, would you have passed it off as my first period?"

He nods like there's absolutely nothing wrong with that. "It would be much easier for you to not know the truth if it happened."

"You don't get to make that decision for me!" I holler. "I'm a *person*, Viorel. Not a pet. It's my fucking body, even if your blood is coursing through it! I have a right to know what's happening to me, and a right to feel whatever I feel about it!"

Viorel's soft expression doesn't change as he ponders my words. "Okay," he says. "I'm sorry."

My mouth opens to unleash another argument I've loaded, but his words have me mashing my lips together and gritting my teeth. "You're sorry?"

"Yes." He tilts his head.

I tighten my fists at my sides. "You're not going to tell me I'm being dumb, and I should listen to you because you know best as my master, or some shit?"

His brows lift, and he shakes his head. "No, not at all. I thought I was helping you by mitigating your suffering, but you made a good argument for your autonomy. I overstepped, so I'm sorry."

Tears well in my eyes, voice croaking as I say, "You weren't waiting until I'm further along, so I have no choice but to keep it, so you have another living thing to torture Denendrius with?"

"I've no concern about Denendrius's role in your pregnancy or how it affects him."

A flood of tears escapes my burning eyes. I hunch over and sob.

"Oh . . ." Viorel sighs. "Marianna, come lie down."

I feel violated, like Denendrius has done this on purpose against my will. I suppose he has, what with letting me believe I couldn't get pregnant, not putting an ounce of thought into prevention, and brushing me off whenever I mentioned I wasn't sure if I was ready, like he didn't take me seriously.

I stumble to the bed and curl up on my side with my knees to my chest to weep. Viorel sits on the edge of the bed near me as I empty myself, a hand resting on the blanket a few inches away like he wants to offer a comforting touch but doesn't want to upset me.

"You didn't get a choice in making it," Viorel starts softly. "But it's yours now, in *your* body, being made of *you*. Only you can choose what to do with it now. But that *choice* is fully yours. Denendrius is rotting in a cell, and he will do nothing more than he already has."

"Denendrius would want me to keep it," I sob. "He would be so happy to know he's done this to me."

There's no humor in Viorel's rebuking laughter. "He *does not* want you to keep it, I promise you. When he tried to drink you to death, he knew you were pregnant. He wants both you and that baby dead."

I sniffle hard and brush tears away, only smearing them across my soaked cheeks. My deep breath is shaky but comes easier with the freedom of Viorel's words.

It doesn't matter what I choose then, Denendrius will be unhappy either way.

My fingers stroke the soft velvet of the blanket, my eyes trained on Viorel's hand so close to mine. I hold my breath as he places his long and cold, slender fingers over mine, the tips of his pointed nails pressing into the velvet. They're pretty and provide a short distraction. I think of how elegant they would look playing violin or pressing the keys of a piano.

"You'll be all right, Marianna," Viorel says as his hand slips away, forcing my focus back on myself.

I squeeze my eyes closed, pushing tears past my wet lashes.

"How is it my body only starts working when he crashes back into my life?"

Viorel sighs. "It's possible you had a condition Denendrius's healing resolved."

"Like what?" I brush tears away from my eyes.

"Since vampire venom cannot restructure underdeveloped organs, I suspect it was something curable. Perhaps something with your pituitary gland, like a tumor or cyst."

There's a pause in my tears, and my heart pounds with terror. "A tumor? Could it have been from the cure? Denendrius was having seizures and going blind. His doctor wanted to check for a brain tumor. Could I have died if he didn't heal me?"

"They're usually benign," he assures me. "But tumors, as a side effect of the cure, would not surprise me since the cure causes massive DNA disruptions and changes."

We're silent for a long moment until my reality has me choking on sobs again.

"Do you know how pregnant I am?" I choke out.

"I can't say for sure, and it's more difficult to know since we cannot count from a last bleed . . . but you're about five weeks along."

"You can tell from tasting my blood?" I exhale a shuddery breath and lower my knees a bit, back aching from the tight position.

"Hormones increase in your blood as pregnancy progresses, and I've tasted enough in my eternity to know what all the minute variations mean."

The flood of emotion is relentless, but I wipe my eyes. "I don't know what to do. I wish I weren't pregnant to begin with." My eyes meet his. "I'm paralyzed with indecision."

"I think you should keep it." He pats my hand as he looks down at it. "But you have two choices. If you want to keep it, I will make sure you are well taken care of. Otherwise, there's termination."

My brow furrows. "Have an abortion . . .?"

He pats my hand again. "Yes. Do you have moral qualms?"

"No, but how would I see a doctor when you won't let me leave—"

"I would make you sleep and take care of it," he interrupts. "It would be quick and painless."

I ponder that for a long minute as he studies me.

"What about adoption?" I whisper. The idea of glimpsing her in the castle occasionally is appealing.

"Marianna . . ." Viorel says carefully. "By proxy, I've marked the baby. My blood flows through both of you and is helping it grow, so I cannot allow anyone else to have it."

My eyes widen on him and I'm cold with horror over the idea of some half-vampire creature inside my fragile body.

His smile is shaky, like he's trying to hide it. "Nothing like that, Marianna. It will be human. I can't say the ways *my* blood will affect it, but vampire blood has never caused harm to the unborn."

"But your blood is different."

His eyes sparkle. "There's no reason to believe it would negatively impact it when my blood never harmed a tiny newborn like Tatiana."

"That's different," I argue.

"Well, perhaps it will make it immune to illness, or give it iron bones."

"You think so?"

He nods, a soft smile on his lips. "Mark aside, there are no consequences for humans consuming immortal blood."

"And you'd really be okay with me keeping it? Why? It's Denendrius's."

"It's yours."

The reality weighs on me. "Yeah . . . I guess. But it ties me to him." Tears spring in my eyes, my lids feeling paper thin from constant rubbing.

"In which way? The baby is not a string connecting you to him. It's a separate entity holding a mixture of DNA. It's merely borrowed material. He has no hold over you and the baby, no claim to it. The baby will be no more Denendrius than you are your mother."

"What if I have her, and it hurts to look at her? What if I hate her because of what he did to me? He *raped* me. Maybe not when she was conceived . . . but that's still my rapist's baby."

"*Her?*" Viorel leans closer, eyes wide and glittering with curiosity.

I swallow and clench the blanket. "Ziggy's friend had a vision of Denendrius murdering me in front of our two-year-old daughter in three years. I must be having a girl."

His eyes sparkle as he ponders the news, then says, "You may feel those things, or nothing close. I will not convince you that keeping . . . *her* . . . would be simple, given how she came to be, but perhaps having a daughter would have a much different impact on you than having a son."

I nod, understanding what he means.

"Either way, I find it hard to believe *you* would resent her for something she had nothing to do with. You might see her and feel nothing but awe that something so precious came from you. You might see yourself as a child and want to shower her with the love you didn't have."

"What if she looks all like him and nothing like me?"

The corner of his lip lifts in a little smile. "Unlikely. Perhaps there may be physical reminders of him, but he is here in the dungeon. You will never escape reminders of him in this castle. Besides, with how genetics work, she may come out looking like neither one of you, instead resembling an ancestor."

"True." I bite my bottom lip. "He's so close . . . You don't think it'd cause problems with her?"

"They locked your mother up but an hour away from you. Did you have a desire to entertain her, knowing how she was?"

I half-shrug. "Only once, when I had questions. But it was a waste of time and I never wanted to see her again."

"Anything pertaining to Denendrius is easily manageable," Viorel promises.

Narrowing my eyes, I study his calm face. "Why do you want me to have this baby? Why are you trying to convince me to keep it?"

His brows twitch. "Does it seem like I'm trying to convince you? I'm sorry. Truly, I want you to make your own decision. I'm simply answering your questions."

Sitting, I wipe the drying tears off my cheeks. "Tell me why, if it's not to torture Denendrius?"

He lowers his head a bit, a nervousness in the way his eyes flick away and back to mine. "My blood is helping her grow, will course through her as she develops. I will feel her becoming a person as you feel her grow. That makes me her father in a way, doesn't it?"

My lips fall apart, and I lean back a bit in shock. "You want to be her *father*? Why?"

"I've given it much thought since Mateo calmed me down. It would be nice to raise a child as my own for once, and this will be as close as someone in my condition can be to fathering one."

I lift my brow. "In twelve thousand years, you've never tried fatherhood out?"

"A child is a lot to lose," he whispers. "And I lose everybody. I've been a surrogate father to hundreds of children, but I've never marked a pregnant woman and gone on that journey as if it's my own."

I swallow and pick at my nail, trying to imagine how life would be playing house with him. The reality is undefined, but any man would be a better father than Denendrius. I would rather have Viorel claim her as his own—and all the benefits attached—than raise her alone, with only Denendrius to fill the empty role in her mind. "Okay," I say quickly, like he might change his mind with his next breath.

He leans closer. "*If* you decide to keep her. I just want you to be happy."

Yet even after the moon switches spots with the sun and reappears for another night, I'm no closer to a decision.

I huff as I throw myself down in my chair across from Viorel as he sits at the table scrutinizing a new wooden puzzle.

"Every time I tune into your head, you're cycling through the same thoughts . . ." He glances up at me from a piece in his hand, the corner of his lip lifting. "Are you done pacing from room to room, chair to chair, bed to bed, or will this continue through the day as well?"

Resting my elbow on the chair arm, I plop my chin on my palm and huff. "I want both equally, though I mostly wish I wasn't pregnant in the first place and didn't have to decide."

"You don't have to decide tonight." He clicks the puzzle piece into place. "But you are limited for time."

"I wish I could have both, walk back and forth between the two realities at will. Decide which one I like best." I gnaw at my cheek and rest back in the chair.

He leans back in his chair too, ignoring the puzzle as he folds his hands on his lap. "What scares you the most about it?"

I close my eyes and flop my head back against the wood. "I don't know."

"Figure it out," he says simply, "and we'll start there."

There are too many things I'm equally scared about, so I start with, "What if I change my mind after I have the baby, and wish I hadn't taken on such an enormous responsibility?"

"It won't be an enormous responsibility for you. I will take an equal share in caring for it, as I said. Besides, Ainsley and the other ladies in the nursery will be tickled over the idea of caring for a newborn since they haven't seen one in years, and I'm sure your aunt would help at least a little."

I can't help the doubtful quirk of my brow. "You didn't say you'd take equal share. You said you'd be its father. I thought you meant in title, and I figured by help, you meant hold it occasionally."

He shakes his head playfully, a sweet smirk curling his lips. *"You assumed."*

My laugh is tired. "Can you blame me? Why should I think you have a modern preference for fatherhood when you're having me wear archaic dresses and trying to help me by withholding knowledge about my body?"

His lips purse. "Hmm. Fair," he says before his face returns to its seriousness. "But I mean it. You won't face the woes of motherhood. My blood will make pregnancy a breeze. No nausea. No uncomfortable misery. I'll take your pain away during childbirth. I'll heal you, so recovery will be nonexistent. You will never have to be sleep deprived and you'll always have time for yourself. I'll ensure your experience as a mother is as easy and ideal as I can make it. Parenting will be simpler with my abilities. I will know her needs despite her not being able to communicate and am quite good at comforting children."

It all sounds too good to be true, even if I have no reason not to believe him.

"What if I'm a terrible mom?" I frown.

"You won't be. Ainsley will teach you, and it's not like I'm lacking in knowledge."

"I guess." There's no way to argue with that. "I was okay at taking care of my foster siblings."

"Let yourself think about what it might be like. The good things." He smiles to himself and continues working on his puzzle.

I try. I do my best to ignore the thought of Denendrius as I imagine myself holding a little baby and teaching her to walk down the long halls of the castle.

This *is* the best place—nearly the best situation, disregarding Denendrius's role in this—to have a baby. I'll get all the joys of motherhood without too many of the avoidable negatives.

A small smile slips onto my lips until a gutting realization has my stomach dropping. "You'll never let her leave the castle because of your mark, will you?"

His lips tighten into a thin line as he looks up at me. "No, Marianna, I'm sorry."

I stare at my lap and wring my fingers together. "I don't think it's fair to give birth to her, then."

"She will not know of the human world," Viorel argues. "She will not know what she's missing. The children here are happy."

"She'll grow up," I counter. "Talk to the other vampires and learn about it. She will blame us for keeping her under lock and key like a princess in a tower."

"Perhaps she will understand. She will never experience the darkness of the human world, either. Never have to worry about being an outcast with me as her father. She will never starve, freeze, or experience poverty."

I stare him right in the eyes as I say, "Tatiana grew up like that, didn't she? And she still yearned to experience the world so much she—"

He stands abruptly and walks past me, gown sweeping against the floor as he leaves the room.

"Viorel . . ." I close my eyes.

"You've had nothing, and now you demand *everything*," he says tersely from the other room.

"Don't be a dick because you're mad I'm right."

His tired voice comes from the doorway behind me. "I want

to give you the freedom you want, as bad as you want it, Marianna. But I *cannot*."

"You're painfully paranoid," I whisper, refusing to open my eyes to turn and look at him.

"My fears are not imagined or unjust. I am profoundly aware of the dangers and possibilities coming with the unpredictability of existence, and I do my best to lessen the extent of potential harm. You cannot comprehend the betrayals and injustices I've witnessed in my time."

It's such a sad, suffocating way to view life. I can't even be mad at him. "I know how awful the world can be, Viorel. I had a gang hunting me and I *still* left the house, despite knowing I could get shot or grabbed at any moment. What's the point of living if you're *not living?*"

He's quiet for so many moments that I open my eyes and peek around the back of the chair to see if he's gone.

But he stands there, the reflection of candlelight flickering in his unblinking eyes. "I'm a prisoner to time. Everyone I've ever loved or cared for has died, and the moments with them went as quickly as they came. Please don't blame me for wishing to extend the little time I'm granted. Please be thankful for what I can give you, considering all you lacked before coming here."

I straighten in my chair and release a slow breath, reminding myself again that if it weren't for me being here, I'd still be blood marked and with Denendrius. I don't want to imagine the sort of abuse and treatment from having a baby with him. Never mind the fact I'd be dead in three years anyway if they hadn't found us. Should I really complain about being stuck in a *massive* castle when the alternative is dead?

I suppose there *are* smaller and worse places than a castle to grow up in. The castle has more to offer than most towns and schools do. A massive library with unfiltered knowledge, hobby rooms well-stocked with supplies, healthy food constantly available. A melting pot of cultures and people. She can learn history from the mouths of those who lived it. She could learn anything she wants here.

Closing my eyes again, I force myself to swallow the truth. I really can't have everything. It's not realistic.

At least this life is adjacent to the normal one I want. Riches, friends and family, a nice house, and someone to have a family with. Besides, I may never get another chance to have a baby.

"Okay," I whisper. "I'll keep her."

XXXII

Stepping into the grand room, I'm greeted with the residual of dozens of dropping conversations and the intense crackle of flames in the fireplace. Eyes cut toward me and away, faces turning to me in curiosity or making a point to look away at a book or their sofa seat mate as to not seem prying.

God fucking damn it.

I grit my teeth and pretend I'm oblivious to their attention on me, that I *can't possibly know* what's running through their minds.

By the time I reach the center of the room, my heart is spasming, and it takes everything in me not to snap at the nearest vampire for glancing at me for a few moments too long. But I say nothing. I don't want to risk the retorts I'm sure most of them have waiting on their tongues.

There are no foul sneers or cursed wishes, but there are no congratulations either.

By the time I reach the staircase, I wonder what the fuck is wrong with me for letting this go on. Am I crazy for not begging

Viorel to cut Denendrius's baby out of me? Is everyone behind me thinking I should?

I keep my eyes forward as I force my aching, exhaustion laden legs to make the climb to Carol and Derek's room.

Derek opens the door as I reach it. He does a poor job of hiding the concern on his face as he ushers me in and shuts the door behind me.

"Hey, honey . . ." Carol's tone is gentle, like I'm cracked glass waiting for the wrong octave to shatter.

"I decided to keep the baby," I tell them as I cross the room and crawl onto the end of the bed, Derek tailing me.

Carol merely gives me a tight-lipped flinch of a smile. Derek's brows twitch up as he leans against the side of the bed and loosely crosses his arms. "Were you given other options?" he asks me, as his eyes flicker to Carol.

Of course, they both think I should abort. I can't blame them.

I half shrug. "Viorel offered an abortion, but I can't bring myself to do it no matter how much I hate Denendrius. Part of me wants to get rid of her because it's Denendrius's, but she's mine, too. If I get rid of her because of something to do with him, it's another thing he's controlling. Denendrius wants a baby, but he would rather the baby and me die now. I can't consider Denendrius in my decision."

Carol and Derek share a glance.

"Her?" Carol's tight and nervous gaze flickers over my torn expression.

I explain Patricia's vision, how Ziggy called me when Denendrius and I were on the road running away and warned me. I expect a gender reveal to elicit a small smile from Carol, but pity remains in her eyes and the lines of her frown.

Derek gives me a tight-lipped smile and nods. "Adoption?"

"The baby is marked by proxy," I explain, my voice tired. "Viorel can't have her adopted."

Derek frowns. His eyes are bright with worry as he searches my face, his brows deeply furrowed.

There's a slight shake to Carol's head, like she hates what she's hearing, but doesn't want to outright admit I should abort. "A baby is hard, especially as a single mother. I would help, but it's hard when you're downstairs most of the time. Have you thought about what it might be like to raise a baby in isolation?"

With a reassuring smile, I say, "Viorel will step up as her father and be fully involved. He said he'll make motherhood easy for me."

They're no less stressed. If anything, my words have only made the line between Derek's brows more severe. Carol's lips twist in concerned thought.

"Marianna . . ." He pushes out a noisy sigh and tightens his arms against his chest as he grimaces. "I think you should think about it a little longer."

I gnaw at my cheek, worries forming like acid bubbles in my gut. What if *they* hate her? My breath becomes a stone in my throat and a grimace contorts my face. I mash my lips together and force myself to think of a way to change the topic before panic can set in again.

"What?" they ask in sharp, unified concern.

I gulp it down and manage to breathe. "In other news, Viorel thinks I was a child vampire. Either something happened in those one or two extra years I can't remember, or I was never Bonnie's daughter to begin with."

Her face pales with horror.

"Why does he think that?" Carol asks, white rimming her eyes.

I rattle off the list of reasons and tell her how Mateo is looking for answers. She blows out a shaky breath and gives her head a slow shake.

"You need a hug," she decides as she twists off the side of the bed and thuds onto the carpet.

I can't blame her for being wordless. I wouldn't know what to say either, after having all this dumped on me.

When she rounds the bed and constricts me with a hug, I lean into her—into the sharp fragrance of citrus and florals locked in her tight and poofy curls—and close my eyes with the realization she's never hugged me this way before. Not since I was a child, perhaps.

"Do you wish you'd stayed in Lorimer?" I whisper. "Wish you had sent me away instead of your other foster kids?"

Her head shakes gently against the side of mine. "No. When you were a little girl, I decided you were my niece. I spent years after we lost you trying to get you back, to no avail. I wasn't about to have you torn out of my life a second time."

"Even though I'm pregnant with a monster's baby and could have who knows what lurking in my past?"

"Even then," she whispers.

I squeeze her back and fill my lungs as she tells me she's going to be here for me, no matter what I choose to do. It's the first time I can remember hearing those words, and all I can do is hope nothing detaches itself from the dark to challenge them.

A girl is waiting outside Derek's door when I step out. My hands instinctively curl into fists before the bright smile meeting her canary yellow painted lids—rich and bold against her dark skin—has me heaving out a breath and reducing my panic to mere worry.

She holds out a large bar of chocolate to me, the gold wrapper shining under the candlelight.

Her French accent is so thick I strain to understand. "For

you, Marianna. You only know of America, I heard. I have this from France. I want you to have something sweet today."

I accept the chocolate, something hot and acidic—embarrassment, perhaps—brewing in my gut. "Thanks a lot." My smile is pained. "I'll probably devour the entire bar in one go."

She gives me a little bow to go with her grand grin, before making a pleased sound as she wanders away.

I take the long way to Laurentius's hall to avoid the grand room. My palms sweat with worry about what he might say to me.

When I near the downstairs door, I dart past it like being too close to it might cause Viorel to revoke permission to sleep upstairs with Rayonne today.

I swear I hear whispering in Laurentius's room when I approach his door, but it opens as I reach it, and I don't have time to take in his face before he swoops me into a tight hug and drags me into his room.

"I'm keeping it," I blurt as the door thuds shut behind us.

He releases me, taking a small step back to mull me over with his worried eyes. No words pass through his thinly pressed lips.

"Viorel thinks I should, and I agree. He wants to claim the baby as his own, and this is probably the only chance I'll ever get to have one," I continue, wringing my fingers together in front of myself while I try to convince both him and me.

There's a strange twinge in his crimson eyes, his deep swallow visible as he nods. "Of course."

My heart beats uncomfortably at the base of my throat. "What are you thinking?"

When he doesn't answer, acidic worry burns a hole in my gut as he instead takes my hand and brings me onto his bed to hold me.

With Laurentius sitting propped against the headboard and me alongside him with my head resting on his tense shoulder, all I can do is hope he's not thinking about anything too awful.

"Do you still want to be with me?" The disappointment is thick in his voice, like he's sure I'll reject him now.

"I was hoping." I bite the edge of my lip and scrape the gold wrapper away from my chocolate bar with my thumb.

His arms tighten around me. "I wasn't sure. It sounds like you have new plans with Viorel now."

I can't help my strangled chuckle. "Oh. He only wants to be the father. He's not interested in me like that. I'm just his familiar."

"Hmm." Laurentius plants a kiss on my head. "Okay."

"So, you don't think I should get rid of it?" I take a bite of my chocolate bar, rich cocoa melting on my tongue.

He places another kiss between the strands of my hair. "I think you should do whatever is right for you."

I exhale anxiety deep from my lungs and nibble on my chocolate bar while Laurentius holds me close. He strokes my bare arm, leaving goosebumps behind under his cool touch.

When I'm halfway through the massive chocolate bar and nausea is creeping into me, I leave it on Laurentius's nightstand and oblige him to a trip to the library.

We cuddle up on a sofa. He writes Hebrew in one of his notebooks while I pick through a monstrous book about the Middle Ages written by a now deceased clan member. I'm only able to attain partial focus, as I can't shake the feel of eyes lingering on me. I catch a few sets peering at me over the handful of hours we relax and fret over what I know they're thinking.

I know everyone knows I'm pregnant with Denendrius's baby, yet nobody dares speak to me about it. Their silence is for the best, since most of them are probably waiting for Viorel to deal with my pregnancy quietly so they won't have Denendrius's spawn living amongst them.

We meet Carol and Derek in the dining hall for our midnight meal, sitting out of immediate sight in the left corner against a purple velvet drape decorating the stone wall. The stares continue as we wait for our plates to be prepared. I focus my attention on the feel of Laurentius's hand on my thigh and how my timed breaths agitate the tear drop flame of the red pillar candle on our table. I'm too focused on my attempt to block out the feeling of being watched that I don't notice Laurentius set my plate in front of me until he nudges it and tells me it's Shakshuka.

I train my gaze on the dish, the mouth-watering flavor of tomatoes, peppers, and eggs, distracting, but can't shake the feel of being watched.

"Everybody is staring at me," I mouth to Derek.

He cuirks a brow and looks around over his shoulder. "Are you sure? I haven't noticed."

Laurentius and Carol give me the same puzzled stare.

I heave out a breath and shovel food into my mouth, refusing to believe I'm imagining it.

But soon I can't handle the eyes on me anymore, and I stand abruptly and announce that I'm going to my room alone to think and wait until they release Rayonne from the ward. I leave Laurentius with a kiss—which inexplicably has Carol bright with a grin—only to be stopped outside of the dining hall by three vampire girls with soft smiles and avoidant eyes. They say little past offering a tin of caramel fudge to me, but I understand it must be a sympathy gift, and how the chocolate likely was too.

XXXIII

A gnawing feeling in my gut has me halting in the middle of the hall as I approach my bedroom door. It tells me to turn around. *Tells me someone is right behind me, watching me.*

I spin, my wide gaze landing on an ivory skinned girl with black curls and bangs standing at the top of the stairs. She hastens down the hall in a black and red lace dress that's larger than life. With her bright smile and scarlet eyes, she fits into the surrounding scenery.

"Rayonne." My knee wobbles, relief nearly whisking me off my feet.

"Good to know my influencing abilities work as they used to," she says with a cherry-lipped grin.

"Almost scared the shit out of me—" Her colliding hug forces the breath from my lungs.

"It's so good to be here. To be me again," she says. "I've got you to thank for that."

I step back as she releases me, my brow furrowed as I shake my head. "No, Rayonne. I almost ruined everything."

"The mark nearly ruined everything." She links her arm with mine and we continue to the bedroom. "Really, there wasn't anything to ruin, anyway. The *only* reason we are here is because you contacted Alaire and Edmond. Who knows who Agatha and her bosses were working for since it wasn't Viorel. Plus, there's no way I would have kept Denendrius under control until I found a contact to turn him in myself."

I blow out a breath and squeeze my tin of fudge. "Fine. We'll chalk it up to teamwork."

Her laugh is musical, and my heart stutters as she uses her renewed strength to swing me gently into the room.

I quirk a brow as she thuds on the bed closest to the door, her suitcase strewn about it.

"The other smelled like you, so I assumed you claimed it."

I grin and plop down on the edge beside her. "Good guess."

She looks around the room and draws in a shaky breath. Her black-rimmed eyes water, but she hides her emotion with a wider smile. "I wish Alessander and Thomas were here with me." Her smile falters. "Sometimes I feel guilty for escaping that burning church, how I should have let Denendrius give me the same fate as them."

"You're allowed to be happy," I tell her. "You don't have to be trapped in the past."

She links her pale fingers together on her lacy lap. "I know." She exhales and we're quiet for a beat before she asks, "How are you?"

"I don't really know how to answer," I whisper. "How was the ward?"

She releases an exaggerated sigh. "Noisy. But otherwise, not too bad. Kind of what I imagine a mental hospital to be like."

My brows lift. "That doesn't sound fun."

Rayonne dismisses my worry with a wave of her hand. "It was fine. The room was comfortable, and I could leave it to socialize. We'd play weird games to help self-control. They'd put us in a room with a human and whoever went the longest without losing it, and could walk out before doing so, won. We'd compete to see who could make our chalice of blood last the longest."

It's strange to think Laurentius was once down there, locked in a little room and playing games of will.

I nod, completely unsure how to respond or what questions to ask with my own life busying my mind.

"Oh!" Her bright eyes widen. "I heard the annual ball is soon, and you're seeing a man already?"

"I haven't heard about a ball."

She smirks. "Well, you're coming. Bring the man, and I'll help you get a dress."

"Okay," I agree, the romantic idea of Laurentius and me dancing not enough to soothe the raw ache of my soul right now.

"Also, you told me how you didn't want to think about dating vampire men. It's been a handful of weeks, and you already have a boyfriend?"

I shrug. "I didn't seek him out. It happened, and I really like him, so I'm not about to pass him up."

Rayonne tilts her head and frowns. "But you're unhappy. What is it?"

The circumstances of my new life spill out of me. The fact Viorel thinks I'm a year or two older, the sun and garlic harming me, and how it made him realize I was likely a vampire.

I spit the worst out before my throat closes. "And I'm pregnant."

Her head pulls back. "What?"

Staring, I wait for my words to register.

Her hands move to cover her mouth. "Oh my god." She stares at me. "I'm so sorry, but *oh my god.*"

I draw my lips into my mouth.

Her eyes water, and she waves her hand in front of her face to save her makeup. "I'm so sorry, Marianna, but . . ."

My eyes lower. "Tell me about it."

I unload all of it on her, how Laurentius was the one to tell me, and how Viorel knew for weeks. How I think I'm having a baby girl because of Patricia's vision, and how absolutely terrified I am.

Tears at bay, she asks, "What are you going to do?"

"I think I'm going to keep it. Viorel offered an abortion, but . . ." I shake my head.

"You've decided in a day?" She frowns.

"Viorel thinks I should, and I can't find a reason other than Denendrius to disagree. I always thought I'd maybe want my own, far in the future if I ever got married, but it won't happen. This is my only chance to have a child, so I will not let Denendrius's role ruin it."

"What if you fall in love with a human boy here?"

I scrunch my nose. "Date another marked human? That's basically all there is for guys. Seems weird, to be honest. I don't even know if Viorel would allow it, considering any baby I have would automatically be marked."

She blows out a breath between her lips. "Fair enough."

I'm sheepish as I say, "Besides, knowing I might have been a vampire already . . . I might turn when Viorel lets me so I can regain those memories. I already can't see the sun or have garlic. Besides, do I really want to grow old here? I don't think there's *a single* elderly person here. Definitely no elderly vampires."

She snorts. "The transformation weeds out the elderly."

A single, dull beat of laughter falls out of me. "I know I didn't want to think about dating vampire men before, but I'm wanting the eternal love vampirism provides. It would be nice to have a family *forever*. I've barely had one for a full year."

"Are you and Viorel . . ." She cocks a brow like I'm supposed to know what she means.

"What?"

"Romantic? *Intimate?*"

A twisted laugh escapes me. "No. He doesn't see me like that. If I hadn't been Denendrius's blood slave, he would have no interest in me. I'm just a familiar."

She narrows her eyes doubtfully and wipes one of them. "Ah yes, because it's normal for a man of his status to accept any man's child as his own. *Especially his enemy's.*"

I shrug. "He sees it as an opportunity for fatherhood."

"If you say so . . ." She pulls in a long breath, a tear darting from the corner of her eye she quickly swipes away. "I'm your friend, so I'll be here for you . . ." She winces. "It's just hard knowing Denendrius is having a child when he murdered mine."

I swallow a knot. "If it makes you feel any better, it's tormenting him. He really doesn't want me birthing her. Viorel's mark is permanent too, so there's no hope for Denendrius to benefit from her existence."

A shaky smile fights its way to her face, more tears brimming her eyes. She makes a noise that's half-sob, half-laugh. "That does make me feel better."

She gives me another long hug, then apologizes for her tears and the mess on her bed.

We're silent as she unpacks her belongings, and when I can stand it no longer, I tell her about the castle. The library with thousands of books, the weed field, the movie nights.

Contagious excitement spills out of her, and she almost has me convinced the future is bright with worry-free fun.

Then there's a knock on the door.

"Come in," Rayonne calls.

The door swings open, Lucia's serious eyes landing straight on mine.

"Is it true?" she says, a line of wetness on her lower lashes.

I gulp and nod, a loud gasp rushing out of me as she appears at my side and wraps her arms around me.

"*Wow,*" she breathes.

My hands hover reluctantly in the air. "Is this a pity hug?"

There are tears in her chuckle. "No. I'm just so unbelievably jealous."

My head jerks. "Jealous?"

She pulls away from me and wipes her eyes with the sleeve of her cinnamon-brown long sleeve. "You get to have a baby."

"But it's Denendrius's," I whisper.

A strangled chuckle escapes her. "Who cares? It's *a baby*. I haven't seen a baby in decades."

Lucia sticks around to hang out with Rayonne and me, filling us with castle history and century old gossip. They both join me for breakfast with Carol, Derek, and Laurentius—where I swear clan members are still noticing me far too much—before Rayonne and I return to our room to sleep.

A sweet kiss from Laurentius lingers on my lips as I crawl into bed and blow my candle out. Rayonne's snuffed out next.

"We did it," she whispers. "We made it."

I fall asleep with an ember of jealousy warming my gut. Though I'll always be thankful to have escaped Denendrius, I wish I had the same clean slate she does.

XXXIV

I dream of stares turning into violent confrontations and vile insults. My deep worries play out throughout the day. Clan members demanding abortion and leaving when Viorel doesn't comply. Nobody sees *my* daughter. They don't see a little human girl. They see Denendrius. A monster who is reaching from the depths of the dungeon to plague their peaceful eternities. Those who stuck around are cruel. The other children bully her, and I live knowing it's my fault.

When I wake, I stare blankly across the room with tears in my eyes. I question all my choices until the vividness of the dream fades with the arrival of night. I'm quiet through dinner, picking at my Chicken Paella and unable to ignore the glances.

"Fuck this," I snap finally as I stand from my chair.

Derek and Carol share the same perturbed brow quirk, oblivious of the tension in the air. Laurentius stands with me as Rayonne looks around for whoever has caused my outburst.

I march downstairs to Viorel.

"When are you going to say something about the baby to

the clan? It's fucking tense up there, Viorel. Everyone knows." I cross my arms in the doorway of a back room stuffed with boxes and crates as Viorel rummages around for something.

"I was giving you opportunity to change your mind," he says. "And I'd say it would be best to wait in case of miscarriage, but it appears everyone already knows."

I huff. "I'm keeping her. So please clear the air, because I can't stand another minute up there under their scrutiny."

"If you're so sure, we'll make an announcement as soon as I'm finished here."

My heart pounds and I wipe my sweaty palms on my jeans. "I'm sure."

There's a beat of silence filled with rummaging.

"What are you looking for?"

"My wood carving tools. Mateo didn't pay attention while moving everything." He grunts in annoyance. "I want to carve a cradle for her."

"Really?" My heart flutters as my cheeks fill with warmth. "Wow."

My heart slows a bit, his dedication soothing the edge of my nerves. If he's so committed already, perhaps I really have nothing to worry about.

"There it is . . . tossed haphazardly in a drawer." He sighs, though is smiling as he appears in front of me. "Shall we?"

All it takes is guards escorting Viorel and me to the grand room, and clan members collect in whispering bunches.

I stand with weak legs next to Viorel in front of the roaring fireplace, watching as the room fills with hundreds of vampires and their humans. My heart pounds so hard I'm dizzy, unable to make anyone out in the sea of faces before me and collecting on the stairs and in the mouths of hallways.

When Viorel adjusts slightly at my side like he's ready to speak, the shift to complete silence has my ears ringing.

My throat and tongue are stark dry as Viorel thanks everyone for their attention.

"It's clear you've all heard how Marianna is with child," Viorel starts.

Scattered nods.

"I have laid claim to this child and expect it to be treated as my own flesh, as I have made it of my blood," Viorel declares.

My leg buckles as I await my nightmare to come to fruition, but right myself before I think anyone notices.

"Those of you who take issue with this turn of events, I implore you to speak now."

Crickets.

"Not one of you?" His heavy gaze flickers over faces, like he's picking through their thoughts for signs of dispute.

Nobody speaks, many shaking their head to verify their positions.

"Splendid." Viorel smiles. "Anything else? Inquiries? Comments?"

"Does she know the gender?" a woman—masked by the crowd—shouts from somewhere near the back.

There's a hushed stream of voices exchanged as Viorel looks to me for permission. Enough words stand out to me to know someone overheard me telling Carol how I think I'm having a girl. Someone says to zip it, reminding them it's rude to gossip even if you can't help overhearing.

I give Viorel a why-the-fuck-not shrug and nod.

He wraps his arm around me, his hand on my hip as he turns back to the crowd. "A seer predicted a baby girl. Make of that what you will."

There's a few *I told yous* to my right, and the clan becomes an ensemble of chatter.

To my relief, there's not even a whisper of Denendrius's name.

The congratulations pour in.

Once Viorel has dismissed the clan and guards have escorted us back to his chambers, he turns to Seth.

"Malcolm and his familiar are taking a vacation tomorrow." A scowl darkens his expression. *"Ensure they do not return."*

Seth gives him a hard nod before closing the iron door behind him.

"Why?" I ask as I rake my fingers through my hair, my heart thumping with giddiness instead of anxiety now.

Sure, the idea of having a child is still nerve-wracking, but the clan's excitement and support lulls the fearful, questioning voice in the back of my head.

He scowls, the corner of his lip twitching in disdain. "They wish you and the baby ill will and think I'm a dolt for allowing you both to live."

I gulp. "Most of the clan isn't opposed, right?"

"Indeed. Many are neutral, focused on themselves but without ill will, but most are quite excited." He chuckles. "You will hear name suggestions, but don't feel pressured to accept any of them."

Overwhelmed, my mind goes blank. "Right. I get to decide on a name for her."

Maybe I will take their suggestions into consideration. I can't help but think baby name books are the one thing the library won't have.

I spend the rest of the night downstairs as the reality of my choice settles in. Viorel tries to relax me, telling me I have months to prepare. The fact he's already sketching a baby cradle doesn't make her birth feel any less imminent. It will be an opulent swinging cradle with its many gilded carvings and stained wood. When he asks for my thoughts, I laugh. It's already far beyond my imagination. Still, I suggest a sheer canopy, and he draws it held in the beak of a dove.

I assess my room for space later while awaiting my breakfast. Viorel planned for baby clothes by giving me a giant wardrobe, but the idea of not having my room stay *mine*—I can't imagine where else I'd put her stuff—makes me gnaw at my cheek. Thankfully, Viorel assures me I can keep my space, and he'll clear another room out for her, though she'll have to sleep at either of our bedsides for a year minimum.

Pressure on my pelvis slowly draws me awake. My waking mind races, eyelids flying open. My gaze rakes uselessly at the darkness, my sight refusing to return no matter how much I search it.

I try shifting under the weight on me. My hands tangle in the blankets while trying to rip them free to push the weight away. Wriggling is useless. I'm pinned.

"Viorel?" My voice comes out panicked and crisp in the silence.

A candle on his bedside ignites, giving me enough light to see Viorel lift his head off my pelvis. His blinks are slow, eyes dull with sleep.

"What's wrong?" he whispers.

I get my hands free, now able to see how the blanket wraps around them. "What the hell are you doing?"

He sits upright and straightens a section of his long hair that was against my body. "I could hear her tiny heartbeat."

"Oh," I breathe, adrenaline dissipating. "Really? Cool."

He gives me a sleepy smile.

"I don't mind if you do that," I decide. "But you scared me."

He studies my face before resting his head back on my pelvis, though he doesn't let the full weight of it press on me.

"Is she still healthy?" I ask.

"Yes," he murmurs. "Her heart sounds normal."

My smile is small, though I wish I could get an ultrasound.

He tucks his hand beneath his ear and inches my top up to press his cold face against my skin. "Is that all right?"

I nod, the temperature soothing.

"I had such a pleasant dream," Viorel whispers, his eyes starry. "I dreamed I had a son."

I rub my eyes. "Are you hoping I have a boy instead?"

"A second child," Viorel clarifies with a tickled smile. "But I'll be happy with either."

"What did you dream?"

He closes his eyes, his serene smile bright. "In my dream, this baby and him were toddlers, about the same age. He had thick and long brown hair like mine and beautiful brown eyes. A bit of a tan. I think he was made of me. They were giggling together in the garden, running around the bushes to find Laurentius. We must have been playing hide and seek."

I smile. "Sounds like a good dream."

He nods and rests his hand flat against my side, half tucked under my shirt. "I can't help but contemplate what she might look like had we made her together."

My heart skips a beat.

Rayonne was right.

"How long have you felt like this?" Could he have originally asked me to keep the baby to spite Denendrius, or has he felt like this all along? Was he developing feelings for me when he marked me despite my pregnancy?

Viorel holds my gaze with half-lidded eyes, the candlelight casting shadows against his face. "I first noticed how beautiful you were after Ainsley helped bathe you." His eyes search my face before he adds, "And I realized I wanted to keep you for me —not only to upset him—as I was digging through your life. I found you quite interesting. I had intended to mark you and send you upstairs, until then. But when I tasted your pregnancy ..." He shakes his head.

I merely stare at him, mind a whirlwind of disjointed

thoughts.

He makes an uncertain grunt before he says, "If I had controlled my harsh tongue with you in the beginning, might you love me back?"

His words send a jolt through me. "You love me?"

He presses his teeth and fangs into his bottom lip, a crease between his brow as he closes his eyes.

"I don't know what to say." My heart beats at the base of my throat. "I've been thinking you only mildly like me."

"I was not lying when I said I never hated you. You were a close target, and I was hurting. I know it's no excuse."

Unable to untangle my thoughts or feelings, I blurt, "I'm falling in love with Laurentius."

"I know," he whispers. "I feel it."

My tongue is too limp to form a response, even if my brain could form one right now.

"Unrequited love isn't so bad," he claims. "Love is pain, Marianna. It's painful now, but it would only be more painful if you loved me back—kissed me, made love to me—and then died. Really, you're doing me a service by mitigating my pain and sparing me such torture."

"I'm not going to die," I assure him.

His chuckle is pained. "You will, darling. It's just a matter of time. Everyone I've ever cared for has died."

Playfully, I roll my eyes. "Well, I'm going to become a vampire someday. If I survive the transformation, who says you won't die before me?"

"Ha. Given my history, that's unlikely."

"The unlikely happens all the time," I counter.

The humor drains from his face, claret eyes opening and holding mine. "Yes, it's true."

I swallow against my dry throat and squeeze my eyes closed, only peeking when Viorel replaces his weight with the soft blanket.

XXXV

Viorel's admission last night plays over in my head through my evening bath and dinner. He gives me space, digging around in back rooms until giving up on whatever he was doing and settling at his puzzle table where I attempt to read. Despite his undeniable attractiveness, and his desire to play father to my baby, I never thought he could have *genuine* feelings for me. It never crossed my mind to think of him in such a way either, despite acknowledging his beauty.

Now I can't help but curiously entertain the thought. What would it be like to be with him as more than a familiar?

I try to keep a leash on my thoughts, training my eyes on the book in my lap while sitting across from Viorel as he draws music notes on a stiff piece of paper. No matter how hard I try, the words are like black smudges beneath my faraway gaze.

Distracting myself with thoughts of Laurentius only works briefly. I remember his soft kisses and wet tongue, and before I can stop myself, I'm imagining Viorel's lips on mine and his pretty hands trailing over my bare skin. Wondering what his lips might feel like brushing against my thighs . . .

Sudden heat between my legs draws me back to reality, and I'm acutely aware of my thumping heart and shallow breath. I'm frozen with hot embarrassment. Viorel's attention remains on his music, but I know he could be listening to my thoughts, noticing my bodily reactions to them, or feeling the creeping lust running through me.

I close my book and silently excuse myself to my bedroom to get away from him, though I know it doesn't make much difference.

I busy my hands with clean clothes, pulling them from a canvas bag and hanging them on velvet hangers before putting them on the bar. Through the process, my mind remains cottony as ideas tug at me.

The sound of Viorel's chair shifting against the floor in his reading room has my heart drumming and my hands shaking.

In the corner of my eye, I catch him in my doorway. He stands watching me as I fumble to zip up a sweater. I can't bear to acknowledge his presence, even when I take the hanger and turn toward my wardrobe.

I know he heard my thoughts without either of us verifying it aloud. As tantalizing as the idea of being with him is, it's equally terrifying. I don't believe he'd be rough and dominating. It's the simple fact he's *Viorel*. It's all the power making him who he is. Being clothed in the same vicinity as him is intimidating enough, never mind naked and—

And fuck, now I'm thinking about him like that again, and he's standing right there.

I'm too breathless to ask what he wants. I'd rather he divert my train of thought, speak up about some random topic and pretend he didn't notice the past few minutes.

His gaze is so heavy my knees are ready to buckle.

What's he waiting for?

It's barely been a couple minutes, but it feels like he's been standing there—and me pretending I don't notice him—for an obscene amount of time. The situation feels claustrophobic.

From the corner of my eye, I think of the space in the doorway and wonder if I can slip past him. If I say I need the bathroom, he'll let me pass . . .

I hold my breath and turn. Viorel's standing in front of me, and I flinch back against the wardrobe with my heart palpitating. Surging adrenaline zaps my throat dry and has me dizzy.

My wide, unblinking eyes are locked straight ahead, his silk-covered chest filling my sight. My brain loses connection with my body, and I know I wouldn't be able to move even if I wanted to.

"Marianna," he murmurs.

I think if I look up, he'll kiss me. I don't hate the thought, despite the terror knotting my stomach.

I can't breathe when his icy fingertips brush over my neck. For a split second, I think he's putting his hand around my throat until his fingers curl around the back of my neck and his thumb pushes against my jaw to tilt my head back.

Viorel inches closer with parted lips, his breath a winter breeze fanning against my mouth as my heart spasms in my chest. I wet my lips and swallow against my tightening throat as I watch his fangs instead of meeting his heavy gaze.

When his nose brushes against mine, I let my eyes fall closed. A sheet of tingles washes over me as our lips touch.

He slides his hand up through my hair, spreading his fingers against the side of my head to hold me in place. He breathes a cold sigh into me as he slips his lips between mine and leans his body against me. A shiver runs through my weak limbs as I respond to his gentle kisses. I relax against the wardrobe and carefully raise my shaky arms to curl around his neck.

I can't string a coherent thought together. The feel of his

gentle lips on mine and his hand creeping up the side of my body occupies the entirety of my mind.

I'm so bewitched by him and the hot tingles running through me, I don't notice I'm no longer in my bedroom until Viorel tilts my head back and I open my eyes as he runs his lips down my throat.

The sight of damp stone glistening with the weak reach of sunlight above my head stuns me still. Damp air passes in and out of my lungs with my labored breaths, the soft rush of water filling my ears.

We stand in the shadows on damp, moss-covered rocks in the entrance of a cave, a gentle sheet of white water falling from overhead a handful of yards behind Viorel. The waterfall empties into a shallow, thin river snaking through large smooth rocks and lined with trees.

"Wow," I breathe, the sight stealing my attention away from how Viorel showers my throat in voracious kisses.

I shudder when he returns his soft lips to mine, his arm circling my torso while the other cups the back of my head to hold it in place. With beseeching kisses, he grips me to him like I'm the first girl he's ever loved. Like he's desperate to expose his heart to me and terrified I might refuse to open mine to him.

But my thudding heart splits open, the feeling pouring through me hot and overwhelming. It's a harrowing sensation I want to sink my nails into. The feel of his body against mine and his ravaging lips causing an emotion to swell in me only comparable to pain. And yet, I don't want it to stop.

I lay my hands on his chest and clutch his velvet gown in my fingers. My muscles tremble, and I can barely breathe. I dread the thought of him pulling away. Dread a moment as romantic as kissing beneath a waterfall in the gentle gold glow of day ending.

But then Laurentius crashes through my flurry of thoughts, and my body burns with guilt. I think of how good Laurentius makes me feel, and a stroke of panic seizes my heart at the thought of ruining our budding relationship.

"Don't think of him," Viorel whispers against my lips. "Laurentius would have to accept it. He knows I'm your master. He knows you belong to me."

Master.

The word makes my ears burn and I freeze.

All it does is remind me that no matter my feelings and Viorel's, we will never be equals. He'll always hold unwavering, limitless power over me, just as he does over everyone else. I'll have nothing normal with him like I could with Laurentius. Vampirism aside, Laurentius could be my equal.

"*Stop,*" I gasp against his lips.

His kisses falter, and he pulls away to stare at me with tormented eyes.

I turn my head and wipe my tears with the back of my hand. "Bring me back to my room."

Viorel's lips fall apart, his unblinking, distant gaze burning into mine.

"*Please,*" I croak, remembering how he once teased he could keep me here as long as he likes.

The hard stone of my room appears beneath my feet, Viorel's lips still against mine as his body holds mine against the wardrobe. I turn my head to break our kiss. His sigh is full of disappointment, but he steps back.

"I can't wrap my head around why you'd want me," I whisper, my confusion making me nauseous. "I'm sure you've had dozens of amazing and beautiful partners throughout your existence."

"Yes," he says as he turns my face back to his. His adoring, desperate eyes bore into mine. "Now I want another."

The backs of my eyes burn with another flash of guilt. I want to wrap my arms around him and pull his body against me.

He wets his lips and leans closer, but I turn my face away.

"I really like Laurentius," I whisper. "I'm sorry."

Viorel takes a step away from me and clasps his hands behind his back as he nods. "Don't apologize. I wasn't lying when I said I can't seem to learn my lesson. If I can't numb my heart, it's best if you refuse to indulge it."

I stand in guilty, stunned silence as he vacates my room and disappears left down the dark hall.

Laurentius's face lights up as he opens his door for me and plants a welcoming kiss on my lips before I can confess. I wince as he recoils.

"Viorel and I made out." The words drop off my tongue the moment he closes the door behind me.

"Yeah, I can taste that."

"I don't really know what to say," I admit. "I didn't mean for it to happen."

He takes a step closer. "Are you here to tell me you're breaking things off?"

"I don't know." I wring my fingers together in front of me. "But I had to tell you. I really like you Laurentius, and I don't want to hurt you."

He studies me. "You have feelings for him."

My sigh is loud. "No, I—"

He lifts his brows, a sharp hurt—perhaps minor annoyance at my denial—in his eyes.

I heave out a noisy breath and drop my hands to my sides. "Okay, yeah. But it's not the same as how I feel about you. I don't know how to explain it." Still, I try. "Being with you is like . . . peace and freedom. I feel like we're on even ground— vampirism aside. We can be silly and weird together. We can hang out like best friends, watch movies and play games. I've never feared you, and you make me feel safe in different ways than Viorel does."

"But?"

"But Viorel is . . ." Butterflies flutter in my stomach. "Viorel is captivating. My feelings for him are consuming and urgent, but I'll *always* be beneath him. He's a rose I keep pricking myself on. He's like poetry that makes me experience both turmoil and bliss. We laugh together and have fun, but it's not like how you and I do."

The disappointment etched in Laurentius's face makes me wish I could take back all my feelings.

"I'm sorry." I hang my head.

He shakes his head roughly. "Don't be. Viorel is literally an angel, so I'd be more concerned if he didn't enrapture you."

"But I don't know who to pick," I admit.

Pain pools in Laurentius's eyes. "Him. You pick him, Marianna."

"But I like you too."

"It doesn't matter. You love him, I can tell. Besides, Viorel is your master, and he wants you. Viorel will raise your baby with you. He can take better care of you—literally ensure the safety of your soul for all eternity. It makes the most sense for you to be with him."

"I want you both," I whisper, knowing how selfish the thought is. But they both offer me things the other can't. The idea of having both feels like completeness. If I were in love with two human men, I wouldn't even consider fighting to keep both. But there is nothing normal about my world, and I no longer have the needs of a normal human girl.

His eyes glisten as a shaky smile shapes his lips. "He would never agree to it, but I would"—He grimaces—"share you. Then you wouldn't have to pick."

Doubtful, my brows hike. "You would be okay with me being with another man at the same time as you?"

He rubs the back of his neck. "No. I'd be okay with you being with *Viorel* and me. Viorel is more than just a man."

"But he'd never agree," I reaffirm.

Laurentius lowers his eyes and stuffs his hands in the pockets of his leather pants. "That's why you're picking him."

"You can't decide for me," I retort, crossing my arms. "I'm picking you. I want to be your girlfriend."

He rests his hand on the edge of a snake tank. "I can remove myself as an option."

His words are like a knife in my gut. "You don't want to be with me anymore?"

"Don't say it like that," he whispers. "I don't want you to have to pick, but I'll still be here for you."

I merely shake my head and stumble out of his room, taking the long way to rush upstairs to my room hoping to find Rayonne. I'd have spoken to her first if it didn't jeopardize Laurentius hearing the news from my mouth.

When I give a warning knock and push the door open, the sight of Glitch doing origami on my bed surprises me enough for the urgency of my mission to falter.

"Hey, Marianna," Rayonne greets with cheer. "Glitch was looking for you. I don't know anyone, and Carol and Derek are busy, so I invited her to hang out."

"Viorel and I kissed," I blurt as I shut the door behind me.

Lucia's jaw drops, her eyes wide with delight.

"What was it I was saying yesterday?" Rayonne gloats.

"It's not funny," I snap. "I like Laurentius, and I hurt him."

"It's not cheating," Rayonne assures me as she adjusts the lace of her flowing black skirt. "You two didn't agree to be exclusive, and love between a vampire and the one they've marked pulls rank over anything else."

"Cheating or not, I hurt him," I argue. "I told him what happened and admitted to wanting both of them, and he cut things off with me so I don't have to choose."

Glitch folds the edge of a red paper. "So be with Viorel."

"But I like Laurentius. What if I only like Viorel because of the mark?" I wander deeper into the room, too stressed to sit on either bed.

Rayonne folds her arms across her chest and shrugs. "Clearly, Viorel hasn't made you a blood slave if you could be with Laurentius, despite Viorel's feelings for you. But I suppose, by the mark's nature, it's not possible to be completely free of mind. When you're a vampire, you can't help but think of your human often since you're connected to their feelings, so they inevitably end up thinking of you too. Whether that forces mutual feelings or not is up to the vampire's true intentions. But if he's good to you, what does it matter? It's not as if his mark is going away."

"That's not reassuring." I scowl.

She smiles. "Derek feared similarly. He refused to overwrite Ziggy's mark for two weeks because he worried he'd be forcing Carol to return his love, despite how she already loved him when Ziggy marked her. He worried his mark would entrap her, erase any possibility of her making her own choice to stay in the relationship. But she said if he's good to her and loves her properly, then what does it matter? She'd be unlikely to fall out of love in a happy relationship, anyway."

I mull over her words for a moment before a little gasp leaves me. "Wait. Denendrius was aware of all my feelings when he was still a vampire . . . He could feel my anger, my grief, my sadness?" Alaire and Edmond never mentioned that part about the mark, though I suppose I was only curious how it affected *me.*

She bobs her head in half-agreement. "Ziggy and Lance said he's emotionally disturbed, so it's possible he couldn't separate his feelings from yours. Denendrius was new to blood marking if you were his first. It's difficult to manage another set of emotions. I can't fathom how Ziggy and Lance manage multiple. Denendrius couldn't handle his own emotions, never mind unregulated emotions like yours. You two were probably in a negative feedback loop—feeding off one another's anger—until his mark became strong enough to influence you completely."

That might explain why he never thought to check on me when I was a child. Perhaps he couldn't tell his suffering from my own.

I bite my bottom lip. "It would have amplified the positive emotions too . . ."

"Yes," she verifies. "Mutual happiness feels like elation."

I bet a feeling like that could create an obsession. If we were having the time of our lives for the twelve days he stole from my childhood . . .

Well, it's no wonder he wanted that feeling back.

Desperate to evade thoughts of Denendrius, I race back around to my feelings for Viorel. "So, you think I should accept my feelings and not worry about their source?"

"Yes," Glitch chimes in, shaking her head like she can't understand why I'm questioning it.

"He's the *king,* Marianna." Rayonne articulates. "The most powerful vampire in the world wants *you,* and you're hung up on a pariah priest?"

I swallow. "But I like Laurentius."

"But you like Viorel?" Glitch asks.

"Yes," I admit with a frustrated shake of my head. "But my feelings for them are different."

Rayonne approaches me and rests her hands on my shoulders as she holds my gaze. "I'm all for true love, trust me. But Viorel is a *king*. Imagine what your eternity could be like at his side. You are blood bonded to him, and as much as you like Laurentius, you will never have as deep of a bond with him as you can Viorel."

I remember how blood sharing with him felt like ecstasy,

and how consuming it was to kiss him. Even when I was Denendrius's blood slave—willing to die for him—I never felt such a way from a simple kiss.

When I groan, she titters and plunks on the edge of my bed next to Glitch.

I throw my head back in frustration. "Why the fuck does Viorel even like me?" At least I can accept Laurentius liking me. We make sense together. Viorel loving someone like me is unfathomable.

Rayonne shrugs. "Why did Alessander choose to turn and wed a plain farm girl like me, when he was a rich and sophisticated man?"

Glitch releases a playfully blissful sigh. "The heart wants what the heart wants, Marianna."

I scowl. "My heart wants both."

Glitch playfully rolls her eyes while Rayonne lifts her chin and says, "Well, you can't have both."

I groan and drag myself over to them, flopping face first on my bed and making Glitch giggle.

Rayonne nudges Glitch, murmuring, "She once told me she didn't even want to think about dating vampire men, and now she thinks she can have two."

I groan louder and hide from both Viorel and Laurentius in our room until Seth drags me back downstairs for sunrise.

My heart spasms as the lock falls into place behind me.

"Come here, Marianna," Viorel calls softly from the bathroom, the sound of rippling water echoing with his voice.

I hold my breath, stepping over the drained bodies of two men as I make my way from the sitting room.

I push the door open and stop stunned at the sight of him.

Viorel relaxes in the bath, chest deep in a mixture of steaming water and blood. His teeth are stained when he smiles, likely from the bodies in the sitting room, since the one beside the tub has a slit throat.

"Uh—" I blink and twist my hands in front of myself as I lean against the sink to face him. "Are you okay?"

He tilts his head, then understanding fills his eyes as he looks between the bloody water and the body. He chuckles. "Oh. Yes, I suppose this would look strange."

I quirk a brow. "Seems like a waste of blood."

He releases a bark of laughter. "I appreciate how that's your primary concern."

"What do you want to talk to me about?" I glue my gaze to the stone beneath my feet. I'm sure I already know.

"I listened to you rethink your conversation with Laurentius on the way down here," he explains softly.

I'm unsure what to say, no closer to choosing between them.

"I truly love you," he croons, the words making my limbs warm.

But a knot forms in my throat.

"I know you have budding feelings for me," he continues, his tone delicate. "I won't make you pick."

"I can see myself with both of you," I mumble, unable to meet his eyes.

"You've only been here for a few weeks, and there are many things occurring in your life currently. It is illogical to make a choice so quickly for underdeveloped feelings. I will accept any love you may offer me, and I will let you and Laurentius explore one another's hearts as well. If it's true you want us both, so be it."

I gape at him. "You would seriously be fine with me being Laurentius's girlfriend *and* being with you?"

"Laurentius is hardly a threat to me," Viorel says with a tickled smile. "Plus, he makes you *so* happy. I love how you feel when you're together, and I understand what draws you to him. But I admit I would kill any other man for even uttering the idea."

I heave out a deep breath. "Rayonne thinks I need to pick."

He scoffs playfully. "Rayonne has only ever loved one man in her entire existence."

Though he's got a point, all it does is make me sigh.

"It's possible—though rare—to truly love two at once," Viorel assures me. "I have, once. It doesn't mean you love either less, just differently. Sometimes it happens in this world."

Relief fills me. "Would you even let me pick Laurentius over you?"

His face is serious. "Yes. It would pain me, but that's what I get for letting my familiar keep control of her own mind and heart. I have nobody but myself to blame."

"You want me to be happy, even if it's not me being romantic with you?" I verify. I think of how Denendrius believes the exact opposite, that we should both die if we can't be together.

He holds a bloody hand out to me. "Yes, I do."

My heart hammers as I join his side—standing inches from the drained body—and place my hand in his. He pulls it to his cold lips for a kiss, my flesh wet with crimson.

Viorel's lips curl with a devilish smile. "Care to join me?"

His hand tightens on mine when I try to scramble back like he might pull me in.

"Ew, no way." I stick my tongue out in disgust, though can't help my amused smile.

"He was free of disease, I promise . . ." His smile turns into a wide grin as he tugs me closer.

"Fuck no." Laughter bubbles out of me, my grin painful as he stretches me across the tub, the curved porcelain edge digging into my hip bones. I plant my free hand on the other side, but it's slippery from bloody handprints and I can't grip it.

"Stop, I'm going to fall in," I plead, but my laughter doesn't make my words convincing.

"Such a *human* reaction, to giggle at the threat of being submerged in the blood of my victim," he jests.

Before I can respond, I lose my balance. The liquid is slick against my skin as I plunge into it, but at least he has the decency to stop my head from going under.

He holds me captive on his lap as I scramble to get out, blood and hot water clinging to my clothes and painting my skin. When I sigh and accept it, he gently grabs my jaw and crashes his mouth against mine.

I melt into him and let my eyes fall closed, breathing in the metallic scent of the air and tasting it on my tongue. His moan vibrates against my lips, and I gasp for breath as he moves his mouth to my throat. I shudder when he runs the tip of his tongue against my flesh to lap up blood, and bite down on my bottom lip when he lifts my hand from the bloody water to suck each of my fingers clean. When his hungry eyes travel down my body as he licks his lips, I can't help but imagine him licking each intimate place clean.

But his lips find mine, and we kiss until the bath cools.

XXXVI

The next week goes smoothly without more life-shattering news.

Laurentius is elated with Viorel's willingness to let me keep my relationship with him and is convinced he's being rewarded for centuries of loyalty, and we continue as if nothing happened.

Rayonne, Lucia, and I spend most of our time together when I'm upstairs and not with Laurentius, though there are a few days where he joins us for films and banter. Lucia and Rayonne end up forming the beginning of a friendship themselves when I'm downstairs. Rayonne is just as eager to tell Lucius to mind his own business, especially when she knows he's going against Viorel's wishes. Lucius has eased off on trying to drag her from the castle, but he's begun a new mission of trying to pull her from us, like he thinks if he's rude and annoys us enough with interruptions, we'll stop being her friend. Perhaps it's worked for him in the past and is why she isn't close to anyone. He works on her when they're alone—

she tells us—by telling her we'll bore of her or get fed up with her "brokenness." We tell her he's wrong, but it's not as effective as the few times we stick by her side during her bouts of memory loss and confusion. What must seal the truth is the day she forgets us both after going comatose for thirty minutes and calls us both liars—screams at us to leave her alone—when we explain what happened since she doesn't recall struggling with memory loss and doesn't even know where she is. She finds us later, sobbing, and all we can do is forgive her.

When I'm not upstairs, I spend a good portion of time either on Viorel's lap or in his bed making out with him. Then I read or play video games while he writes music and plays violin. Though our sessions are long and full of heat, he doesn't try touching me despite how often my mind plays with such ideas. I'd think he was taking things slow if I wasn't sure he was getting off on winding me up. Laurentius won't do more than kiss me either, but he's started a habit of slapping my rear when I least suspect it and doesn't give a damn who notices.

Despite being pregnant, I've never felt physically better. Viorel's blood is likely responsible for the lack of symptoms like morning sickness. I still wouldn't know if nobody told me and keep checking my stomach in the full-length mirror despite Viorel telling me it could be weeks before I show.

To my surprise, Viorel feels guilty for keeping my pregnancy from me and how the discovery ruined one of my nights upstairs and offers another.

"How would you feel about Lucia being our roommate?" I pull my blankets tight around myself. "I asked Viorel, and he'll deal with whatever mess Lucius makes over it."

Rayonne stirs in her bed. "It's a good idea. I think Lucia's father is abusing her," Rayonne whispers, her words snaking around my throat and constricting my breath.

"Do you mean . . .?" I chew at my cheek and shift under the covers, the space beneath them clammy.

"I . . ." Her inhale is noisy. "I want to be wrong, but I've seen and heard enough to think something is off. Haven't you? He never let her have her own room, and she sleeps in odd places around the castle. He wants to be the only one taking care of her when she's having spells of confusion and memory loss."

I scowl.

"He doesn't have a wife—or any partner—and apparently hasn't had one since his died millenniums ago, and he is far too interested in what she's up to all day. He comes across as jealous when others are with her."

"Could he be doing *that* with nobody knowing? You'd think after so many centuries someone would have heard something or shunned him." Or not. Mostly, I don't want to think about how Rayonne could be right.

"I don't know. What if not all her dissociative episodes are from a Child of Stars intervening with her transformation? What if she has some sort of dissociative amnesia from abuse?"

"Is it possible for vampires to have psychiatric problems?" Then I think of Denendrius and well . . .

"I think some carry over from being human, if it's not something venom can heal. Venom doesn't erase physical scars from when you were human or replace a missing kidney, but heals what it can—cancers, disease—and builds off your frozen state. Derek is convinced Viorel suffers from agoraphobia. From gossip, it sounds like Laurentius had schizophrenia when he was human. Denendrius is a nutcase with a serious antisocial personality disorder. Ziggy is a box of worms I can't even get into, but I'm sure a psychiatrist would love him."

My brow furrows, and I can't help but wonder what Viorel's life might have been like before he was turned. He was likely kidnapped and could have been held for some time by whatever vampire tinkered with his mind to wipe it clean. Has he always been paranoid, or has it worsened with age?

"Either way, we should get her away from him tomorrow," I whisper.

She agrees, and we wish one another a good sleep. I'm left with my noisy thoughts about how Lucius could be a rapist. I want to charge into their room now and pull her out, but things won't go my way when I have no evidence. There's no guarantee she would admit—if she even remembers—to him hurting her if we confronted him. We could end up making things harder on her.

Now pregnant, the idea of hurting your own child in such horrendous ways is even more unfathomable. How could you hurt a piece of you? You might as well be hurting yourself. What kind of father abuses his own fifteen-year-old daughter? I suppose it's common. Even thousands of years ago, people were hurting their children. Even Denendrius's father was hurting his own fifteen-year-old daughter.

My mind freezes with a cold realization, and a sour idea unfurls itself inside me.

I stitch together the commonalities between Lucia and Denendrius's little sister, Adelia, as I fight to get a breath past my drumming heart.

Brown hair. Tall. Fifteen. Brown eyes; Denendrius said they all looked alike despite him being adopted, and that was the color of his. Born in the city of Rome nearly two thousand years ago. Had younger sisters. Abusive father who was—might be—raping her. I think of the bracelet Adelia made for Denendrius, and how Lucia is fond of the hobby.

Oh god. No wonder he wants to leave with Lucia now that Denendrius is here.

"What's wrong?" Rayonne murmurs, sleepy.

The reminder of Rayonne's presence forces some of reality back into me.

It can't be.

Right?

There's no possibility that of the thirty-seven people Denendrius ripped into, his father and sister survived, right? That because she lost much of her memory from Child of Stars interference, he renamed them, concocted a new life for them, and eventually hid in a castle in the one place he could be sure Denendrius wouldn't find them on his own, right?

I flop back down on my pillow, trying to talk sense into myself. Rome was massive, and clearly full of vampires. Could Lucia really be the only fifteen-year-old with an abusive father who was born there two-thousand years ago and later bit by a Darkling?

The thoughts keep me awake all night, and the more I try to convince myself I'm crazy, the more I do the opposite.

So, to ease my paranoid mind, I keep my lips sealed until I know without a doubt I'm not desperately trying to distract myself from my own problems.

When night comes, I bolt out of bed before Rayonne is fully awake and search for Seth or Asil. It takes me an hour until I track Asil down, but when I do, I blurt, "I need to talk to Denendrius."

He clicks his tongue in disapproval. "Why? I'll have to ask Viorel."

"I have more questions about the time he kidnapped me." The lie comes out with ease, but I know one of two things will happen if I tell the truth. Either Viorel will wave my theory off from little evidence, or he'll confront Lucius and if it's untrue, I've made myself look crazy and given Glitch more problems.

Thankfully, Asil fetches permission without me.

"He's actually letting me?" I walk down the hall at Asil's side.

Asil runs his hand over his beard. "He said each time you visit, you return hating Denendrius a little more. It pleases him and causes Denendrius more distress."

"Are you alive?" I lean against the risen stone of the oubliette, Asil standing quietly nearby.

Denendrius limps out of the shadows of his cell.

"Unfortunately." Something half smile, half grimace contorts his face. "I missed you."

Crossing my arms, I say, "Tell me about your father."

Asil furrows his brow at me, clearly realizing I've duped him. Thankfully, he only crosses his arms.

Denendrius's single beat of laughter is painfully high. "They've sent you to torture me today, have they?"

"Please."

He lays down on his belly, then grunts and flips over to his back as he tilts his jaw up to look at me upside down. "No."

I close my eyes, inhale deeply, then grit my teeth. "Can you tell me his name, at least? I came all the way down here to see you."

"He gave Adelia the feminine version of his preferred name. Now, you should be able to figure it out on your own."

I sneer at him. "How?"

Denendrius closes his eyes and spreads his bare arms out across the stone. He flattens his palms and picks at something on the stone with his fingernail. "Maybe you should have paid attention in history class."

"Denendrius," I snarl.

He chuckles.

"This is fucking serious."

Sighing, he smiles. "I'm sure it is, sweetheart."

I grit my teeth and turn. "Fine, I'm leaving." He doesn't deserve any elaboration if he's going to be like this.

"Tria nomina," Denendrius starts. "There was a question about it on your quiz. You skipped it."

He saw my history quiz? How often did he go rooting through my school files?

I turn back around. "Fine, take the longest possible way around to the answer to keep me here longer."

His grin grows. "When I was human, the naming conventions for girls were relaxing. But they often gave girls the feminine version of their father's name. Though they named my youngest two sisters after other family members, my father named Adelia after himself."

"Still not helpful."

"Think about it," he says. "What's my father's name?"

I scowl and sift through the onslaught of information. As Asil looks down at me and parts his lips to offer the answer, it clicks in my mind and slips off my tongue. "Adelius."

He tsks. "You could have passed that quiz. What a shame."

"Adelius," I repeat. "What does he look like?"

Asil looks at me sideways before turning his body toward me. But he doesn't demand answers, merely peers between Denendrius and me.

Denendrius laughs. "Why does Huarsar want to know about my father so much?"

"*Viorel* doesn't," I snap. "I do. I'm curious and wanted to see you about it. I can't visit *just because*."

There's a long silence making me huff and glance toward the exit.

"He hated how I looked like my sisters and mother and passed for their blood but was glad I looked nothing like him. I was his first son, and he wouldn't give me his name, was holding out for a son of his own. I was backup." He laughs. "Three daughters. He hated me more with each one. Mother named me after some distant, plebeian friend of her own father's. I used to get teased."

Lucius is blond. And with Lucia's long medium-brown hair—practically the same cold shade—and her lankiness, she really would look like a blood relative next to him.

I swallow, my heart thudding heavier in my chest with his words. I tell myself not to feel sorry for him, but as much as I hate him, I can't help but remember how awful it felt to see tears flooding those warm brown eyes.

"What does he look like?" I refuse to acknowledge his attempt to garner my pity.

Denendrius stares up at the stone like he wishes the castle would crush him. "Why did he hate me so much? I knew other boys adopted into rich families, and their fathers loved them and were thankful to have their love returned. As a boy, I tried for years to earn his love. He wouldn't give it. He hated me since I was a baby. Why?"

"Maybe he knew you were worthless and destined to ruin everything when your mother brought you home. She found you stuffed in a pot and left on a side road like trash . . . Maybe he would have been better off without a son at all." I don't care for my own words, but I swallow down the foul aftertaste of them. As awful as his father must be, and as unfair as it is to hate a little baby for no reason, Denendrius does not deserve consolation.

He deserves to hurt.

"*Yeah,*" Denendrius breathes, tears glistening in the candlelight as they run down his temples. "That's probably it."

Asil confronts me once we've left the dungeon, his words thick with disappointment. "Explain, Marianna. *You lied.*"

I shake my head, digging myself deeper. "I was too angry to

ask him my questions, but I know he *hates* thinking about his father and I've never gotten him to say his name aloud, so I was hoping I could hurt him."

Asil blows out a heavy breath. "Okay." He holds his palms up and shrugs. "Sorry."

He doesn't push the matter further, merely asks me if I need anything else and meanders off for his rounds when I don't.

Alone, I begin my search for Lucia, knowing her father will hunt for her if they're not already together. I don't want to involve Rayonne in my hunch or say it aloud to anyone until I've proven it.

I spend an hour searching, but she's not in any of our regular places, and the few people I ask claim to not have seen her either. As I'm ready to park my ass by their bedroom door to wait, Ainsley's voice rings across the grand room as she calls my name.

She stands in the hall before the staircase, her hand on her hip and the index finger of the other beckoning me.

Sighing, I hasten across the room to her and walk at her side toward the nursery.

"Why are you avoiding me?" she asks, her pink lips in a faux pout before she smiles. "Viorel told me you refused to join him when he came to visit the children yesterday."

"I don't know." Another lie.

Ainsley tucks a blond curl behind her ear. "Nervous about motherhood?"

"Nervous is an understatement."

Her light laugh is bright. "No experience with children?"

I shrug. "I took care of my foster siblings well enough. But I've never even held a baby."

She smiles fondly down at me. "It will all be swell. I was a midwife when I was human, so I'll deliver her for you with Viorel's help. We'll teach you everything you need to know."

My heart thumps when the sound of children playing fills

my ears, and soon we're facing two steel doors with ornamental cutouts to mask how they're basically cell doors.

"Stay close," she warns gently as an unfamiliar guard—a man with a well-trimmed beard, wearing a turban, opens a door for us.

Chaos.

A massive room the size of the dining hall lies before me, brightly lit with electrical lamps. Crafts cover the walls, open steel doors—with the same decorative designs as the main one —across the room leading to brightly lit rooms full of bunk beds and dressers. Toys are strewn across the room, smears of paint and glue on rows of wooden tables to the right. A sippy cup of blood leaks onto the carpet a few feet away from me.

"Give me back my bear!" A tiny girl screeches to my left, disappearing in a blur to reappear across the room on the red roof of a park-sized wooden play center. She shoves a boy off and he's suddenly on his feet, waving her bear in the air. When the little girl glowers daggers, he drops the bear and clutches his head as he cries out in pain until she unlatches her gaze from him and scales down the side of the play center.

Ainsley sighs at my side but smiles.

The children become significantly more terrifying when I realize some have abilities too.

Did I have abilities? Or was I a Darkling? Did I act wild like some of these children, or calm like the few scattered about reading, coloring, or playing independently?

I estimate thirty children in the room alone. None appear under four, though most look between eight and ten. There are very few black eyes, which makes sense if most adults die during the Darkling transformation, but the colored eyes make it more difficult to tell the potential humans apart from the Children of Stars.

A slender man in a cardigan calls out, "Clean up, movie in fifteen minutes!"

I swear each time I blink, some of the mess disappears. The Legos are gone. *Blink.* Tables wiped. *Blink.* A little boy picks up dolls with the wave of his hand. *Blink.* A girl is scaling the wall to pick balls of colored clay off the ceiling. *Blink.*

"Hi, can I play with the baby when she comes out of your tummy?" A little boy—maybe five—with red hair and freckles stares up at me, his toes against mine.

I flinch in surprise. "You scared me."

He giggles, his blue eyes bright.

"Go help Andre make popcorn, Timothy," Ainsley says, eyes twinkling with adoration.

He pulls a disgusted face but agrees and hops off.

Ainsley tells me she has something to show me, and motions for me to follow her. We pass by a tall separating wall on the left and walk by a colorful reading nook with floor to ceiling bookshelves stuffed with kid books.

A little girl is curled up in a child size recliner. She looks five or six but is halfway through a well-read copy of *The Odyssey.* Ainsley asks her if she wants to join the others for the film in the playroom, but she merely shakes her head without looking away from her book.

"Did you have children of your own?" I ask as we near another section full of rooms.

She half-smiles. "I had two girls and a boy. My daughters died of typhus when they were seven and nine, but my son grew up strong. I tried not to meddle in his life after I died, but I saw enough to know he married and had his own children before I met Mateo."

"How did you meet Mateo?"

We pause in front of a wooden door adorned in decorative steel bars.

"It was about three-hundred years ago, Viorel sent me home to London to retrieve an immortal child. We were on board a British vessel en route to France when a storm took us off course and sank the ship. We were swimming for shore when a Spanish pirate ship intercepted us." She opens the door into a dark room, the dusty air making me sneeze.

"The captain asked us to remain aboard in exchange for pay and blood. They sunk Neptune's Curse—Denendrius's ship, I'm sure you know, though I didn't then—a week prior and were convinced he would return to kill them since they also took a girl they found in the captain's quarters. I sympathized but had duties."

My heart pounds. "A girl?"

Ainsley lights a candle and gives me a sad nod. "Yes. She was bitten and bruised, but jumped ship and drowned during the night despite how they were going to leave her at the next port."

I survey the room, studying the antique crib with a thick layer of dust on it to distract myself from the thought of Denendrius keeping some girl in his cabin to torment.

"Anyway," she continues softly. "Mateo was part of the crew. He was smitten with me and requested I take him home. He was so kind to the child and handsome, I obliged."

"How did he end up a guard?" I peer at the old chests, also blanketed with dust.

She chuckles. "He couldn't handle not taking orders from someone. Was always asking the guards for tasks or ways he could help around when he was my familiar. Viorel made him a guard when he turned, and eventually put him in charge."

I'm about to ask another question when she playfully shakes her head at me and tells me we'll chat more about it another time.

Ainsley lights another candle across the room, the outline of a pile on the floor more defined. My heart thumps when my eyes adjust. The sight of bags of baby clothes, antique toys, books, and other small baby items makes my hands sweat.

"There's an out-pour of excitement for you," she says as she grins and motions down at the pile. "You don't have to take anything you don't want—much of it is outdated and likely no use to you anyway—but there is a box of handmade items."

"People brought this stuff for me?" I whisper, dumbfounded.

"Yes. Some are items clan members used for their own children when they were human. There's a desire to bring back items for you as well. Do you have a theme decided for a nursery, so they have some direction while shopping?"

I don't have to think about it. "An ocean theme. Dolphins. Beaches. Mermaids."

Her black eyes sparkle in the candlelight. "How lovely."

Emotion burns in my eyes, my throat thick. "People really aren't upset with me having Denendrius's baby?"

Ainsley makes a pitying *tsk* and turns to me. "Oh, Marianna. Of course not. You would not believe the excitement and support. Perhaps they've been less direct with you . . . but they fear overwhelming and upsetting you, considering the delicacy of the situation. You should know a baby shower is being planned. They are having Jacob bake you cake."

My throat tightens, nose burning as wetness wells in my eyes. I don't want to cry—I'm so tired of being fucking sad—but there's an ache in my heart, like the muscle has rubbed itself raw against my ribcage.

Their kindness feels like a mistake. Who would do something like that for *me?*

Ainsley drapes her arm around me and rests her head atop mine, voice feathery as she whispers, "In this world, Marianna, families are not biological. There are very few blood-related vampire families. Our families are adopted, chosen. And in our world, a baby is a baby, no matter who or where they came from. You and she are part of our family now. *Forever.*"

XXXVII

I spot Lucius as I enter the grand room, furious and with long strides propelling him forward toward his hall. I race after him, my swift steps unable to move me fast enough to catch up.

With the two of us alone in the hall, I know he must smell me following him.

"Adelius!" I bark as he reaches his door, anticipating for him to look at me like I'm crazy or search the hall for whoever possesses the name.

His hand halts halfway to the knob as he lifts his head and stares at the wooden door mere inches from his face while pushing out a long breath. He takes the knob and throws the door open. I flinch as he slams it shut, stunned still in my tracks.

Wrangling my breath, my feet match the pace of my hammering heart as I cross the hall and throw his door open with no regard to his privacy or my safety. I gamble on whether he wants to add harming me to the trouble he's about to find himself in, and feel my odds are quite good.

"Get out," he snarls, as he pulls a suitcase from beneath the bed and tosses it on the mattress, moving so swiftly around the room the items seem to appear on their own in the suitcase.

I step deeper into the room. "It's your fault you feel the need to run from your son, Adelius. Are you scared, even with him behind bars? You deserve whatever you fear might happen to you."

He comes to a standstill at the side of the bed and takes a heavy step toward me, a warning in his eyes.

I lift my chin. "You won't do anything to me, you fucking prick. You want out of this castle, not tossed deeper into it. Besides, I'm technically carrying your grandchild."

He lets out a dark chuckle as he shakes his head and arranges clothes for more space. "I have no grandchildren. All my daughters are dead—in one form or another—and Denendrius isn't my son."

"You adopted Denendrius," I remind him.

He laughs. "I adopted a dog too."

"I bet you treated it better," I snap.

He smiles and wanders over to a shelf to collect a few old and dusty hardbacks. "It's difficult for a dog to disappoint its master."

As much as I hate Denendrius, I can't help the wet sheen coating my eyes before I blink it away. I understand the pain and anger of never being wanted. Perhaps that's why Denendrius liked my adoptive parents, Vianna and Kenneth, so much and trusted them enough to give me back to them after kidnapping me. They loved me, and he must have recognized it and wanted me to have the experience. Though, I guess he couldn't care quite enough to stop vampires from killing them.

"Somehow I hate you more than him," I spit. If Adelius had been a proper father, none of this would have happened to me. "He never had a fucking chance with a father like you."

"Not my fault," Adelius says plainly as he smirks and places the books in his suitcase before opening his side drawer and rooting through it.

"He didn't get like that by himself. It's not a coincidence you're both rapists."

"Did you know Denendrius had quite a reputation in the brothels?"

Surely, he can't expect me to have an actual response to his attempt at steering the negative light from himself.

"My wife and I liked to be rough with one another. He saw sometimes, tried to copy on the slaves once he was old enough to get it up—"

My scoff silences him. "I think what you mean to say is he saw you assaulting your wife, right? I bet he witnessed everything you did to her since he was a baby."

He ignores my remark. "I needed them fit to work, and they were mine, not his. I gave him money and sent him to the brothels. He spent a lot of time there through his teens and until he disappeared. Did you know that?"

"He told me he used to go to brothels." Acid bubbles in my stomach. "So what?"

He sucks at his teeth. "Apparently, he was a perfect gentleman to the girls *until* he was paying with his own money. I think he was on his best behavior, so I wouldn't cut him off if he made trouble. Then I heard things, how he liked to choke the girls a bit, how he paid them extra to let him do what he wanted. Not enough to get banned, but enough that the brothel owner told me he was concerned Denendrius would escalate and strangle a girl to death." Adelius laughs. "I talked to Denendrius, and he wasn't truly harming the girls, just frightening them a little. No real problem."

"He started strangling girls to death," I tell him, tone serrated. "When he was a vampire."

Adelius shrugs. *Fucking shrugs.*

He chuckles. "He did not learn from me. But I suppose I

shouldn't be surprised, considering the little shit strangled my dog when he was ten."

I gape at him.

"He complained about the dog all the time." Adelius smirks before adopting a mocking, whiny voice. *"Why does he get to eat before me, Tata? Why did you give him the last of the meat instead? Why do you hug him, Tata, and not me?"*

I'm so choked with anger I can't form words. The backs of my eyes burn with tears.

Denendrius never had a fucking chance with a monster like this raising him.

"You favored your dog over your own son. No wonder he killed it out of jealousy."

"I beat the bastard so hard he was bedridden for two weeks." An airy, single beat of laughter escapes him. *"Little shit."*

"You're failing to explain how this isn't all your fault," I growl. "You created a fucking serial killer."

"I did nothing to make him like this," Adelius says simply.

"No? Being abused and emotionally neglected from infancy, viewing violence, the beatings you gave him, having jealous tendencies fueled by you taking him in and acting like you never wanted him, had *nothing* to do with how he ended up?"

"No," Adelius dares say. "From a baby, I knew he was a waste. All he did was cry. *Cry, cry, cry.* First fucking thing I heard when my wife brought him home. He was always inconsolable, no matter what she or the slaves did. He'd cry so hard he'd go blue and pass out."

"Viorel should throw you into the dungeon," I declare. "Put you in a cell with Denendrius and see how you fare after what you did to him and for assaulting Adelia."

"I don't think Viorel cares so much about human morality, or he would have had half the men removed from general population already, and he wouldn't be loaning out his familiar to the priest."

"Loaning me out?" I snarl through gritted teeth. My hands curl into fists at my sides.

A hint of a smile curls his lips. "Is that not the most accurate way to describe it? He has you downstairs for a while and then sends you up for the priest to fuck?"

I can't help but recoil from his words.

Are those his thoughts, or does the entire castle agree?

I lift my nose. "That's not how it is. I'm dating Laurentius out of my own free will. *Not that it's any of your business.*"

He shrugs, a condescending chuckle slipping past his little smirk as he gathers a few articles of clothes and carefully folds them into his suitcase. "What a coincidence you're most keen on one of Viorel's favorites. He claims he has none, but it's hard not to see the favoritism with all he's gotten away with. What would have been a death sentence for any of us was a mere two years in the ward. I bet if you weren't under Viorel's spell, you'd see how crazy Laurentius is alongside everyone else. Even the Catholic Church didn't want him, and they are usually fine with their priests *bending morals.*"

"I like Laurentius because he respects me and is genuinely good at heart, despite the violent ways he reacted to *being tormented.*" I swallow a burning lump of fury. "It has nothing to do with how Viorel feels about him."

"Sure." He looks me up and down and smirks.

"What?" I snarl.

"You look a lot like her," he says. "I hope you don't think Denendrius picked you because he thought you were special. You're not."

"Like who?" I demand, wanting to see if Adelius's memory matches with all Denendrius's stories.

"Mariana's mother. Denendrius never shut up to his mother about Marciana and her daughter." He shakes his head. "He had the gall to speak of divorcing the prospects I had for him once Mariana was of age, as if I'd ever approve. Said he'd kill me if I refused. You'd think he'd be happy the girls thought he was a sweetheart, treated him like a celebrity for fighting. But no, that wasn't good enough. He had to obsess over a poor girl and her *perfect family.*"

"God, you're bitter. I'm not surprised you had to threaten and beat your wife to scare her out of divorcing you."

He zips his bag up.

"You think the guards are going to let you leave?" I cross my arms.

"I don't need permission." He stares at me with the sharp and wild eyes of a man with nothing to lose.

"You're not taking her," I snarl as I twist and bolt away to the steel door, banging on it for the attention of whatever guard is closest to hear.

Sascha answers. "What's wrong?"

The words come out on a single breath. "Viorel, right now."

Her eyes widen some, then she nods and swiftly hooks her arm through mine to guide me down. The iron door creaking open sounds so far away, the steps swiftly moving up them thudding.

"Turn her around," Viorel roars.

Sascha spins us, and we're scrambling back up the stairs. There's a static sound—a satellite phone—and Seth giving orders in Romanian. My heart hammers in my ears as my thoughts race over the past few hours. The feel of Viorel's hand touching my waist only has my heart skipping and my breath more uneven, knowing chaos is moments away from unfolding.

When the steel door opens for us, Viorel gently pulls me to his side as Sascha drops behind. I do my best to match his swift steps as a group of guards surrounds us. We walk in uniform down the hall toward a commotion in the grand room. There's a stream of whispers below Adelius's spewing anger.

"Unhand her!" Viorel bellows a moment before we turn the corner to take in the scene.

Adelius stands at the castle doors demanding a pair of guards to drive them past the veil. He grips a fistful of Adelia's hair as she sobs and pleads for him to let go. There are suitcases at his feet.

Clan members stand back in clumps, some moving aside as we hasten toward them. Once we reach the halfway mark, Adelius finally notices the silence and falls into his own, his hand unclenching from Adelia's tangle of hair as he turns to face Viorel.

Tears streak Adelia's face. She scrambles toward us, so swiftly she disappears past a guard and reappears, hiding behind Viorel before one of them can stop her. I reach for her, and she holds onto my arm and presses herself against him and me.

Viorel's even voice booms through the room. "Why so eager to leave?"

Adelius squares his shoulders. "I would have left with the others, but Lucia has been resistant."

"She's not required to leave," Viorel says. "She doesn't want to."

"She's my daughter," Adelius says, a careful edge to his tone. "I must look after her."

Viorel flexes his hand at his side. "What makes you think you have more authority over her life than I? I am your king. I am hers. Do I not look after her? Do I not provide a safe home and blood for her?"

Adelius stares at him, lips parted dumbly.

"You do nothing for her," Viorel snarls. "You do not care for her in ways that matter. She runs from you in fear and to me for protection."

"I'm sorry," is all Adelius chokes out.

"You avoided my question, *Adelius,*" Viorel starts. One of Adelius's eyes twitch. They flicker to the gathered crowd and back to Viorel, who continues with, "What has you so eager to leave now that Denendrius is here? Do you fear him escaping? Or is it you fear the clan discovering Denendrius's father is hiding amongst them?"

A murmur erupts around us that a couple of guards quickly squash.

Behind me, Adelia squeaks, *"He's not my real father?"*

The depth of her ignorance has me holding my breath. I'm not sure if her theory is better, or worse. Would it be better to assume the man who has claimed he's your father for centuries wasn't? And he merely found you turning and pretended to be? If that's what she believes, I wish it could be true. It would be far easier than discovering you are Denendrius's sister.

My heart slams into my chest when I notice the eyes raking over us—*her*—as the obvious truth falls into place.

"He's her brother?"

"He has a sister?"

"Poor girl. To have to grow up with that . . ."

"What kind of father raises a monster like him?"

The confusion—concern—is a hurricane around us and has Adelia battling for breath and looking up at me with saucer-wide eyes, like she wants *me* to tell her it's not true.

"Fine," Adelius boots her suitcase toward us. "I'll leave without her."

Viorel's dark laugh has the hair standing up on the back of my neck, the chill of the sound giving me goosebumps.

A twisted smile twitches on Viorel's lips. "You're not leaving this castle again."

The metallic clang of chains has heads turning in unison. I keep my eyes locked on Adelius.

"What is this . . ." Adelius breathes in horror as his eyes widen below his furrowed brow.

"Take him at once," Viorel instructs the guard.

"On what standing?" Adelius demands, no effort to hide the shake in his voice.

"Treachery," Viorel proclaims. "You came into my home under false pretenses while hiding your identity from me, even once you knew I was searching for Denendrius. You made yourself a recluse so I would not question your frequent absences from the clan, and my presence, so you could hide your thoughts from me."

"That's it? You're damning me to the dungeon because of white lies? He's not even my blood! He's hardly my son. Is it so wrong to seek refuge from a madman, to opt for a fresh start?"

"Blood doesn't matter," Viorel tells him. "I have access to your thoughts, Adelius, and though you claim refuge and fresh beginnings, your mind is far more honest. So no, that is *not all*."

To my surprise, he doesn't run or protest as a guard clasps garlic-infused shackles around his wrists. He tears Adelius's shirt off to allow the chains they wind around his torso to contact his skin. He grits his teeth as his skin blisters.

He must know fleeing is futile.

"Then what else?" Adelius cringes against the pain of his blistered wrists and stomach.

"You have harmed members of this clan."

Adelius's eyes flicker to Adelia and back to Viorel. Yet he scoffs and says, "Who?"

"Myself, for starters. You know what else you've done. I'm disgusted to have to experience such memories in your thoughts."

"*You?* How have lies brought you harm?" Adelius demands.

Viorel bristles beside me, his voice low with bridled fury. "You have a hand in my niece's death. You created the poison she succumbed to."

Adelius gapes at Viorel. "*Denendrius?* You're going to blame me for how he is?" Adelius snarls in disbelief. *"Punish me for how he turned out after I wasted years raising him?"*

"Yes, Adelius," Viorel snaps, voice thick with impatience. "You were the fly that first birthed maggots on the corpse of his psyche. You created a place where foul things go to breed and feed. Now he is naught but a rotted, vile thing. A skeleton of what a man should be."

"He is not like that because of me!" Adelius bellows.

"Your memories prove otherwise." Viorel flicks his gaze away from Adelius and nods a command at a guard.

Adelia shakes in her skin, one hand gripping my shirt, the other Viorel's gown as guards escort Adelius—blathering as he fights forced steps—away.

XXXVIII

"I once asked him if I had an older brother," Adelia whispers from where she lies curled up on the sofa in Viorel's sitting room. "I remembered a room in our villa belonged to a man, how it felt safe, and I knew he was family but couldn't remember how. Father told me he was a cousin that was killed when we were attacked, how I only had younger sisters. I've been having strange dreams since you and him arrived."

It's her first utterance in three hours. She collapsed on the stairs on the way down, and before then I didn't think it was possible for vampires to have panic attacks. I sat on the coffee table to offer her comfort.

The moment Sascha helped her to the sofa, I told Adelia everything I knew—everything Denendrius told me about her—upon request.

I told her how they were close growing up, how Denendrius would attempt to protect her from their father's abuse, the bracelet she made him, and how he ran home when he was turned. How she gave him a hug, and he tore into her.

Tears pour from her onyx eyes. "Can I meet him?"

Dread like thick, black sludge rots my stomach and is heavy in my veins. My heart stutters.

"He's evil." The words rush out of me. "You're better off not knowing him."

She blinks tears out of her vision. "He's the only one who can tell me the truth about my human life."

"He's a liar." My tone is desperate, pleading with her to reconsider her request.

"He's my *brother*. Maybe he'll tell me the truth."

My eyes fly to Viorel, who sits proper in his chair with the shadow of fury across his composed face, and hope he'll talk sense into her.

"Okay," Viorel breathes.

I inhale a raspy breath, eyes widening on him.

You're going to let him meet his sister? I think at him.

Viorel eyes are dull as they lock with mine. *It's for her, not him. She's lived a lie for centuries. Let her exhaust her only option for peace. She deserves it, especially after living with her abuser under my care for so long.*

Panic wreaths around my throat, and though I know none of this is about me, the fact she wants anything to do with the man who brutally abused me—brother or not—stings.

I can't feel my legs when I stand, Adelia's tight grip on my arm only makes the feel of sinking through the floor worse.

We return upstairs with a shield of guards, the vacant halls thick with darkness. I dread Denendrius's reaction to seeing his sister alive. Will he be happy? I don't want him to be happy. At least knowing his father is alive and out of reach will torment him.

When we reach the dungeon, the steel door groans open and Adelia stares down the steps like she's looking down the throat of a snake. She hugs closer to me as we descend the stairs, stiff at my side when we reach the bottom. Her eyes dart from cell to cell as we move, like she's never seen the dungeon before. Perhaps she hasn't.

I hold my breath when we step down into Denendrius's section.

He sits hunched over with his back against the bars, bare skin streaked in fresh, slick blood. I squint through the faint candlelight to make out what he's doing, eyes popping wide at how he's messily feasting on his own wrist. Adelia stares at me with terror-filled eyes.

"Denendrius," Viorel calls curtly.

Denendrius's unblinking, crazed and scarlet eyes pin me as he turns, his bloodied fangs lifting out of his vein. He licks his lips, labored breaths passing between them.

I can't gather enough air to speak, frozen as I wait for the sight of Adelia to register in his broken mind.

Denendrius's gaze grazes over Adelia as he looks at Viorel and rasps, "What do you want now?" He wipes blood from his lips with the back of his streaked forearm and smears crimson across his cheek.

"Curious." Viorel narrows his eyes, head tilting as he clasps his hands behind his back.

"*What?*" Denendrius spits through grit teeth, bloodied venom spraying through the bars and making Adelia flinch beside me.

"She's real," Viorel says. "She's not a hallucination."

Denendrius's eyes fly to Adelia, and he gingerly rises to his feet like the movement might send her running. We wait for him to say something—anything—but he merely stands frozen like he's seeing a ghost.

I give her a supportive nudge forward, hoping his appearance and behavior is enough to make her rethink her choice to meet him, and stop any future requests. "Talk."

"A-are you really my brother?"

He nods vacantly.

A frail smile quivers on her lips, her voice a weak murmur as she explains how she's been in the castle for centuries, unaware of her identity after a Child of Stars tried to save her from turning into a Darkling but corrupted the process instead.

"You've been alive for . . ." Tears dart down Denendrius's bloodied cheeks, a thousand yards in his unblinking eyes. His voice is barely a whisper. "You didn't look for me? You didn't . . ."

"I'm sorry," she squeaks, hugging herself. "I couldn't remember you."

"Why?" Denendrius demands of Viorel. "Why do I only know she's alive now?"

Adelia looks up at me. "Marianna has been helping me stand up against my father. She followed a hunch that I wasn't who I thought."

"Your fath—?" Something breaks in Denendrius's mind as the word turns to mush on his tongue, the disconnection visible in his feral eyes as he drags his gaze to Viorel. He's monotone as he says, *"He's here?* Let me kill him."

Viorel exhales an airy laugh. "You don't deserve the satisfaction. He'll rot in his own cell. Like father, like son."

Denendrius screams ear-shattering Latin, venom spraying from his lips as he kicks the cell door's lock panel with his bare heel. The thuds reverberate through the room, metal groaning in protest.

"Bleed the rest of his strength," Viorel orders, voice dripping with annoyance.

Viorel ushers Adelia and me into the dungeon hall, half the guards remaining with us. The cell door crashes closed between us and Denendrius's section, and we watch as they enter his cell and wrangle him. He's frothing with fury, and it takes all four of them to splay him out on the ground, his anger making up for the lack of strength from his thirst. They force a metal bit between his teeth, straps of leather around his head holding it in place.

We return upstairs before they haul Denendrius out to bleed.

"This is my fault, isn't it?" Adelia cries, her voice echoing in the empty hall. "If I hadn't forgotten, I could have helped him. He wouldn't have hurt so many people."

"No." Viorel's gaze is stony. "Don't have the thought again."

I shake my head. "He's sick, Glitch. He always has been, even when he was human. There's nothing anybody could have done to help him."

Tears spill over her lashes and bead down her cheeks. "But I could have tried. I had centuries to remember, and my useless brain wouldn't let me. How could I not remember *my brother?* If I had remembered, he could have protected me from Father all these years . . ."

Her words send a ripple of unease through me, and I take a discreet step away from her. I tell myself she's merely in pain. How could she not be?

"You know he deserves to be down there, right?" I ask, terrified she might disagree.

Relief weakens me when she nods and chokes out, *"I know."*

Viorel turns his gaze to Seth. "Take her to Rayonne's chamber."

She wipes her cheeks with the heel of her hand. "Can I see him again?"

There's no warmth in Viorel's eyes when he says, "I'm sorry, but no."

Her lips shake, but she nods and walks off with Seth.

Viorel and I stand in silence, my heart thumping wildly in my ears.

"I'm glad you're not letting her see him again," I admit before pulling in a shaky breath.

Low, Viorel says, "She remembered him. Not fully, but enough. I don't want to encourage anything."

"Smart—"

Viorel turns to me, fury in his eyes. "You will not see Denendrius again either, unless it is from my side. Do you understand? You lied to me."

I fight the urge to bow my head, my eyes locked on his. "I understand."

"You *are not* a guard or a bounty hunter," he scolds. "You put yourself at risk by confronting Adelius alone. Should you uncover other conspiracies in the future, you are to lay them at my feet immediately."

My hands ball into fists at my side, and I gulp down the venom on my tongue as I grit my teeth.

Viorel lifts his chin. "We will deal with them together."

Hands relaxing at my sides, my well of adrenaline runs dry. "Together?"

He gives me a single, firm nod. "Together."

I spend the rest of the day fighting for sleep. Anger is like a knife in me, slicing deeper and longer with each unsettled twist and turn on the mattress until I'm sitting upright with grit teeth and shaking hands begging for blood.

Denendrius doesn't deserve to be angrier than me. He doesn't deserve to be furious over his father's survival and crimes when he let himself become a worse man than the one he despised. He should have never got to meet his sister, been given a reason to feel anything but desolation and fear.

Viorel rolls over beside me, candles coming alight and casting shuddering shadows over his hard expression.

"Let me torture the fuck out of Denendrius," I choke out, my jaw tense and aching from the pressure of fury.

"There's nothing on Earth I'd rather see more right now," he murmurs with a bitter smile as he takes my stiff hand and kisses it.

A vicious grin curls Viorel's lips as guards escort us to the dungeon. Hate and fury drives me down the steep steps and forward through the sour stench and past the rows of unfortunate souls.

Denendrius—wan and bled—lies in wait for me, limbs held in place by the soldered steel cuffs on the table of a torture cell. He's bare aside from his boxers, the unhealing gashes from where they bled him inspiring.

Viorel lowers himself into a wooden chair near the bars and at the end of Denendrius's body. He grins as Denendrius rocks his head sideways to meet his eyes before he rolls them away and back to me as I circle the table.

"Great," Denendrius rasps. "You've convinced her to torture me. Of course."

Viorel holds his palms up to refute his claim. "It was her idea."

I clench my fist at my side and would slam it into his chest if I wouldn't receive the pain of the blow instead of him. "He doesn't have to make me hurt you, Denendrius. You've done enough to convince me."

"I love you." Denendrius tries to catch my hard gaze. "You know how much I love you, right?"

"Shut the fuck up," I snarl. "We'll see how much you love me once I'm done with you."

He swallows and gives me a floppy nod. "Do what you must do, sweetheart. I can take it. Nothing you do can hurt as bad as what they've done."

I lift my chin, staring down my nose at him. "I hope that's not true."

He winces. "It is."

I swallow against a burn in my chest. He's right. Nothing I

can do will ever get the point across to him. I can't hurt him nearly as bad as they have. What can I do to him that will matter? What can I do to make him understand how badly he hurt me?

"It doesn't matter," I decide. "As long as you hurt. As long as it's *me* making you hurt."

I look back at Viorel, who sits tall with anticipation and eyes bright with excitement, before I scan the wall of equipment.

"Do *whatever* you desire, Marianna," Viorel encourages. "There are no limits, so long as he continues to grasp life in wait for more suffering."

The options are overwhelming, half the devices so foreign to me I can't fathom their purpose. My hands know blades and guns, and I've sat in on waterboarding and cow-prod zaps.

So, I grab a knife with a dull, nicked blade and follow the eye-stinging stench of garlic to a metal basin in the back to dip it.

He grits his teeth in fury as I burrow the tip of the blade into his stomach.

"Huarsar, *you bastard*," he snarls as I carve the first letter—*B*—into his stomach.

Viorel scoffs before a laugh slips past his lips. "This is not my fury, Denendrius. This is all Marianna. Give her some credit."

Eyes narrow in concentration, the blade snags and tears his flesh as I carve. I wipe my hand across the choppy workmanship to reveal the oozing letters across his abdomen. He strains to lift his head and peer down at the word.

BITCH.

Denendrius slackens on the table, his watery eyes holding mine as he turns his head toward me. There's no fury left on his face. He swallows the last of it down and exhales disbelief.

"Why would you write that?" A wet sheen coats his eyes.

I clench my jaw and jerk toward him—he doesn't flinch—to say, "Because you're a little bitch for everything you did to me."

He relaxes his head back onto the table, staring up at the ceiling. "Okay," he whispers, and I swear there's an edge of relief to his voice.

"Dungeon bitch," Viorel says low with a twisted snicker. "Perhaps I should let her carve it back into you each time it heals, so you never forget it. Perhaps next time, she can burn it into your flesh."

Denendrius closes his eyes, lip curling back in fury as he pulls against the steel restraints.

"You can think whatever you like about me, Denendrius." Viorel smiles. "I don't have to listen."

"I'm going to get out," Denendrius proclaims, a heavy exhale through grit teeth sending venom spraying onto his bloodied lips. "And when I do, I'm coming for you, Huarsar."

Viorel gives him a tickled smile. "Your previous escape was a fluke, rat. There are no more traitorous guards in this castle you can threaten to bring you through the veil, and you used your only trick. My guards know you'll try to sink your teeth into them the first chance you get, and it took you over three-hundred years to come up with the plan to begin with. The same mistakes will not be made again."

"No, but you'll make different mistakes." Denendrius's barking laugh has me taking a long step back, and Viorel scowling in annoyance. "You're already making new mistakes."

"For a man who has found himself in my dungeon twice now, you're grossly overestimating your power, rat," Viorel spits.

"You took sixteen-hundred years to recapture me," Denendrius rebukes. "A fluke. Perhaps you're overestimating *your* power. Your years don't make you more intelligent."

Viorel sighs, unbothered by Denendrius's insults. "Sixteen hundred years is but a drop in the bucket of time. You are not the first man to upheave my life. You are *nothing.* Do not think you are so important that I would dedicate each of my thoughts and breaths toward the task. I am a patient man. I knew you would make the task easy for me eventually, and I opted to enjoy my life while I waited."

"You think I'm really going to give up and let you torture me for eternity? You think I'm going to stay in a cell knowing you're abusing and raping the love of my life? Forcing her to have our baby so it can suffer too? That my sister is upstairs, and my father is alive?"

"Indeed," Viorel grumbles, then to me says, "He's talking far too much."

I swing my gaze over Denendrius, my blade thirsty for blood. I bring it down through the soft spot between his collarbones and he gurgles.

I lean close to his ear. "It's hard to love someone who hurts you, isn't it?"

I yank the knife out of his throat and straighten as he squirms and gags until breath is passing in and out of him without him choking on blood.

His voice is hoarse when he speaks, breezy like air is leaking through the unhealed wound in his throat. "*No. That's the difference between you and me, sweetheart. I can't stop loving you, even when you do things that make me want to kill you. Even when you get me imprisoned. I love you uncondi-tionally.*"

I exhale a heavy breath. "If you and I had the same understanding of love, you'd change your mind."

He coughs, blood spraying up from his mouth and landing in specks on his face. "One day you'll understand," he says. "When I get out, I'll make up for everything. We'll have another life for ourselves as we did in Bellevue. This time will be better. I know underneath Huarsar's mark, you're dying to get out of this place. I know you don't want to hurt me."

The candles flicker, our shadows fluttering against the stone walls as I stare down at him. I clench the knife in my hand, thoughts of Bellevue swirling in my memory. The morning sun as it crept through the white curtains covering the long window beside our bed comes to mind, the way the heat laid over top of me in the early morning. How it cast silhouettes of branches and leaves across the wall for me to watch dance as I worked up the strength to slip out from beneath the warm covers. The dungeon is colder then, my stomach sour with homesickness for a place I know I'm too terrified to return to.

Viorel shifting in my peripheral vision breaks me from my thoughts. I blink and focus on Denendrius.

"You took everything from me. You ruined *my entire life,* Denendrius. If it weren't for you and your evil, I would have had a normal life with Vianna, Kenneth, and Carol. I would be in school right now, or at home resting with fucking parents instead of standing in a cold, stinky dungeon across the world torturing a man who doesn't even deserve to keep breathing." I pull in a breath, my heart drumming to the beat of grief in my chest. "Viorel saved my life. I am barely worth anything to humans, never mind vampires, and he still took me when he probably would have been better off drinking me dead. He clothes me, feeds me, takes care of me. *Keeps me safe from you.*"

Denendrius swallows, no fire in his half-lidded eyes. I swear he looks as though he *feels sorry for me.* He looks like he wishes he could save me. "You are alive and with him because it tortures me," Denendrius whispers. "He knows it."

With a slow shake of my head, I disagree. "I will never understand the way your heart loves. I can't even comprehend the hate it carries for innocent people."

When Denendrius parts his lips to speak, I take the blade in both hands and drive it up between his ribs before twisting it. The effort of shifting the blade in his thick insides has sweat beading on my forehead. He grunts and mashes his lips together.

"You created this, Huarsar." Denendrius chokes out. "You created this pain for yourself. I wasn't like this before you gave me to your guards like a steak to a pack of dogs. What did I suffer for? For two weeks of bloodshed in my newborn panic? My creator abandoned me. How was I supposed to know the rules? How was I supposed to think clearly when I hardly understood I was a vampire? When I was so thirsty it's almost all I could think about?"

"You made an impressive amount of chaos in two weeks, rat."

He doesn't react as I pull the blade from his body, only his breath changing when I press the tip of the blade between two ribs on his side and use the weight of my body to drive it into him. His pain is barely evident in his voice. "You could have helped me, but you were too angry about the inconvenience. Don't pretend like you cared about any of the humans I killed. I was worth something in Rome, did you know that? I was a gladiator. Maybe I would have been so grateful for your help, for your guidance when I didn't have my creator's, that I would have fought to protect you."

When Viorel only returns purposeful silence, Denendrius continues with, "You didn't punish my creator for what he did to me either. You should have. Should he not have known better than to dump a human without knowing if they were dead? If he had guided me, I never would have cried out for attention. Your guards merely took his word that I was dangerous, and you accepted one fleeting thought of mine as proof. You said you can't fully trust thoughts, but you punished me for a thought crime. How can you blame me for wishing death toward the man who left me for dead? You were lazy with your judgment. You wanted to sweep the problem away, and I was already there at your feet."

A bored frown weighs on Viorel's lips. "Are you done?"

Denendrius's lip trembles and I can't help the sourness

rolling through me at his words. I do my best not to give them any merit, to trust Viorel wouldn't condemn a man to an eternity of suffering without a damn good reason.

Viorel sighs and taps his finger on the wooden arm of the chair. "You can ponder the past all you want. It changes nothing. You had lifetimes to right your ways after you escaped my clutch, and you strayed deeper into darkness. That is not my fault. You chose to pillage, rape, maim, and kill. Why? Because I had you tortured? No, you liked it. There was something dark laying dormant inside you."

"Do you know what lengths your men went to torment me?" Denendrius chokes out.

"How my prisoners suffer is not my concern." Viorel smirks and emphasizes, *"They're prisoners."*

I wince at Viorel's words, unable to help old feelings from my days in juvenile detention when I was fourteen from returning. All I did was steal a car for my overage brothers, and the guards spoke to me like I was shit on their shoes. Some girls were in there for theft or minor possession, and still they treated us like grown men who committed atrocities. Guards sexually assaulted multiple girls at the center, and nobody did anything. *"Because we're criminals,"* one girl had said at the lunch table when another asked why the warden wasn't taking the mistreatment seriously.

"Then you fed that monster," Denendrius whispers. "You made me stop caring. Sixteen hundred years may seem like many, but those three hundred and twelve felt infinitely longer. It changed my mind in ways I can't describe. You made me what I am."

Viorel sucks at his teeth. "What are you hoping to achieve with this conversation, Denendrius? I have no regard for your feelings or well-being."

Denendrius's eyes drift to me and back to Viorel. "I know."

I lower my head, the heaviness of Denendrius's gaze on me.

It doesn't matter who's right. It makes no difference if there could be a crumb of truth in a few of Denendrius's accusations.

Viorel chuckles, and he stands in my peripheral vision. "You will never have her love or understanding, rat," Viorel says. "You will rot in my dungeon until you are a husk not even worth poking at for curiosity's sake."

Denendrius's eyes widen on the empty air beyond the cell, his muscles tightening beneath his blood slick flesh as he pulls against his restraints.

Viorel follows his gaze, a wicked smile on his lips and coldness in his eyes. "Did you miss him?"

My brows furrow. Nobody is there but the guards.

Denendrius grits his teeth as he huffs and feebly writhes on the table in a futile attempt to break free. "I killed him!" he snarls, venom spraying past his lips.

With mock disbelief, Viorel says, "Did you? Then how could he *possibly* be here?"

Denendrius wriggles harder against his restraints, wild eyes following the unseen man through the door of the cell.

"He missed you." The ice in Viorel's voice sends chills through me. "He's waited centuries to spill your blood and make you quiver in fear again."

"I killed him in Sirmium the last time he came near me!" Denendrius croaks.

"Are you sure?" Viorel furrows his brow.

"Get away!" Denendrius bellows, spraying Latin threats at the empty air.

I see him for just a moment. A man larger than Denendrius with thick muscles, black eyes, and a scar down half his face. He walks up to Denendrius's side and rests his hand on his stiff chest.

Then, there's nobody there.

Denendrius ceases fighting, falling limp against the table, his hands and feet loose in their restraints. His gaze is far away

—hopeless—despite being settled toward something to his right. He winces and closes his eyes, his lips mashed together as he turns his head away.

Viorel leans down to Denendrius's ear and whispers, *"You cannot kill what lives inside you forever."*

Denendrius whimpers, the sound making my gut roil. I turn my face away.

Viorel chuckles, a sharp stroke of fear in me as he drapes his arm across the back of my shoulders. The darkness surrounding Viorel has my heart hammering despite knowing he won't harm me.

Viorel guides me from the cell. I can't help but peek over my shoulder. Denendrius quivers, mumbling Latin pleas.

I wish I could hurt him as badly as Viorel can. I can't help but feel outdone, like Viorel has overshadowed me.

"What was that?" I whisper as we tread down the hall.

"Mental anguish." Viorel's voice is saturated with hate.

When we reach the door, Denendrius's furious bellow makes me flinch.

"Huarsar!" he roars, a twisted laugh following that makes me think he understands none of the past few minutes were real. *"I'll kill you!"*

"Again, should we?" Viorel proposes.

I merely swallow and nod, the feel of my soaked hands heavy at my sides.

XXXIX

When night returns, I help Adelia relocate to my and Rayonne's room, since she prefers to stay with us despite her father's imprisonment. Laurentius and Rayonne help her move furniture, the three of them refusing to let me carry anything heavy since I'm pregnant. It makes me feel weak, but I'm not sure even the strongest humans could lift the solid wooden dresser, vanity, and wardrobe. With my bed shifted over, there's more than enough space for hers, but she refuses to move it and would rather sleep on the floor. She doesn't have to explain her issues with it. It's easy to understand. Rayonne offers to switch with her, but she doesn't want it in the same room. Thankfully, it's not too difficult for a guard to track down another, since so many were vacated.

The move is tense—at least it feels as much to me—and Adelia is eerily quiet. I anticipate sympathy for Denendrius each time her lips part, but she doesn't say much aside from whispered thanks, and to tell us which items she wants moved.

Once fully moved in, she spends the next three days hidden

away in her mind, offering sparse conversation while Rayonne and I hangout near for emotional support. Neither one of us knows what to say to her. What could you possibly say to someone trying to unravel nearly two thousand years of their life? Yet we answer her questions and discuss her new thoughts and realizations along with her, like how she can have a boyfriend now, travel wherever she wants, and do whatever she wants. She asks us if we still want to be her friend despite her being Denendrius's sister, and we confirm it changes nothing.

But when she asks, *"Does this mean I'm going to be an aunt, Marianna?"* I set her straight—albeit bluntly—and carefully ease myself from the room to cuddle Laurentius in his before returning downstairs to reset with Viorel.

"Your friends request your presence upstairs to prepare for the ball," Viorel calls from his reading room.

My hands freeze on a pair of blue and gray footy pajamas as I unfold them from a pile of recently purchased garments on my bed. "I totally forgot about it with all the chaos. I don't really want to go . . ."

"I suspect Laurentius will be painfully disappointed if you don't," Viorel teases.

My heart thrums at the thought of seeing Laurentius dressed formally and twirling me around in an old gown. "Yeah, you're right." I sigh and drop the little bunch of fabric in a heap. "Will you come dance with me too?"

"I'll be awaiting you here when you tire."

"Yeah, whatever." I roll my eyes, his refusal a stinging needle prick in my chest. The idea of him in something lace and silk while slow dancing with me to old music is painfully romantic.

I inhale sharply when he appears at my side, tucking my

hair behind my ear and kissing my temple. "It's not personal," he promises. "I'm simply—"

"Yeah, fine," I mumble. "Don't bother explaining."

My forced smile is tense, and I walk around him without another word.

Heading toward my room, giggles ring behind the door, so plentiful they spill from beneath it and into the hall.

Rayonne is helping Adelia lace up the back of her champagne ball gown when I enter, the white lace of her ruffled quarter sleeves swaying with the force. Rayonne wears a lacy black ball gown, her back curls pinned up with a few loose curls around her face. Adelia has her hair pinned similarly.

Adelia's reflection smiles at me in her full-length mirror between my vanity and hers, her hands clutching either side of it to counteract Rayonne's force. "I didn't think you were going to come."

I shrug. "I forgot."

"I thought you might," Rayonne teases with a sigh. "You're lucky Viorel had a dress made for you."

My heart thumps. He had a dress made for me? And yet he won't dance with me.

My eyes travel to the mass of black and red hanging over the side of my bed. Once she laces Adelia up, they're shoving me in my dress. It's sleeveless and a more modern interpretation of a ball gown. Its base is garnet silk, the corset and two-tiered poufy skirt, each draped with transparent black tulle adorned in lace trim. Red diamonds decorate the stiff corset, matching the tear-drop necklace Adelia clasps around my neck. I don't object to the dramatic black eyeshadow Rayonne brushes on my lids, or the crimson gloss Adelia insists on. I hate the way it feels on my lips, but I look elegant.

Standing in the mirror, the only thing I can imagine improving my reflection is scarlet eyes staring back.

Perhaps red is my color.

Adelia appears at my side, chin lowered sheepishly as her eyes meet mine in the mirror. Her hands are behind her back.

I raise my brow in question.

"You'll probably think it's silly . . ."

"Show her," Rayonne insists, her grin blinding.

"Close your eyes," Adelia whispers.

I obey, wrinkling my nose in confusion until something cold and heavy circles my head. She shoves a pin onto either side to hold it in place.

My eyes fly open and widen at the ostentatious tiara on my head. It's dainty but made of vicious black metal peaks and rubies of alternating size set in elegant swirls.

"Wow," I breathe, looking like a dark princess from some Gothic fairy tale.

"I picked it up a few centuries ago, but I've never encountered a time when I needed it. I think it better suits someone like you."

I carefully turn my head side to side, watching the candlelight hit the diamonds and silver. "Someone like me?"

"Royalty," she clarifies. "You understand you are, right? You're Viorel's."

My brow furrows and I give my head a risky little shake. "That doesn't make me royalty."

In unison, they both say, "You're wrong."

A knock calls for our attention, Rayonne welcoming Laurentius before I'm fully turned.

The sight of him has my cheeks burning and my stomach warm with my first burst of genuine excitement for the night. The dark red tailcoat he wears over his black blouse is simple, the faint pattern of his high-waisted, laced pants the fanciest thing on him.

"You look beautiful, Marianna." His gaze trails over me, his smile warm.

"You're pretty fucking hot yourself," I assure him as I cross the room and take his hand.

He exhales a breath of laughter and draws me in for a kiss before we walk from the room with our fingers laced. Rayonne and Adelia link arms behind us.

The haunting harmony of violins, piano, and cello is clearer in the hall, the sound accompanied by a low stream of chatter as it carries up the stairs.

Pausing at the top of the stairs, I stare over the stone balcony at the bustling room below. There's a small ensemble organized near a grand piano in the far corner, hundreds of dancing forms in between.

I'm buzzing with excitement. "It's like a movie."

Laurentius gives me a toothy smile and tugs on my hand. "Come dance with me like we're in one."

"I don't know how to dance," I warn him as I skip after him in my flats.

"I'll teach you!"

When we reach the bottom step, he hooks his arm around my waist and spins me onto the floor.

Adelia and Rayonne pair off, play fighting for the woman's role as they move across the floor to waltz.

Laurentius guides me in their wake. When we find space, he takes my hand, placing his other arm beneath mine as he rests his hand on my back.

I pay careful attention as he teaches me to waltz, Rayonne and Adelia twirling nearby and offering tips and themselves as example. My steps are sloppy, out of sync from his for a handful of bubbly, romantic songs until something clicks and I turn into a giggling princess each time he spins me away before pulling me in and stealing a kiss.

"I love you," I tell him when my cheeks are burning from my wide smile and my heart feels too full for the space in my chest.

This time, Laurentius says it back.

The more we step in twirling circles, the more surreal it all becomes. I forget about my life before the castle. With the aroma of flowers and burning firewood filling my lungs, I forget about the stench of heroin and the dirty city. About the bite of knuckles against my body, and the pressure of being held down. It's possible I can't recall what it looks like where I came from. In fact, I'm not so sure America exists at all. With the music and the hypnotic ring of elated laughter and colorful, old gowns and suits, it would be easy to believe my old life was simply a nightmare. After all, if I were to dart outside and look for it, there would be no evidence I'm wrong.

For a while, I convince myself I'm a royal girl who has lived in the castle all her life. It's not far-fetched with the bright chords filling my ears, the silk hugging my body, and the blood surging like power through my veins.

For hours, I'm not Marianna Cortez. There's a real chance I never really was.

Either way, I'm now a girl who has *everything*.

Looking over, Adelia is light on her feet, her new freedom detectable in her smooth steps and serene smile. Rayonne sways like a peaceful current moves through her. Carol and Derek find us and dance at our sides and chatter for a few songs before disappearing back into the merry-go-round of dancers.

Laurentius twirls me, a moment of confused panic entering me with a gasp as his hand disconnects from mine. An arm hooks around my waist from the other side, my body pulled still as I'm dropped into a dip.

My heart is light in my chest. "Viorel."

His charming smile plucks my heartstrings and I practically gasp in delight when he bends down and presses a kiss against my throat.

"I hope you've saved a few dances for me, darling," he says, as he straightens me on my feet.

I swallow a knot and nod as I take him in, twirling my finger in a strand of his long hair as he stands so close the smell of rose perfume fills my nose. He's wearing a frilly black blouse with lace around his throat and poufy sleeves cinched at the wrists, tucked into black pants tied at his waist.

Laurentius watches on with a tickled smile as Viorel clutches my hand and presses his palm against my back. The sharp uptick of rapid violin chords and mellow piano tones has my heart thumping. They're a breathtaking combination of hope and anguish that has my clutch on Viorel tightening as he walks us in a tight circle.

"You came."

"You were having a grand amount of fun, and I became jealous and wished to be a part of it." His smile is soft, though I don't miss the flicker of unease hiding in his twinkling eyes. There's a serious uptick in guard presence, my nose wrinkling at the beep of a satellite phone behind me.

"Well, thank you," I whisper.

"I'm glad I did." He winks and strokes his hand across the silky side of my corset. "Because you look absolutely *ravishing* tonight."

I bite my lip to subdue a coy smile.

When I close my eyes as he pulls me in for a kiss as the song ends softly, I open them to an empty room, the only sound the ensemble and our lonely steps.

A manage a calm breath as a fresh song fills the air, a fluttering of piano chords and gentle cello behind playful violin.

"The tiara's a nice touch." He pulls my hand to his lips for a kiss.

I feel the next bout of fluttering piano chords in my chest. "You think so?"

He holds me close, and our bodies relax as we swing side to side. "Yes, it's quite fitting."

A tickled noise vibrates in the back of my throat. I sigh and dance until the lack of people has the air feeling colder.

"I liked all the people," I admit as the end of the song trickles into the start of another. "Less lonely with their laughter."

They return with a blink; a wide circle of observers having formed around us. We spin into a joyous, sunny tune, though Viorel's wandering gaze when I face him tells me he's only half with me.

His eyes level with mine as the song ends. "Care to return downstairs with me?"

A stressed laugh strangles me. "But I'm having fun."

As he pulls my body against his, our steps merely shifting, his plea passes through my mind. *Please . . .*

Shaking my head against his chest, I inhale deeply and force it back out.

Please don't make me. I was having so much fun, I think at him.

A gap forms between our bodies as he draws away. His paranoid eyes hold mine. "Okay, you may stay. I won't ruin your night."

He bows and kisses my hand before placing it back in Laurentius's and giving a guard on my far right a long, hard stare. I'm too choked to protest, but nearly do when my emotion must cause his single, faltering step as he walks away with all but the guard he gave psychic orders. My eyes sting as he disappears.

The room is emptier with him gone, though the amount of people is mostly unchanged. I nearly wish Viorel had remained downstairs—or joined at the beginning and shared dances— instead of arriving to give me a taste of what I've been missing all night.

I dance a while longer with my face pressed against Laurentius's comforting form, so thankful to have his love. He holds me until my heavy mood has me swaying against the music. I leave when there's only an echo of chords thinning in the room's air.

Viorel's still dressed up, standing between the foot of his bed and the organ when I drag myself to his chambers.

"Care to dance?" he asks, hand outstretched.

My shoulders hunch as I sigh. "I danced for hours. My feet hurt. You could have stayed longer if you wanted to dance more."

His hand remains waiting. "Please."

I drag my feet toward him. "*Fine.* Let's just spin around in the silence—"

A low, haunting hum fills the room, a key on the organ lowering without his touch. My heart stutters in surprise.

He smirks. "You were saying?"

I gulp and place my hand in his, a collection of dark chords filling the air as he pulls me close. My heart thumps as we sway in the candlelight, a slow, wistful song vibrating through me. It's bitter sorrow and desperate, aching love. A warm darkness. A hand clutching mine when everything else has slipped away into a chasm of cold.

Resting my head on his silent chest, I close my eyes and move with him to the music. He wraps his free arm around me, the other still clutched in mine at our side.

"I love you," he murmurs in my ear. "I'm keeping you forever."

"Okay." I'm weightless in his arms. "I won't fight you."

"When the soil is ash, and the trees are pillars of fire, I will fill you with whatever remains in my veins. I will give you the very last of me."

Emotion has tears welling beneath my lids, and I release a breathy chuckle to mask it. "You love me so much already?"

"My soul knows the rhythm of your quick heart as well as it

knows the faded beat of mine, experiences each emotion rocketing through it alongside my own. Since the moment I first shared myself with you, I have known you twice as long as you've known me." He spins me in a circle that has my hair flitting. "And I dream, my love. Vision or fantasy, it *does not matter.* Each one draws me deeper into your arms."

I rest my hand on his chest, a thin tear slipping from beneath my lashes. The first happy tear in my life. It's the first time love has made me cry without leaving a bruise.

"Forever," he echoes, the words escaping from the depth of his chest. "Until the gray sky of ruination gives us days of freedom while we await the quietus of the sun crashing through us."

"You really think we'll live so long?" The music is so deep in my core it's like it moves me by itself.

"I believe we're doomed to," he proclaims, with a smile in his voice. "But therewithal, it means there will be no two who love as long as we."

It's a hauntingly romantic idea, and I dance with it, feel it moving in the swelling air around me.

"I wrote this song for you," he whispers. "I'm glad it moves you."

I ache for a much more intimate dance with him, starving with the thought of our bare bodies writhing against one another on his bed. For his soft touch to play with me as passionately as he plays this song, for him to fill me so deeply with pleasure I sing.

Viorel shoves me against the organ with his body, the music stopping in an abrupt clash of chords. My heart spasms and his hooked finger lifts my chin as I'm tilting my head back. He crashes his lips against mine, our labored breaths as rapid as our sloppy kiss. I wrap my arms around his neck while he pushes me harder into the organ with his body, his hands tight on my waist and holding me firmly to him.

My heart beats at the base of my throat, my weak knees knocking together. I grip him to keep standing as my body melts against his.

I inhale sharply against his lips as he spins me until we've swapped places. He walks me backward, untying my corset and dropping it on the floor before my calves touch the bones of his bed frame. He leans forward and lays me as gently as glass on the mattress with my legs dangling over the edge. The smell of roses surrounds me, and I splay my arms out and feel the fresh, soft petals on the velvet blanket.

My chest rises and falls beneath the lacy, thin, black camisole covering me. The heat of his wanting gaze dries my throat. My breath is still in my chest as he strokes his hand down the front of my chest, goosebumps rising on my bare arms at the cold of his soft touch.

I watch with heavy curiosity as he pulls his blouse off and sets it at the end of the bed. My gaze traces over his toned chest and stomach, my fingers twitching to touch his pale skin as I raise them toward his body. He patiently waits for my touch as his hand pushes the frilly, thin straps of my camisole down my shoulders.

He shudders, muscles twitching beneath the pads of my fingers when I press them against his cold chest and stroke down his chest and abdomen.

When he pulls my camisole down, my breath catches. I fight the urge to cover myself as he shimmies it off with my heavy skirt and lacy black underwear, leaving me trembling and naked.

Viorel exhales a lustrous *"oh"* as his eyes trail over me. My face fills with heat, a gasp falling past my lips when his hand takes turns exploring my breasts.

Nervous trembles course through my limbs, my legs weak as he nudges them apart with his knee so he can stroke his hand between my legs. Heat spreads through my body at his touch and pools in my groin. When his knuckle sneaks inside me, I stiffen at the thought of his sharp nails poking inside me. He promises he won't.

His voice comes low as he unlaces his pants and slides them off. "Lay your head on the pillow."

It takes a few painful, rapid breaths before my brain obeys. Naked, he crawls over me with starving eyes sending my heart running. He lowers his head for a soft kiss that slowly grows rougher. I curl one arm around his neck, the other clutching the blanket at my side. When his lips trail across my jaw and down my throat, I bask in the feel until a sharp pinch has me crying out. It's a needle prick compared to the first time he bit me, but the surprise makes up for it.

He pulls away, fangs slick with blood, eyes locked on the wetness spreading from my throat. I'm frozen as his hand cups the back of my neck to angle me off the pillow while his gaze follows the hot stream trickling across my collarbone and creeping down the center of my heaving chest.

Though pain is absent from my neck, it doesn't stop my wide eyes or the terrified, cold surge of adrenaline drowning my senses. I'm dizzy until his soft eyes snap to mine, the hint of a smile on his lips as he angles me higher off the bed, so the river of crimson runs between my legs.

I squeeze my eyes closed as he lays my head on the pillow and delicately kisses the wound, his tongue sending a shiver through me as he licks the trail of blood clean. Reaching up, my fingers glide over my healed flesh.

My eyes pop open and a moan rolls out of me when he licks the mess between my legs. Groaning, I put my hand on his head until pleasure has my eyes rolling back.

When he moves away from me and stands on the floor, I swallow against my dry throat and lift a shaky brow. He gives me a mischievous smile and beckons me with a blood-stained finger. Gulping, I twist onto my shaky arms and legs and crawl over. He punctures his wrist with his nail and drizzles blood over himself as my mouth waters. I lick my lips as he takes a fistful of my hair, a moan vibrating from him as I clean up the mess while gazing up into his fond eyes.

But once he reaches under me and rubs between my legs, I can't focus on anything else. He guides my quivering body back onto the mattress and stretches out beside me, splitting kisses between my parted lips and chest.

"Sing for me," he commands softly, shoving the teasing knuckle of his finger inside me, his thumb rubbing me faster.

My moan is musical as my legs quake. His hand moves so fast I can't catch my breath. Ecstasy winds like a tight string inside me, closer to snapping with each turn of his thumb. He stops too soon, clicking his tongue and telling me I'm not allowed to finish yet as I pant and lie limply.

Viorel positions himself between my angled legs and I bite down on my bottom lip, focusing on even breaths that catch with the feel of him slowly sliding inside me. If his tormented moans didn't make my toes curl and heat blossom beneath my skin, my nerves might've made me stiffen.

I feel synchronized with him in every possible way as we make love, from our bodies to our minds. It's nice having him in my thoughts. He knows the moment a touch is too hard or too soft, too slow or too quick. He doesn't pull away or alter his movements as he finds the right spots, and he's quick to adjust before I can decide if I should ask him to.

I'm crazed with passion, my nails digging into the flesh of his back as my heart aches so deeply with love for him that my eyes burn.

I love him.

I love him. I love him. I love him.

Digging my nails deeper, I wish they could bite into his skin so I can drink up the beads of blood and have more of him inside me.

His chest falls as he releases a heavy breath, his lips parted for the gasps that follow. He crushes his chest against mine, burying his face in my neck as he rests his forearms on either side of my turned head on the pillow. I brace myself when his icy breath pulses against my throat, his slit wrist muffling my grunt as he bites into me.

I capture his forearm in my hand to lock it in place, nerves alight as I lap him up. Pleasure floods into me, his enjoyment seeping in with his blood.

Somewhere between my thoughts and reality, his voice comes to me. *I love you.*

I want his blood to replace mine, and for mine to course through him and give him the strength to love me so closely over and over again.

The feel—the connection—is celestial.

I let out a deep, muffled moan of pleasure as stars explode across my sight. My knees lock as my legs kick out, my entire body spasming under him and making him whine and groan against me. A thin tendril of crimson escapes past his lips that he quickly catches with the tip of his tongue. There's so much release—the bliss agonizing—my consciousness nearly unravels with me.

As he straightens and continues thrusting, his half-lidded, drunken eyes hold mine as he brings my wrist to his mouth and bites me. A moan escapes his bloody, parted lips, and a few scarlet drops drip from the corner of them and land between my breasts as he tries to lick his flooded lips clean. A surge of pleasure strengthens the shake in my limbs as he leans against me and collects the droplets with the tip of his stained tongue.

The pleasure is unbearable. If I could catch my breath, I might cry out. Black shudders at the fringes of my vision.

"Fuck," he hisses in my ear as he paws at the blanket next to my side. His whine turns into a gasp before he stiffens and shudders as his nails tear the blanket.

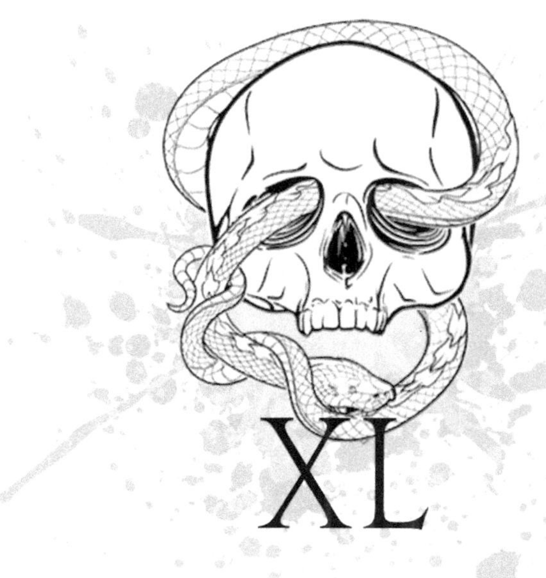

XL

Viorel's nails gingerly trace lines up and down my back, drawing me awake. The single flickering flame on his night-stand focuses in my vision past his bare chest. I adjust my cheek on his chest and untangle my leg from his, my arm draped over him.

"You're not sleeping?" I rub my eyes. Hours must have passed.

"No," he murmurs, placing a kiss on the top of my head.

I pull the blanket up over my shoulder to ward off the chilly air. "Why?"

He doesn't respond until I drift. "Have you thought of a baby name?"

I yawn. "I can't think of anything I like other than Aeliana. Don't remember where it came from, but it's pretty. Maybe an old library book, or a clan member suggested it."

"Hm." He nuzzles his cheek into my hair. "It's a Roman name from the gens, Aelia. They were a plebeian family, but under Emperor Hadrian there was a settlement called Pons

Aelius. I recall hearing the augmented cognomen Aelianus. The feminine derivative would be Aeliana."

I'm too close to slipping back under to understand what he's talking about. Does he like the name?

"I do. Have you considered a male name in case the vision was wrong?"

"No, but Aelius works, if that's the guy version."

"It would work," he agrees.

Viorel traces the tip of his nail across the back of my forearm. I shiver.

His breath caresses my ear as he says, "Aelius's roots mean sun."

My smile is warm. "That's what I'll name her then. Aeliana. She'll be the only sun in my world."

There's tense guilt in his silence.

"It's not your fault," I remind him, my thumb stroking the smooth skin of his stomach.

He pulls in a deep breath through his nose and noisily releases it.

I close my eyes. "It's not."

Viorel stiffens and curses beneath his breath a few moments before someone's panicked hammering on the door has my eyes flying open. Adrenaline shoots through me and I jerk upright as the candles come alight.

The iron door muffles Asil's pained holler.

Viorel slides out of bed, sharp eyes dark as he casually redresses.

"What's happening?" I demand, heart stuttering with each thudding knock.

"Dress," he commands as he pulls open his wardrobe.

I throw the blanket off myself. "Where are we going?"

He pulls a dark, golden crown from the top shelf and places it upon his head. The thick band is adorned in a handful of black and crimson diamonds amongst a florid design, the wide and long points of the crown lethal. "To pluck weeds."

When Viorel opens the iron door, the acrid stench of garlic radiating off Asil makes my eyes water. Asil straightens from a slump against the wall and wipes a trail of blood from the corner of his mouth into his thick beard. The chest of his black shirt is soaked, his hand wet with blood.

"Mutiny," Asil heaves out as he twists back onto the stairs.

My eyes widen, but my vision is ripped from me as we follow up the steps. I suspect it's Viorel's doing, since there's no sign of Sascha.

Viorel's silent as we walk, like he's already heard Asil's recount in his thoughts.

There's the sound of a violent commotion as the steel door opens before my eyes. A trio of guards flanks us as we march down the hall toward the grand room.

It's packed, people turned toward an uproar in the center. A man's yelling incoherently through the sounds of a beating.

The crowd scatters as we approach, leaving a bloodied and furious vampire man alone in the center. He scrambles for a bloodied dagger, but a clan member swiftly kicks it out of reach and a guard snags it.

"Bend to your knee," Viorel commands, black velvet cloak flitting against the floor behind him until he comes to an abrupt stop in front of the man. I stand half behind Viorel, trying to navigate the flurry of mumbles and whispers around us.

The vampire grits his teeth, fangs bared. "I will bow no longer—" His pale, bloodied face twists in pain, his jaw stretching wide as he crumbles to his knees under the agony of Viorel's stare.

"You call for death and Death shall answer!" Viorel roars.

He stiffens and thuds on his side, eyes rolled back as slow jerks ripple through him.

"What's he been blabbering about?" Viorel questions the crowd, vicious eyes pinned on the vampire as he twitches breathlessly.

A handful of vampires half-trip over one another to get closer, a woman getting a word in first, saying, "He was sullying your name, said you hid the fact you were Huarsar so you wouldn't have the fault of him when recruiting a new clan to serve you in rebuilding. He planned to breach the steel door and stabbed Asil when stopped. He wanted us to help him strip you of your power."

"Others planned to aid him, but fled the castle," another man interjects.

Viorel's lip twitches, chin lifting as he looks down at the man. His seizing halts, a groan rolling out of him as he slowly shifts to his hands and knees. Fearfully shaking, he carefully lifts his head of black hair to gaze up widely at Viorel.

"I hid *nothing*, Mitchell. Nobody cared to inquire. I took another name to avoid danger following me to a new clan, to ease possible nerves about my ability to protect. I haven't cared to deny the truth, or attempted to cover it now, have I? The *only* mistake I made in Sirmium was not weeding out traitors like you swiftly enough. They brought death upon my entire clan."

Mitchell presses his lips into a tight line.

As Viorel's lips part, a man shouts from across the room behind us. "Mitchell said you're betraying us by allowing Denendrius's child to live. He wants it and Marianna killed."

A bitter cold radiates from Viorel that has my skin pricking with goosebumps. "For two hundred years I housed you, fed you, kept you safe, and *this is what I get*?" he bellows, voice ricocheting across the room. "I will not let your poisonous ideas spread and strangle the peace in my home. I will not let you plant terror in the minds of my *family!*"

Mitchell cowers under Viorel's lethal glare, eyes closed like he's waiting patiently for death.

"That's *my* child!" Viorel roars. *"Mine!"*

Mitchell's lip quivers.

"You could have left if you had a change of heart," Viorel spits. "Now, you're not going anywhere, lest you take your nonsense with you."

Viorel steps back as a guard arrives with manacles and chains. Mitchell fights to twist free as he's chained, but he's stuck in place until he's yanked to his feet and shoved forward. He curses Viorel as he's dragged through the crowd toward Sascha, who waits at the entrance door. She pulls it open as the metal grate lifts, and they shove Mitchell inside.

Viorel clasps his hands behind his back as he turns to Asil and Seth, who are standing nearby awaiting orders. "Round up the clan, humans included."

Guards disappear down each hall, hordes of vampires returning with bewildered expressions as they collect with the others. Soon the room is packed with bodies. A guard blocks each exit. Someone brings chairs for Viorel and me, and we sit before the crowd near the fire. I search for my family, friends, and Laurentius, but can't spot them.

Silence spreads across the room, all eyes on Viorel. I glance at him, waiting for his announcement, but he's silent while his hard gaze flickers over everyone.

The minutes drone on. At first, I think we're awaiting more people, but enough time passes to debunk the idea. The lengthy passage of time gnaws at me as we sit before the unmoving crowd.

Then a woman bolts. Guards take her down as she screams damning, ill wishes at Viorel and me. She's shackled and thrown in the entry hall with Mitchell.

Viorel doesn't break his silence, doesn't look toward her as he picks through the crowd.

I settle in my chair, understanding how we're waiting for weak links to break.

A guard grabs a man in the front row a handful of minutes later. His thoughts must have damned him, as he didn't speak a word until he's dragged away hollering.

We wait for so long humans waver on their feet, a few—likely already weak blood slaves—fully collapsing. Guards bring blood for Viorel, and water for me, and even once our chalices are empty, they continue to pick off clan members. Soon, I'm brought food. With over a thousand eyes on us, I feel like too much of a dick to eat. Yet Viorel commands me to, saying how me and the baby shouldn't suffer for the disloyal few. They strike three more clan members down after his words.

Someone whispers something to a loved one and is assaulting by them. A few more try fleeing and are subdued by those nearest. Guards pick others off while standing silently and do nothing but plead and beg as they're dragged away. A few crumple to their knees in agony until they're dealt with.

One Darkling is brave enough to attempt attack, though I don't realize what's happening until he's writhing on the floor at our feet with a dagger in his hand. He's swiftly dragged into the entrance hall as well.

Nobody steps in to challenge the guards. Some vampires or humans cry when their loved ones or masters are torn from the clan, but most curse them for their betrayal.

Finally, after another long stretch where nobody is ousted, Viorel smiles and says, "Thank you for your enduring faith in me, and for your aid in keeping peace and balance in our home. If you wish to observe punishment against those who have endangered your lives, join me in the garden."

My heart hammers when Viorel takes my hand as I rise to my feet. Vampires disperse down the halls, a relieved and happy murmur filling the air. There's laughter, words of disbelief that anyone would dare betray Viorel, and expressions of thankfulness.

A group of guards takes volunteers to aid them in moving the traitors, a handful escorting Viorel and me through the main rear exit.

My steps slow as I take in the two long rows of tall, sharpened wooden stakes erected in the middle of the grassy field. One is centered at the end.

"Holy shit," I whisper.

The clan regroups in the garden, the crowd as plentiful as it was in the grand room, now spread out. A thin, cottony sheet of fog lies atop the grass, the moon bright overhead.

I hug Viorel's arm as he walks us to the centered stake. We watch as they drag the traitors out to the stakes, struggling while shrieking or crying until they're pinned down to have their throats slashed. I count fifty-three traitors being bled, including the few who ran before we arrived upstairs. The air fills with gushing and gurgling as blood seeps into the grass and soil. As throats heal, they're slit again, energy spilling out of them until their bodies are too weak to mend the wound.

Furious screaming echoes from the front of the castle as Mitchell is wrangled around the corner and dragged down the aisle of gore. His steps squelch, his beige slacks soaking up crimson as he's marched to us.

"This is a fucking cult!" he spits at Viorel, venom spewing past his bloodied and busted lips as he's kicked to his knees. He tries to right himself with his shackled hands, but the guard kicks him onto his side and rests the heel of his boot on the side of his head as Mitchell bellows, "You're all fucking sheep following a deranged cult leader!"

Viorel is unfazed as he holds his palm up. A guard places a bloodied military bayonet in his hand, and I release my grip on him as he assesses the blade. The guard backs away from Mitchell as Viorel squats. He grabs a fistful of his short black hair and roughly twists his head toward the traitors. My heart skips a beat at the sudden sound of his spine crunching. Though he remains conscious, he's unmoving.

"Look what you made me do," Viorel scolds with a curled lip. "You poisoned their minds, turned them against their family and convinced them to renounce me and their home, to condemn us. Now they must suffer with you. Soon, they will die. You will watch."

A guttural groan crawls up Mitchell's throat as Viorel releases a deep, twisted laugh. "You want to destroy my family and our home, murder my love and my child, dethrone me, but *I'm the villain? I'm the one who must be stopped?*" He rests the blade against Mitchell's throat, the slick metal glinting in the moonlight. "After tonight, I hope not a soul dares agree with you."

Viorel tears into Mitchell's throat with the blade, sawing through his pallid skin like it's butter. Maroon bubbles from the gory slit and floods the grass. He gurgles and twitches, red eyes wide with lucid panic.

My heart hammers as I take a step back from the slowly growing pool of blood, the earth soaking it up as it nears the toes of my black flats. Adrenaline courses through me, my muscles spasming with excited twitches as the clan erupts with brutal cheers.

Viorel stands and takes my hand, pulling me away from Mitchell. He lifts his chin, staring in concentration at Mitchell and down the row of traitors.

Their limp bodies lift off the ground, rising above the stakes —they must be a dozen feet tall—and hovering. I hold my breath, unblinking as I await their fall. The suddenness has me gasping as, in sync, their bodies pierce the stakes. The sharp, jagged edges tear through their throats, chests, or mouths. Blood drizzles down the bark-covered stakes, weak moans and whimpers echoing as gravity has bodies shifting and snagging.

I'm light and hot with exhilaration as Viorel's grip tightens on mine. I soak up the sight of their skewered, dripping bodies.

They wanted to take everything from me. And for what? What did I do to them?

Viorel's low snarl has the hair standing on my bare arms. *"Burn."*

Fire engulfs each of them. Furious orange flames burning what only the sunlight can finish. Weak moans of agony emit from sizzling bodies.

The crowd murmurs in excitement behind us.

Viorel's arm embraces me as he buries his face in my hair. His psychic words circle my mind. *I'd burn every one of them if it kept you warm.*

I close my eyes—the bright flames glowing through my lids—and pull in a deep breath as I lean into him. The acrid stench of their burning bodies singes my nostrils and fills my lungs as I take it deep into myself.

Their suffering smells like safety.

Leaving Mitchell to sizzle in the sun would be a mercy, and Viorel is not so merciful. Viorel gouges his eyes and cuts his tongue out before guards drag him back into the grand room. They soak his scorched body in garlic and hang him from the iron chandelier with hooks through his wrists. Viorel orders for whoever attempts to aid him to join him. But he remains alone, only strong enough to moan in agony for two weeks until the clan bores and he becomes an obnoxious decoration. After they take him down, Viorel flays him in the center of the grand room before digging his heart out with his bare hands and feeding it to the fire. Then, he wires Mitchell's skull to the post of his bedframe.

It feels safer knowing there are no more unruly, pricking weeds in my beautiful garden.

July smears into August, and I become accustomed to my new routine of doing nothing much more than enjoying myself with my friends and family.

Glitch doesn't speak another word about Denendrius as she slowly cracks out of her cocoon. She's so carefree I fear it's an act, but her episodes of confusion and memory loss lessen with the passing days.

Mateo briefly returns to stuff Agatha in a cell. I don't have time to speak with him, but Viorel tells me about my mother's death. I feel nothing when he recounts how they dosed her with LSD before chasing her through the woods and doling out a meticulous beating. She has already been dead to me for a long time.

I'm unsure how to feel upon hearing how my birthdate is wrong, though my mother couldn't offer specifics. I must have been right about her being too high to know when she gave birth to me.

With Mateo continuing his search for Alaire and Edmond's

last residence, all I can do is wait and hope for more information. Before leaving Lorimer, they found their van in a police impound lot and their laptop in evidence. Despite how Denendrius left it at the warehouse—where the police began investigating—he took the time to clean my blood off the floor.

From the sound of things, Ziggy and Lance used Agatha as their personal punching bag. No doubt for convincing Rayonne to leave their clan to help find Denendrius, for betraying Rayonne by turning her back, plus all the deaths Agatha caused when Ziggy and members of his clan came to our rescue when Agatha had Venganza Roja kidnap us for her. They yanked her teeth and fangs out, only giving her drops of rat blood to keep her responsive. It's far kinder than what Viorel does to her for working for the men who impersonated his own. He takes a day to flay her and remove all organs but her heart and brain, despite how she gives up their names and location the moment he steps into the room with surgeon's tools. I suspect he's more violent with her for exactly that reason. There's not a loyal bone in her body.

The two men Agatha worked for are brought in two weeks later. They were trying to track Denendrius down for their clan leader—a *literal* Nazi from WW2—after him and *"his Russian soldier friend"* destroyed their camp and medical experiments before killing all of them. Sergei was a newborn and accidentally left their clan leader alive.

They're brave and haughty until they meet Viorel, who takes their loyalties personally and has them horrifically tortured for a month nonstop despite not having any useful information about their leader to give up.

October comes like a punch in my gut, and I find myself in the throes of past trauma again when a group of unfamiliar guards—satellite phones on their hips telltale of their positions —enter the grand room with a group of thirty-six bewildered immortal children.

Immortal children Viorel has had a group of men looking for five years after he caught wind of a trafficking ring. They found them—and the six immortal traffickers who made and sold them—in a brothel on an island east of Brazil. Viorel sends the group of men back out to try tracking down the other two-hundred-and-fifteen children they discovered evidence of sales for.

Life upstairs becomes trickier with their arrival. I avoid the new children—all Children of Stars who travel together in clumps—as much as possible, reminded of my own pain each time I glimpse them. Being in their presence wouldn't be so difficult if they didn't wear the horror of their experiences in their dull eyes and on their quiet lips. Some of them were in Hell for decades or centuries.

But one night I notice the oldest girl—skinny, golden-haired, and fifteen—isn't with them in the grand room and think nothing of it until Viorel is sending every guard to tear through the castle for her. They don't find her in the castle. They don't find her in the garden or the stable, though they catch her scent as fresh as the last dawn on a tree in the forest. Nobody has to say what happened, because everybody knows nobody would attempt fleeing the castle through the confusion of the veil right before sunrise.

Viorel spends the entire night after with her traffickers in the dungeon while I pick at blanket threads in my room upstairs. The tense air spares no space for conversation, so thick in the halls you could cut through it. When I'm brought downstairs with Viorel, he spends the morning scrubbing blood off himself.

We both sleep better that day.

After a few weeks, a few children liven, and I glimpse books in their hands and brief flashes of smiles on their lips. Some appear more distraught than when I first saw them, and I hate how I've experienced the hurricanes within their cloudy gazes.

A handful of them look to me for comfort, convinced I'm the future vampire queen after overhearing chit-chat between their abusers over my missing poster they took in hopes it would be memorabilia worth something one day. According to a seer on the outside, word is I'm to be a powerful vampire, supposedly the evidence in how I fought blood-slavery and betrayed my master backing up the claims.

But the only power I find to comfort them is spilling the pain of my own dark past. Despite how the words practically choke me, I tell them what my mother did, but how much better my life has been since coming to the castle. They seem to take comfort in knowing I can relate and are more hopeful since they've observed how happy I seem these days.

Saying the words aloud helps me too, because I realize *I am okay*. Not fully, but more than I ever have been. And if I can be this amount of okay after a decade, maybe I can fully heal after a handful more.

Come November, Viorel tightens restrictions. By the time I'm six months pregnant, I'm lucky if I'm allowed upstairs for a few hours, even with a guard glued to my side. Though he doesn't protest the baby shower clan members have put together for me, he's rigid in his chair next to mine the entire time I eat red velvet cake and open a mountain of gifts.

If he weren't genuinely terrified for my safety, I might think of his need to control me as abuse. But I can't argue when he says all it takes is a split second for someone to kill Aeliana. Sure, he could fix me if I get hurt, but there's absolutely nothing anybody could do for the baby.

Thankfully, Viorel is reasonable to allow guests for a few hours, so I can see everyone in my close circle. I spend most nights tucked in bed next to Viorel, his hand on my stomach and his face buried in my hair, though there are a few days— days where he can't seem to fall asleep and is overtaken by grief and the urge to wear a path in the stone—where Viorel lets

Laurentius slip into my bed beside me instead. He's too afraid of hurting me and the baby to touch me, anyway.

One of those nights, I half-wake to Viorel standing at my bedside, overlooking Laurentius. He stares down fondly at him as he sleeps, his long nails pushing the overgrown hair away from Laurentius's serene face.

I understand then why Viorel doesn't mind me sharing my affection with him, why he doesn't mind the taste of Laurentius on my lips, and why he's his favorite clan member.

I scoot closer to Laurentius and pat the space behind me.

Want to crawl in? I think at him.

Caught, he sets his jaw as he inhales deeply while slipping around the side of the bed to creep on beside me. He buries his face in my hair and sighs.

Despite so many reminders of my pregnancy, my lack of growing stomach and absence of symptoms makes it difficult to fully believe. A little part of me wonders if I'm pregnant at all, even with the stolen, portable ultrasound machine and heart monitor a clan member gifted to me.

Ainsley swears it's normal for some women to hardly show, how I should be grateful I don't have to replace most of my clothing since my belly only sticks out like I gorged myself on Christmas turkey. Part of me wishes I were big and round, yet I can't complain about keeping my figure. But maybe the pregnancy would be easier to believe, and I'd feel more like a mom-to-be. At least I understand the stories of women who didn't know they were pregnant.

But then one night I feel her. A strange fluttering. Viorel must have heard it, as he rolls over in bed and puts his hand on my stomach. It's the first time I feel like a mom. The first time it really hits that there's a tiny person growing inside me.

XLII

January fourteenth creeps up on me like a winter storm.

I'm leaving the dining room with Laurentius's hand in mine when I spot Mateo pushing a dolly of corrugated office boxes, a few guards carrying small stacks behind him.

My heart leaps into my throat, and I drop Laurentius's hand and move as fast as my body allows across the room. He keeps up beside me.

"Hey," I greet Mateo breathlessly as I fight to keep up with his long strides toward the steel door. "You found Alaire and Edmond's place? Is there something about me in one of those boxes?"

"Hello, Marianna." His head twitches toward me, but his eyes remain straight ahead, his expression deadpan. "Viorel must go through them."

I gasp for breath, Laurentius hooking his arm through mine and telling me to slow down.

"But did you find anything about me in them?" I press.

He's stoic, not a look in his staring eyes betraying his

461

thoughts or feelings. "Viorel will talk to you after he searches the boxes."

"Can you answer my—"

He out-walks me and I stop while Laurentius sighs in disapproval beside me. My lungs fight against me, and I realize panic has settled into me and it's not a lack of stamina. Dread surrounds me, wet and cold and making me clench my teeth.

"Deep breath," Laurentius murmurs from beside me. "Need to sit?"

"He found something," I squeak. I turn to face Laurentius, the movement shaking tears loose. They streak my cheeks. "What could he have found? He won't even meet my eyes."

Laurentius pulls me into his arms, my little baby bump stopping me from pressing against him as tightly as I wish I could. "Whatever it is, I'm here for you," he whispers, arms tight across my back.

Peeking over the side of Laurentius's biceps, I notice a few clan members casting curious gazes toward us.

I drag Laurentius to the steel door, hoping to return downstairs anyway.

Laurentius knocks on the door for me, and I hold my breath until Sascha cracks it open and peeks out.

"You can't come down right now," she tells me.

Stunned, my lips part in disbelief. "Why not?"

"I don't know," she says. "Mateo said, 'Don't let her down here.'"

The ache to be downstairs away from everyone makes tears flow faster. "I need Viorel."

Her lips twist in sympathy, and she shoots a glance over her shoulder. "Okay. I'll go over Mateo's head."

I smile a little, even as she locks the door behind her. I lean into Laurentius and wipe my face with the sleeve of my sweater while I wait.

"She's coming back," Laurentius says a few agonizing minutes later.

My heart stumbles as the door unlocks, and she peeks out at me, something odd in her eyes when they meet mine. Her smile twitches like it's forced. "Viorel says to stay upstairs for now. Everything's fine, don't worry. But he has *boxes and boxes* to go through, so it'll be noisy all day. Sleep with Laurentius, or in your room upstairs."

I gawk at her, my heart thudding so hard I worry it's going to fail.

"If you need something from downstairs, I can get it for you," she offers.

The room spins, my lips and tongue numb as I say, "Can't I see Viorel quick?"

"Sorry, no." She inches the door closed and I grimace as it locks.

I twist to stare at Laurentius. "They've locked me out . . ." Panic builds like pressure in my head, an old feeling returning to me. I think of the nights my foster mom, Pam, locked me out of the house. The cold nights in the shed or walking in the dark to my friend Manny's house. How he'd give me his bed while he sold heroin out of his living room. It was always too late to get in touch with Jenna, Camille, or Daina, and it wasn't worth the stress of going to a youth shelter when I knew they'd call my social worker.

Somehow, despite having a bedroom upstairs and a boyfriend I can crash with, it still feels like they locked me out of my only home. Perhaps it's the rejection, the fact Viorel doesn't want me downstairs with him.

Laurentius clicks his tongue in pity and grabs my hand, walking me down the hall to his room.

I hold my worries on my tongue until we're at his bedside, only the habitat lamps illuminating the chilled space.

"What if he doesn't want me anymore?" I whisper, too little breath to speak louder.

He kisses the back of my hand and helps me onto his bed. "You're overthinking it."

My voice shoots up an octave. "Am I?" I lick salty tears off my lips. "What if he found something so horrible, he's changed his mind?"

A small smile curls at the corners of Laurentius's lips, his maroon eyes soft. "What could possibly be so horrible?"

"I don't know." I throw my hands up and let them thud against the blanket. "What if I was a monster? What if my parent sold me to some vampire who made me his little immortal toy, and that's how I spent centuries?"

"Or it could be something simple."

"Mateo knows," I choke. "And whatever it is, he can't look me in the eye over it."

"Perhaps Mateo saw something upsetting in those boxes unrelated to you."

"No, it was about me. I know it."

Laurentius rests his forehead against mine and smooths my hair against the side of my face. His cool breath is soothing against my hot cheeks.

"Why doesn't Viorel want me down there? Why doesn't he want to comfort me?"

"Because he knows I'll take care of you while Mateo catches him up. They brought in dozens of boxes. Viorel is going to be overwhelmed, so let him sort things out with Mateo so he can give you his full attention. He's probably thinking of the easiest way to break whatever news they've found."

"Maybe," I whisper, something sharp shooting through my heart with each gush of blood.

He pulls away and plants a soft kiss on my forehead. "Lay down and we'll cuddle."

I toss and turn all night, agonizingly uncomfortable. My

hips hurt in ways they haven't before. Resting on either side is unbearable. My stomach is suddenly too heavy to lay comfortably on my back. I whimper and whine all night, my emotion and physical pain making it feel like razor blades are embedded in my chest. I blame Laurentius's bed for a while since I've become accustomed to sleeping on Viorel's memory foam mattress, but even with Laurentius arranging pillows around me—between my knees, against my back—it's no use.

Someone must hear me complaining and take pity on me—or they want me to shut up so they can rest—as a black-eyed man knocks quietly in the middle of the day and offers his familiar's hot water compress and some ginger tea. I graciously take it, though it only dulls the aches for a short while.

"There's something wrong," I cry once I've fought through three quarters of the day sleeplessly. My head pounds from exhaustion. "I've never hurt so bad before."

There's a hint of concern in his voice when he asks, "Are you cramping?"

"No. It feels like someone's trying to tear my legs off from my hips and like she's trying to kick through my ribs. If I wasn't so frustrated, tired, and stressed, it wouldn't be so bad," I growl.

He adjusts his knees in the crook of mine, his breath grazing my cheek. "Okay. As long as it doesn't feel like labor."

A craving wakes and twists around inside my gut. A transient surge of intense need that comes with images of needles and the vinegary stench of impending relief. The shame for thinking of heroin when I have a baby inside me is short-lived once I'm dizzy with the breathlessness of pain.

"What does Viorel usually do when you feel like this?" Laurentius asks. "I'm out of ideas."

I realize why this pain is unfamiliar. I let out a flat laugh. "He gives me his blood every morning, through the night, and before bed. He's close to me all day, his healing hands always on some part of my body while I sleep."

Laurentius blows out a breath. "Yeah, so I'm practically useless right now."

Shaking my head, I say, "No. Holding me—comforting me —is exactly what I need."

Hours pass before Mateo knocks on the door in the evening, cracking it open with no regard to privacy, to say, "You may come down now."

I grit my teeth as Laurentius helps me sit. Hugging myself for warmth, I shift off the bed and wince as I walk to Mateo, pinning my eyes to his and refusing to break away. He holds my gaze this time, and there's nothing but heavy exhaustion in his.

"Were you up all day with Viorel?" I ask.

"I haven't slept in four days," he mumbles.

I'm not sure what to make of that.

After a kiss goodbye, Laurentius crawls back into bed for a proper rest.

Mateo and Sascha escort me downstairs. I lower my gaze upon walking into the sitting room. The scattered pages and notebooks across the floor, table, and sofa call for my attention, but Viorel asks for it instead. I can't bear to look at him as his lower half comes into my line of sight. He places his hands on my waist. The pain in my body evaporates, but I still can't bring myself to meet his eyes despite how his touch assures me he doesn't hate me. My tongue is in a knot. I don't want to know what's in his eyes and ponder what has put the emotion there.

"You didn't sleep," he murmurs. "I'm sorry."

I sniffle. *Tell me,* I think at him.

Instead, he guides me to his bed and has me sit on the mattress.

"Rest for a while." His voice is delicate, but there's something restrained in it putting me on edge.

I keep my eyes on my lap, even when he takes my hand and presses his wintry lips to the back of it. "I'm sorry for putting you out. Mateo and I had much to discuss."

I find my voice. "What did they discover about me?"

"Now, now," he starts. "You're practically sick with exhaustion. Sleep."

Gritting my teeth, I bite back my protests as he maneuvers me beneath the blankets and brushes my hair from my face as I rest my head on his pillow. Tears leak from the corners of my eyes, the soft thud of them hitting the pillow near my ears making me squeeze my lids closed.

"I can't sleep not knowing," I argue, hands in fists on the blanket.

My eyes pop open at the feel of his wrist on my lips, and I gulp him up. With his blood flowing over my tongue, all my discomfort washes away. My body finally accepts the idea of sleep, rushes toward it, despite how my mind fights to stay awake to plead for the truth.

"You must," he whispers, as I drift.

All I can think as I fall asleep is he's found something so horrible he wants to make sure I get one last sleep in before I can't bear to close my eyes again.

Viorel is sitting on the edge of the bed as I wake, staring off blankly at the wardrobe.

"What time is it?" I demand.

"It's five in the morning," he says.

"So, tell me," I urge, clearing my dry throat.

His chest rises and falls with a sigh, and he turns his head to look at me while I prop myself up against the headboard with the pillow and hug the blanket to myself for comfort.

"Viorel . . ."

He wets his lips, something like pain etched into his face—like he doesn't want to tell me—as he reaches out to rest his hand on my leg over the blanket. He parts them to speak.

My head throbs so hard his words don't make it to my ears, the pain making me dizzy for a moment. I screw my eyes closed as I fight the disorientation. When I clear my throat, the tissue is so dry it's like I swallowed thumbtacks.

I rub my wet eyes. They're sore to the touch.

Viorel must have noticed, and is waiting for me to catch my bearings, because his lips are a silent line now.

"Go on," I choke out, pushing wet strands of hair off my tacky cheeks. I'm unbearably exhausted again, like I never slept at all. "Please."

His breaths are noticeably quicker, a dam of emotion in his eyes as he looks away toward the sitting room and back at me.

"You were born on May thirteenth, and this upcoming birthday will be your nineteenth. Your mother, Bonnie, had you alone at home. Her boyfriend Julio convinced her to keep you, despite being sure you were a client's baby. They kept you a secret, and you spent the extra time unaccounted for as similarly as before you were first taken away. You were a quick learner, and Julio spent hours homeschooling you, hoping you would have a chance. It was a client of your mother's who reported your existence to the police. He disliked how your mother was turning tricks and had you starving and living in squalor. After the first time authorities removed you from the home, Julio was working on bribing the judge to have you returned to her, despite the agency believing it was best to terminate her parental rights. After Carol's sister and husband were killed, Julio put money in the right hands, and they returned you to her. You know the rest of your unfortunate time with her."

I stare at him, heart thudding crookedly. "When was I a child vampire?"

There's something hollow in his eyes when he limply says, "You weren't. I was wrong."

I lick my dry lips, salty tears transferred to my tongue, and heave out a breath from my sore lungs. I tuck my feet under the disheveled blanket, my body aching like I was in a fight. It's worse than when I came down here. My face feels puffy and my head pounds.

He looks away, like he can't bear to look at me. Like he's trying to hide his face.

"Viorel . . ."

He faces me, all composed aside from his unsettled eyes.

"You're lying to me," I accuse, panic trickling into my veins. "And you're doing an offensively poor job for someone who has had such a long time to learn to lie."

He smiles, but it doesn't meet his eyes. "Are you disappointed to hear all that?"

"What's so bad about the truth that you've decided to lie?" My voice cracks.

At the sound of papers shuffling in the sitting room, I throw myself out of bed and dart to the room, wanting to hear it from Mateo.

"What did you find?" I demand before my raw throat has me coughing. My heart thumps so fast my knees are weak.

He sits on the sofa and doesn't turn to me as he swiftly picks a navy-blue leather notebook off the couch and drops it in a box. "Viorel told you."

"Viorel told me a lie!" I bark. "Tell me the truth."

He adjusts the rings on his fingers. "It's okay to be disappointed, Marianna."

I spin at Viorel's featherlight touch on my waist and stare up at him with pleading eyes and a painful frown.

"Go sit, and think about what I've said," he murmurs. "Where is your trust in me, Marianna?"

I close my eyes, my lids feeling paper thin, and pull in a breath intended to calm me but doesn't do more than burn my lungs.

"I feel like shit," I tell him. "Why do I feel like shit?"

He takes my hand and walks me back to the bed, but I don't climb back on, standing on my sore legs beside it.

"Isn't it better to know you were simply human?" he asks, reaching up to tuck my hair behind my ear.

"But you were so sure," I whisper. "Everything you said made sense—"

"I was wrong," he says with delicate finality.

Slowly, I shake my head like I can loosen the confusion constricting my thoughts. "How?"

"I'm not infallible, Marianna."

With the way he forces his eyes to stay steady on mine, he must have. "It's true I was a child vampire, isn't it, Viorel?"

Them not jumping to fill the silence only has the panic clawing my breath back, and tears build behind my sore eyes. *"What did you find?"* I squeeze out, building hysteria choking me. "It's the only thing that makes sense. How else can you explain how my body fought Denendrius's mark, how I can't be hypnotized? Why does my body react to your blood? Make it so sunlight and garlic hurt me?"

Bewilderment flashes through his eyes before he sets his jaw and swallows it away. "Marianna—"

"Tell me!" I wail, a hot blade twisting in my chest, burning me so deeply I want to scream. *"Tell me."*

Mateo mutters something from the other room and exhales despondently. Viorel blinks away a damp film over his claret eyes.

"Tell me, please." I gasp, sharp breaths stabbing at my lungs. "I know you're lying. You found something horrible, didn't you? You're trying to save me from the truth by telling me something you know I'd prefer . . . but I can't feel anything for that story aside from knowing it's a lie."

The truth is in Viorel's white-rimmed eyes and parted lips. So horrible it must be that even he can't shake the words loose.

Viorel shifts so close and presses his body against mine that

I'm expecting him to hold me to deliver some awful news. He must think it will have me collapsing. Instead, his hands cradle my face and angle my head up toward his.

My breath hitches. "*Please.* What did you find?"

Viorel's claret eyes are a deep void I succumb to. "*Believe me,*" he murmurs. A warm rush of thoughts enters me, and my breath comes easy again. I relax under Viorel's comforting touch. He breaks our gaze and kisses me on the forehead. "Know I would do nothing to harm you."

He's right. There's no reason for him to lie about me having been a vampire. After everything I've been through in my brief life, he should know I can handle any truth. There can't be anything more nightmarish than what's already happened to me he'd have to shield me from.

I heave out a relieved breath and wipe my eyes, feeling a little silly for my meltdown. "Okay. I'd probably lose it if I had to find out my past was a bigger tragedy than it already is."

Viorel turns his head, staring across the room as he takes purposeful breaths.

I let a chuckle bubble out of me. "Sorry for being a regular, boring human. I know you both were hoping I was some miraculously cured vampire child."

"There's no need to apologize for anything, Marianna," Viorel assures me with a soft smile.

"Do you still want me knowing I'm not special?" I bite my lip.

"Of course." Viorel's fingernails graze my cheekbone on the way to tuck my hair behind my ear. "Being special can be over-rated. It doesn't bother me to know you're a *normal* human girl."

My cheeks burn. "Well, that makes me *feel* special, at least."

Viorel's smile is tired. "How about a warm bath to relax? I'm sure you could use it."

I heave out a breath and nod in agreement. Viorel takes my arm and walks me to my room to collect my bathrobe.

As I drape the poofy thing over my arm and close the door of my wardrobe, I notice the clock on my nightstand. "It's ten a.m.?"

Confusion has my head swiveling to Viorel. He said it was five, and there's no way more than twenty minutes have passed . . .

"No, it's not," Viorel says with a tickled smile, his tone bright and teasing. "How would that make sense?"

"But—" I look back at the clock and my heart skips. The hands are at 5:13 now.

"Tired girl . . ." He clicks his tongue at me. "Have a bath, and back to bed you go."

XLIII

Tangled in fuzzy nightmares of Denendrius, the sound of my crying wakes me as I thrash. Viorel wraps his arms around me, gently shushing my strained, hysterical sobs.

There's something broken in his voice when he whispers, *"You're okay."*

Ragged breaths choke me, my chest aching as I fight to keep it in my lungs and break out of my disorientation. Viorel whispers for me to take deep breaths, and Aeliana's strong kicks remind me of where I am.

He strokes my hair away from my sweaty forehead when I'm calm and curled up at his side. I press my hand against the side of my stomach, the little feet kicking back from the inside still so odd.

As we lie in the warm glow of candlelight, I dig into my cluster of dreams, trying to untangle the dark threads that seem to have no definition or end. I can't remember what any of them were about but can't shake the urge to see him, despite how the idea makes me want to puke. Like when you can't help but check for a monster beneath your bed, even if the sight of it will terrify you.

I blow out a long breath. "Can I visit Denendrius?"

He flinches. "Why would you want to?"

"I need to make sure he's hurting," I admit.

"I don't think it's a good idea anymore."

I wipe my eyes. "Why not? You said you didn't mind because I come back hating him a little more each time."

Viorel stares blankly across the room.

I scowl. "You won't even let me torture him again?"

A wicked smile creeps across Viorel's lips. "Okay. It would do you good to *hate him more.*"

By the time we reach his cell with a team of silent guards and Mateo, I'm unbearably nauseous, despite the fresh relief of knowing I can fully leave my past behind me. I wipe my clammy hands on my yoga pants for the fifth time as another chill floods me. Perhaps my heightened sense of smell and the dungeon stench choking me are to blame.

Denendrius is hunched against the wall of his cell as we enter, his eyes dull as they settle on us. His lips are parted like it's too much effort to keep them together.

Viorel seats me in the chair across from Denendrius's cell and stands by my side, Mateo on my other side.

"Why the smug smile, Huarsar?" Denendrius rasps, his voice like rusty nails in my ears.

"I'm simply enjoying the *immensity* at which you have fucked your entire life." A tickled chuckle bubbles from him. "You have no idea how confounding the mistakes you've made are."

Denendrius blinks at him, too dazed to react properly. His gaze shifts to me and rests on my stomach. "Why are you here, Marianna?"

I swallow a knot, not fully knowing myself.

But I find myself telling him, "It turns out I wasn't a child vampire after all." I'm weightless with relief saying those words aloud.

Denendrius's eyes narrow. "I thought he was sure of it. It made sense to me."

I shrug. "He made a mistake."

"No, you didn't," Denendrius says, eyes narrowing on Viorel.

I don't bother looking up to assess Viorel's expression. "Yes, he did. It's fine. I'd rather be normal and fully human, anyway."

"He hypnotized you," Denendrius accuses, pointing a finger at me.

Viorel strokes the back of my head as the accusation brings the heat of my blood to a simmer. Denendrius tenses.

I grit my teeth. "Fuck you, no I wasn't."

His narrow eyes study my face as he leans closer to the bars. "Yeah, you were," he says, matter of fact. "I've done my fair share of hypnotizing. *And. You. Were.*"

"He didn't hypnotize me," I snarl as Mateo takes a warning step forward.

Viorel sighs. "You're not nearly as perceptive as you believe, rat."

"What was so bad about the truth?" Denendrius demands.

"Nothing," I snap.

He shakes his head, lip curling with disgust. "I wonder what else he's done to you. I bet he hypnotizes you often—" His head snaps back against the wall as he grits his teeth in pain.

"Care to lose your tongue again, rat?" Viorel warns. "Have you forgotten who you're speaking to?"

Denendrius gasps for breath as Viorel releases him from imagined pain, then chokes out, "When I escape, I'll turn you once we've built our family. Then all Huarsar's lies will unravel, and you'll remember the truth."

Viorel's dark laugh is taunting. "So arrogant to think such a thing could transpire."

Denendrius's lips twitch to expose a fang. "Then I hope my baby dies during childbirth and takes Marianna with her."

My heart stutters at his words despite knowing he's thought them all along.

"My baby," Viorel corrects calmly before clicking his tongue in condescending disapproval. "I see you're set on losing more than your tongue tonight."

Denendrius narrows his eyes, a dark grin pulling at the corners of his lips. "Come, show me how angry you are."

Viorel releases a bark of laughter that has my ears ringing. "I'm much too preoccupied to waste my energy on you, what with *becoming a father* and all. I've only come down because Marianna wanted to see how you're suffering."

Denendrius's expression darkens, hate burning in his scarlet glare.

"Is he suffering enough?" Viorel asks me.

"No," I snarl.

Denendrius sets his jaw.

"What do you suppose we should do?" The corner of his lip draws back in a wry smile as I look up at him.

I straighten in the chair. "Have the guards beat him. I want to hear his bones break."

I'm out of breath and mildly dizzy when we return from the dungeon, grabbing onto Viorel's outstretched arm as he offers it to me and guides me to his bed. Exhaustion smacks into me and my hands shake as he helps me lower myself to the edge of the mattress.

As he sits beside me, I blow out a lung-emptying breath and gasp to refill them. "I'm still so tired." I complain, wincing with an ache that starts in my lower back.

Viorel rubs the pain away, and I relax against his touch.

"Pregnancy and stress will do that. I can rid you of aches, but not the need for proper sleep."

"At least watching Denendrius get the shit kicked out of him was good stress-relief." The crunch and snap of his bones breaking replays in my mind. If it hurt, he bit back his cries, but he couldn't hide the sound of his body breaking.

He smirks and nods in agreement as he rests his hand on my stomach and gently feels around. Aeliana doesn't kick. I suspect she's sleeping and waiting until I do to jam her little toes into me.

"Also, it's an immense relief knowing I don't have an entirely different past to unravel while I'm trying to adjust to a whole new one." I blow out a breath.

"Yes." Viorel kisses the back of my hand.

I think of opening the packages of baby toys in Aeliana's nursery to give myself something to do. With all the free time I've had downstairs, everything has been ready for her for weeks. It still hasn't stopped me from wandering in there and finding a better way to reorganize.

Or maybe I could get my watercolors out and paint another oceanic scene to hang beside the other two I've done—one of dolphins, another of killer whales—in their silver frames.

"Or you could sleep." Viorel winks.

"Fine." I crawl under the covers with him and snuggle close as he offers his wrist. The soothing trickle of blood down my throat has me asleep before his wrist parts from my lips.

I wake with a sharp ache in my abdomen that swiftly passes. The candle on Viorel's bedside is burned down while he rests on his back, blankly staring up. Shadows flicker across his haunted face.

"What's wrong?" I whisper, placing my hand on his chest.

He unclasps his hands from where they rest on his stomach and places one over mine. "Sleep has escaped me since Mateo returned."

"Why?"

His exhale is deflating.

"Is something from Alaire and Edmond's files bothering you? There must have been all sorts of horrible things from testing the cure on children."

When he nods, it's so slight I nearly miss it.

"What did you find?" A tense line forms between my brows. "I'm curious too."

He loudly empties his lungs, chest lowering beneath our hands. "They gave the cure to dozens of children, and most died after consumption. Of the few who woke human, half died within a short handful of weeks or years in different flavors of horrible. Only three made it past ten years old. One girl developed minor health issues but was admitted to a psychiatric ward at sixteen after she began remembering her previous life as an eight-year-old vampire and became vocal about it. She was obsessed with the idea of blood drinking and couldn't keep down food. She became emaciated and committed suicide. One boy was left disabled. Aside from severe hemophilia and a host of other medical issues, he was immobile and unable to communicate. He died during a seizure at nineteen. But there was another girl who was practically a miracle."

"The other girl lived longer?"

"She was a success. Nearly zero physical health issues, and the issues she had almost completely resolved near adulthood."

My brow furrows. "Was she a vampire for a shorter time? Were they all the same type of vampire?"

He shakes his head. "The first girl was a Child of Stars for two years. The boy was immortal for almost four hundred, and the other girl was nearly two thousand years old. Both were Darklings."

I mouth my amazement and frown. "Like rolling dice."

"Completely unpredictable," he agrees.

"What's her story?"

He's silent for a few beats before he sighs. "Alaire and Edmond approached her parents after they were all caught in a park at night. They willingly gave their daughter up, so Alaire and Edmond permitted them to live. The child was growing miserable as the world advanced, as she saw everything she was missing out on. She became obsessed with being a normal human child. Seeing the lives of human children on TV had her aching to be like them. She wanted friends, wanted to ride the bus and go to school with them. Play in the sunshine. Eat candies and treats. She wanted to grow up. Her parents tried to remove the television, but it was too late. She turned violent and frequently had to be restrained. She would sob for days, cry and beg for the idealized human life she built in her head and did not understand why she couldn't have it, or why she knew no other children like her. They had to return the TV to pacify her. Her parents just wanted her to be happy."

"Wow," I murmur. "Her parents must have loved her to give her up."

"Yes, they did."

I nuzzle my cheek into his shoulder. "Did she get what she wanted? Did she have a good life?"

"She was being adopted, last Alaire and Edmond knew. But no, in the end, she did not have the life they all hoped for. Last they checked, she had quite a scarring, miserable experience growing up as a human."

"All that to live miserable as a human? Fuck. I'm glad you didn't find anything about me in there," I whisper, eyes burning at the idea. "Thankfully, I've always been human, even if I'm an abnormal one. I know what it's like to so desperately want to be normal you drive yourself crazy. I can't imagine the regret she must have had knowing she gave up loving parents for a life of misery. That would hurt so bad. Personally, I don't think I'd be able to come back from something like that."

"Yes." He swallows hard as he closes his eyes and lifts my hand to his lips for a kiss.

My smile is small as I notice the wetness on his lashes. My chest warms seeing how he's capable of such sadness. "It's sweet you care about immortal children so much."

"They're the most innocent creatures, and they suffer the most." Viorel kisses my hand again as I wipe his eyes with the back of my free one.

My lips twist in thought. "Did Alaire and Edmond have more notes about her? What happened to her?"

He pauses. "No, they wrote nothing else. They must have died before they were able."

I click my tongue in disappointment. "*Damn.* Well, I hope she gets another chance if she's still alive. I feel bad for her. It doesn't seem like the cure benefited any of them, even if they considered her successf—" I gasp as another sharp ache ricochets through my stomach.

He reaches under my shirt and rubs his cold palm over my belly.

I test a smile but end up cringing with another painful contraction. "Braxton Hicks, like Ainsley warned about?"

"No." I can't read his blank expression. His hand slips away from my body as my abdomen tightens again.

I gasp with another slice of pain as something cold and sinister slams into me, sinking through my sweaty skin and wringing my bones. Dread sits on my chest. I'm dizzy, even with my eyes closed, and a flash of heat envelopes me.

Warm wetness gushes out of me like my bladder failed, but it feels too thick to be pee.

"W-what was that?" I stutter as my heart races. "Did my water break?

"No." I can't focus on his flat expression as he throws himself out of bed. "Don't sit up and don't move. Stay awake."

Viorel darts from my side, my ears barely registering the

sound of the iron door opening and his faraway shouts—like he's run up the stairs—for Seth to get Ainsley and Mateo.

The fact he's left the room and *gone up the stairs* without a single guard has panic kicking at my heart and my breath fighting me. I grit my teeth at the squeezing pain in my stomach. Darkness shudders at the edges of my vision.

He's calm when he returns. I almost miss the flares of panic in his unblinking, calculating eyes.

"You must have the baby now." He climbs onto the bed and pulls the blankets away from me. "Ainsley is coming with medical equipment."

I don't have enough breath to express my horror. I'm only thirty-five weeks along.

Viorel strips my crimson-soaked pajama pants and panties off and tosses them aside.

Aeliana hasn't kicked in a while. The realization has me gagging, and my nausea nearly has me spewing.

"Her heart is still beating. She'll be okay," he promises me as he pushes my shirt off my stomach, the pain disappearing with his touch. "But you're rapidly losing blood and could die if we don't immediately deliver her."

I don't have the breath to ask him what's happening. My thoughts become looser, the gaps between them filling with panic and the urge to rest my eyes. There's no pain—just the quick growth of warm blood around me—and I worry I'm dying.

"I'm taking your pain," he whispers. "You're not dying on me."

The room goes dark, though I can't tell if I've closed my eyes or if I'm about to pass out.

"Don't sleep," he tells me, but I can feel myself drifting from his voice.

Ainsley's voice surrounds me like a dream, and I feel Viorel gently shifting beneath me. I suspect I'm propped up against him between his legs, but I can't be sure until he brushes my sweaty hair away from my forehead as my weak head rolls back and forth against his abdomen.

The faint taste of his blood appears on my tongue, but I can't feel my lips—or any part of me anymore—to know he's given me his wrist.

Viorel's panicked voice sounds so far, like I'm underwater. *"Mateo, stand closer to us. Be prepared to turn her if it comes to it. Death may not take her from me."*

Ainsley says something about an incision before the vague clang of metal. *"Give her your blood again and be ready to heal her."*

Mateo speaks, but I can only hear the comforting tone of his voice.

"You'll be okay." Viorel's promise snakes around what's left of my consciousness. *"One way or another."*

I lose touch with the room around me, mind circling around the taste of his blood and how it numbs my fear of if Aeliana and I will survive. It feels like laying on my back in the water, though I can feel nothing but the waves trying to tug me away through the dark void around me.

"Don't go to sleep," Viorel whispers as I struggle to taste the blood flowing over my tongue. *"Marianna, please stay with me. I love you."*

It seems like such an unfair, impossible task to ask of me.

XLIV

My eyes snap open. A shot of adrenaline courses through me with the memory of fighting to stay awake while Ainsley worked to deliver Aeliana. *All the blood.* I jerk upright in Viorel's bed, scrambling to get the white duvet from my room and an unfamiliar sheet off to see my stomach.

It's flat. There are no scars or signs of injury when I lift my shirt. It's like I was never pregnant. Swinging my legs off the bed and bounding to my feet, I don't feel like someone who just gave birth, either.

I think of how Viorel wanted Mateo to turn me should I begin to die, and recall being swept under by a flood of darkness.

Oh god, am I dead?

The drumming of my heart in my chest and ears dissolves the idea.

"Marianna," Viorel calls softly from somewhere near the sitting room. "You're all right. Come see your baby girl."

Relief floods me at verification of her survival, and I'm

flying across the room before I consciously decide to and stopping hard in the mouth of the sitting room. Gasping for breath, my eyes lock on Viorel and the bundle of white fabric he clutches against his chest. He sits on the sofa with formula and glass bottles laid out on the coffee table.

"Come see," he murmurs.

Terror chains me to the floor. What if she looks like Denendrius? What if I hate her when I see her? What if all I can think about every time I look at her is what he did to me?

"Marianna," Viorel presses with a soft smile. "It's all right. Come hold her."

I shake my head, a flood of tears rushing down my cheeks.

What if I see her and wish she were never born? What if I just ruined my life? What if I brought her into the world to suffer?

I take a step back as Viorel stands, turning my face toward the wall as he slowly moves toward me.

When he lowers Aeliana from his chest, I squeeze my eyes closed.

"Marianna..." There's a pained twinge in his voice.

His hand tries to lift my arm and shape it like he plans on having me cradle her, but I pull away and hug myself.

"Please don't reject her..." Viorel pleads quietly.

I back away, sick with dread, like a nightmare has sprung up around me.

"I can't look at her," I cry, choking on a breath. My heel hits the foot of the pew and I grab onto a wooden edge to catch myself.

Eyes firmly shut, I straighten and find Viorel's body against mine, his arm hooked around my lower back, a warm lump between us. "She's been looking for you," Viorel says. "When you were unconscious, I had to rest her on your chest so she'd stop crying. She keeps thinking of your voice."

"Really?" I choke.

"Of course," Viorel whispers. "She's your baby. Your womb is all she's known for months. She yearns for you."

His words give me pause, my thoughts calming enough to manage a full breath.

"Does she know you since she has your blood?" I hope she wants him too, and that there isn't some biological part of her seeking Denendrius's presence.

I can tell he's smiling when he says, "Yes. She knows my voice."

"How long was I out?" I crack an eye open, focusing on a faded pink elephant on the white blanket.

"About thirty-six hours," Viorel says. "Carol came down for a couple of hours after she was born. She sat with you, as Ainsley and I tended to Aeliana."

A squeaky, "Oh," is all I can manage.

"They think she's beautiful," Viorel murmurs. "I know you'd agree. There's nothing to fear, I promise."

I wipe at my tears. "Okay," I agree, only because of the pool of guilt forming in me for the thought of upsetting Aeliana when it was my choice to have her.

Holding my breath, I lower myself onto the pew and shape my arms the way Ainsley taught me will dolls. I stiffen at her weight, my eyes wide and heart racing as I process the sight of her.

With her in my arms, I find I don't hate her at all. It's me I hate, for not giving her a choice in having a monster for a father, for all the grief she might receive for his evil. I hate myself for making Denendrius's dream come true of having his own baby, when all he's done is ruin mine.

"She's *yours*," Viorel reminds me as he sits at my side. "You're allowed to have your child, Marianna. Denendrius does not matter."

I stare at her little face and pudgy cheeks as I digest his words and force myself to accept that she's really mine, and not an extension of Denendrius I've been carrying. I force myself to search for that truth in her face.

A copy of my cinnamon eyes stares up at me, a replica of my own lips parted for little breaths. I skate my finger down her little nose and across the curve of her upper lip and slight cupid's bow. Gentle, I give her chubby, olive-toned cheeks a squish.

My heart thrums as my eyes become slick with tears.

"She has his hair." I run my fingers across the little loose brown curls and cough away the emotion building in my throat.

Viorel's silent as he studies my face.

"That's okay," I decide as I release a slow breath. "He has nice hair. Hair can't be evil."

Viorel circles his arm around my back. "Nobody will lend much thought to his role in her existence when she's full of my blood and born to someone as special as you."

I can't help but laugh. "Special."

"Yes, truly," Viorel whispers. "I'm quite fortunate to be part of this."

"I'm lucky to be here with you," I murmur.

For a fleeting moment, I'm euphoric as I trick myself into thinking we're a normal family with Aeliana in my arms and Viorel pressed at my side as he stares down at her in awe. I wonder what Viorel would be like as a human while wishing he were Aeliana's biological father.

Reality is far more surreal. It feels impossible to be holding my own baby, and someone—*him* of all men—has found me good enough to love.

I exhale my anxieties as Viorel leans his forehead against the side of my head. His arm tightens around my back, the other resting against the side of Aeliana's head.

"I thought I was going to lose you both," he whispers. "I was petrified. There was nothing I could have done to save her."

Aeliana closes her eyes, so I run my finger down her tiny nose and her little pink lips part. "She's perfect."

"Yes," Viorel agrees with a blissful sigh. "Completely healthy too. She's practically identical to a full-term baby, so she likely would have wanted out soon anyway. We might have been wrong about her due date, but I'm going to let myself believe my blood caused her to develop faster."

"What happened?"

"You had a severe, full placental abruption and would have died had I not been able to stabilize you. You likely would have died in a modern hospital."

"Why did that happen?" Since I was alive for Denendrius to kill in Patricia's vision, this probably never would have happened in Bellevue.

"There isn't always a cause, but stress or physical trauma can increase risks."

"I haven't been *that* stressed," I argue. "And definitely no physical trauma."

He doesn't say anything, and I don't know what to say either. I'm just so fucking grateful to be *here*.

I still can't fathom how me—a tiny blip in his existence— can be so important. It's almost silly, though it fills me with warmth.

"You're not a blip. I want to keep you for eternity. Both of you."

"You haven't changed your mind about taking Denendrius's baby as your own?" I ask, unable to help worry the novelty of her might wear off.

"She's *mine*," he says as he straightens, red eyes practically sparkling as he gazes down at her. "I'm her father. I helped make her. I've done more for her development with my blood than any other father ever could. I don't think a mark could be deeper. I could feel her creeping into existence."

His answer—the conviction in it—has my shoulders lowering and my breath passing easier.

Viorel keeps true to his promise of making motherhood as easy as possible for me, but I feel useless compared to him most days. Aeliana spends most of her time sleeping, and everything is easy when she's awake, thanks to Viorel. She rarely cries since he always knows what she wants and how to fix it. He's quick to attend to her thirst, and heals every growing ache and upset, gassy stomach. And when there's seemingly no reason for her cries, he simply gives her blood and she's peacefully snoozing again.

He takes on the responsibility of most day feedings and changes since his immortal body doesn't need sleep to function the way mine does, and the feel of her restlessness wakes him before she ever has a chance to cry and wake me. I make it up to him, sharing my blood with him, since his lack of sleep has him thirstier. I'm so well rested, it's only fair.

Despite all he does, she still cries for me, desperate to have me hold and rock her. It's strange being needed—wanted—so badly.

For the first month, we spend a good portion of our time holding her. She loves my warm arms and even prefers Viorel's cold ones to her cradle. As cozy as he's made it for her, she still spends hours sleeping on one of our chests.

Viorel gives me plenty of opportunities to go upstairs for a *"break"*, but he's made things so easy for me I don't find myself desperate for one. I find I enjoy reading or playing video games with Aeliana in my lap, though I spend plenty of time upstairs with my family and friends since I refuse to lose myself to simply being *mommy*.

Creaking draws me awake and I roll over to find Viorel rocking back and forth in the rocking chair between the bed and his wardrobe, unblinking and lost in haunted thoughts as he holds Aeliana in his lap with a bottle of milk tinged pink with his blood.

"What's wrong?" I rub my eyes.

He blinks, my voice pulling him from the fog. "Do you recall when I spoke of having visions in my sleep, though they are often easily ignored as dreams?"

I nod.

"I had a nightmare, but I know with certainty it was not a dream."

I prop myself up on my elbow. "What did you see?"

He closes his eyes and leans his head back. "You and Aeliana . . . *miserable and hating me.*"

"Because you won't let us leave the castle?"

A sour, pained smile flashes across his lips. "The fact you can already guess . . ." His frown is heavy. "You were both immortal. Black eyed. Her not much younger than you and looking so much like you. You both hated me. Her more than you, though she began to resent you for having already known the outside world. She was suicidal, and I still wouldn't budge. You and I couldn't be in a room together without fighting. The clan began to reassess the idea of me being a fair man. Even *Laurentius* was beginning to resent me for your pain, but I was crippled with terror over the mere thought of either of you leaving and dying." A single thin tear runs from the corner of his eye. "You tried to take her and leave—you had no plans to return—and I was crying while trying to restrain you in the garden. My obsession with your safety was stronger than my love for you."

My heart thumps with terror.

"I can't bear that future," Viorel rasps. "I fear it more than all our deaths."

Tears well in my own eyes, my voice pleading. "I don't want that to happen."

"It *can't* happen," Viorel whispers. "I don't want to succumb to such paranoia that I become that man."

I pull in a shaky breath, waiting for him to tell me how he plans on changing things. Waiting for him to say the *only thing* capable of fixing the future before it breaks.

He pulls in a shuddering breath as he opens his watery eyes. "I will grant you freedom once you're immortal. I will have Mateo turn you in no sooner than three years. Give you and Aeliana a chance to know one another . . . in case you don't survive the transformation or die beyond the veil. Anything can happen since we're attempting to alter the future, so your survival is not guaranteed. Aeliana can travel once she's immortal as well."

His words of doom barely faze me. Warmth floods me and I can't help the elated grin crossing my face or the excited breaths rushing in and out of me. I want to jump for joy, but resort to an awkward, blanket-restricted dance.

"I love you," I gush, the happiness bubbling out of me. "I know how hard it must be to even consider it, so I hope you know how *fucking much* your effort means to me."

Viorel gives me a shaky smile, his eyes glistening. He mouths, *"I love you too."*

"What about you?" I press my teeth into my bottom lip and gaze at him with slipping hope.

He draws in a deep breath and adjusts his grip on the glass bottle, Aeliana momentarily peeking through half-lidded eyes as she sleeps. "In two nights, we will leave Aeliana with Carol and Ainsley while I take you horseback riding into the woods for a picnic."

I'm speechless, unblinking, and half-convinced I'm still fast asleep.

"Guards will monitor us from afar, but I'll order them to stay out of our sight."

Maybe Ziggy was right. Maybe Viorel lets me leave the castle this summer despite his current plan, and this is the first step to him making that decision.

XLV

I inhale toxic nail polish fumes as Adelia slathers the rose-pink varnish on her toenails a mere foot from where I rest my head on my bed upstairs. Rayonne throws garments in her beaten suitcase, giddy with excitement as she flies around the room to collect the most necessary items of the few she owns.

"Are you sure you don't want to see Egypt with us, Glitch?" Rayonne asks for the third time as she stuffs a handful of socks into her suitcase.

After receiving an impromptu invitation from another group of girls an hour ago, she'll be spending the day sleeping over in their room before their trip tomorrow.

Glitch wrinkles her nose. "And leave Marianna alone?"

I flick my eyes into the back of my head and push out a dramatically playful sigh. "I already said I won't be alone. I literally have four other people I see regularly, not including the baby that would miss me."

Swirling the tip of the nail polish brush around the rim of

the bottle, she sighs and says, "I'd still feel bad leaving you behind."

"I don't!" Rayonne sticks her tongue out past her black-painted lips.

"Wow, rude," I tease.

Rayonne carries a shit-eating grin as she folds a lacy skirt into her suitcase. "You get to be jealous of me leaving the castle, and I get to be jealous the most powerful vampire in the world is in love with you and raising a cute little baby with you."

"Fair." I smile and bite my bottom lip.

Despite all I have now, and the happiness filling me more often these days, I can't help the painful twang ricocheting through my swollen heart as I stare longingly at Rayonne's quickly filling suit-case. Even if Viorel keeps his word and lets me leave the castle—assuming Death brings me home after my walk with him—three years is still so long. And who knows if I'll even have enough control as a newborn vampire to travel. Adjusting to immortality could add a few more years before I'm capable of leaving.

A sigh swells in my throat as Rayonne closes and latches her suitcase before scurrying over for hugs and goodbyes. I release it once the door latches behind her, her flurry of excite-ment having whisked away some of mine.

I sit on the bed and wrap my arms around my knees. When I turn to Adelia, her serious eyes are already pinned to my face. How long was she studying me?

"Looks like you get the room to yourself for two weeks." I trill my lips.

"You're upset." Her mouth forms a taut line as she pulls in a deep breath that has her chest lifting.

I shrug. "Eh. It would be nice to see Egypt is all."

Her gaze is downcast in thought, her shoulders curled forward. "It's so unfair," she whispers. "I love Viorel with all my heart, but he doesn't understand how painful it is to be trapped here. I haven't left the castle in decades. I don't know what the world is like out there aside from things I've heard."

"You're not trapped here," I argue, knowing she means me. "You can plan a trip with Rayonne."

I wish I could tell her I probably won't be trapped here forever, but I keep my lips sealed as Viorel requested. He plans on having us sneak out for our horse ride and picnic, so nobody knows. I'm sure I'll be able to tell her things are changing eventually. Maybe I'll plan a surprise trip for her, me, and Rayonne.

Her eyes lock with mine. "But you're my best friend. I would want you to come. I would feel awful leaving you behind, knowing you feel trapped."

"That doesn't change the fact I'm not allowed to leave." Not yet, at least. "You would have to go without me, and I wouldn't be hurt. I haven't even been here a year yet, and it's not so bad. It's not like I would have ever been able to travel if I never came here. Besides, I technically have more now than I ever did. And you *deserve* to get out and explore."

Tears well in her eyes and spill over. "I'm so sad for you, Marianna. To be trapped here forever, hardly allowed outside. Only sometimes allowed upstairs. It's wrong. One day, you're going to feel like this too knowing there's a whole, changing world out there you're forbidden from being part of."

I straighten my legs and lean back on my hands, unsure of what else to say but, "It's fine, Glitch. Why don't we watch a movie, or something?"

A shuddering, unsure noise leaves her. "I've been thinking about Denendrius and Huarsar and Tatiana—"

"Why?" The inquiry sounds more like a snappy demand, but it's the foul taste of hearing her talk about her brother and the reminder she felt for him—even for a moment.

Glitch whips her head away from me, like my gaze can wound her. When she speaks, her voice carries away from me. "I think I figured out how he escaped the veil."

Confusion wrinkles between my brows. "Yeah . . . he was smuggled out by corrupt guards he threatened."

By the way she shakes her head, she seems so sure I'm wrong. "No. It was Tatiana's blood."

Unease sends my heart scrambling behind my ribcage. "Says who?"

Glitch talks into her shoulder, and I fight the urge to give her a yank so I can see her face. "Think about it. Denendrius *supposedly* cannibalized the guards to find his strength to escape. I've shared blood with my father before, and though it gives you more strength than human blood, it doesn't give you the type of strength one would need to escape a fortress built and guarded by *Viorel*."

"I was told he feigned weaker than he was and surprised a guard who came into his cell. Back to full strength, iron and stone wouldn't have been able to contain him. He was a gladiator. He would have had the skill and strength to fight off the guards. Plus, he used Tatiana *as a human shield*."

She shakes her head again, and I set my jaw as frustration floods me.

"Viorel's blood is different from other vampires. I can tell from the smell of your blood; how it mingles with his. His is powerful . . . *He's powerful.* It makes sense why you can't go in the sun and why garlic hurts you, and why it made him think you might be more than human."

"He said his blood has never done that to his past familiars," I argue.

"Maybe not two-thousand years ago . . . but now? Vampires only grow stronger as they age."

I twist my ouroboros bracelet around my wrist, unable to argue. "So, you think Denendrius escaped his cell and got through the veil by drinking her blood?"

She nods, blank face and tormented eyes turning back to mine.

I lean away from her. "Either way, who gives a fuck? Why are we talking about Denendrius? How much time have you spent thinking about him?"

Her hands strike forward and wind around my wrists, holding them against the bed.

"What the fuck," I breathe as I fail to twist from her steel grasp. I first think she's merely gripped me faster and harder than she hoped. "Adelia, let me go."

But tears fill her eyes as she shifts to her knees, and I find myself recovering from the dizziness of being swiftly sprawled on my back and straddled. My eyes widen as she clamps her hand around my throat, only tight enough to subdue the impending bellow for help.

Tears flurry down her cheeks. "You're my best friend, Marianna. You were there for me when *nobody else was*. You helped free me. Now it's my turn to help free you."

My eyes widen, a tendril of air curling down my esophagus. Enough to slow the budding pressure in my head, but too little for words. I wriggle uselessly, my free hand batting at her body like my fist is made of soft rubber. She's young and small but is no weaker than the Darkling men I've encountered.

"I'm so sorry for hurting you," she cries, cold tears peppering the bridge of my nose and cheeks as she leans over me, her hair grazing my skin as she grabs my water bottle off the nightstand. "But I need your blood."

Both hands now free, I shove and kick at her to no avail. She empties it on the floor, crying another apology as she allows me a single gulp of air before stealing my wrist. Opening my vein with her sharp fingernail, she presses the wide mouth of the bottle over the gushing wound. I watch in horror as the clear plastic fills with crimson.

In that moment, I understand why Viorel is so terrified of me being unprotected and why he's so nervous about being attacked. I understand how justified he is in locking me away, and how catastrophic my freedom could be. I understand what he meant about how sharing my blood would bring serious consequences . . . *and that the consequence wouldn't be a punishment he doles out.*

But it's too late.

Panic or blood loss has me faint and the room swims as she caps the bottle.

The sight of her pulses in my vision. Her eyes widen as she bites into my other wrist, her black eyes flicking back in ecstasy. Her hand loosens on my throat, but I still can't breathe. Blood creeps into the whites of her eyes as the veins burst, the veins beneath her lower lashes swelling and protruding angry and red beneath her pale flesh.

She looks as monstrous as Denendrius did when Viorel accidentally shared the vision of him raping and drinking from Tatiana.

Unconsciousness smites me, my senses reduced to ringing ears and darkness.

An explosion rattles me, a chorus of shrieks lurching me awake. My eyes open to darkness, my hunched back pressed against the same hardness below my rear and bare feet. A heavy weakness pounds through me. It's molasses in my veins, so thick my heart shudders instead of beating properly and I can barely get my arms and legs to obey me. I slide sideways into the same hardness—*wood*—when I try to shift my body.

"Marianna!" Rayonne hollers beyond the darkness.

The memory of Adelia attacking me and draining my blood seizes my thoughts.

The darkness to my right opens to my dim room, the cold air entering the wardrobe I now understand Adelia left me in.

Rayonne stands in the opening, her blood-spattered face and wide eyes telling me my nightmare has just begun.

My rubbery tongue flops around in my mouth as I attempt to ask her what happened. *I fear I already know.*

"We need to get out of here right now!" She maneuvers her arms under my weak legs and between my back and the wardrobe wall.

He appears halfway across the bedroom, bloodied body half masked by darkness. His shadowed gaze is unblinking and locked on me.

I grunt as I struggle to unknot my tongue, fight to tell her how Denendrius is standing right behind her. My tongue lolls around behind my teeth, a slurring sound tumbling past my lips as I play tug of war with my head and gravity.

As her eyes widen on me with the understanding of danger, Denendrius clears the space. The image of his hand protruding from the front of her chest with her heart gripped in his fist is seared into my eyes before I can fully comprehend what's happened.

His demon eyes lock with mine as he dislodges his hand from her chest cavity and lets her body thud against the floor. The whites of his eyes are flooded crimson, furious veins spider webbing from beneath his lower lashes.

Betrayal chokes me.

Adelia gave him my blood. Viorel's blood.

Adelia set him free.

In that instant, I know what I must do if I want to live.

"You came for me." The words curl off my tongue with a cry. I hope he can twist my tear-soaked cheeks and terror into something meaningful to him. "I'm sorry. He made me say those things. Made me hurt you."

He wraps his arm around me and pulls me in a tight, crushing hug against his chest. "I know, sweetheart."

"I thought we'd be apart forever." I release fearful tears and don't hide the pain in my voice. "I thought I'd have to live through his torture for eternity."

"He'll never touch you again," Denendrius says, voice monotone.

"He's got Aeliana!" I sob, moving my desperate, shaky hands to his blood-slick chest and pushing away to meet his lifeless eyes. "Denendrius, Huarsar's got our baby. You've got to kill him and take her."

"Where's his chamber?" Denendrius grabs my arm and pulls me from the wardrobe.

My weak ankles protest with the weight of my body, rolling in defiance. Denendrius hooks his arm around my waist and my stomach roils at the feel of his cold chest against mine. He's wearing a splattered pair of jeans he must have stolen.

"I'll take you to him," I choke out as the room whirls around me.

If only Denendrius knew I plan to lead him to his death.

All I can hope is Viorel remains in his chamber, Aeliana with him.

The room shifts, the chaos of the grand room enveloping me. There are a dozen fights and people fleeing. Torn bodies—both vampires and humans—are scattered over the furniture and in pools of shining blood. It coats the floor in thick puddles, like the aftermath of a rainstorm. It's cold beneath my bare feet, the liquid rippling around my toes. Many of the vampires are unfamiliar to me, the few with broken shackles and gaunt appearances telling me *Denendrius must have emptied the dungeon.*

"Which way?" Denendrius demands.

I point toward the hall as panic chokes me at the thought of Carol and Derek dead or dying. Laurentius may have better odds of making it through alive since he's a Darkling, though he'll likely be targeted—

My heart seizes when I spot Laurentius brawling with another man on the blood-streaked carpet near the mouth of the hall. A man tosses him into the wall, the scene rapidly changing with Laurentius on top of him doling out punches.

Denendrius follows my eyes to Laurentius before I can look away, bristling as he grips me tighter and drags me along.

"Rapist priest," he snarls beneath his breath.

"Forget him," I beg, planting my feet to stop him. The slick blood under my soles only makes moving me easier for him. "Please, Denendrius! He's not worth it! We need to get Aeliana from Viorel before he kills her."

"Priest!" Denendrius bellows, his voice breaking apart several fights, his presence sending them rushing away, including the man who had been fighting to pin Laurentius down.

"I'm sorry," Laurentius says as he squares up and holds his ground, shaking hands up in defense as Denendrius tightens his grip on my arm and charges toward him.

Knowing I can't say the words aloud without undue pain to myself, I catch Laurentius's wide gaze and mouth, *"Run!"*

"Pray, priest!" Denendrius bellows as Laurentius stumbles backward a few steps. "Pray!"

"Denendrius, don't!" I shriek, my heart beating so hard it feels like it shreds itself against the hard bone of my ribs. "We're wasting time!"

Laurentius's eyes flicker to me. "I'm sorry!" he cries as he spins to flee down the hall.

I don't have time for my breath of relief knowing he won't try fighting Denendrius, because before he's turned, Denendrius has him sprawled face first on the floor.

"Please!" Laurentius begs, as Denendrius flips him onto his back and straddles his chest. "I didn't rape her, I swear!"

"You'll pray," Denendrius snarls. He rips the rosary from Laurentius's neck and dangles it in front of his eye to inspect the cross before balling it up in his fist and looking down at Laurentius. "And you'll die."

"No!" I shriek. "Denendrius, no! *We're wasting time!*"

Laurentius prays loudly in Latin. I hear Lucifer's name as

Denendrius pins his arms down at his sides—outstretched like he's on a cross—with his knees. He thrashes uselessly as Denendrius pries his jaw open and stuffs the balled-up rosary down his throat, gagging him as he forces it down with his fingers while snarling at Laurentius to swallow it.

I'm useless and may as well be a shrieking ghost batting at Denendrius until he disappears from Laurentius and reappears in a flash of combat with Mateo down the hall. I can't tell who's winning, though catch Denendrius's furious words over how Mateo's crew sunk his ship and stole his women. He must be talking about the girl they found in the captain's quarters, and me.

I risk Denendrius seeing me help Laurentius and drop to my knees, my fumbling hands searching for a way to help. But the rosary is gone as Laurentius rolls onto his hands and knees, crying and mumbling about how he'll have to cut it out of himself.

The rapid firing of an automatic gun has my eyes flying wide. It cuts through a chorus of screams and furious roars. Bodies scatter in the grand room, vanishing from sight like they don't want to find out if the shooter is friend or foe.

My sight smears with icy hands on my shoulders. I stupidly hope Mateo or Laurentius has taken me and ran, but Denendrius's unhinged eyes lock on mine as he holds me against the wall.

"Where—"

"The steel door down the hall you were fighting the priest—"

Disorientation comes in a wave, the steel door—hanging off its hinges—revealed as it pulls away. A thick trail of blood and unidentifiable ground organs leads down the stone stairs.

I grip to Denendrius's arm to stay standing. "I don't know how to get there from here. They always blinded me."

A dark smile twists over Denendrius's lips as he inhales a

deep breath through his nose. "Easy. I'll follow the scent of death."

He drags me along with Darkling speed and we abruptly stop at the top of a familiar, narrow and steep stairway.

I stifle my shriek as Denendrius drags me over Sascha's body. She's sprawled down the stairs, her blue eyes brimmed with blood, her neck only attached to her body by bits of shredded flesh. Her chest has a crater where her heart once was.

I can't breathe as we near the bottom of the stairs, the smell of something charred—flesh and hair, dare I think—choking me. Fear and hopelessness pound through me at the sight before us.

I suspected Viorel barricaded himself behind the iron door with a bunch of guards and Aeliana. Perhaps I thought he'd be expecting Denendrius, knowing he would have gone straight for me, and would simply open the door and have Denendrius taken care of in a matter of minutes. Perhaps I thought all I needed to do to find safety was get here.

The iron door is off its hinges, a carpet of half-charred bodies padding the fire-lit landing and carrying on into the sitting room of smashed furniture. Furious hollers—one of them Viorel's—echo with smashing furniture and pained gurgling.

I feel outside myself—numb—as I search the visible faces while Denendrius forces me to walk on top of the bodies, hoping I don't find guards amongst the mass of unfamiliar vampires I guess came from the dungeon. I'm sorely disappointed.

Asil's barely recognizable. His body is pinned beneath two others, half his face torn.

We move past the sitting room, and I spot Seth's corpse splayed over Viorel's puzzle table. His eyes are void of life, a gaping hole in his chest and a blade jutting from his throat.

"Marianna!" Viorel bellows, the desperation pounding off the stone and slamming into me.

A vicious smile twists onto Denendrius's lips, darkness in his eyes.

We come to a hard stop at the end of the hall, and I gape at the open passage I've never seen before, in the middle of the empty floor space before the cell. A bloodied vampire scrambles up a set of steps, his feet flying out from under him. He saves himself with a roll, Viorel occupied with whoever grunts in combat with him.

Aeliana screams, a shrill, pained sound that has me grinding my teeth and flying forward against Denendrius's grip.

Viorel snarls something in Romanian as a man comes flying up the stairs, back slamming against the wall and unable to move out of a pursuing hatchet's path. The sharp edge collides with his throat, the sound of the metal hitting the stone as it parts the man's head from his body, making the hair stand up on the back of my neck.

With the door smashed, the guards dead, and the fact Viorel is fighting as Aeliana screams, I come to a world-shattering understanding that Viorel is *holding our baby* and fighting against every vampire come to cut down the king.

The secret passage vanishes, Denendrius stiffening at my side as his gaze flits over the room for Viorel.

He spins, hand catching the bloodied, sharp tip of a wooden stake mere millimeters from his heart.

Viorel stands at the end of the hall, scarlet eyes wild with unbridled rage. Blood spatter is across his face, the ends of his hair soaked. He cradles Aeliana in one of his arms, her little kicking feet and crimson stained hands bloody, reaching for him. Half the blanket she's bundled in is soaked.

Viorel's voice ricochets through my head. *She's all right. I healed her.*

Denendrius throws the stake back, and it bursts into flames

and flies back at him like a boomerang. I gasp as Denendrius yanks me in front of him, but it halts before it can drive into me and clatters in a heap of singed wood on the stone.

Viorel's eyes are wide. He grits his teeth, baring his fangs as he glowers at Denendrius before his head snaps toward the commotion of voices and storming feet coming down the stairs.

I love you, he thinks at me as he spins and flees into the sitting room—away from the door—in a flurry of silk and bloodied brown hair.

Tears spill over my lashes and my heart is swollen at the base of my throat as Denendrius roars and charges after him, dark laughter bubbling out of him.

I expect to find Viorel standing in a corner ready to defend himself—and Denendrius must too—but there's a dark doorway next to Viorel's throne where a simple wall used to be, and our confusion has us stopping short.

The flurry of war cries grows louder; prisoners hungry for Viorel's blood. They'll be upon us in moments.

Denendrius drags me forward and grabs a cutlass sword from the chest of a corpse, and we dash into the darkness of the secret passage.

The candlelight of the sitting room vanishes once we step inside, leaving us trapped in the stale and dust-thick air.

Our steps crunch and echo as we stalk forward through the dense dark.

"Aeliana's scent stops in the air here . . ." He releases me and slams his hands against the stone wall, feeling up and down on both sides of the passage. "Huarsar must be masking a branch. Prepare to be ambushed."

I yelp as Denendrius yanks my back tight against his chest and angles the blade of the wet sword across my throat.

"I won't let you die, I promise," Denendrius whispers in my ear.

My drumming heart and ragged breaths fill the tense air as

Denendrius walks us forward, turning us in slow circles as he moves forward like he's expecting Viorel to come through the wall.

Tendrils of weak moonlight reach into the tunnel from above. Denendrius tightens his grip on me, the cold metal of the sword kissing my flesh, ready to bite into it as we walk to the light and look up at the starry sky through a square hatch in the ground. The biting cold wafts against my face and I shiver.

My knees buckle as Denendrius bends his, and then we're outside barefoot in the snow. The secret tunnel disappears, soft and powdery snow in its place.

"Come out, come out, wherever you are," Denendrius sings as he rotates us.

I shiver and scan the widely spaced trees of the forest, eyes widening on shifting shadows and every branch the harsh breeze cuts through. The castle pokes out of the trees in the distance, the sound of chaos leeching into the woods like haunting whispers. Smoke billows from some windows, quick flashes of lights paired with the echo of sporadic shots emitting from others.

My vision pulses with darkness like a thick cloud consumes the moon. I'm wracked with nauseous dread and confusion at the fuzzy sight of my fingers digging into the bloodied snow below me, the hot puddle quickly growing as I choke on wet heat. I can't get a breath in, a gurgle rolling in my throat with each failed attempt.

"No!" Viorel roars as he appears on Denendrius's sword, up to the hilt at his sternum and narrowly missing Aeliana as she shrieks. His eyes are glued to me, hardly aware of the blade piercing him.

My lungs scream for air, gushes of crimson melting the snow near my hands and making me lift them to my throat. There's a necklace of a gash from the sword. Fire rages in my stomach, and I press my hand against the pain. My shirt is soaked, another stream gushing between my numb fingers.

I concentrate through the consuming black shuddering at the fringes of my vision as the sword melts like goop in Denendrius's hand; the metal leaking down Viorel's gown. With a furious swipe of his hand, Viorel sends Denendrius skidding sideways through the snow and landing in a crumpled heap.

Viorel bolts to me and drops to his knees as he promises I'll be okay, resting Aeliana—wailing—in the snow against my bloodied side. She vanishes the second he moves his hands from her to place them on my slashed throat and wounded stomach.

Denendrius appears handfuls of meters away. He cradles Aeliana in his arms, little feet kicking against his bloody chest, as he looks at her in astonishment. Horror shakes me at the sight of them together, more profound than the slowly fading pain embedded in my body.

"My baby," he murmurs. "She looks just like us, Marianna."

Viorel's gaze switches frantically between Denendrius and my wounds, the panic clear in his eyes. If he interferes before I'm properly healed, I'll bleed out and die, and there's little he can do from here that won't result in Aeliana getting hurt.

I can see on Viorel's face—in his misty eyes and rapid breath—that he's living his worst nightmare.

Denendrius bites into his wrist, my protest gurgling as he rests the bloody incisions against Aeliana's little lips. I brace myself for his reaction when his mark fails to overwrite Viorel's. His furious roar has tears cascading down my cheeks as it echoes through the woods. I blink them away to clear my sight of Aeliana.

Denendrius sobs, but the emotion only shows in his jerking shoulders and labored breaths. He stares at Aeliana like he's found the world's greatest riches and must give them up.

"I love you. Your tata loves you, Aeliana," Denendrius chokes out as he lifts her forehead to his. *"Tata will save you and mama."*

I can't help but think it sounds like a goodbye.

My eyes fight to catch Viorel's while I try to bring words to my tongue, but the blood refuses to clear from my throat despite how I try swallowing it down. It fills the space between my cheeks and beneath my tongue before it spills over my bottom lip.

Leave me, I think at him.

His eyes jerk to mine. "No," he breathes.

Save Aeliana. Go get her.

He's not going to steal her. He's going to kill her.

He disappears from my side as Aeliana's screaming cuts off sharply, but I finally manage a breath.

My chest heaves with heavy breaths as I grab my healed throat.

The scene changes before me, Denendrius writhing in the snow as Viorel stares down at him with Aeliana in his arms. But as I move to stand, they're gone.

I waver weakly, frozen in place as a new scene unfolds.

Denendrius and Viorel are no longer alone in combat. I swear I glimpse Mateo.

Flashes of shadows weave through the trees, pained bellows and battle cries bounding between them.

My vision shifts in a blur of snow and brown bark, the castle even farther now. Denendrius wraps his arm around my chest, pinning my arms at my side. He whispers an apology in my ear, claiming hurting me was the only way to draw Viorel out.

The cold clings to me as I watch in bewilderment with chattering teeth as bodies appear scattered around us, Viorel and Aeliana only visible in flashes.

Blood streaks the pure snow, pools and spatters continuously appearing with corpses.

A beheaded body lies twenty feet away. Another is staked on a tree branch. The smell of burning clothes and hair comes with the sight of a vampire fleeing into the woods. A girl lies ashen and half-decomposed on my left. Two dozen more lie mangled, my fuzzy brain unable to grasp their wounds.

Aeliana's cries have me gritting my teeth, though her bouts of silence make my chest swell with panic. I don't want to know how many times Viorel has had to heal her.

I gasp at Viorel's pained outcry as he tumbles in the snow, white kicking up around him. He jerks backward—dragged by an invisible force—and the horrible fact he's not immune from other vampires attacking him with their abilities has my heart thudding in my stomach.

Then he's on his feet. Aeliana lies in the crook of one arm while he uses the other to hold a scraggly vampire man high in the air by his throat. Mateo appears behind the man and shoves a stake into his heart.

Viorel sweeps his arm across himself, and a few grunts paired with tumbling in snow come from behind me. Fury flares in his eyes as they lock on us, and Denendrius buckles and grunts in pain. But somehow, he remains on his feet.

I fear Denendrius's strength with my blood—Viorel's blood—coursing through him.

"Bring the veil down!" Denendrius commands through grit teeth.

"Never!" Viorel snarls as he kicks a man square in the chest and rolls over to protect Aeliana as another vampire attempts to clamber onto him, and instead lands where Viorel lay a second before.

Denendrius tightens his grip on me, and my legs give out. "The sun's coming up in thirty minutes! One way or another, this veil will be lifted!"

"You're not leaving with her, rat! I'd rather we all burn," Viorel snarls, throwing his hand to the side and sending a vampire

flying backward as he slips from behind a tree to attack. He swings his hand to the left, his fist connecting with the face of another vampire.

Black explodes across my vision as Denendrius tears into my throat. The faint sound of battle and a withering clan in the distance seep into my unconsciousness. Will there be a home left for those who survive this?

Viorel's face adjusts in my vision as he kneels next to me in the scarlet snow, the blurry sight of Denendrius and Mateo brawling in the snow behind him. His wrist is against my lips, his blood slowly filling me. I want to protest—tell him he needs his blood—but with Adelia draining me, Denendrius wounding me and drinking from me, I can barely blink.

I can see in Viorel's dull eyes how exhausted he is. It's hard to grasp the reality that he's not limitless. Even the world's oldest vampire can only fight for so long, and I know he's been using most of his energy to keep such a massive veil up to stop the escaped prisoners from leaking into the rest of the world. He's been fighting a nonstop onslaught of vampires alone and has probably taken down hundreds by now. And how much of his energy has he given to me through his blood? How much has he used to heal me? To heal Aeliana? To heal *himself?*

I struggle to turn my head to break my lips from his flesh. I'd rather he keep his strength for himself so he can protect Aeliana.

His voice rings in my heavy head. *Drink, or you'll die. Aeliana still needs her mother. I've got some fight left in me yet.*

He holds Aeliana against his chest, delivering a kiss to the bundle. But when he hangs his head, I doubt his strength for a moment until flames in my peripheral and a shriek takes my attention. Viorel's wrist disappears from my lips, the sweet taste of his blood keeping my eyes open.

A tree is alight, hungry flames devouring the wood as a body plummets from the snapping branches and writhes as it burns. When I look back at Viorel, he's shoving a vampire off him, a dripping heart in his hand.

"What is that . . ." Denendrius stops fighting as he stares off into the distance past Viorel and me. Mateo throws his arms around Denendrius, and they land on the ground. Mateo curses as Denendrius sinks his fangs into his arm, and they both roll away from one another and fumble toward a stake that zips through the air and into the snow.

Dread pounds through me as Denendrius tears the stake from Mateo's grip and plunges it into Mateo's heart. He goes slack and Denendrius laughs until he's looking around the woods in confusion, like he's no longer seeing them.

As Viorel braces himself to stand, his eyes and jaw widen, and he nearly topples over me with our baby until he catches himself. My heart stops, my half-lidded gaze landing on the sharp wooden tip protruding through his chest. Tears lick my cheeks, despite how he stays conscious.

His eyes roll back, and a shiver ripples through him as he grunts and wraps his hand around the end to pull it out. Blood oozes from the wound and takes a concerning number of seconds to heal.

Viorel stands and spins, gasping for breath as he sweeps his arm through the air and sends ten more vampires tumbling into the snow as they dart from different directions. He grits his teeth, face twisting in pain as he falls backward and claws at a vampire clambering over him and Aeliana.

Denendrius rushes forward, yanking me to my feet and along through the trees. His touch injects hot adrenaline into my frosty veins. I think he's going to attack Viorel, but then we're past him, and I'm looking back at Denendrius as his feet fly out from under him and he lands on his chest, me on my side with my arm burning from the force of Denendrius's fall.

"A highway," Denendrius mumbles as he stands and pulls me to my feet. "There's a highway."

"A highway?" I don't check for one myself. I'm ill with the idea of the veil falling with Viorel.

I see something half as bad instead.

Viorel brawls with a vampire three times his size, his war cries squeezing the breath from me as he and the Darkling are a blur of fists and flashing silver blades. A scraggly looking man with stringy hair and a shackle on his ankle picks up Aeliana—shrieking—from the snow.

I fight against Denendrius's grip for the first time.

"Put her down!" I shriek, my volume tearing at my vocal cords. *"You put her down!"*

He holds her against his chest instead, ignoring my demands and Viorel's threats as he fights the sharp steel with his bare hands. He lowers himself into the snow, cradling her between his chest and risen knees as he rocks and twitches. "Pardon me," the vampire begs in a thick and rough accent, his risen voice raw with thirst. "Pardon me, and I'll protect her while you fight. I'll bow if you pardon me."

The giant of a vampire sends Viorel flying onto his back, and he quickly turns to dodge the bloodied blade that disappears into the white earth.

If he's lowered the veil, he's stretched to his limits and must be desperate to conserve the rest of his energy.

With Denendrius's wicked smile as he drags me toward the twist of gray asphalt in the distance, I understand this was his plan all along.

Cause a prison break that sends hundreds of vengeful men bolting to punish their torturer and use the havoc they wreck to bide his time in finding me.

He didn't care about killing Viorel. He rather safely stood by to watch and use me as a pawn.

Didn't care about fighting to retrieve Aeliana—after all, how could he keep her with Viorel's permanent mark?

Perhaps he knows he doesn't stand a chance against him.

No, he wanted to weaken Viorel enough for him to drop the veil so he could flee with me, Viorel and our baby's deaths mere bonuses.

Viorel screams my name, too trapped in battle and protecting Aeliana—who shrieks in terror or pain—to move more than a few feet toward us at a time. When Denendrius's legs buckle beneath him and he lands with a thud in the snow, he's quickly able to recover from Viorel's weakened protest. I wonder how resistant Denendrius's body is to Viorel's powers with the stolen blood running through him. Surely, he should be capable of doing more to him, right?

I look over my shoulder and stare up at the moonlit, snow-covered peaks and points of the towering castle—*my home.* Flames flicker in windows, black smoke billowing from the other side of it like the garden's on fire. We're so far it would take me hours to get home if I slipped free from Denendrius's grasp.

The pain in my chest is so severe I nearly check to see if Denendrius has injured me again.

As we reach the highway, a car slows a few yards from us and jerks to a halt, a man and woman scrambling out, their heavy breaths billowing in the air as they stare aghast at the castle atop the hill.

They notice us, eyes bulging and faces as pale as the snow at the sight of Denendrius.

As Denendrius flinches forward to attack, two vampires lunge from the woods and slam their bodies against the metal, their fangs latched onto the human's throats as a third, red-eyed girl catches up.

She circles the car, blistering eyes studying it like she's completely unsure of what it is. She sniffs at it and scowls before all three of them vanish across the highway into the woods.

Denendrius sweeps me off the ground and bolts toward the car, yanking the back door open before trying to swing me in.

I kick my bare foot against the frame, the protest dumb and automatic.

"Get in the car!" Denendrius hollers as I kick my legs against the frame, needing a few more moments, hoping to see the veil return so I know Viorel is safe.

"But Aeliana!" I cry as he wrestles me into the backseat, my eyes locked on the castle behind him.

Nobody is coming from the woods to save me right now. So many of the guards are dead, and they'll help Viorel and Aeliana before they make their way to me. Perhaps Mateo will come running if Viorel has a chance to unstake him.

Denendrius is fucking escaping with me, and nobody is coming to stop him just yet. My only chance is to go with him willingly until the guard can recover enough to band together and track me down.

He flicks the child lock on and slams the door.

Viorel . . .

Denendrius appears in the driver's seat and the car peels away.

Tears blur my sight, my heart pounding harder with each second the gray stone walls remain visible. My jaw hangs as I struggle to breathe, my face twisted in horror.

"*Viorel,*" I mouth.

Would I feel it if he died, like he would if I did? Would it feel as excruciating as it does now? Or *worse?* I can't imagine a pain worse than this.

I gasp as the castle disappears; the space filled with snow-covered trees like it was never there at all.

Like I merely imagined my happiness, and I've been with this monster all along.

Viorel's alive . . . but my home is *gone.*

The car comes to a screeching stop.

The passenger door flies open and Adelia scrambles into the seat, screaming at Denendrius in Latin as she sobs and stares at him with tormented eyes.

Adelius's name passes between their furious voices before Adelia cries, "*I promise I got him past the veil when it came down!* But even injured, he's stronger than me. He ran!"

"Hope we get him before the sunlight does," Denendrius growls as she pulls her knees to her chest and sobs.

I don't understand how she can be so upset. This is her fault. Brother or not, Denendrius was in the dungeon for a reason.

My wail is ear piercing, the grief a nail bomb in my chest, so painful I swear I'm dying. I curl into a ball on the backseat as sobs wrack and shatter me.

But I think of the vision Ziggy told me about, how I was lying in his bed looking at a CD this summer. *How the vision was so sure.* If I'm with Ziggy, it must mean I get away from Denendrius. I think of the rumors beyond the walls, how one of the new vampire children's abusers gossiped about a seer saying I would be powerful. Viorel's vision of me trying to leave the castle as an immortal must mean I make it home.

I promise myself I'll find a way back no matter if they come true, though I know I'll have to crawl through Hell to get there.

This time, Denendrius will not rot in a dungeon. *He'll rot in the fucking ground with all the other wriggling worms.* I'll put him there myself.

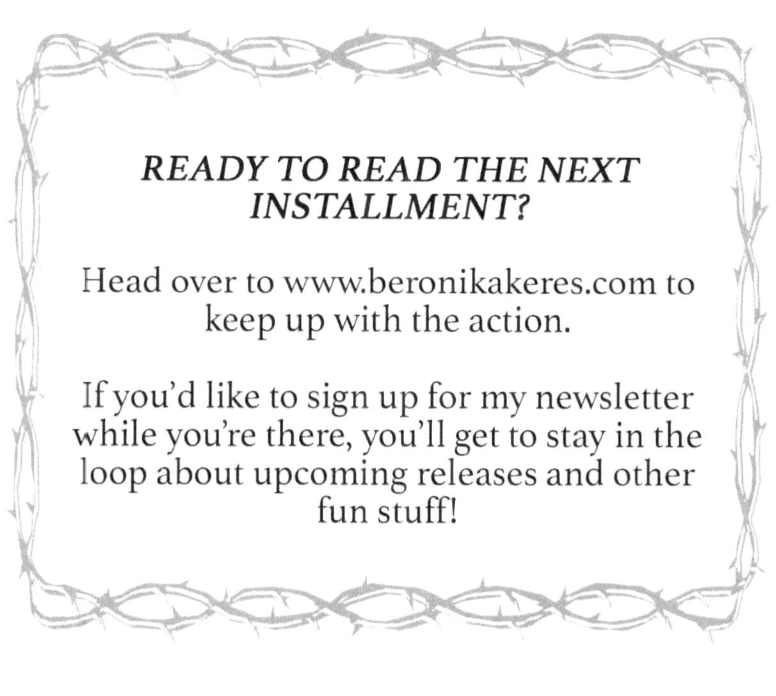
READY TO READ THE NEXT INSTALLMENT?

Head over to www.beronikakeres.com to keep up with the action.

If you'd like to sign up for my newsletter while you're there, you'll get to stay in the loop about upcoming releases and other fun stuff!

ABOUT THE AUTHOR

Beronika Keres is the Canadian author of the dark fantasy thriller series, Cracked Coffins. She decided in the second grade that she wanted to be an author and has spent her life honing her craft and pursuing her dream. She can often be found chasing plot bunnies and writing books.

When she's not writing, she enjoys spending time with her family, or listening to some gothic rock, punk, or metal while working on her newest spike and patch covered project.

www.beronikakeres.com

facebook.com/AuthorBeronikaKeres

instagram.com/beronikakeres

tiktok.com/@beronikakeres

bookbub.com/authors/beronika-keres

goodreads.com/BeronikaKeres

www.ingramcontent.com/pod-product-compliance
Lightning Source LLC
Chambersburg PA
CBHW050842210726
48290CB00004B/1052